PRASE FOR

"A thrilling, action-packed fantasy ... ...bitious heroine's rise from poverty to ruthless military commander makes for a gripping read, and I eagerly await the next installment."

—Julie C. Dao, author of *Forest of a Thousand Lanterns*

"A blistering, powerful epic of war and revenge that will captivate you to the bitter end."

—Kameron Hurley, author of *The Stars Are Legion*

"I have no doubt this will end up being the best fantasy debut of the year. . . . I have absolutely no doubt that [Kuang's] name will be up there with the likes of Robin Hobb and N.K. Jemisin."

—BookNest

"The best fantasy debut of 2018. . . . This year's Potter."

—Wired

"The 'year's best debut' buzz around this one was warranted; it really is that good."

— B&N Sci-fi and Fantasy Blog

"Debut novelist Kuang creates an ambitious fantasy reimagining of Asian history populated by martial artists, philosopher-generals, and gods. . . . This is a strong and dramatic launch to Kuang's career."

—*Publishers Weekly*

"The book starts as an epic bildungsroman, and just when you think it can't get any darker, it does. . . . Kuang pulls from East Asian history, including the brutality of the Second Sino-Japanese war, to weave a wholly unique experience."

—*Washington Post*

"[*The Poppy War* is a] strikingly grim military fantasy that summons readers into an East Asian–inspired world of battles, opium, gods, and monsters. Fans of Ken Liu's *The Grace of Kings* will snap this one up."

—*Library Journal* (starred review)

"This isn't just another magical, fantasy world with artificially fabricated stakes. Rin's journey and the war against the Federation feel incredibly urgent and powerful. . . . R.F. Kuang is one of the most exciting new authors I've had the privilege of reading."

—the Roarbots

THE
POPPY
WAR

R. F. KUANG

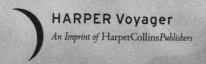
HARPER Voyager
An Imprint of HarperCollins Publishers

FIRST HARPER VOYAGER PAPERBACK EDITION PUBLISHED 2019.

Designed by Paula Russell Szafranski
Interior art © by Mariyana Lozanova/Shutterstock, Inc.
Map by Eric Gunther and copyright © 2017 Springer Cartographics

Library of Congress Cataloging-in-Publication Data has been applied for.

ISBN 978-0-06-266258-3

23 24 25 26 27 LBC 40 39 38 37 36

This is for Iris

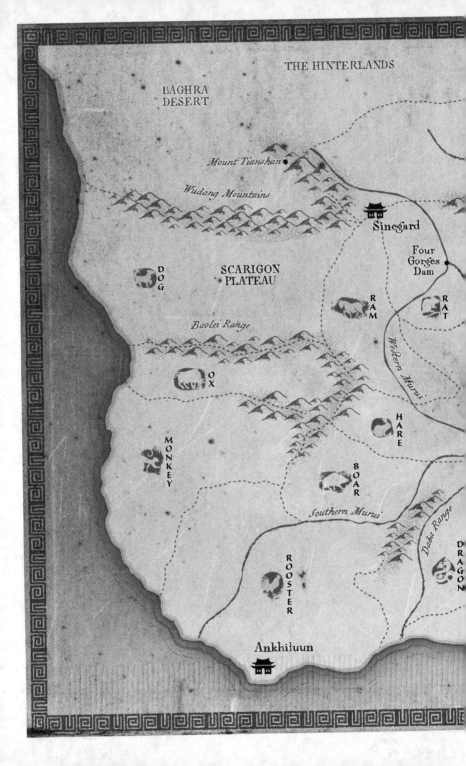

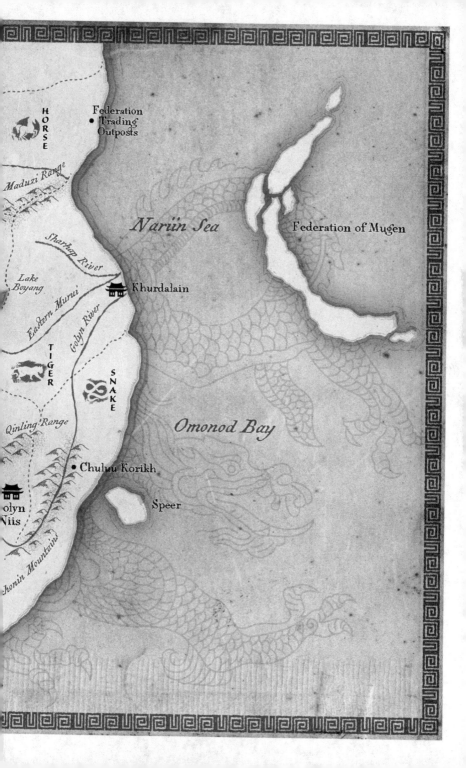

PART I

CHAPTER 1

"Take your clothes off."

Rin blinked. "What?"

The proctor glanced up from his booklet. "Cheating prevention protocol." He gestured across the room to a female proctor. "Go with her, if you must."

Rin crossed her arms tightly across her chest and walked toward the second proctor. She was led behind a screen, patted thoroughly to make sure she hadn't packed test materials up any orifices, and then handed a formless blue sack.

"Put this on," said the proctor.

"Is this really necessary?" Rin's teeth chattered as she stripped. The exam smock was too large for her; the sleeves draped over her hands so that she had to roll them up several times.

"Yes." The proctor motioned for her to sit down on a bench. "Last year twelve students were caught with papers sewn into the linings of their shirts. We take precautions. Open your mouth."

Rin obliged.

The proctor prodded her tongue with a slim rod. "No discoloration, that's good. Eyes wide open."

"Why would anyone drug themselves *before* a test?" Rin asked as the proctor stretched her eyelids. The proctor didn't respond.

Satisfied, she waved Rin down the hallway where other prospective students waited in a straggly line. Their hands were empty, faces uniformly tight with anxiety. They had brought no materials to the test—pens could be hollowed out to contain scrolls with answers written on them.

"Hands out where we can see them," ordered the male proctor, walking to the front of the line. "Sleeves must remain rolled up past the elbow. From this point forward, you do not speak to one another. If you have to urinate, raise your hand. We have a bucket in the back of the room."

"What if I have to shit?" a boy asked.

The proctor gave him a long look.

"It's a twelve-hour test," the boy said defensively.

The proctor shrugged. "Try to be quiet."

Rin had been too nervous to eat anything that morning. Even the thought of food made her nauseated. Her bladder and intestines were empty. Only her mind was full, crammed with an insane number of mathematical formulas and poems and treatises and historical dates to be spilled out on the test booklet. She was ready.

The examination room fit a hundred students. The desks were arranged in neat rows of ten. On each desk sat a heavy exam booklet, an inkwell, and a writing brush.

Most of the other provinces of Nikan had to section off entire town halls to accommodate the thousands of students who attempted the exam each year. But Tikany township in Rooster Province was a village of farmers and peasants. Tikany's families needed hands to work the fields more than they did university-educated brats. Tikany only ever used the one classroom.

Rin filed into the room along with the other students and took her assigned seat. She wondered how the examinees looked from above: neat squares of black hair, uniform blue smocks, and brown wooden tables. She imagined them multiplied across identical classrooms throughout the country right now, all watching the water clock with nervous anticipation.

Rin's teeth chattered madly in a staccato that she thought everyone could surely hear, and it wasn't just from the cold. She clamped her jaw shut, but the shuddering just spread down her limbs to her hands and knees. The writing brush shook in her grasp, dribbling black droplets across the table.

She tightened her grip and wrote her full name across the booklet's cover page. *Fang Runin.*

She wasn't the only one who was nervous. Already there were sounds of retching over the bucket in the back of the room.

She squeezed her wrist, fingers closing over pale burn scars, and inhaled. *Focus.*

In the corner, a water clock rang softly.

"Begin," said the examiner.

A hundred test booklets were opened with a flapping noise, like a flock of sparrows taking off at once.

Two years ago, on the day Tikany's magistracy had arbitrarily estimated to be her fourteenth birthday, Rin's foster parents had summoned her into their chambers.

This rarely happened. The Fangs liked to ignore Rin until they had a task for her, and then they spoke to her the way they would command a dog. *Lock up the store. Hang up the laundry. Take this packet of opium to the neighbors and don't leave until you've scalped them for twice what we paid for it.*

A woman Rin had never seen before sat perched on the guest's chair. Her face was completely dusted over with what looked like white rice flour, punctuated with caked-up dabs of color on her lips and eyelids. She wore a bright lilac dress dyed with a plum-flower pattern, cut in a fashion that might have suited a girl half her age. Her squat figure squeezed over the sides like a bag of grain.

"Is this the girl?" the woman asked. "Hm. She's a little dark—the inspector won't be too bothered, but it'll drive your price down a bit."

Rin had a sudden, horrifying suspicion of what was happening. "Who are you?" she demanded.

"Sit down, Rin," said Uncle Fang.

He reached out with a leathery hand to maneuver her into a chair. Rin immediately turned to flee. Auntie Fang seized her arm and dragged her back. A brief struggle ensued, in which Auntie Fang overpowered Rin and jerked her toward the chair.

"I won't go to a brothel!" Rin yelled.

"She's not from the brothel, you idiot," Auntie Fang snapped. "Sit down. Show some respect to Matchmaker Liew."

Matchmaker Liew looked unfazed, as if her line of work often involved accusations of sex trafficking.

"You're about to be a very lucky girl, sweet," she said. Her voice was bright and falsely saccharine. "Would you like to hear why?"

Rin clutched the edge of her chair and stared at Matchmaker Liew's red lips. "No."

Matchmaker Liew's smile tightened. "Aren't you a dear."

It turned out that after a long and arduous search, Matchmaker Liew had found a man in Tikany willing to marry Rin. He was a wealthy merchant who made a living importing pig's ears and shark fins. He was twice divorced and three times her age.

"Isn't that wonderful?" Matchmaker Liew beamed.

Rin bolted for the door. She hadn't made it two steps before Auntie Fang's hand shot out and seized her wrist.

Rin knew what came next. She braced herself for the blow, for the kicks to her ribs where bruises wouldn't show, but Auntie Fang only dragged her back toward her chair.

"You will *behave*," she whispered, and her clenched teeth promised punishment to come. But not now, not in front of Matchmaker Liew.

Auntie Fang liked to keep her cruelty private.

Matchmaker Liew blinked, oblivious. "Don't be scared, sweet. This is exciting!"

Rin felt dizzy. She twisted around to face her foster parents, fighting to keep her voice level. "I thought you needed me at the shop." Somehow, it was the only thing she could think to say.

"Kesegi can run the shop," Auntie Fang said.

"Kesegi is *eight*."

"He'll grow up soon enough." Auntie Fang's eyes glittered. "And your prospective husband happens to be the village import inspector."

Rin understood then. The Fangs were making a simple trade: one foster orphan in exchange for a near monopoly over Tikany's black market in opium.

Uncle Fang took a long draught from his pipe and exhaled, filling the room with thick, cloying smoke. "He's a rich man. You'll be happy."

No, the *Fangs* would be happy. They'd get to import opium in bulk without bleeding money for bribes. But Rin kept her mouth clamped shut—further argument would only bring pain. It was clear that the Fangs would have her married if they had to drag her to the bridal bed themselves.

They had never wanted Rin. They'd taken her in as an infant only because the Empress's mandate after the Second Poppy War forced households with fewer than three children to adopt war orphans who otherwise would have become thieves and beggars.

Since infanticide was frowned upon in Tikany, the Fangs had put Rin to use as a shopgirl and opium runner since she was old enough to count. Still, for all the free labor she provided, the cost of Rin's keep and feed was more than the Fangs cared to bear. Now was their chance to get rid of the financial burden she posed.

This merchant could afford to feed and clothe Rin for the rest of her life, Matchmaker Liew explained. All she had to do was serve him tenderly like a good wife and give him babies and take care of his household (which, as Matchmaker Liew pointed out, had not one but *two* indoor washrooms). It was a much better deal than a war orphan like Rin, with no family or connections, could otherwise hope to secure.

A husband for Rin, money for the matchmaker, and drugs for the Fangs.

"Wow," Rin said faintly. The floor seemed to wobble beneath her feet. "That's great. Really great. Terrific."

Matchmaker Liew beamed again.

Rin concealed her panic, fought to keep her breathing even until the matchmaker had been ushered out. She bowed low to the Fangs and, like a filial foster daughter, expressed her thanks for the pains they had gone through to secure her such a stable future.

She returned to the store. She worked silently until dark, took orders, filed inventory, and marked new orders in the ledger.

The thing about inventory was that one had to be very careful with how one wrote the numbers. So simple to make a nine look like an eight. Easier still to make a one look like a seven . . .

Long after the sun disappeared, Rin closed the shop and locked the door behind her.

Then she shoved a packet of stolen opium under her shirt and ran.

"Rin?" A small, wizened man opened the library door and peeked out at her. "Great Tortoise! What are you doing out here? It's pouring."

"I came to return a book," she said, holding out a waterproof satchel. "Also, I'm getting married."

"Oh. Oh! What? Come in."

Tutor Feyrik taught a tuition-free evening class to the peasant children of Tikany, who otherwise would have grown up illiterate. Rin trusted him above anyone else, and she understood his weaknesses better than anyone else.

That made him the linchpin in her escape plan.

"The vase is gone," she observed as she glanced around the cramped library.

Tutor Feyrik lit a small flame in the fireplace and dragged two cushions in front of it. He motioned for her to sit down. "Bad call. Bad night overall, really."

Tutor Feyrik had an unfortunate adoration for Divisions, an immensely popular game played in Tikany's gambling dens. It wouldn't have been so dangerous if he were better at it.

"That makes no sense," said Tutor Feyrik after Rin recounted to him the matchmaker's tidings. "Why would the Fangs marry you off? Aren't you their best source of unpaid labor?"

"Yes, but they think I'll be more useful in the import inspector's bed."

Tutor Feyrik looked revolted. "Your folks are assholes."

"So you'll do it," she said hopefully. "You'll help."

He sighed. "My dear girl, if your family had let you study with me when you were younger, we might have considered this . . . I *told* the Fangs then, I *told* her you might have potential. But at this stage, you're speaking of the impossible."

"But—"

He held up a hand. "More than twenty thousand students take the Keju each year, and hardly three thousand enter the academies. Of those, barely a handful test in from Tikany. You'd be competing against wealthy children—merchants' children, nobles' children—who have been studying for this their entire lives."

"But I've taken classes with you, too. How hard can it be?"

He chuckled at that. "You can read. You can use an abacus. That's not the kind of preparation it takes to pass the Keju. The Keju tests for a deep knowledge of history, advanced mathematics, logic, and the Classics . . ."

"The Four Noble Subjects, I know," she said impatiently. "But I'm a fast reader. I know more characters than most of the adults in this village. Certainly more than the Fangs. I can keep up with your students if you just let me try. I don't even have to attend recitation. I just need books."

"Reading books is one thing," Tutor Feyrik said. "Preparing for the Keju is a different endeavor entirely. My Keju students spend their whole lives studying for it; nine hours a day, seven days a week. You spend more time than that working in the shop."

"I can study at the shop," she protested.

"Don't you have actual responsibilities?"

"I'm good at, uh, multitasking."

He eyed her skeptically for a moment, then shook his head. "You'd only have two years. It can't be done."

"But I don't have any other options," she said shrilly.

In Tikany, an unmarried girl like Rin was worth less than a gay rooster. She could spend her life as a foot servant in some rich household—if she found the right people to bribe. Otherwise her options were some combination of prostitution and begging.

She was being dramatic, but not hyperbolic. She could leave town, probably with enough stolen opium to buy herself a caravan ticket to any other province . . . but where to? She had no friends or family; no one to come to her aid if she was robbed or kidnapped. She had no marketable skills. She had never left Tikany; she didn't know the first thing about survival in the city.

And if they caught her with that much opium on her person . . . Opium possession was a capital offense in the Empire. She'd be dragged into the town square and publicly beheaded as the latest casualty in the Empress's futile war on drugs.

She had only this option. She had to sway Tutor Feyrik.

She held up the book she had come to return. "This is Mengzi. *Reflections on Statecraft*. I've only had this for three days, right?"

"Yes," he said without checking his ledger.

She handed it to him. "Read me a passage. Any will do."

Tutor Feyrik still looked skeptical, but flipped to the middle of the book to humor her. "The feeling of commiseration is the principle of . . ."

"Benevolence," she finished. "The feeling of shame and dislike is the principle of righteousness. The feeling of modesty and complaisance is the principle of . . . the principle of, uh, propriety. And the feeling of approving and disapproving is the principle of knowledge."

He raised an eyebrow. "And what does that mean?"

"No clue," she admitted. "Honestly, I don't understand Mengzi at all. I just memorized him."

He flipped toward the end of the book, selected another passage, and read: "Order is present in the earthly kingdom when all beings understand their place. All beings understand their place when they fulfill the roles set out for them. The fish does not attempt to fly. The polecat does not attempt to swim. Only when each being respects the heavenly order may there be peace." He shut the book and looked up. "How about this passage? Do you understand what it means?"

She knew what Tutor Feyrik was trying to tell her.

The Nikara believed in strictly defined social roles, a rigid hierarchy that all were locked into at birth. Everything had its own place under heaven. Princelings became Warlords, cadets became soldiers, and orphan shopgirls from Tikany should be content with remaining orphan shopgirls from Tikany. The Keju was a purportedly meritocratic institution, but only the wealthy class ever had the money to afford the tutors their children needed to actually pass.

Well, fuck the heavenly order of things. If getting married to a gross old man was her preordained role on this earth, then Rin was determined to rewrite it.

"It means I'm very good at memorizing long passages of gibberish," she said.

Tutor Feyrik was silent for a moment. "You don't have an eidetic memory," he said finally. "I taught you to read. I would have known."

"I don't," she acknowledged. "But I'm stubborn, I study hard, and I really don't want to be married. It took me three days to memorize Mengzi. It was a short book, so I'll probably need a full week for the longer texts. But how many texts are on the Keju list? Twenty? Thirty?"

"Twenty-seven."

"Then I'll memorize them all. Every single one. That's all you need to pass the Keju. The other subjects aren't that hard; it's the Classics that trip people up. You told me that yourself."

Tutor Feyrik's eyes were narrowing now, his expression no longer skeptical but calculated. She knew that look. It was the look he got when he was trying to predict his returns at Divisions.

In Nikan, a tutor's success was tied to his reputation for Keju results. You attracted clients if your students made it into an academy. More students meant more money, and to an indebted gambler like Tutor Feyrik, each new student counted. If Rin tested into an academy, an ensuing influx of students could get Tutor Feyrik out of some nasty debts.

"Enrollment's been slow this year, hasn't it?" she pressed.

He grimaced. "It's a drought year. Of course admission is slow. Not many families want to pay tuition when their children barely have a chance to pass regardless."

"But I can pass," she said. "And when I do, you'll have a student who tested into an academy. What do you think that'll do for enrollment?"

He shook his head. "Rin, I couldn't take your tuition money in good faith."

That posed a second problem. She steeled her nerve and looked him in the eye. "That's okay. I can't pay tuition."

He balked visibly.

"I don't make anything at the store," Rin said before he could speak. "The inventory isn't mine. I don't get any wages. I need you to help me to study for the Keju at no cost, and twice as fast as you train your other students."

Tutor Feyrik began to shake his head again. "My dear girl, I can't—this is—"

Time to play her last card. Rin pulled her leather satchel out from under her chair and plunked it on the table. It hit the wood with a solid, satisfying smack.

Tutor Feyrik's eyes followed her eagerly as she slipped a hand into the satchel and drew out one heavy, sweet-smelling packet. Then another. And then another.

"This is six tael worth of premium opium," she said calmly. Six tael was half of what Tutor Feyrik might earn in an entire year.

"You stole this from the Fangs," he said uneasily.

She shrugged. "Smuggling's a difficult business. The Fangs know the risk. Packages go missing all the time. They can hardly report it to the magistrate."

He twiddled his long whiskers. "I don't want to get on the Fangs' bad side."

He had good reason to fear. People in Tikany didn't cross Auntie Fang—not if they cared about their personal safety. She was patient and unpredictable as a snake. She might let faults go unacknowledged for years, and then strike with a well-placed poisonous pellet.

But Rin had covered her tracks.

"One of her shipments was confiscated by port authorities last week," Rin said. "And she hasn't had time to do inventory yet. I've just marked these packets as lost. She can't trace them."

"They could still beat you."

"Not so badly." Rin forced a shrug. "They can't marry off damaged merchandise."

Tutor Feyrik was staring at the satchel with obvious greed.

"Deal," he said finally, and grasped for the opium.

She snatched it out of his reach. "Four conditions. One, you teach me. Two, you teach me for free. Three, you don't smoke when you're teaching me. And four, if you tell anyone where you got this, I'll let your creditors know where to find you."

Tutor Feyrik glared at her for a long moment, and then nodded.

She cleared her throat. "Also, I want to keep this book."

He gave her a wry smile.

"You *would* make a terrible prostitute. No charm."

"No," said Auntie Fang. "We need you in the shop."

"I'll study at night," Rin said. "Or during off-hours."

Auntie Fang's face pinched together as she scrubbed at the frying wok. Everything about Auntie Fang was raw: her expression, an open display of impatience and irritation; her fingers, red from hours of cleaning and laundering; her voice, hoarse from screaming at Rin; at her son, Kesegi; at her hired smugglers; at Uncle Fang, lying inert in his smoke-filled room.

"What did you promise him?" she demanded suspiciously.

Rin stiffened. "Nothing."

Auntie Fang abruptly slammed the wok onto the counter. Rin flinched, suddenly terrified that her theft had been discovered.

"What is so wrong with getting married?" Auntie Fang demanded. "I married your uncle when I was younger than you are now. Every other girl in this village will get married by her sixteenth birthday. Do you think you're so much better than them?"

Rin was so relieved that she had to remember to look properly chastised. "No. I mean, I don't."

"Do you think it will be so bad?" Auntie Fang's voice became dangerously quiet. "What is it, really? Are you afraid of sharing his bed?"

Rin hadn't even considered that, but now the very thought of it made her throat close up.

Auntie Fang's lip curled in amusement. "The first night is the worst, I'll give you that. Keep a wad of cotton in your mouth so you don't bite your tongue. Do not cry out, unless he wants you to. Keep your head down and do as he says—become his mute little household slave until he trusts you. But once he does? You start plying him with opium—just a little bit at first, though I doubt he's never smoked before. Then you give him more and more every day. Do it at night right after he's finished with you, so he always associates it with pleasure and power.

"Give him more and more until he is fully dependent on it, and on you. Let it destroy his body and mind. You'll be more or less married to a breathing corpse, yes, but you will have his riches, his estates, and his power." Auntie Fang tilted her head. "Then will it hurt you so much to share his bed?"

Rin wanted to vomit. "But I . . ."

"Is it the children you're afraid of?" Auntie Fang cocked her head. "There are ways to kill them in the womb. You work in the apothecary. You know that. But you'll want to give him at least one son. Cement your position as his first wife, so he can't fritter his assets on a concubine."

"But I don't want that," Rin choked out. *I don't want to be like you.*

"And who cares what you want?" Auntie Fang asked softly. "You are a *war orphan*. You have no parents, no standing, and no connections. You're lucky the inspector doesn't care that you're not pretty, only that you're young. This is the best I can do for you. There will be no more chances."

"But the Keju—"

"*But the Keju*," Auntie Fang mimicked. "When did you get so deluded? You think *you're* going to an academy?"

"I do think so." Rin straightened her back, tried to inject confidence into her words. *Calm down. You still have leverage.* "And you'll let me. Because one day, the authorities might start asking where the opium's coming from."

Auntie Fang examined her for a long moment. "Do you want to die?" she asked.

Rin knew that wasn't an empty threat. Auntie Fang was more than willing to tie up her loose ends. Rin had watched her do it before. She'd spent most of her life trying to make sure *she* never became a loose end.

But now she could fight back.

"If I go missing, then Tutor Feyrik will tell the authorities precisely what happened to me," she said loudly. "And he'll tell your son what you've done."

"Kesegi won't care," Auntie Fang scoffed.

"I raised Kesegi. He loves me," Rin said. "And you love him. You don't want him to know what you do. That's why you don't send him to the shop. And why you make me keep him in our room when you go out to meet your smugglers."

That did it. Auntie Fang stared at her, mouth agape, nostrils flaring.

"Let me at least try," Rin begged. "It can't hurt you to let me study. If I pass, then you'll at least be rid of me—and if I fail, you still have a bride."

Auntie Fang grabbed at the wok. Rin tensed instinctively, but Auntie Fang only resumed scrubbing it with a vengeance.

"You study in the shop, and I'll throw you out on the streets,"

Auntie Fang said. "I don't need this getting back to the inspector."

"Deal," Rin lied through her teeth.

Auntie Fang snorted. "And what happens if you get in? Who's going to pay your tuition, your dear, impoverished tutor?"

Rin hesitated. She'd been hoping the Fangs might give her the dowry money as tuition, but she could see now that had been an idiotic hope.

"Tuition at Sinegard is free," she pointed out.

Auntie Fang laughed out loud. "Sinegard! You think you're going to test into Sinegard?"

Rin lifted her chin. "I could."

The military academy at Sinegard was the most prestigious institution in the Empire, a training ground for future generals and statesmen. It rarely recruited from the rural south, if ever.

"You *are* deluded." Auntie Fang snorted again. "Fine—study if you like, if that makes you happy. By all means, take the Keju. But when you fail, you *will* marry that inspector. And you will be grateful."

That night, cradling a stolen candle on the floor of the cramped bedroom that she shared with Kesegi, Rin cracked open her first Keju primer.

The Keju tested the Four Noble Subjects: history, mathematics, logic, and the Classics. The imperial bureaucracy in Sinegard considered these subjects integral to the development of a scholar and a statesman. Rin had to learn them all by her sixteenth birthday.

She set a tight schedule for herself: she was to finish at least two books every week, and to rotate between two subjects each day. Each night after she had closed up shop, she ran to Tutor Feyrik's house before returning home, arms laden with more books.

History was the easiest to learn. Nikan's history was a highly entertaining saga of constant warfare. The Empire had been formed a millennium ago under the mighty sword of the merciless Red Emperor, who destroyed the monastic orders scattered across the continent and created a unified state of unprecedented size. It was the first time the Nikara people had ever conceived of themselves as a single nation. The Red Emperor standardized the Nikara language, issued a uniform set of weights and measurements, and built a system of roads that connected his sprawling territory.

But the newly conceived Nikara Empire did not survive the Red Emperor's death. His many heirs turned the country into a bloody mess during the Era of Warring States that followed, which divided Nikan into twelve rival provinces.

Since then, the massive country had been reunified, conquered, exploited, shattered, and then unified again. Nikan had in turn been at war with the khans of the northern Hinterlands and the tall westerners from across the great sea. Both times Nikan had proven itself too massive to suffer foreign occupation for very long.

Of all Nikan's attempted conquerors, the Federation of Mugen had come the closest. The island country had attacked Nikan at a time when domestic turmoil between the provinces was at its peak. It took two Poppy Wars and fifty years of bloody occupation for Nikan to win back its independence.

The Empress Su Daji, the last living member of the troika who had seized control of the state during the Second Poppy War, now ruled over a land of twelve provinces that had never quite managed to achieve the same unity that the Red Emperor had imposed.

The Nikara Empire had proven itself historically unconquerable. But it was also unstable and disunited, and the current spell of peace held no promise of durability.

If there was one thing Rin had learned about her country's history, it was that the only permanent thing about the Nikara Empire was war.

The second subject, mathematics, was a slog. It wasn't overly challenging but tedious and tiresome. The Keju did not filter for genius mathematicians but rather for students who could keep up things such as the country's finances and balance books. Rin had been doing accounting for the Fangs since she could add. She was naturally apt at juggling large sums in her head. She still had to bring herself up to speed on the more abstract trigonometric theorems, which she assumed mattered for naval battles, but she found that learning those was pleasantly straightforward.

The third section, logic, was entirely foreign to her. The Keju posed logic riddles as open-ended questions. She flipped open a sample exam for practice. The first question read: "A scholar traveling a well-trodden road passes a pear tree. The tree is laden with fruit so heavy that the branches bend over with its weight. Yet he does not pick the fruit. Why?"

Because it's not his pear tree, Rin thought immediately. *Because the owner might be Auntie Fang and break his head open with a shovel.* But those responses were either moral or contingent. The answer to the riddle had to be contained within the question itself. There must be some fallacy, some contradiction in the given scenario.

Rin had to think for a long while before she came up with the answer: *If a tree by a well-traveled road has this much fruit, then there must be something wrong with the fruit.*

The more she practiced, the more she came to see the questions as games. Cracking them was very rewarding. Rin drew diagrams in the dirt, studied the structures of syllogisms, and memorized the more common logical fallacies. Within months, she could answer these kinds of questions in mere seconds.

Her worst subject by far was Classics. It was the exception to her rotating schedule. She had to study Classics every day.

This section of the Keju required students to recite, analyze, and compare texts of a predetermined canon of twenty-seven books. These books were written not in the modern script but in the Old Nikara language, which was notorious for unpredictable grammar patterns and tricky pronunciations. The books contained poems, philosophical treatises, and essays on statecraft written by the legendary scholars of Nikan's past. They were meant to shape the moral character of the nation's future statesmen. And they were, without exception, hopelessly confusing.

Unlike with logic and mathematics, Rin could not reason her way out of Classics. Classics required a knowledge base that most students had been slowly building since they could read. In two years, Rin had to simulate more than five years of constant study.

To that end, she achieved extraordinary feats of rote memorization.

She recited backward while walking along the edges of the old defensive walls that encircled Tikany. She recited at double speed while hopping across posts over the lake. She mumbled to herself in the store, snapping in irritation whenever customers asked for her help. She would not let herself sleep unless she had recited that day's lessons without error. She woke up chanting classical analects, which terrified Kesegi, who thought she had been possessed by ghosts. And in a way, she had been—she dreamed of ancient poems by long-dead voices and woke up shaking from nightmares where she'd gotten them wrong.

"The Way of Heaven operates unceasingly, and leaves no accumulation of its influence in any particular place, so that all things are brought to perfection by it . . . so does the Way operate, and all under the sky turn to them, and all within the seas submit to them."

Rin put down Zhuangzi's *Annals* and scowled. Not only did she have no idea what Zhuangzi was writing about, she also couldn't see why he had insisted on writing in the most irritatingly verbose manner possible.

She understood very little of what she read. Even the scholars of Yuelu Mountain had trouble understanding the Classics; she could hardly be expected to glean their meaning on her own. And because she didn't have the time or the training to delve deep into the texts—and since she could think of no useful mnemonics, no shortcuts to learning the Classics—she simply had to learn them word by word and hope that would be enough.

She walked everywhere with a book. She studied as she ate. When she tired, she conjured up images for herself, telling herself the story of the worst possible future.

You walk up the aisle in a dress that doesn't fit you. You're trembling. He's waiting at the other end. He looks at you like you're a juicy, fattened pig, a marbled slab of meat for his purchase. He spreads saliva over his dry lips. He doesn't look away from you throughout the entire banquet. When it's over, he carries you to his bedroom. He pushes you onto the sheets.

She shuddered. Squeezed her eyes shut. Reopened them and found her place on the page.

By Rin's fifteenth birthday she held a vast quantity of ancient Nikara literature in her head, and could recite the majority of it. But she was still making mistakes: missing words, switching up complex clauses, mixing up the order of the stanzas.

This was good enough, she knew, to test into a teacher's college or a medical academy. She suspected she might even test into the scholars' institute at Yuelu Mountain, where the most brilliant minds in Nikan produced stunning works of literature and pondered the mysteries of the natural world.

But she could not afford any of those academies. She *had* to test into Sinegard. She had to test into the highest-scoring percentage of students not just in the village, but in the entire country. Otherwise, her two years of study would be wasted.

She had to make her memory perfect.

She stopped sleeping.

Her eyes became bloodshot, swollen. Her head swam from days of cramming. When she visited Tutor Feyrik at his home one night to pick up a new set of books, her gaze was desperate, unfocused. She stared past him as he spoke. His words drifted over her head like clouds; she barely registered his presence.

"Rin. Look at me."

She inhaled sharply and willed her eyes to focus on his fuzzy form.

"How are you holding up?" he asked.

"I can't do it," she whispered. "I only have two more months, and I can't do it. Everything is spilling out of my head as quickly as I put it in, and—" Her chest rose and fell very quickly.

"Oh, Rin."

Words spilled from her mouth. She spoke without thinking. "What happens if I don't pass? What if I get married after all? I guess I could kill him. Smother him in his sleep, you know? Would I inherit his fortune? That would be fine, wouldn't it?" She began to laugh hysterically. Tears rolled down her cheeks. "It's easier than doping him up. No one would ever *know*."

Tutor Feyrik rose quickly and pulled out a stool. "Sit down, child."

Rin trembled. "I can't. I still have to get through Fuzi's *Analects* before tomorrow."

"Runin. Sit."

She sank onto the stool.

Tutor Feyrik sat down opposite her and took her hands in his. "I'll tell you a story," he said. "Once, not too long ago, there lived a scholar from a very poor family. He was too weak to work long hours in the fields, and his only chance of providing for his parents in their old age was to win a government position so that he might receive a robust stipend. To do this, he had to matriculate at an academy. With the last of his earnings, the scholar bought a set of textbooks and registered for the Keju. He was very tired, because he toiled in the fields all day and could only study at night."

Rin's eyes fluttered shut. Her shoulders heaved, and she suppressed a yawn.

Tutor Feyrik snapped his fingers in front of her eyes. "The scholar had to find a way to stay awake. So he pinned the end of his braid to the ceiling, so that every time he drooped forward, his hair would yank at his scalp and the pain would awaken him." Tutor Feyrik smiled sympathetically. "You're almost there, Rin. Just a little further. Please do not commit spousal homicide."

But she had stopped listening.

"The pain made him focus," she said.

"That's not really what I was trying to—"

"The pain made him focus," she repeated.

Pain could make *her* focus.

So Rin kept a candle by her books, dripping hot wax on her arm if she nodded off. Her eyes would water in pain, she would wipe her tears away, and she would resume her studies.

The day she took the exam, her arms were covered with burn scars.

Afterward, Tutor Feyrik asked her how the test went. She couldn't tell him. Days later, she couldn't remember those horrible, draining hours. They were a gap in her memory. When she tried to recall how she'd answered a particular question, her brain seized up and did not let her relive it.

She didn't want to relive it. She never wanted to think about it again.

Seven days until the scores were out. Every booklet in the province had to be checked, double-checked, and triple-checked.

For Rin, those days were unbearable. She hardly slept. For the past two years she had filled her days with frantic studying. Now she had nothing to do—her future was out of her hands, and knowing that made her feel far worse.

She drove everyone else mad with her fretting. She made mistakes at the shop. She created a mess out of inventory. She snapped at Kesegi and fought with the Fangs more than she should have.

More than once she considered stealing another pack of opium and smoking it. She had heard of women in the village committing suicide by swallowing opium nuggets whole. In the dark hours of the night, she considered that, too.

Everything hung in suspended animation. She felt as if she were drifting, her whole existence reduced to a single score.

She thought about making contingency plans, preparations to escape the village in case she hadn't tested out after all. But her mind refused to linger on the subject. She could not possibly con-

ceive of life after the Keju because there might not be a life after
the Keju.

Rin grew so desperate that for the first time in her life, she
prayed.

The Fangs were far from religious. They visited the village temple sporadically at best, mostly to exchange packets of opium behind the golden altar.

They were hardly alone in their lack of religious devotion.
Once the monastic orders had exerted even greater influence on
the country than the Warlords did now, but then the Red Emperor
had come crashing through the continent with his glorious quest
for unification, leaving slaughtered monks and empty temples in
his wake.

The monastic orders were gone now, but the gods remained:
numerous deities that represented every category from sweeping
themes of love and warfare to the mundane concerns of kitchens
and households. Somewhere, those traditions were kept alive by
devout worshippers who had gone into hiding, but most villagers
in Tikany frequented the temples only out of ritualistic habit. No
one truly believed—at least, no one who dared admit it. To the
Nikara, gods were only relics of the past: subjects of myths and
legends, but no more.

But Rin wasn't taking any chances. She stole out of the shop
early one afternoon and brought an offering of dumplings and
stuffed lotus root to the plinths of the Four Gods.

The temple was very quiet. At midday, she was the only one inside. Four statues gazed mutely at her through their painted eyes.
Rin hesitated before them. She was not entirely certain which one
she ought to pray to.

She knew their names, of course—the White Tiger, the Black
Tortoise, the Azure Dragon, and the Vermilion Bird. And she knew
that they represented the four cardinal directions, but they formed
only a small subset of the vast pantheon of deities that were worshipped in Nikan. This temple also bore shrines to smaller guardian
gods, whose likenesses hung on scrolls draped over the walls.

So many gods. Which was the god of test scores? Which was the god of unmarried shopgirls who wished to stay that way?

She decided to simply pray to all of them.

"If you exist, if you're up there, help me. Give me a way out of this shithole. Or if you can't do that, give the import inspector a heart attack."

She looked around the empty temple. What came next? She had always imagined that praying involved more than just speaking out loud. She spied several unused incense sticks lying by the altar. She lit the end of one of them by dipping it in the brazier, and then waved it experimentally in the air.

Was she supposed to hold the smoke to the gods? Or should she smoke the stick herself? She had just held the burned end to her nose when a temple custodian strode out from behind the altar.

They blinked at each other.

Slowly Rin removed the incense stick from her nostril.

"Hello," she said. "I'm praying."

"Please leave," he said.

Exam results were to be posted at noon outside the examination hall.

Rin closed up shop early and went downtown with Tutor Feyrik half an hour in advance. A large crowd had already gathered around the post, so they found a shady corner a hundred meters away and waited.

So many people had accumulated by the hall that Rin couldn't see when the scrolls were posted, but she knew because suddenly everyone was shouting, and the crowd was rushing forward, pressing Rin and Tutor Feyrik tightly into the fold.

Her heart beat so fast she could hardly breathe. She couldn't see anything except the backs of the people before her. She thought she might vomit.

When they finally got to the front, it took Rin a long time to find her name. She scanned the lower half of the scroll, hardly daring to breathe. Surely she hadn't scored well enough to make the top ten.

She didn't see *Fang Runin* anywhere.

Only when she looked at Tutor Feyrik and saw that he was crying did she realize what had happened.

Her name was at the very top of the scroll. She hadn't placed in the top ten. She'd placed at the top of the entire village. The entire *province*.

She had bribed a teacher. She had stolen opium. She had burned herself, lied to her foster parents, abandoned her responsibilities at the store, and broken a marriage deal.

And she was going to Sinegard.

CHAPTER 2

The last time Tikany had sent a student to Sinegard, the town magistrate threw a festival that lasted three days. Servants had passed baskets of red bean cakes and jugs of rice wine out in the streets. The scholar, the magistrate's nephew, had set off for the capital to the cheers of intoxicated peasants.

This year, Tikany's nobility felt reasonably embarrassed that an orphan shopgirl had snagged the only spot at Sinegard. Several anonymous inquiries were sent to the testing center. When Rin showed up at the town hall to enroll, she was detained for an hour while the proctors tried to extract a cheating confession from her.

"You're right," she said. "I got the answers from the exam administrator. I seduced him with my nubile young body. You caught me."

The proctors didn't believe a girl with no formal schooling could have passed the Keju.

She showed them her burn scars.

"I have nothing to tell you," she said, "because I didn't cheat. And you have no proof that I did. I studied for this exam. I mutilated myself. I read until my eyes burned. You can't scare me into a confession, because I'm telling the truth."

"Consider the consequences," snapped the female proctor. "Do you understand how serious this is? We can void your score and have you jailed for what you've done. You'll be dead before you're done paying off your fines. But if you confess now, we can make this go away."

"No, *you* consider the consequences," Rin snapped. "If you decide my score is void, that means this simple *shopgirl* was clever enough to bypass your famous anticheating protocols. And that means you're shit at your job. And I bet the magistrate will be just thrilled to let you take the blame for whatever cheating did or didn't happen."

A week later she was cleared of all charges. Officially, Tikany's magistrate announced that the scores had been a "mistake." He did not label Rin a cheater, but neither did he validate her score. The proctors asked Rin to keep her departure under wraps, threatening clumsily to detain her in Tikany if she did not comply.

Rin knew that was a bluff. Acceptance to Sinegard Academy was the equivalent of an imperial summons, and obstruction of any kind—even by provincial authorities—was tantamount to treason. That was why the Fangs, too, could not prevent her from leaving—no matter how badly they wanted to force her marriage.

Rin didn't need validation from Tikany; not from its magistrate, not from the nobles. She was leaving, she had a way out, and that was all that mattered.

Forms were filled out, letters were mailed. Rin was registered to matriculate at Sinegard on the first of the next month.

Farewell to the Fangs was an understandably understated affair. No one felt like pretending they were especially sad to be rid of the other.

Only Rin's foster brother, Kesegi, displayed any real disappointment.

"Don't go," he whined, clinging to her traveling cloak.

Rin knelt down and squeezed Kesegi hard.

"I would have left you anyway," she said. "If not for Sinegard, then to a husband's house."

Kesegi wouldn't let go. He spoke in a pathetic mumble. "Don't leave me with *her*."

Rin's stomach clenched. "You'll be all right," she murmured in Kesegi's ear. "You're a boy. And you're her son."

"But it's not fair."

"It's life, Kesegi."

Kesegi began to whimper, but Rin extracted herself from his viselike embrace and stood up. He tried to cling to her waist, but she pushed him away with more force than she had intended. Kesegi stumbled backward, stunned, and then opened his mouth to wail loudly.

Rin turned away from his tear-stricken face and pretended to be preoccupied with fastening the straps of her travel bag.

"Oh, shut your mouth." Auntie Fang grabbed Kesegi by the ear and pinched hard until his crying ceased. She glowered at Rin, standing in the doorway in her simple traveling clothes. In the late summer Rin wore a light cotton tunic and twice-mended sandals. She carried her only other set of clothing in a patched-up satchel slung over her shoulder. In that satchel Rin had also packed the Mengzi tome, a set of writing brushes that were a gift from Tutor Feyrik, and a small money pouch. That satchel held all of her possessions in the world.

Auntie Fang's lip curled. "Sinegard will eat you alive."

"I'll take my chances," Rin said.

To Rin's great relief, the magistrate's office supplied her with two tael as transportation fare—the magistrate had been compelled by Rin's imperial summons to cover her travel costs. With a tael and a half, Rin and Tutor Feyrik managed to buy two places on a caravan wagon traveling north to the capital.

"In the days of the Red Emperor, an unaccompanied bride carrying her dowry could travel from the southernmost tip of Rooster Province to the northernmost peaks of the Wudang Mountains." Tutor Feyrik couldn't help lecturing as they boarded the wagon. "These days, a lone soldier wouldn't make it two miles."

The Red Emperor's guards hadn't patrolled the mountains of Nikan in a long time. To travel alone over the Empire's vast roads was a good way to get robbed, murdered, or eaten. Sometimes all three—and sometimes not in that order.

"Your fare is going toward more than a seat on the wagon," the caravan leader said as he pocketed their coins. "It's paying for your bodyguards. Our men are the best in their business. If we run into the Opera, we'll scare them right off."

The Red Junk Opera was a religious cult of bandits and outlaws famous for their attempts on the Empress's life after the Second Poppy War. It had faded to myth by now, but remained vividly alive in the Nikara imagination.

"The Opera?" Tutor Feyrik scratched his beard absentmindedly. "I haven't heard that name for years. They're still out and about?"

"They've quieted down in the last decade, but I've heard a few rumors about sightings in the Kukhonin range. If our luck holds, though, we won't see hide or hair of them." The caravan leader slapped his belt. "I would go load up your things. I want to head out before this day gets any hotter."

Their caravan spent three weeks on the road, crawling north at what seemed to Rin an infuriatingly slow pace. Tutor Feyrik spent the trip regaling her with tales of his adventures in Sinegard decades ago, but his dazzling descriptions of the city only made her wild with impatience.

"The capital is nestled at the base of the Wudang range. The palace and the academy are both built into the mountainside, but the rest of the city lies in the valley below. Sometimes, on misty days, you'll look over the edge and it'll seem like you're standing higher than the clouds themselves. The capital's market alone is larger than all of Tikany. You could lose yourself in that market . . . you will see musicians playing on gourd pipes, street vendors who can fry pancake batter in the shape of your name, master calligraphers who will paint fans before your eyes for just two coppers.

"Speaking of. We'll want to exchange these at some point."

Tutor Feyrik patted the pocket where he kept the last of their travel money.

"They don't take taels and coppers in the north?" Rin asked.

Tutor Feyrik chuckled. "You really have never left Tikany, have you? There are probably twenty kinds of currency being circulated in this Empire—tortoise shells, cowry shells, gold, silver, copper ingots . . . all the provinces have their own currencies because they don't trust the imperial bureaucracy with monetary supply, and the bigger provinces have two or three. The only thing everyone takes is standard Sinegardian silver coins."

"How many can we get with this?" Rin asked.

"Not many," Tutor Feyrik said. "But exchange rates will get worse the closer we get to the city. We'd best do it before we're out of Rooster Province."

Tutor Feyrik was also full of warnings about the capital. "Keep your money in your front pocket at all times. The thieves in Sinegard are daring and desperate. I once caught a child with his hand in my pocket. He fought for my coin, even after I'd caught him in the act. Everyone will try to sell you things. When you hear solicitors, keep your eyes forward and pretend you haven't heard them, or they'll hound you the entire way down the street. They're paid to bother you. Stay away from cheap liquor. If a man is offering sorghum wine for less than an ingot for a jug, it's not real alcohol."

Rin was appalled. "How could you fake alcohol?"

"By mixing sorghum wine with methanol."

"Methanol?"

"Wood spirits. It's poisonous stuff; in large doses it'll make you go blind." Tutor Feyrik rubbed his beard. "While you're at it, stay away from the street vendors' soy sauce, too. Some places use human hair to simulate the acids in soy sauce at a lower cost. I hear hair has also found its way into bread and noodle dough. Hmm . . . for that matter, you're best off staying away from street food entirely. They sell you breakfast pancakes for two coppers apiece, but they fry them in gutter oil."

"*Gutter oil?*"

"Oil that's been scooped off the street. The big restaurants toss their cooking oil into the gutter. The street food vendors siphon it up and reuse it."

Rin's stomach turned.

Tutor Feyrik reached out and yanked on one of Rin's tight braids. "You'll want to find someone to cut these off for you before you get to the Academy."

Rin touched her hair protectively. "Sinegardian women don't grow their hair out?"

"The women in Sinegard are so vain about their hair that they'll imbibe raw eggs to maintain its gloss. This isn't about aesthetics. I don't want someone yanking you into the alleys. No one would hear from you until you turned up in a brothel months later."

Rin looked reluctantly down at her braids. She was too dark-skinned and scrawny to be considered any great beauty, but she had always felt that her long, thick hair was one of her better assets. "Do I have to?"

"They'll probably make you shear your hair at the Academy anyway," said Tutor Feyrik. "And they'll charge you for it. Sinegardian barbers aren't cheap." He rubbed his beard as he thought up more warnings. "Beware of fake currency. You can tell a silver's not an imperial silver if it lands Red Emperor–side up ten throws in a row. If you see someone lying down with no visible injuries, don't help them up. They'll say you pushed them, take you to court, and sue you for the clothes off your back. And stay away from the gambling houses." Tutor Feyrik's tone turned sour. "Their people don't mess around."

Rin was starting to understand why he had left Sinegard.

But nothing Tutor Feyrik said could dampen her excitement. If anything, it made her even more impatient to arrive. She would not be an outsider in the capital. She would not be eating street food or living in the city slums. She did not have to fight for scraps or scrounge together coins for a meal. She had already secured a position for herself. She was a student of the most prestigious academy in all of the Empire. Surely that insulated her from the city's dangers.

That night she cut off her braids by herself with a rusty knife she'd borrowed from one of the caravan guards. She jerked the blade as close to her ears as she dared, sawing back and forth until her hair gave way. It took longer than she had imagined. When she was done, she stared for a minute at the two thick ropes of hair that lay in her lap.

She had thought she might keep them, but now she could not see any sentimental value in doing so. They were just clumps of dead hair. She wouldn't even be able to sell them for much up north—Sinegardian hair was famously thin and silky, and no one wanted the coarse tresses of a peasant from Tikany. Instead, she hurled them out the side of the wagon and watched them fall behind on the dusty road.

Their party arrived in the capital just as Rin was starting to go mad from boredom.

She could see Sinegard's famous East Gate from miles off—an imposing gray wall topped by a three-tiered pagoda, emblazoned with a dedication to the Red Emperor: *Eternal Strength, Eternal Harmony.*

Ironic, Rin thought, for a country that had been at war more often than it had been at peace.

Just as they approached the rounded doors below, their caravan came to an abrupt halt.

Rin waited. Nothing happened.

After twenty minutes had passed, Tutor Feyrik leaned out of their wagon and caught the attention of a caravan guide. "What's going on?"

"Federation contingent up ahead," the guide said. "They're here about some border dispute. They're getting their weapons checked at the gate—it'll be a few more minutes."

Rin sat up straight. "Those are Federation soldiers?"

She'd never seen Mugenese soldiers in person—at the end of the Second Poppy War, all Mugenese nationals had been forced out of their occupied areas and either sent home or relocated to limited diplomatic and trading offices on the mainland. To those Nikara born after occupation, they were the specters of modern history—always lingering in the borderlands, an ever-present threat whose face was unknown.

Tutor Feyrik's hand shot out and grabbed her wrist before she could hop out of the wagon. "Get back here."

"But I want to see!"

"No, you don't." He gripped her by the shoulders. "You *never* want to see Federation soldiers. If you cross them—if they even think you've *looked* at them funny—they can and will hurt you. They still have diplomatic immunity. They don't give a shit. Do you understand?"

"We *won* the war," she scoffed. "The occupation's over."

"We *barely* won the war." He shoved her back into a sitting position. "And there's a reason why all your instructors at Sinegard care only about winning the next one."

Someone shouted a command at the front of the caravan. Rin felt a lurch; then the wagons began to move again. She leaned over the side of their wagon, trying to catch a glimpse up ahead, but all she could see was a blue uniform disappearing through the heavy doors.

And then, at last, they were through the gates.

The downtown marketplace was an assault on the senses. Rin had never seen so many people or *things* in one place at one time. She was quickly overwhelmed by the deafening clamor of buyers haggling with sellers over prices, the bright colors of flowery skeins of silk splayed out on grand display boards, and the cloyingly pungent odors of durian and peppercorn drifting up from vendors' portable grills.

"The women here are so *white*," Rin marveled. "Like the girls in wall paintings."

The skin tones she observed from the caravan had moved up

the color gradient the farther north they drove. She knew that the people of the northern provinces were industrialists and business-men. They were citizens of class and means; they didn't labor in the fields like Tikany's farmers did. But she hadn't expected the differences to be this pronounced.

"They're pale as their corpses will be," Tutor Feyrik said dis-missively. "They're terrified of the sun." He grumbled in irritation as a pair of women with day parasols strolled past him, accidentally whacking him in the face.

Rin discovered quickly that Sinegard had the unique ability to make newcomers feel as unwelcome as possible.

Tutor Feyrik had been right—everyone in Sinegard wanted money. Vendors screamed at them persistently from all directions. Before Rin had even stepped off the wagon, a porter ran up to them and offered to carry their luggage—two pathetically light travel bags—for the small fee of eight imperial silvers.

Rin balked; that was almost a quarter of what they'd paid for a spot on the caravan.

"I'll carry it," she stammered, jerking her travel bag away from the porter's clawing fingers. "Really, I don't need—let go!"

They escaped the porter only to be assaulted by a crowd, each person offering a different menial service.

"Rickshaw? Do you need a rickshaw?"

"Little girl, are you lost?"

"No, we're just trying to find the school—"

"I'll take you there, very low fee, five ingots, only five ingots—"

"Get lost," snapped Tutor Feyrik. "We don't need your ser-vices."

The hawkers slunk back into the marketplace.

Even the spoken language of the capital made Rin uncomfort-able. Sinegardian Nikara was a grating dialect, brisk and curt no matter the content. Tutor Feyrik asked three different strangers for directions to the campus before one gave a response that he understood.

"Didn't you live here?" Rin asked.

"Not since the occupation," Tutor Feyrik grumbled. "It's easy to lose a language when you never speak it."

Rin supposed that was fair. She herself found the dialect nearly indecipherable; every word, it seemed, had to be shortened, with a curt *r* noise added to the end. In Tikany, speech was slow and rolling. The southerners drew out their vowels, rolled their words over their tongues like sweet rice congee. In Sinegard, it seemed no one had time to finish his words.

Even with directions, the city itself was no more navigable than its dialect. Sinegard was the oldest city in the country, and its architecture bore evidence of the multiple shifts in power in Nikan over the centuries. Buildings were either of new construction or were falling into decay, emblems of regimes that had long ago fallen out of power. In the eastern districts stood the spiraling towers of the old Hinterlander invaders from the north. To the west, blocklike compounds stood wedged narrowly next to one another, a holdover from Federation occupation during the Poppy Wars. It was a tableau of a country with many rulers, represented in a single city.

"Do you know where we're going?" Rin asked after several minutes of walking uphill.

"Only vaguely." Tutor Feyrik was sweating profusely. "It's become a labyrinth since I was here. How much money have we got left?"

Rin dug out her coin pouch and counted. "A string and a half of silvers."

"That should more than cover what we need." Tutor Feyrik mopped at his brow with his cloak. "Why don't we treat ourselves to a ride?"

He stepped out onto the dusty street and raised an arm. Almost immediately a rickshaw runner swerved across the road and halted jerkily in front of them.

"Where to?" panted the runner.

"The Academy," said Tutor Feyrik. He tossed their bags into the back and climbed into the seat. Rin grasped the sides and was about to pull herself in when she heard a sharp cry behind her. Startled, she turned around.

A child lay sprawled in the center of the road. Several paces ahead, a horse-drawn carriage had veered off course.

"You just hit that kid!" Rin screamed. "Hey, *stop!*"

The driver yanked the horse's reins. The wagon screeched to a halt. The passenger craned his neck out of the carriage and caught sight of the child feebly stirring in the street.

The child stood up, miraculously alive. Blood trickled down in tiny rivulets from the top of his forehead. He touched two fingers to his head and glanced down, dazed.

The passenger leaned forward and uttered a harsh command to the driver that Rin didn't understand.

The wagon turned slowly. For an absurd moment Rin thought the driver was going to offer the child a lift. Then she heard the crack of a whip.

The child stumbled and tried to run.

Rin shrieked over the sound of clomping hooves.

Tutor Feyrik reached toward the gaping rickshaw runner and tapped him on the shoulder. "Go. *Go!*"

The runner sped up, dragged them faster and faster over the rutted streets until the exclamations of bystanders died away behind them.

"The driver was smart," said Tutor Feyrik as they wobbled over the bumpy road. "You cripple a child, you pay a disabilities fine for their entire life. But if you kill them, you pay the funeral fee once. And that's only if you're caught. If you hit someone, better make sure they're dead."

Rin clung to the side of the carriage and tried not to vomit.

Sinegard the city was smothering, confusing, and frightening.

But Sinegard Academy was beautiful beyond description.

Their rickshaw driver dropped them at the base of the mountains at the edge of the city. Rin let Tutor Feyrik handle the luggage and ran up to the school gates, breathless.

She'd been imagining for weeks now what it would be like to ascend the steps to the Academy. The entire country knew how Sinegard Academy looked; the school's likeness was painted on wall scrolls throughout Nikan.

Those scrolls didn't come close to capturing the campus in reality. A winding stone pathway curved around the mountain, spiraling upward into a complex of pagodas built on successively higher tiers. At the highest tier stood a shrine, on the tower of which perched a stone dragon, the symbol of the Red Emperor. A glimmering waterfall hung like a skein of silk beside the shrine.

The Academy looked like a palace for the gods. This was a place out of legend. This was her home for the next five years.

Rin was speechless.

Rin and Tutor Feyrik were given a tour of the grounds by an older student who introduced himself as Tobi. Tobi was tall, bald-headed, and clad in a black tunic with a red armband. He wore a dedicatedly bored sneer to indicate he would rather have been doing anything else.

They were joined by a slender, attractive woman who initially mistook Tutor Feyrik for a porter and then apologized without embarrassment. Her son was a fine-featured boy who would have been very pretty if he hadn't had such a resentful expression on his face.

"The Academy is built on the grounds of an old monastery." Tobi motioned for them to follow him up the stone steps to the first tier. "The temples and praying grounds were converted to classrooms once the Red Emperor united the tribes of Nikan. First-year students have sweeping duty, so you'll get familiar with the grounds soon enough. Come on, try to keep up."

Even Tobi's lack of enthusiasm couldn't detract from the Academy's beauty, but he did his best. He walked the stone steps in a rapid, practiced manner, not bothering to check whether his guests were keeping pace. Rin was left behind to help the wheezing Tutor Feyrik up the perilously narrow stairs.

There were seven tiers to the Academy. Each curve of the stone pathway brought into view a new complex of buildings and training grounds, embedded in lush foliage that had clearly been carefully cultivated for centuries. A rushing brook sliced down the mountainside, cleaving the campus neatly in two.

"The library is over there. Mess hall is this way. New students live at the lowest tier. Up there are the masters' quarters." Tobi pointed very rapidly to several stone buildings that all looked alike.

"What about that?" Rin asked, pointing to an important-looking building by the brook.

Tobi's lip curled up. "That's the outhouse, kid."

The handsome boy snickered. Cheeks burning, Rin pretended to be very fascinated by the view from the terrace.

"Where are you from, anyway?" Tobi asked in a not-very-friendly tone.

"Rooster Province," Rin muttered.

"Ah. The south." Tobi sounded like something made sense to him now. "I guess multistory buildings are a new concept to you, but try not to get too overwhelmed."

After Rin's registration papers had been checked and filed, Tutor Feyrik had no reason to stay. They said their goodbyes outside the school gates.

"I understand if you're scared," Tutor Feyrik said.

Rin swallowed down the massive lump in her throat and clenched her teeth. Her head buzzed; she knew a dam of tears would break out from under her eyes if she didn't suppress it.

"I'm not scared," she insisted.

He smiled gently. "Of course you're not."

Her face crumpled, and she rushed forward to embrace him. She buried her face in his tunic so that no one could see her crying. Tutor Feyrik patted her on the shoulder.

She had made it all the way across the country to a place she had spent years dreaming of, only to discover a hostile, confusing city that despised southerners. She had no home in Tikany or Sinegard. Everywhere she traveled, everywhere she escaped to, she was just a war orphan who was not supposed to be there.

She felt so terribly alone.

"I don't want you to go," she said.

Tutor Feyrik's smile fell. "Oh, Rin."

"I hate it here," she blurted suddenly. "I *hate* this city. The way they talk—that stupid apprentice—it's like they don't think I should be here."

"Of course they don't," said Tutor Feyrik. "You're a war orphan. You're a southerner. You weren't supposed to pass the Keju. The Warlords like to claim that the Keju makes Nikan a meritocracy, but the system is designed to keep the poor and illiterate in their place. You're offending them with your very presence."

He grasped her by the shoulders and bent slightly so that they were eye to eye. "Rin, listen. Sinegard is a cruel city. The Academy will be worse. You will be studying with children of Warlords. Children who have been training in martial arts since before they could even walk. They'll make you an outsider, because you're not like them. That's *okay*. Don't let any of that discourage you. No matter what they say, *you deserve to be here*. Do you understand?"

She nodded.

"Your first day of classes will be like a punch to the gut," Tutor Feyrik continued. "Your second day, probably even worse. You'll find your courses harder than studying for the Keju ever was. But if anyone can survive here, it's you. Don't forget what you did to get here."

He straightened up. "And don't ever come back to the south. You're better than that."

As Tutor Feyrik disappeared down the path, Rin pinched the bridge of her nose, willing the hot feeling behind her eyes to go away. She could not let her new classmates see her cry.

She was alone in a city without a friend, where she barely spoke the language, at a school that she now wasn't sure she wanted to attend.

He leads you down the aisle. He's old and fat, and he smells like sweat. He looks at you and he licks his lips . . .

She shuddered, squeezed her eyes shut, and opened them again.

So Sinegard was frightening and unfamiliar. It didn't matter. She didn't have anywhere else to go.

She squared her shoulders and walked back through the school gates.

This was better. No matter what, this was a thousand times better than Tikany.

"And then she asked if the outhouse was a classroom," said a voice from farther down in the line for registration. "You should have seen her clothes."

Rin's neck prickled. It was the boy from the tour.

She turned around.

He really was pretty, impossibly so, with large, almond-shaped eyes and a sculpted mouth that looked good even twisted into a sneer. His skin was a shade of porcelain white that any Sinegardian woman would have murdered for, and his silky hair was almost as long as Rin's had been.

He caught her eye and smirked, continuing loudly as if he hadn't seen her. "And her teacher, you know, I bet he's one of those doddering failures who can't get a job in the city so they spend their lives trying to scrape a living from local magistrates. I thought he might die on the way up the mountain, he was wheezing so loud."

Rin had dealt with verbal abuse from the Fangs for years. Hearing insults from this boy hardly fazed her. But slandering Tutor Feyrik, the man who had delivered her from Tikany, who had saved her from a miserable future in a forced marriage . . . that was unforgivable.

Rin took two steps toward the boy and punched him in the face.

Her fist connected with his eye socket with a pleasant popping noise. The boy staggered backward into the students behind him, nearly toppling to the ground.

"You *bitch*!" he screeched. He righted himself and rushed at her. She shrank back, fists raised.

"Stop!" A dark-robed apprentice appeared between them, arms flung out to keep them apart. When the boy struggled forward anyway, the apprentice quickly grabbed his extended arm by the wrist and twisted it behind his back.

The boy stumbled, immobilized.

"Don't you know the rules?" The apprentice's voice was low, calm, and controlled. "No fighting."

The boy said nothing, mouth twisted into a sullen sneer. Rin fought the sudden urge to cry.

"Names?" the apprentice demanded.

"Fang Runin," she said quickly, terrified. Were they in trouble? Would she be expelled?

The boy struggled in vain against the apprentice's hold.

The apprentice tightened his grip. "Name?" he asked again.

"Yin Nezha," the boy spat.

"Yin?" The apprentice let him go. "And what is the well-bred heir to the House of Yin doing brawling in a hallway?"

"She punched me in the face!" Nezha screeched. A nasty bruise was already blossoming around his left eye, a bright splotch of purple against porcelain skin.

The apprentice raised an eyebrow at Rin. "And why would you do that?"

"He insulted my teacher," she said.

"Oh? Well, that's different." The apprentice looked amused. "Weren't you taught not to insult teachers? That's taboo."

"I'll kill you," Nezha snarled at Rin. "I will fucking *kill* you."

"Aw, shut it." The apprentice feigned a yawn. "You're at a military academy. You'll have plenty of opportunities to kill each other throughout this year. But save it until after orientation, won't you?"

CHAPTER 3

Rin and Nezha were the last ones to the main hall—a converted temple on the third tier of the mountain. Though the hall was not particularly large, its spare, dim interior gave an illusion of great space, making those inside feel smaller than they were. Rin supposed this was the intended effect when one was in the presence of both gods and teachers.

The class of first-years, no more than fifty in total, sat kneeling in rows of ten. They twisted their hands in their laps, blinking and looking around in silent anxiety. The apprentices sat in rows around them, chatting casually with one another. Their laughter sounded louder than normal, as if they were trying to make the first-years feel uncomfortable on purpose.

Moments after Rin sat down, the front doors swung open and a tiny woman, shorter even than the smallest first-year, strode into the hall. She walked with a soldier's gait—perfectly erect, precise, and controlled.

Five men and one woman, all wearing dark brown robes, followed her inside. They formed a row behind her at the front of the room and stood with hands folded into their sleeves. The apprentices fell silent and rose to their feet, hands clasped behind them and heads tilted forward in a slight bow. Rin and the other first-years took their cue and hastily scrambled to their feet.

The woman gazed out at them for a moment, then gestured for them to sit.

"Welcome to Sinegard. I am Jima Lain. I am grand master of this school, commander of the Sinegardian Reserve Forces, and former commander of the Nikara Imperial Militia." Jima's voice cut through the room like a blade, precise and chilly.

Jima indicated the six people arrayed behind her. "These are the masters of Sinegard. They will be your instructors during your first year, and will ultimately decide whether to take you on as their apprentices following your end-of-year Trials."

The masters were a solemn crowd, each more imposing than the last. None of them smiled. Each wore a belt of a different color—red, blue, purple, green, and orange.

Except one. The man to Jima's left wore no belt at all. His robe, too, was different—no embroidery at the edges, no insignia of the Red Emperor stitched over his right breast. He was dressed as if he'd forgotten orientation was happening and had thrown on a formless brown cloak at the last minute.

This master's hair was the pure white of Tutor Feyrik's beard, but he was nowhere near as old. His face was curiously unlined but not youthful; it was impossible to tell his age. As Jima spoke, he dug his little finger around in his ear canal, and then brought his finger up to his eyes to examine the discharge.

He glanced up suddenly, caught Rin staring at him, and smirked. She hastily looked away.

"You all are here because you achieved the highest Keju scores in the country," said Jima, spreading her hands magnanimously. "You have beaten thousands of other pupils for the honor of studying here. Congratulations."

The first-years cast awkward glances at one another, uncertain of whether they should be applauding themselves. A few tentative claps sounded across the room.

Jima smirked. "Next year a fifth of you will be gone."

The silence then was acute.

"Sinegard does not have the time nor resources to train every child who dreams of glory in the military. Even illiterate farmers can become soldiers. But we do not train soldiers here. We train *generals*. We train the people who hold the future of the Empire in their hands. So, should I decide you are no longer worth our time, you will be asked to leave.

"You'll notice that you were not given a choice of a field of study. We do not believe this choice should be left in the hands of the students. After your first year, you will be evaluated for proficiency in each of the subject tracks we teach here: Combat, Strategy, History, Weaponry, Linguistics, and Medicine."

"And Lore," interrupted the white-haired master.

Jima's left eye twitched. "And Lore. If, in your end-of-year Trials, you are found worthy of one track of study, you will be approved to continue at Sinegard. You will then attain the rank of apprentice."

Jima gestured to the older students surrounding them. Rin saw now that the apprentices' armbands matched the masters' belts in color.

"If no master sees fit to take you on as an apprentice, you will be asked to leave the Academy. The first-year retention rate is usually eighty percent. Look around you. This means that this time next year, two people in your row will be gone."

Rin glanced around her, fighting a rising swell of panic. She had thought testing into Sinegard was a guarantee of a home for at least the next five years, if not a stable career afterward.

She hadn't realized she might be sent home in months.

"We cull out of necessity, not cruelty. Our task is to train only the elite—the best of the best. We don't have time to waste on dilettantes. Take a good look at your classmates. They will become your closest friends, but also your greatest rivals. You are competing against each other to remain at this academy. We believe it is through that competition that those with talent will make themselves known. And those without will be sent home. If you deserve it, you will be present next year as an apprentice. If you aren't . . . well then, you should never have been sent here in the first place." Jima seemed to look directly at Rin.

"Lastly, I will give a warning. I do not tolerate drugs on this campus. If you have even so much as a whiff of opium on you, if you are caught within ten *paces* of an illegal substance, you will be dragged out of the Academy and thrown into the Baghra prison."

Jima fixed them with a last, stern look and then dismissed them with a wave of her hand. "Good luck."

Raban, the apprentice who had broken up Rin and Nezha's fight, led them out of the main hall to the dormitories on the lowest tier.

"You're first-years, so you'll have sweeping duties starting next week," Raban said, walking backward to address them. He had a kind and soothing voice, the sort of tone Rin had heard village physicians adopt before amputating limbs. "First bell rings at sunrise; classes begin half an hour after that. Be in the mess hall before then or you miss breakfast."

The boys were housed in the largest building on campus, a three-story structure that looked like it had been built long after the Academy grounds were seized from the monks. The women's quarters were tiny in contrast, a spare one-story building that used to be a single meditation room.

Rin expected the dorm to be uncomfortably cramped, but only two other bunks showed signs of habitation.

"Three girls in one year is actually a record high," Raban said before he left them to settle in. "The masters were shocked."

Alone in the dorm, the three girls warily sized one another up.

"I'm Niang," offered the girl to Rin's left. She had a round, friendly face, and she spoke with a lilting accent that belied her northern heritage, though it was nowhere as indecipherable as the Sinegardian dialect. "I'm from the Hare Province."

"Pleased," the other girl drawled. She was inspecting her bed-sheets. She rubbed the thin off-white material between her fingers, made a disgusted face, and then let the fabric drop. "Venka," she said begrudgingly. "Dragon Province, but I grew up in the capital."

Venka was an archetypical Sinegardian beauty; she was pretty in a pale way, and slim as a willow branch. Rin felt coarse and unsophisticated standing next to her.

She realized both were watching her expectantly.

"Runin," she said. "Rin for short."

"*Runin.*" Venka mangled the name with her Sinegardian accent, rolled the syllables through her mouth like some bad-tasting morsel. "What kind of name is *that*?"

"It's southern," Rin said. "I'm from Rooster Province."

"That's why your skin's so dark," Venka said, lip curling. "Brown as cow manure."

Rin's nostrils flared. "I went out in the sun once. You should try it sometime."

Just as Tutor Feyrik had warned, classes escalated quickly. Martial arts training commenced in the second-tier courtyard immediately after sunrise the next day.

"What's this?" Master Jun, the red-belted Combat instructor, regarded their huddled class with a disgusted expression. "Line up. I want straight rows. Stop clumping together like frightened hens."

Jun possessed a pair of fantastically thick black eyebrows that almost met in the middle of his forehead. They rested on his swarthy face like a thundercloud over a permanent scowl.

"Backs straight." Jun's voice matched his face: gruff and unforgiving. "Eyes forward. Arms behind your backs."

Rin strained to mirror the stances of her classmates in front of her. Her left thigh prickled, but she didn't dare scratch it. Too late, she realized she had to pee.

Jun paced to the front of the courtyard, satisfied that they were standing as uncomfortably as possible. He stopped in front of Nezha. "What happened to your face?"

Nezha had developed a truly spectacular bruise over his left eye, a bright splotch of violet on his otherwise flawless mien.

"Got in a fight," Nezha mumbled.

"When?"

"Last night."

"You're lucky," Jun said. "If it had been any later, I would have expelled you."

He raised his voice to address the class. "The first and most important rule of my class is this: do not fight irresponsibly. The techniques you are learning are lethal in application. If improperly performed, they will cause serious injury to yourself or your training partner. If you fight irresponsibly, I will suspend you from my class and lobby to have you expelled from Sinegard. Am I understood?"

"Yes, sir," they answered.

Nezha twisted his head over his shoulder and shot Rin a look of pure venom. She pretended not to see.

"Who's had martial arts training before?" Jun asked. "Show of hands."

Nearly the entire class raised their arms. Rin glanced around the courtyard, feeling a swell of panic. Had so many of them trained before the Academy? *Where* had they trained? How far ahead of her were they? What if she couldn't keep up?

Jun pointed to Venka. "How many years?"

"Twelve," said Venka. "I trained in the Gentle Fist style."

Rin's eyes widened. That meant Venka had been training almost since she could walk.

Jun pointed to a wooden dummy. "Backward crescent kick. Take the head off."

Take the head off? Rin looked doubtfully at the dummy. Its head and torso had been carved from the same piece of wood. The head hadn't been screwed on; it was solidly connected to the torso.

Venka, however, seemed entirely unperturbed. She positioned her feet, squinted at the dummy, and then whipped her back leg around in a twist that brought her foot high up over her head. Her heel cut through the air in a lovely, precise arc.

Her foot connected with the dummy's head and lobbed it off, sent it flying clean across the courtyard. The head clattered against the corner wall and rolled to one side.

Rin's jaw fell open.

Jun nodded curtly in approval and dismissed Venka. She returned to her place in the ranks, looking pleased.

"How did she do that?" Jun asked.

Magic, Rin thought.

Jun stopped in front of Niang. "You. You look bewildered. How do you think she did that?"

Niang blinked nervously. "*Ki*?"

"What is *ki*?"

Niang blushed. "Um. Inner energy. Spiritual energy?"

"Spiritual energy," Master Jun repeated. He snorted. "Village nonsense. Those who elevate *ki* to the level of mystery or the supernatural do a great disservice to martial arts. *Ki* is nothing but plain energy. The same energy that flows through your lungs and blood vessels. The same energy that moves rivers downstream and causes the wind to blow."

He pointed up to the bell tower on the fifth tier. "Two servicemen installed a newly smelted bell last year. Alone, they never would have lifted the bell all that distance. But with cleverly placed ropes, two men of average build managed to lift something many times their weight.

"The principle works in reverse for martial arts. You have a limited quantity of energy in your body. No amount of training will allow you to accomplish superhuman feats. But given the right discipline, knowing where to strike and when . . ." Jun slammed his fist out at the dummy's torso. It splintered, forming a perfect radius of cracks around his hand.

He pulled his arm away. The dummy torso shattered into pieces that clattered to the ground. "You can do what average humans *think* impossible. Martial arts is about action and reaction. Angles and trigonometry. The right amount of force applied at the proper vector. Your muscles contract and exert force, and that force is dispelled through to the target. If you build muscle mass, you can exert greater force. If you practice good technique, your force disperses with greater concentration and higher effectiveness. Martial arts is no more complicated than pure physics. If that confuses you, then simply take the advice of the grand masters. Don't ask questions. Just obey."

History was a lesson in humility. Stooped, balding Master Yim began expounding on Nikan's military embarrassments before they had even finished filing into the classroom.

"In the last century, the Empire has fought five wars," Yim said. "And we've lost every single one of them. This is why we call this past century the Age of Humiliation."

"Upbeat," muttered a wiry-haired kid in the front.

If Yim heard him, he didn't acknowledge it. He pointed to a large parchment map of the eastern hemisphere. "This country used to span half the continent under the Red Emperor. The Old Nikara Empire was the birthplace of modern civilization. The center of the world. All inventions originated from Old Nikan; among them the lodestone, the parchment press, and the blast furnace. Nikara delegates brought culture and methods of good governance to the islands of Mugen in the east and to Speer in the south.

"But empires fall. The old empire fell victim to its own splendor. Flush with victories of expansion in the north, the Warlords began fighting among themselves. The Red Emperor's death set off a series of succession battles with no clear resolution. And so Nikan split into the Twelve Provinces, each headed by one Warlord. For most of recent history, the Warlords have been preoccupied with fighting each other. Until—"

"The Poppy Wars," said the wiry-haired kid.

"Yes. The Poppy Wars." Yim pointed to a country on Nikan's

border, a tiny island shaped like a longbow. "Without warning, Nikan's little brother to the east, its old tributary nation, turned its dagger on the very country that had given it civilization. The rest you know, surely."

Niang raised her hand. "Why did relations sour between Nikan and Mugen? The Federation was a peaceful tributary in the days of the Red Emperor. What happened? What did they want from us?"

"Relations were never peaceful," Yim corrected. "And are not to this day. Mugen has always wanted more, even when it was a tributary. The Federation is an ambitious, rapidly growing country with a bulging population on a tiny island. Imagine you're a highly militaristic country with more people than your land can sustain, and nowhere to expand. Imagine that your rulers have propagated an ideology that they are gods, and that you have a divine right to extend your empire across the eastern hemisphere. Suddenly the sprawling landmass right across the Nariin Sea looks like a prime target, doesn't it?"

He turned back to the map. "The First Poppy War was a disaster. The fractured Empire could never stand up against well-trained Federation troops, who had been drilling for decades for this enterprise. So here's a puzzle for you. How did we win the Second Poppy War?"

A boy named Han raised his hand. "The Trifecta?"

Muted snickers sounded around the classroom. The Trifecta—the Vipress, the Dragon Emperor, and the Gatekeeper—were three heroic soldiers who had unified the Empire against the Federation. They were real—the woman known as the Vipress still sat on the throne at Sinegard—but their legendary martial arts abilities were the subject of children's tales. Rin had grown up hearing stories about how the Trifecta had single-handedly flattened entire Federation battalions, leveraging storms and floods with their supernatural powers. But even she thought it sounded ridiculous in a lecture about history.

"Don't laugh. The Trifecta were important—without their political machinations, we might never have rallied the Twelve Provinces," said Yim. "But that's not the answer I'm looking for."

Rin raised her hand. She had memorized this answer from Tutor Feyrik's history primers. "We razed the heartland. Pursued a strategy of slash and burn. When the Federation army marched too far inland, their supply lines ran out and they couldn't feed their armies."

Yim acknowledged this answer with a shrug. "Good answer, but false. That's just propaganda they put in the countryside textbooks. The slash-and-burn strategy hurt the rural countryside more than it hurt Mugen. Anyone else?"

It was the wiry-haired boy in the front who got it right. "We won because we lost Speer."

Yim nodded. "Stand up. Explain."

The boy shoved his hair back and stood. "We won the war because losing Speer made Hesperia intervene. And, uh, Hesperia's naval abilities were vastly superior to Mugen's. They won the war over the ocean theater, and Nikan got looped into the subsequent peace treaty. The victory wasn't really ours at all."

"Correct," Yim said.

The boy sat, looking immensely relieved.

"Nikan did not win the Second Poppy War," Yim reiterated. "The Federation is gone because we were so pathetic that the great naval powers to the west felt bad for us. We did such a terrible job defending our country that it took *genocide* for Hesperia to intervene. While Nikara forces were tied up on the northern front, a fleet of Federation ships razed the Dead Island overnight. Every man, woman, and child on Speer was butchered, and their bodies burned. An entire race, gone in a day."

Their class was silent. They had grown up hearing stories about the destruction of Speer, a tiny island that punctuated the ocean between the Nariin Sea and Omonod Bay like a teardrop, lying just beside Snake Province. It had been the Empire's only remaining tributary state, conquered and annexed at the height of the

Red Emperor's reign. It held a fraught place in Nikan's history, a glaring example of the massive failure of the disunited army under the Warlords' regime.

Rin had always wondered whether the loss of Speer was purely an accident. If any other province had been destroyed the way Speer had, the Nikara Empire wouldn't have stopped with a peace treaty. They would have fought until the Federation of Mugen was in pieces.

But the Speerlies weren't really Nikara at all. Tall and brown-skinned, they were an island people who had always been ethnically separate from the Nikara mainlanders. They spoke their own language, wrote in their own script, and practiced their own religion. They had joined the Imperial Militia only at the Red Emperor's sword point.

This all pointed to strained relations between the Nikara and the Speerlies all the way up through the Second Poppy War. So, Rin thought, if any Nikara territory had to be sacrificed, Speer was the obvious choice.

"We have survived the last century through nothing more than sheer luck and the charity of the west," said Yim. "But even with Hesperia's help, Nikan only barely managed to drive out the Federation invaders. Under pressure from Hesperia, the Federation signed the Non-Aggression Pact at the end of the Second Poppy War, and Nikan has retained its independence since. The Federation has been relegated to trading outposts on the edge of the Horse Province, and for the past nearly two decades, they've more or less behaved.

"But the Mugenese grow restless, and Hesperia has never been good about keeping its promises. The heroes of the Trifecta have been reduced to one; the Emperor is dead, the Gatekeeper is lost, and only the Empress remains on the throne. Perhaps worse, we have no Speerly soldiers." Yim paused. "Our best fighting force is gone. Nikan no longer possesses the assets that helped us survive the Second Poppy War. Hesperia cannot be relied upon to save us again. If the past centuries have taught us anything, it is that

Nikan's enemies never rest. But this time when they come, we intend to be ready."

The noontime bell marked lunch.

Food was served from giant cauldrons lined up by the far wall—congee, fish stew, and loaves of rice flour buns—distributed by cooks who seemed wholly indifferent to their jobs.

The students were given portions just large enough to sate their growling stomachs, but not so much that they felt fully satisfied. Students who tried to pass through the line again were sent back to their tables empty-handed.

To Rin, the prospect of regular meals was more than generous— she'd frequently gone without dinner in the Fang household. But her classmates complained to Raban about the single portions.

"Jima's philosophy is that hunger is good. It'll keep you light, focused," explained Raban.

"It'll keep us miserable," Nezha grumbled.

Rin rolled her eyes but kept her mouth shut. They sat crammed in two rows of twenty-five along the wooden table near the end of the mess hall. The other tables were occupied by the apprentices, but not even Nezha had the nerve to attempt to sit among them.

Rin found herself crammed between Niang and the wiry-haired boy who had spoken up in History class.

"I'm Kitay," he introduced himself, once he'd finished inhaling his stew.

He was one year her junior and looked it—scrawny, freckled, with enormous ears. He also happened to have achieved the highest Keju score in Sinegard Municipality, by far the most competitive testing region, which was especially impressive for someone who had taken it a year early. He had a photographic memory, he wanted to study Strategy under Master Irjah once he got past the Trials, and didn't she think Jun was kind of an asshole?

"Yes. And I'm Runin. Rin," she said, once he let her get a word in.

"Oh, you're the one Nezha hates."

Rin supposed there were worse reputations to have. In any case, Kitay didn't seem to hold it against her. "What's his problem, anyway?" she asked.

"His father is the Dragon Warlord and his aunts have been concubines to the throne for generations. You'd be a prick too if your family was both rich *and* attractive."

"Do you know him?" Rin asked.

"We grew up together. Me, Nezha, and Venka. Shared the same tutor. I thought they'd be nicer to me once we were all at the Academy." Kitay shrugged, glancing at the far end of the table, where Nezha and Venka appeared to be holding court. "Guess I thought wrong."

Rin wasn't surprised that Nezha had cut Kitay out of his social circle. There was no way Nezha would have stuck around anyone half as witty as Kitay—there were too many opportunities for Kitay to upstage him. "What'd you do to offend him?"

Kitay pulled a face. "Nothing, except beat him on the exam. Nezha's prickly about his ego. Why, what did you do?"

"I gave him that black eye," she admitted.

Kitay raised an eyebrow. "Nice."

Lore was scheduled for after lunch, and then Linguistics. Rin had been looking forward to Lore all day. But the apprentices who led them to the class looked like they were trying not to laugh. They climbed the winding steps to the fifth tier, higher up than any of their other classes. Finally they stopped at an enclosed garden.

"What are we doing here?" Nezha asked.

"This is your classroom," said one of the apprentices. They glanced at each other, grinned, and then left. After five minutes, the cause of their amusement became clear. The Lore Master didn't show. Ten minutes passed. Then twenty.

The class milled around the garden awkwardly, trying to figure out what they were supposed to do.

"We've been pranked," suggested Han. "They led us to the wrong place."

"What do they grow in here, anyway?" Nezha pulled a flower down to his nose and sniffed it. "Gross."

Rin took a closer look at the flowers, then her eyes widened. She'd seen those petals before.

Nezha recognized it at the same moment that she did.

"Shit," he said. "That's a poppy plant."

Their class reacted like a startled nest of dormice. They scurried hastily away from the poppy plant as if mere proximity would get them high.

Rin fought the absurd urge to burst out laughing. Here on the other side of the country was at least one thing she was familiar with.

"We're going to be expelled," Venka wailed.

"Don't be stupid, it's not *our* poppy plant," Kitay said.

Venka flapped her hands around her face. "But Jima said if we were even within ten paces of—"

"It's not like they can expel the entire class," Kitay said. "I bet he's testing us. Seeing if we really want to learn."

"Or testing us to see how we'll react around illegal drugs!" Venka shrilled.

"Oh, calm down," Rin said. "You can't get high just by touching it."

Venka did not calm down. "But Jima didn't say she had to catch us high, she said—"

"I don't think it's a real class," Nezha interrupted. "I bet the apprentices are just having their bit of fun."

Kitay looked doubtful. "It's on our schedule. And we saw the Lore Master, he was at orientation."

"Then where were his apprentices?" Nezha shot back. "What color was his belt? Why don't you see anyone walking around with *Lore* stitched into their armbands? This is stupid."

Nezha stalked out through the gates. Encouraged, the rest of the class followed him out, one by one. Finally Rin and Kitay were the only ones left in the garden.

Rin sat down and leaned back on her elbows, admiring the

variety of plants in the garden. Aside from the blood-red poppy flowers, there were tiny cacti with pink and yellow blossoms, fluorescent mushrooms glowing faintly in the dark corners under shelves, and leafy green bushes that emitted a tealike odor.

"This isn't a garden," she said. "This is a drug farm."

Now she *really* wanted to meet the Lore Master.

Kitay sat down next to her. "You know, the great shamans of legend used to ingest drugs before battle. Gave them magical powers, so the stories say." He smiled. "You think that's what the Lore Master teaches?"

"Honestly?" Rin picked at the grass. "I think he just comes in here to get high."

CHAPTER 4

Classes only escalated in difficulty as the weeks progressed. Their mornings were devoted to Combat, Medicine, History, and Strategy. On most days Rin's head was reeling by noon, crammed with names of theorems she'd never heard and titles of books she needed to finish by the end of the week.

Combat class kept their bodies exhausted along with their minds. Jun put them through a torturous series of calisthenics—they regularly ran up the Academy stairs and back down, did handstands in the courtyard for hours on end, and cycled through basic martial arts forms with bags of bricks hanging from their arms. Every week Jun took them to a lake at the bottom of the mountain and had them swim the entire length.

Rin and a handful of other students had never been taught to swim. Jun demonstrated the proper form exactly once. After that, it was up to them not to drown.

Their homework was heavy and clearly meant to push the first-years right up against their limits. So when the Weapons Master, Sonnen, taught them the correct proportions of saltpeter, sulfur, and charcoal necessary to mix the incendiary fire powder that powered war rockets, he also had them create their own impromptu missiles. And when the Medicine Master, Enro, assigned them to learn the names of all the bones in the human body, she also expected them to know the most common patterns of breakage and how to identify them.

It was Strategy, though, taught by Master Irjah, that was their hardest course. Their first day of class he distributed a thick tome—Sunzi's *Principles of War*—and announced that they were to have it memorized by the end of the week.

"This thing is massive!" Han complained. "How are we supposed to do the rest of our homework?"

"Altan Trengsin learned it in a night," said Irjah.

The class exchanged exasperated looks. The masters had been singing the praises of Altan Trengsin since the start of the term. Rin gathered he was some kind of genius, apparently the most brilliant student to come through Sinegard in decades.

Han looked as irritated as she felt. "Okay, but we're not Altan."

"Then try to be," said Irjah. "Class dismissed."

Rin settled into a routine of constant study and very little sleep; their course schedules left the first-years with no time to do anything else.

Autumn had just started to bite at Sinegard. A cold gust of wind accompanied them as they raced up the steps one morning. It rustled through the trees in a thunderous crescendo. The pupils had not yet received their thicker winter robes, and their teeth chattered in unison as they huddled together under a large mimosa tree at the far end of the second-tier courtyard.

Despite the cold, Jun refused to move Combat class indoors before the snowfall made it impossible to hold outside. He was a brutal teacher who seemed to delight in their discomfort.

"Pain is good for you," he said as he forced them to crouch in low, torturous endurance stances. "The martial artists of old used to hold this position for an hour straight before training."

"The martial artists of old must have had amazing thighs," Kitay gasped.

Their morning calisthenics were still miserable, but at least they had finally moved past fundamentals to their first weapon-based arts: staff techniques.

Jun had just assumed his position at the fore of the courtyard when a loud shuffle sounded above his head. A smattering of leaves fell down right over where he stood.

Everyone glanced up.

Perched high up on a thick branch of the mimosa tree stood their long-absent Lore Master.

He wielded a large pair of gardening shears, cheerfully clipping leaves at random while singing an off-key melody loudly to himself.

After hearing a few words of the song, Rin recognized it as "The Gatekeeper's Touches." Rin knew it from her many trips delivering opium to Tikany's whorehouses—it was an obscene ditty bordering on erotica. The Lore Master butchered the tune, but he sang it aloud with wild abandon.

"*I can't touch you there, miss / else you'll perish from the bliss . . .*"

Niang shook with suppressed giggles. Kitay's jaw hung wide open as he stared at the tree.

"Jiang, I've got a class," Jun snapped.

"So teach your class," said Master Jiang. "Leave me alone."

"We need the courtyard."

"You don't need *all* of the courtyard. You don't need this tree," Jiang said petulantly.

Jun whipped his iron staff through the air several times and slammed it against the base of the tree. The trunk actually shook from the impact. There was the crackling noise of deadweight dropping through several layers of dry mimosa leaves.

Master Jiang landed in a crumpled heap on the stone floor.

Rin's first thought was that he wasn't wearing a shirt. Her second thought was that he must be dead.

But Jiang simply rolled to a sitting position, shook out his left leg, and brushed his white hair back past his shoulders. "That was rude," he said dreamily as blood trickled down his left temple.

"Must you bumble around like a lackwit?" Jun snapped.

"Must you interrupt my morning gardening session?" Jiang responded.

"You're not doing any gardening," Jun said. "You are here purely to annoy me."

"I think you're flattering yourself."

Jun slammed his staff on the ground, making Jiang jump in surprise. "*Out!*"

Jiang adopted a dramatically wounded expression and hauled himself up to his feet. He flounced out of the garden, swaying his hips like a whorehouse dancer. "*If for me your heart aches / I'll lick you like a mooncake . . .*"

"You're right," Kitay whispered to Rin. "He *has* been getting high."

"Attention!" Jun shouted at the gawking class. He still had a mimosa leaf stuck in his hair. It quivered every time he spoke.

The class hastily lined up in two rows before him, staves at the ready.

"When I give the signal, you will repeat the following sequence." He demonstrated with his staff as he spoke. "Forward. Back. Upper left parry. Return. Upper right parry. Return. Lower left parry. Return. Lower right parry. Return. Spin, pass through the back, return. Understood?"

They nodded mutely. No one dared admit that they had missed nearly the entire sequence. Jun's demonstrations were usually rapid, but he had moved faster just now than any of them could follow.

"Well then." Jun slammed his staff against the floor. "Begin."

It was a fiasco. They moved with no rhythm or purpose. Nezha blazed through the sequence at twice the speed of the rest of the class, but he was one of the only students who was able to do it at all. The rest of them either omitted half the sequence or badly mangled the directions.

"Ow!"

Kitay, parrying where he should have turned, hit Rin in the

back. She jerked forward, knocking Venka in the head by accident.

"Stop!" Jun shouted.

Their flailing subsided.

"I'm going to tell you a story about the great strategist Sunzi." Jun paced along their ranks, breathing heavily. "When Sunzi finished writing his great treatise, *Principles of War*, he submitted the chapters to the Red Emperor. The Emperor decided to test Sunzi's wisdom by having him train a group of people with no military experience: the Emperor's concubines. Sunzi agreed and assembled the women outside the palace gates. He told them: 'When I say, "Eyes front," you will look straight ahead. When I say, "Left turn," you will face your left. When I say, "Right turn," you must face your right. When I say, "About turn," you must turn one hundred and eighty degrees. Is that clear?' The women nodded. Sunzi then gave the signal, 'Right turn.' But the women only burst out laughing."

Jun paused in front of Niang, whose face was pinched in trepidation.

"Sunzi told the Emperor, 'If words of command are not clear and distinct, if orders are not thoroughly understood, then the general is to blame.' So he turned to the concubines and repeated his instructions. 'Right turn,' he commanded. Again, the women fell about laughing."

Jun swiveled his head slowly, making eye contact with each one of them. "This time, Sunzi told the Emperor, 'If words of command are not clear, then the general is to blame. But if words of command are clear, but orders are not executed, then the troop leaders are to blame.' Then he selected the two most senior concubines in the group and had them beheaded."

Niang's eyes looked like they were going to pop out of her head.

Jun stalked back to the front of the courtyard and raised his staff. While they watched, terrified, Jun repeated the sequence, slowly this time, calling out the moves as he performed them. "Was that clear?"

They nodded.

He slammed his staff against the floor. "Then begin."

They drilled. They were flawless.

Combat was a soul-sucking, spirit-crushing ordeal, but there was at least the fun of nightly practice sessions. These were guided drill periods supervised by two of Jun's apprentices, Kureel and Jeeha. The apprentices were somewhat lazy teachers, and disproportionately enthused at the prospect of inflicting as much pain as possible on imagined opponents. As such, drill periods usually bordered on disaster, with Jeeha and Kureel milling around, shouting bits of advice while the pupils sparred against one another.

"Unless you've got a weapon, don't aim for the face." Jeeha guided Venka's hand down so her extended knife hand strike would land on Nezha's throat rather than his nose. "Aside from the nose, the face is practically all made of bone. You'll only bruise your hand. The neck's a better target. With enough force, you could fatally collapse the windpipe. At the very least, you'll give him breathing trouble."

Kureel knelt down next to Kitay and Han, who were rolling around the ground in mutual headlocks. "Biting is an excellent technique if you're in a tight spot."

A moment later, Han shrieked in pain.

A handful of first-years clustered around a wooden dummy as Jeeha demonstrated a proper knife hand strike. "Nikara monks used to believe this point was a major *ki* center." Jeeha indicated a spot under the dummy's stomach and punched it dramatically.

Rin took the bait to speed things along. "Is it?"

"Nah. No such thing as *ki* centers. But this area below the rib cage has a ton of necessary organs that are exposed. Also, it's where your diaphragm is. *Hah!*" Jeeha slammed his fist into the dummy. "That should immobilize any opponent for a good few seconds. Gives you time to scratch out their eyes."

"That seems vulgar," said Rin.

Jeeha shrugged. "We aren't here to be sophisticated. We're here to fuck people up."

"I'll show you all one last blow," Kureel announced as the session drew to a close. "This is the only kick you'll ever need, really. A kick to bring down the most powerful warriors."

Jeeha blinked in confusion. He turned his head to ask her what she meant. And Kureel raised her knee and jammed the ball of her foot into Jeeha's groin.

Mandatory drill sessions lasted for only two hours, but the first-years began staying in the studio to practice their forms long after the period had ended. The only problem was that the students with previous training seized this chance to show off. Nezha performed a series of twirling leaps in the center of the room, attempting spinning kicks that became progressively more flamboyant. A small ring of his classmates gathered around to watch.

"Admiring our prince?" Kitay strolled across the room to stand next to Rin.

"I fail to see how this would be useful in battle," Rin said. Nezha was now spinning a full 540 degrees in the air before kicking. It looked very pretty, but also very pointless.

"Oh, it's not. A lot of old arts are like that—cool to watch, practically useless. The lineages were adapted for stage opera, not combat, and then adapted back. That's where the Red Junk Opera got their name, you know. The founding members were martial artists posing as street performers to get closer to their targets. You should read the history of inherited arts sometime, it's fascinating."

"Is there anything you haven't read about?" Rin asked. Kitay seemed to have an encyclopedic knowledge of almost every topic. That day over lunch he had given Rin a lecture on how fish-gutting techniques differed across provinces.

"I have a soft spot for martial arts," said Kitay. "Anyway, it's depressing when you see people who can't tell the difference between self-defense and performance art."

Nezha landed, crouched impressively, after a particularly high leap. Several of their classmates, absurdly, began to clap.

Nezha straightened up, ignoring the applause, and caught Rin's eye. "*That's* what family arts are," he said, wiping the sweat off his forehead.

"I'm sure you'll be the terror of the school," said Rin. "You can dance for donations. I'll toss you an ingot."

A sneer twisted Nezha's face. "You're just jealous you have no inherited arts."

"I'm glad I don't, if they all look as absurd as yours."

"The House of Yin innovated the most powerful kicking-based technique in the Empire," Nezha snapped. "Let's see how you'd like being on the receiving end."

"I think I'd be fine," Rin said. "Though it would be a dazzling visual spectacle."

"At least I'm not an artless *peasant*," Nezha spat. "You've never done martial arts before in your life. You only know one kick."

"And you keep calling me a peasant. It's like you only know one insult."

"Duel me, then," Nezha said. "Fight to incapacitation for ten seconds or first blood. Right here, right now."

"You're on," Rin started to say, but Kitay slapped a hand over her mouth.

"Oh, no. Oh, no, no." Kitay yanked Rin back. "You heard Jun, you shouldn't—"

But Rin shrugged Kitay off. "Jun's not here, is he?"

Nezha grinned nastily. "Venka! Get over here!"

Venka broke off her conversation with Niang at the other end of the room and flounced over, flushed at Nezha's summons.

"Referee us," Nezha said, not taking his eyes off Rin.

Venka folded her hands behind her back, imitating Master Jun, and lifted her chin. "Begin."

The rest of their class had now formed a circle around Nezha and Rin. Rin was too angry to notice their stares. She had eyes only for Nezha. He began moving around her, darting back and forth with quick, elegant movements.

Kitay was right, Rin thought. Nezha really did look like he was performing stage opera. He didn't seem particularly lethal then, just foolish.

She narrowed her eyes and crouched low, following Nezha's movements carefully.

There. A clear opening. Rin raised a leg and kicked out, hard.

Her leg caught Nezha in midair with a satisfying *whoomph*.

Nezha uttered an unnatural shriek and clutched his crotch, whimpering.

The entire studio fell silent as all heads swiveled in their direction.

Nezha clambered to his feet, scarlet-faced. "You—how *dare* you—"

"Just as you said." Rin dipped her head into a mocking bow. "I only know one kick."

Humiliating Nezha felt good, but the political repercussions were immediate and brutal. It didn't take long for their class to form alliances. Nezha, mortally offended, made it clear that associating with Rin meant social alienation. He pointedly refused to speak to her or acknowledge her existence, unless it was to make snide comments about her accent. One by one the members of their class, terrified of receiving the same treatment, followed suit.

Kitay was the one exception. He had grown up on Nezha's bad side, he told Rin, and it wasn't about to start bothering him now.

"Besides," he said, "that look on his face? Priceless."

Rin was grateful for Kitay's loyalty, but was amazed by how cruel the other students could be. There was apparently no end of things about Rin to be mocked: her dark skin, her lack of status, her country accent. It was annoying, but Rin was able to brush the taunts off—until her classmates started snickering every time she talked.

"Is my accent so obvious?" she asked Kitay.

"It's getting better," he said. "Just try rolling the ends of your words more. Shorten your vowels. And add the *r* sound where it doesn't exist. That's a good rule of thumb."

"*Ar. Arrr.*" Rin gagged. "Why do Sinegardians have to sound like they're chewing cud?"

"Power dictates acceptability," Kitay mused. "If the capital had been built in Tikany, I'm sure we'd be running around dark as wood bark."

In the following days Nezha didn't utter a single word to her, because he didn't have to. His adoring followers wasted no opportunity to mock Rin. Nezha's manipulations turned out to be brilliant—once he established that Rin was the prime target, he could just sit back and watch.

Venka, who was obsessively attached to Nezha, actively snubbed Rin whenever she had the chance. Niang was better; she wouldn't associate with Rin in public, but she at least spoke to her in the privacy of their dorm.

"You could try apologizing," Niang whispered one night after Venka had gone to sleep.

Apologizing was the last thing Rin had in mind. She wasn't about to concede defeat by massaging Nezha's ego. "It was his idea to duel," she snapped. "It's not my fault he got what he was asking for."

"Doesn't matter," Niang said. "Just say you're sorry, and then he'll forget about you. Nezha just likes to be respected."

"For *what*?" Rin demanded. "He hasn't done anything to earn my respect. All he's done is act high and mighty, like being from Sinegard makes him *so* special."

"Apologizing won't help," interjected Venka, who apparently hadn't been asleep after all. "And being from Sinegard *does* make us special. Nezha and I"—it was always *Nezha and I* with Venka—"have trained for the Academy since we could walk. It's in our blood. It's our destiny. But you? You're *nothing*. You're just some tramp from the south. You shouldn't even be here."

Rin sat up straight in her bed, suddenly hot with anger. "I took the same test as you, Venka. I have every right to be at this school."

"You're just here to fill up the quota," Venka retorted. "I mean, the Keju has to *seem* fair."

Annoying as Venka was, Rin scarcely had the time or energy to pay much attention to her. They stopped snapping at each other after several days, but only because they were too exhausted to speak. When training sessions ended for the week, they straggled back to the dormitory, muscles aching so much they could barely walk. Without a word, they shed their uniforms and collapsed on their bunks.

They awoke almost immediately to a rapping at their door.

"Get up," said Raban when Rin yanked the door open.

"What the—"

Raban peered over her shoulder at Venka and Niang, who were whining incoherently from their bunks. "You too. Hurry up."

"What's the matter?" Rin mumbled grumpily, rubbing at her eyes. "We've got sweeping duty in six hours."

"Just come."

Still complaining, the girls wriggled into their tunics and met Raban outside, where the boys had already assembled.

"If this is some sort of first-year hazing thing, can I have permission to go back to bed?" asked Kitay. "Consider me bullied and intimidated, just let me sleep."

"Shut up. Follow me." Without another word, Raban took off toward the forest.

They were forced to jog to keep up with him. At first Rin thought he was taking them deep into the mountainside forest, but it was only a shortcut; after a minute they emerged in front of the main training hall. It was lit up from within, and they could hear loud voices from inside.

"More class?" asked Kitay. "Great Tortoise, I'm going on strike."

"This isn't class." For some reason, Raban sounded very excited. "Get inside."

Despite the audible shouting, the hall was empty. Their class bumbled around in groggy confusion until Raban motioned for them to follow him down the stairs to the basement floor. The basement was filled with apprentices crowded around the center of the room. Whatever stood at the center of attention, it sounded extremely exciting. Rin craned to get a glimpse over the apprentices' heads but could see nothing but bodies.

"First-years coming through," Raban yelled, leading their little group into the packed crowd. Through vigorous use of elbows, Raban carved them a path through the apprentices.

The spectacle at the center was two circular pits dug deep into the ground, each at least three meters in diameter and two meters deep. The pits stood adjacent to one another, and were ringed with waist-high metal bars to keep spectators from falling in. One pit was empty. Master Sonnen stood in the center of the other, arms folded across his broad chest.

"Sonnen always referees," Raban said. "He gets the short straw because he's the youngest."

"Referees what?" Kitay asked.

Raban grinned widely.

The basement door opened. Even more apprentices began to stream inside, filling the already cramped hall to the brim. The press of bodies forced the first-years perilously close to the edges of the rings. Rin clenched the rail to keep from falling in.

"What's going on?" Kitay asked as the apprentices jostled for positions closer to the rings. There were so many people in the room now that apprentices in the back had brought stools on which to stand.

"Altan's up tonight," Raban said. "Nobody wants to miss Altan."

It must have been the twelfth time that week Rin had heard that name. The whole Academy seemed obsessed with him. Fifth-year student Altan Trengsin was associated with every school record, was every master's favorite student, the exception to every rule. He had now become a running joke within their class.

Can you piss over the wall into town?

Altan can.

A tall, lithe figure suddenly dropped into Master Sonnen's ring without bothering to use the rope ladder. As his opponent scrambled down, the figure stretched his arms behind his back, head tilted up toward the ceiling. His eyes caught the reflection of the lamplight above.

They were crimson.

"Great Tortoise," said Kitay. "That's a real Speerly."

Rin peered inside the pit. Kitay was right; Altan didn't look close to Nikara. His skin was several shades darker than any of the other students'; a darker hue, even, than Rin's. But where Rin's sun-browned skin made her look coarse and unsophisticated, Altan's skin gave him a unique, regal air. His hair was the color of wet ink, closer to violet than black. His face was angular, expressionless, and startlingly handsome. And those eyes—scarlet, blazing red.

"I thought the Speerlies were dead," said Rin.

"*Mostly* dead," said Raban. "Altan's the last one."

"I am Bo Kobin, apprentice to Master Jun Loran," announced his opponent. "I challenge Altan Trengsin to a fight to incapacitation."

Kobin had to be twice Altan's weight and several inches taller, yet Rin suspected this would not be a particularly close fight.

Altan shrugged noncommittally.

Sonnen looked bored. "Well, go on," he said.

The apprentices fell into their opening stances.

"What, no introduction?" Kitay asked.

Raban looked amused. "Altan doesn't need an introduction."

Rin wrinkled her nose. "He's a little full of himself, isn't he?"

"Altan Trengsin," Kitay mused. "Is Altan the clan name?"

"Trengsin. The Speerlies put clan names last," Raban explained hastily. He pointed to the ring. "Shush, you'll miss it."

They already had.

She hadn't heard Altan move, hadn't even seen the scuffle begin. But when she looked back down at the ring, she saw Kobin pinned against the ground, one arm twisted unnaturally behind his back. Altan knelt above him, slowly increasing the pressure on Kobin's arm. He looked impassive, detached, almost lackadaisical.

Rin clenched at the railing. "When did—when did he—"

"He's Altan Trengsin," Raban said, as if this were explanation enough.

"Yield," Kobin shouted. "*Yield*, damn it!"

"Break," said Sonnen, yawning. "Altan wins. Next."

Altan released Kobin and offered him a hand. Kobin let Altan hoist him to his feet, then shook Altan's hand once he stood up. Kobin took his defeat with good grace. There was no shame, it seemed, in being defeated by Altan Trengsin in less than three seconds.

"That's it?" Rin asked.

"It's not over," Raban said. "Altan got a lot of challengers tonight."

The next contender was Kureel.

Raban frowned, shaking his head. "She shouldn't have been given permission for this match."

Rin found this appraisal unfair. Kureel, who was one of Jun's prized Combat apprentices, had a reputation for viciousness. Kureel and Altan appeared matched in height and strength; surely she could hold her own.

"Begin."

Kureel charged Altan immediately.

"Great Tortoise," Rin murmured. She had trouble following as Kureel and Altan began trading blows in close combat. They matched multiple strikes and parries per second, dodging and ducking around each other like dance partners.

A minute passed. Kureel flagged visibly. Her blows became sloppy, overextended. Droplets of sweat flew from her forehead every time she moved. But Altan was unfazed, still moving with that same feline grace he had possessed since the beginning of the match.

"He's playing with her," said Raban.

Rin couldn't take her eyes off Altan. His movements were dancelike, hypnotic. Every action bespoke sheer *power*—not the hulking muscle that Kobin had embodied, but a compact energy, as if at every moment Altan were a tightly coiled spring about to go off.

"He'll end it soon," Raban predicted.

It was ultimately a game of cat and mouse. Altan had never been evenly matched with Kureel. He fought on another level entirely. He had acted the part of her mirror to humor her at first, and then to tire her out. Kureel's movements slowed with every passing second. And, mockingly, Altan too slowed down his pace to match Kureel's rhythm. Finally Kureel lunged desperately forward, trying to score a hit on Altan's midriff. Instead of blocking it, Altan jumped aside, ran up against the dirt wall of the ring, rebounded off the other side, and twisted in the air. His foot caught Kureel in the side of the head. She snapped backward.

She was unconscious before Altan landed behind her, crouched like a cat.

"Tiger's tits," said Kitay.

"Tiger's tits," Raban agreed.

Two orange-banded Medicine apprentices jumped immediately into the pit to lift Kureel out. A stretcher was already waiting by the side of the ring. Altan hung in the center of the pit, arms folded, waiting calmly for them to finish. Even as they carried Kureel out of the basement, another student climbed down the rope ladder.

"Three challengers in one night," Kitay said. "Is that normal?"

"Altan fights a lot," said Raban. "Everyone wants to be the one who takes him down."

"Has that ever happened?" Rin asked.

Raban just laughed.

The third challenger turned his shaved head up to the lamplight, and Rin realized with a start that it was Tobi—the apprentice from the tour.

Good, Rin thought. *I hope Altan destroys him.*

Tobi introduced himself loudly, whipping up yells from his Combat classmates. Altan picked at his sleeve and again said nothing. He might have rolled his eyes, but in the dim light Rin couldn't be sure.

"Begin," Sonnen said.

Tobi flexed his arms and sank back into a low crouch. Rather than forming fists with his hands, he curled his knobby fingers tightly as if wrapping them around an invisible ball.

Altan tilted his head as if to say, *Well, come on.*

The match quickly lost its elegance. It was a knockdown, bloody-knuckled, no-holds-barred struggle. It was heavy-handed and abrupt, and full of brute, animalistic force. Nothing was off-limits. Tobi clawed furiously at Altan's eyes. Altan ducked his head and slammed an elbow into Tobi's chest.

Tobi staggered back, wheezing for air. Altan backhanded him across the head as if disciplining a child. Tobi tumbled to the floor, then rebounded with a complicated flipping motion and barreled forward. Altan raised his fists in anticipation, but Tobi threw himself at Altan's waist, pushing both of them back to the ground.

Altan slammed backward onto the dirt floor. Tobi pulled his right arm back and drove his clawed fingers into Altan's stomach. Altan's mouth opened in the shape of a soundless scream. Tobi dug his fingers in deeper and twisted. Rin could see veins protruding from his lower arm. His face warped into an wolf's snarl.

Altan convulsed under Tobi's grip and coughed. Blood sprayed from his mouth.

Rin's stomach roiled.

"Shit," Kitay kept saying. "Shit, shit, shit."

"That's Tiger Claws," said Raban. "Tobi's signature technique. Inherited arts. Altan won't be able to shit properly for a week."

Sonnen leaned forward. "All right, break—"

But then Altan wrapped his free hand around Tobi's neck and

jammed Tobi's face down into his own forehead. Once. Twice. Tobi's grip went slack.

Altan flung Tobi off and lunged forward. Half a second later their positions were reversed; Tobi lay inert on the ground as Altan kneeled atop him, hands pressed firmly around his neck. Tobi tapped frantically at Altan's arm.

Altan flung Tobi away from him in disdain. He glanced at Master Sonnen as if awaiting further instructions.

Sonnen shrugged. "That's the match."

Rin let out a breath she hadn't known she was holding.

The Medicine apprentices jumped into the ring and hauled Tobi up. He moaned. Blood streamed from his nose.

Altan hung back, leaning against the dirt wall. He looked bored, disinterested, as if his stomach weren't twisted into a sickening knot, as if he had never been touched at all. Blood dripped down his chin. Rin watched, partly in fascination and partly in horror, as Altan's tongue snaked out and licked the blood from his upper lip.

Altan closed his eyes for a long time, and then tilted his head up and exhaled slowly through his mouth.

Raban grinned when he saw their expressions. "Make sense now?"

"That was—" Kitay flapped his hands. "How? *How?*"

"Doesn't he feel pain?" Rin demanded. "He's not human."

"He's not," said Raban. "He's a Speerly."

The next day at lunch, all any of the first-years could talk about was Altan.

The entire class had fallen in love with him, to some extent, but Kitay especially was besotted with him. "The way he *moves*, it's just—" Kitay waved his arms in the air, at a loss for words.

"He doesn't talk much, does he?" Han said. "Wouldn't even introduce himself. Prick."

"He doesn't need to introduce himself," Kitay scoffed. "Everyone knows who he is."

"Strong and mysterious," Venka said dreamily. She and Niang giggled.

"Maybe he doesn't know how to talk," Nezha suggested. "You know how the Speerlies were. Wild and bloodthirsty. Hardly knew what to do with themselves unless they'd been given orders."

"The Speerlies weren't idiots," Niang protested.

"They were primitive. Scarcely more intelligent than children," Nezha insisted. "I heard that they're more closely related to monkeys than human beings. Their brains are smaller. Did you know they didn't even have a written language before the Red Emperor? They're good at fighting, but not much else."

Several of their classmates nodded as if this made sense, but Rin found it hard to believe that someone who fought with such graceful precision as Altan could possibly have the cognitive ability of a monkey.

Since arriving in Sinegard, she'd come to learn what it was like to be presumed stupid because of the shade of her skin. It rankled her. She wondered if Altan suffered the same.

"You heard wrong. Altan's not stupid," Raban said. "Best student in our class. Possibly in the entire Academy. Irjah says he's never had such a brilliant apprentice."

"I heard he's a shoo-in for command when he graduates," said Han.

"*I* heard he's doped up," Nezha said. He was clearly unused to not being the center of attention; he seemed determined to undermine Altan's credibility in any way possible. "He's on opium. You can see it in his eyes, they're bloodshot all the time."

"He's got red eyes because he's *Speerly*, you idiot," Kitay said. "All the Speerlies had crimson eyes."

"No, they didn't," said Niang. "Only the warriors."

"Well, Altan's *clearly* a warrior. And his eyes are red in the iris," Kitay said. "Not the veins. He's not an addict."

Nezha's lip curled. "Spend a lot of time staring at Altan's eyes, do you?"

Kitay blushed.

"You haven't heard the other apprentices talk," Nezha continued smugly, like he was privy to special information that they weren't. "Altan *is* an addict. *I* heard Irjah gives him poppy every time he wins. That's why he fights so hard. Opium addicts will do anything."

"That's absurd," said Rin. "You have no idea what you're talking about."

She knew what addiction looked like. Opium smokers were yellowed, useless sacks of flesh. They did not fight like Altan did. They did not *move* like Altan did. They were not perfect, lethal animals of graceful beauty.

Great Tortoise, she realized. *I'm just as obsessed with him myself.*

"Six months after the Non-Aggression Pact was signed, Empress Su Daji formally banned the possession and use of all psychoactive substances within Nikan's borders, and instituted a series of harshly retributive punishments in an attempt to wipe out illegal drug use. Of course, black markets in opium continue to thrive in many provinces, provoking debates over the efficiency of such policies." Master Yim looked up at his class. They were invariably twitching, scratching in their booklets, or staring out the window. "Am I lecturing to a graveyard?"

Kitay raised his hand. "Can we talk about Speer?"

"What?" Yim furrowed his brow. "Speer doesn't have anything to do with what we're . . . Ah." He sighed. "You've just met Trengsin, haven't you?"

"He was awesome," Han said fervently to nods of agreement.

Yim looked exasperated. "Every year," he muttered. "*Every year.* Fine." He tossed his lecture notes aside. "You want to talk about Speer, we'll talk about Speer."

The class was now paying rapt attention. Yim rolled his eyes as he shuffled through a thick stack of maps in his desk drawer.

"Why was Speer bombed?" Kitay asked with impatience.

"First things first," said Yim. He flipped through several sheets of parchment until he found what he was looking for: a wrinkly map of Speer and the southern Nikan border. "I don't tolerate hasty historiography," he said as he tacked it up on the board. "We'll start with appropriate political context. Speer became a Nikara colony during the Red Emperor's reign. Who can tell me about Speer's annexation?"

Rin thought that *annexation* was a light way to put it. The truth was hardly so clinical. Centuries ago the Red Emperor had taken the island by storm and forced the Speerlies into military service, turning the island warriors into the most feared contingent in the Militia until the Second Poppy War wiped them out.

Nezha raised his hand. "Speer was annexed under Mai'rinnen Tearza, the last warrior queen of Speer. The Old Nikara Empire asked her to give up her throne and pay tribute to Sinegard. Tearza agreed, mostly because she was in love with the Red Emperor or something, but she was opposed by the Speerly Council. Legend has it Tearza stabbed herself in desperation, and that final act convinced the Speerly Council of her passion for Nikan."

The room was silent for a moment.

"That," Kitay mumbled, "is the dumbest story I've ever heard."

"Why would she kill herself?" Rin asked out loud. "Wouldn't she have been more useful alive to argue her case?"

Nezha shrugged. "Reasons why women shouldn't be in charge of small islands."

This provoked a hubbub of responses. Yim silenced them with a raised hand. "It was not that simple. Legend, of course, has blurred the facts. The tale of Tearza and the Red Emperor is a love story, not a historical anecdote."

Venka raised her hand. "I heard the Red Emperor betrayed her. He promised he wouldn't invade Speer, but went back on his word."

Yim shrugged. "It's a popular theory. The Red Emperor was famed for his ruthlessness; a betrayal of that sort would not have been out of character. The truth is, we don't know *why* Tearza died, or if anyone killed her. We know only that she did die,

Speer's tradition of warrior monarchs was discontinued, and the isle became annexed to the Empire until the Second Poppy War.

"Now, economically, Speer hardly pulled its weight as a colony. The island exported almost nothing of use to the Empire but soldiers. There is evidence that the Speerlies may not even have been aware of agriculture. Before the civilizing influence of the Red Emperor's envoys, the Speerlies were a primitive people who practiced vulgar and barbaric rituals. They had very little to offer culturally or technologically—in fact, they seemed centuries behind the rest of the world. Militarily, however, the Speerlies were worth their weight in gold."

Rin raised her hand. "Were the Speerlies really fire shamans?"

Muted snickers sounded around the classroom, and Rin immediately regretted speaking.

Yim looked amazed. "They still believe in shamans down in Tikany?"

Rin's cheeks felt hot. She had grown up hearing stories upon stories about Speer. Everyone in Tikany was morbidly obsessed with the Empire's frenzied warrior force and their supposed supernatural abilities. Rin knew better than to take the stories for the truth, but she'd still been curious.

But she had spoken without thinking. Of course the myths that had enthralled her in Tikany only sounded backward and provincial here in the capital.

"No—I mean, I don't—" Rin stammered. "It's just something I read, I was just wondering . . ."

"Don't mind her," Nezha said. "Tikany still thinks we lost the Poppy Wars."

More snickers. Nezha leaned back, smug.

"But the Speerlies had *some* weird abilities, right?" Kitay swiftly came to Rin's defense. "Why else would Mugen target Speer?"

"Because it's a convenient target," Nezha said. "Smack-dab between the Federation archipelago and Snake Province. Why not?"

"That makes no sense." Kitay shook his head. "From what I've read, Speer was an island of little to no strategic value. It's not even useful as a naval base—the Federation would be better off sailing directly over the narrow strait to Khurdalain. Mugen would only have cared about Speer if the Speerlies could do something that terrified them."

"The Speerlies *were* terrifying," Nezha said. "Primitive, drug-loving freaks. Who *wouldn't* want them gone?"

Rin couldn't believe Nezha could be so terribly crass in describing a tragic massacre, and was amazed when Yim nodded in agreement. "The Speerlies were a barbaric, war-obsessed race," he said. "They trained their children for battle as soon as they could walk. For centuries, they subsisted by regularly raiding Nikara coastal villages, because they had no agriculture of their own. Now, the rumors of shamanism probably have more to do with their religion. Historians believe they had bizarre rituals in which they pledged themselves to their god—the Vermilion Phoenix of the South. But that was only ever a ritual. Not a martial ability."

"The Speerly affinity for fire is well documented, though," said Kitay. "I've read the war reports. There are more than a few generals, Nikara and Federation alike, who thought the Speerlies could manipulate fire at will."

"All myths," Yim said dismissively. "The Speerly ability to manipulate fire was a ruse used to terrify their enemies. It probably originated from their use of flaming weapons in nighttime raids. But most scholars today agree that the Speerly battle prowess is entirely a product of their social conditioning and harsh environment."

"So why couldn't our army copy them?" Rin asked. "If the Speerly warriors were really so powerful, why couldn't we emulate their tactics? Why'd we have to enslave them?"

"Speer was a tributary. Not a slave colony," Yim said impatiently. "And we *could* re-create their training programs, but again, their methods were barbaric. The way Jun tells it, you're struggling with general training enough as it is. You'd hardly want to undergo the Speerly regimen."

"What about Altan?" Kitay pressed. "He didn't grow up on Speer, he was trained at Sinegard—"

"Have you ever seen Altan summon fire at will?"

"Of course not, but—"

"Has the very sight of him addled your minds?" Yim demanded. "Let me be perfectly clear. There are no shamans. There are no more Speerlies. Altan is human just like the rest of you. He possesses no magic, no divine ability. He fights well because he's been training since he could walk. Altan is the last scion of a dead race. If the Speerlies prayed to their god, it clearly didn't save them."

Their obsession with Altan wasn't entirely wasted in their lessons, though. After witnessing the apprentices' matches, the first-years redoubled their efforts in Jun's class. They wanted to become graceful, lethal fighters like Altan. But Jun remained a meticulous coach. He refused to teach them the flashy techniques they'd seen in the ring until they had thoroughly mastered their fundamentals.

"If you attempted Tobi's Tiger Claws now, you couldn't kill a rabbit," he sneered. "You'd just as quickly break your own fingers. It'll be months before you can channel the *ki* that sort of technique requires."

At least he had finally bored of drilling them in formation. Their class was now handling their staves with reasonable competence— at least, the accidental injuries were minimal. Near the end of class one day, Jun lined them up in rows and ordered them to spar.

"*Responsibly*," he emphasized. "Half speed if you must. I have no patience for idiotic injuries. Drill on the strikes and parries that you've practiced in the form."

Rin found herself standing across from Nezha. Of course she was. He shot her a nasty smile.

She wondered, briefly, how they could possibly finish the match without harming each other.

"On my count," said Jun. "One, two—"

Nezha launched himself forward.

The force behind his blow stunned her. She barely got her staff up over her head in time to block a swing that would have knocked her out cold—the impact sent tremors through her arms.

But Nezha continued to advance, ignoring Jun's instructions completely. He swung his staff with savage abandon, but also with startlingly good aim. Rin wielded her weapon clumsily; the staff was still awkward in her arms, nothing like the spinning blur in Nezha's hands. She could barely keep her grip on it; twice it almost spun out of her grasp. Nezha landed far more hits than she blocked. The first two—elbow strike, upper thigh strike—hurt. Then Nezha landed so many that she couldn't feel them anymore.

She had been wrong about him. He had been showing off earlier, but his command of martial arts was prodigious and real. Last time they'd fought, he'd gotten cocky. Her lucky blow had been a fluke.

He was not being cocky now.

His staff connected with her kneecap with a sickening crunch. Rin's eyes bulged. She crumpled to the ground.

Nezha wasn't even bothering with his staff anymore. He kicked at her while she was still down, each blow more vicious than the last.

"That's the difference between you and me," muttered Nezha. "I've trained for this my entire life. You don't get to just stroll in here and embarrass me. You understand? You're *nothing*."

He's going to kill me. He's actually going to kill me.

Enough with the staff. She couldn't defend herself with a weapon she didn't know how to use. She dropped the staff and lunged upward to tackle Nezha around the waist. Nezha dropped his staff and tripped over backward. She landed on top of him. He swung at her face; she forced a palm into his nose. They pummeled furiously at each other, a chaotic tangle of limbs.

Then something yanked hard at her collar, cutting off her airflow. Jun pried them apart in an impressive display of strength, held them suspended in the air for a minute, then flung them both to the ground.

"What part of *block and parry* was unclear?" he growled.

"She started it," Nezha said quickly. He rolled to a sitting position and pointed at Rin. "She dropped her—"

"I know what I saw," Jun snapped. "And I saw you rolling around the floor like imbeciles. If I enjoyed training animals, I would be in the Cike. Shall I put in a word?"

Nezha cast his eyes down. "No, sir."

"Put your weapon away and leave my class. You're suspended for a week."

"Yes, sir." Nezha rose to his feet, tossed his staff at the weapons rack, and stalked off.

Jun then turned his attention to Rin. Blood dripped down her face, streaming from her nose, trickling down her forehead. She wiped clumsily at her chin, too nervous to meet Jun's eyes.

He loomed above her. "You. Get up."

She struggled to her feet. Her knee screamed in protest.

"Get that pathetic look off your face. You won't receive any sympathy from me."

She didn't expect his sympathy. But neither was she expecting what came next.

"That was the most miserable display I've seen from a student since I left the Militia," Jun said. "Your fundamentals are horrific. You move like a paraplegic. What did I just witness? Have you been asleep for the past month?"

He moved too fast. I couldn't keep up. I don't have years of training like he does. Even as the words came to her mind, they sounded like the pathetic excuses they were. She opened her mouth and closed it, too stunned to respond.

"I hate students like you," Jun continued relentlessly. The sounds of staves clashing against one another had long died away. The entire class was listening. "You skip into Sinegard from your little village, thinking that this is it—you've made it, you're going to make Mommy and Daddy proud. Maybe you were the smartest kid in your village. Maybe you were the best test taker your tutor has ever seen! But guess what? It takes more than memorizing a few Classics to be a martial artist.

"Every year we get someone like you, some country bumpkin who thinks that just because they were good at taking some *test*, they deserve my time and attention. Understand this, southerner. The exam proves nothing. Discipline and competence—those are the *only* things that matter at this school. That boy"—Jun jerked his thumb in the direction Nezha had gone—"may be an ass, but he has the makings of a commander in him. You, on the other hand, are just peasant trash."

The entire class was staring at her now. Kitay's eyes were wide with sympathy. Even Venka looked stunned.

Rin's ears rang, drowning out Jun's words. She felt so small. She felt as if she might crumble into dust. *Don't let me cry.* Her eyes throbbed from the pressure of forcing back her tears. *Please don't let me cry.*

"I do not tolerate troublemakers in my class," Jun said. "I do not have the happy privilege to expel you, but as Combat Master I can do this: From now on you are banned from the practice facilities. You do not touch the weapons rack. You do not train in the studio during off-hours. You do not set foot in here while I am teaching a class. You do not ask older students to teach you. I don't need you causing any more trouble in my studio. Now get out of my sight."

CHAPTER 5

Rin stumbled out the courtyard door. Jun's words echoed over and over in her head. She was suddenly dizzy; her legs wobbled and her vision went temporarily black. She slid down against the stone wall, hugging her knees to her chest while blood pumped furiously in her ears.

Then the pressure in her chest bubbled up and she cried for the first time since orientation, sobbing with her face pressed into her hands so that no one could hear.

She cried from the pain. She cried from the embarrassment. But mostly she cried because those two long years of studying for the Keju hadn't meant a thing. She was years behind her peers at Sinegard. She had no martial arts experience, much less an inherited art—even one that looked as stupid as Nezha's. She hadn't trained since childhood, like Venka. She wasn't brilliant, didn't have an eidetic memory like Kitay.

And the worst thing was, now she had no way to make up for it. Without Jun's tutelage, frustrating though it was, Rin knew she didn't have a chance of making it past the Trials. No master would choose to take on an apprentice who couldn't fight. Sinegard was primarily a *military* academy. If she couldn't hold her own on the battlefield, then what was the point?

Jun's punishment was as good as an expulsion. She was done. It was over. She'd be back in Tikany within a year.

But Nezha attacked first.

The more she considered this, the faster her despair crystallized into anger. Nezha had tried to *kill* her. She had acted only in self-defense. Why had she been thrown out of the class, when Nezha had gotten off with little more than a slap on the wrist?

But it was so clear why. Nezha was a Sinegardian noble, the son of a Warlord, and she was a country girl with no connections and no status. Expelling Nezha would have been troublesome and politically contentious. He mattered. She did not.

No—they couldn't just do this to her. They might think they could sweep her away like rubbish, but she didn't have to lie down and take it. She had come from nothing. She wasn't going back to nothing.

The courtyard doors opened as class let out. Her classmates hurried past her, pretending they didn't see her. Only Kitay hung behind.

"Jun will come around," he said.

Rin took his proffered hand and stood up in silence. She wiped at her face with her sleeve and sniffed.

"I mean it," Kitay said. He placed a hand on her shoulder. "He only suspended Nezha for a week."

She shrugged his hand off violently, still wiping furiously at her eyes. "That's because Nezha was born with a gold ingot in his mouth. Nezha got off because his father's got half the faculty here by their balls. Nezha's from Sinegard, so Nezha's *special*, Nezha *belongs* here."

"Come on, you belong here too, you passed the Keju—"

"The Keju doesn't mean anything," Rin said scathingly. "The Keju is a ruse to keep uneducated peasants right where they've always been. You slip past the Keju, they'll find a way to expel you anyway. The Keju keeps the lower classes sedated. It keeps us dreaming. It's not a ladder for mobility; it's a way to keep people like me exactly where they were born. The Keju is a drug."

"Rin, that's not true."

"It *is*!" She slammed her fist against the wall. "But they're not going to get rid of me like this. Not this easily. I won't let them. I *won't*."

She swayed suddenly. Her vision pulsed black and then cleared.

"Great Tortoise," said Kitay. "Are you all right?"

She whirled on him. "What are you talking about?"

"You're sweating."

Sweating? She wasn't sweating. "I'm fine," she said. Her voice sounded inordinately loud; it rang in her ears. Was she shouting?

"Rin, calm down."

"I'm calm! I'm extremely calm!"

She was far from fucking calm. She wanted to hit something. She wanted to scream at someone. Anger pulsed through her like a wave of heat.

Then her stomach erupted with a pain like she had been stabbed. She gasped sharply and clutched at her midriff. She felt as if someone were sliding a jagged stone through her innards.

Kitay grasped at her shoulders. "Rin? *Rin?*"

She felt the sudden urge to vomit. Had Nezha's blows given her internal damage?

Oh, fantastic, she thought. *Now you're humiliated and injured, too. Wait until they watch you limp into class; Nezha's going to love that.*

She shoved Kitay away. "I don't need— Leave me alone!"

"But you're—"

"I'm *fine*!"

Rin awoke that night to a deeply confusing sticky sensation.

Her sleeping pants felt cold, the way her pants had felt when she'd been little and peed in her sleep. But her legs were too sticky to be covered in urine. Heart pounding, she scrambled out of her bunk and lit a lamp with shaking fingers.

She glanced down at herself and almost shrieked out loud. The soft candlelight illuminated pools of crimson everywhere. She was covered in an enormous amount of blood.

She fought to still her panic, to force her drowsy mind to think rationally. She felt no acute pain, only a deep discomfort and great irritation. She hadn't been stabbed. She hadn't somehow ejected all of her inner organs. A fresh flow of blood trickled down her leg that moment, and she traced it to the source with soaked fingers.

Then she was just confused.

Going back to sleep was out of the question. She wiped herself off with the parts of the sheet that weren't soaked in blood, jammed a piece of cloth between her legs, and ran out of the dormitory to get to the infirmary before the rest of the campus woke.

Rin reached the infirmary in a sweaty, bloody mess, halfway to a nervous breakdown. The physician on call took one look at her and called his female assistant over. "One of those situations," he said.

"Of course." The assistant looked like she was trying hard not to laugh. Rin did not see anything remotely funny about the situation.

The assistant took Rin behind a curtain, handed her a change of clothes and a towel, and then sat her down with a detailed diagram of the female body.

It was a testament, perhaps, to the lack of sexual education in Tikany that Rin didn't learn about menstruation until that morning. Over the next fifteen minutes, the physician's assistant explained in detail the changes going on in Rin's body, pointing to various places on the diagram and making some very vivid gestures with her hands.

"So you're not dying, sweetheart, your body is just shedding your uterine lining."

Rin's jaw had been hanging open for a solid minute.

"What the *fuck*?"

She returned to the bunks with a deeply uncomfortable girdle strapped under her pants and a sock filled with heated uncooked rice grains. She placed the sock on her lower torso to dull the aching pain, but the cramping was so bad that she couldn't crawl out of bed before classes started.

"Do you want me to get someone?" Niang asked.

"No," Rin mumbled. "I'm fine. Just go."

She lay in bed for the entire day, despairing at all the class she was missing.

I'll be all right. She chanted it over and over to herself so that she wouldn't panic. One missed day couldn't hurt. Pupils got sick all the time. Kitay would lend her his notes if she asked. Surely she could catch up.

But this was going to happen every month. Every gods-damned month her uterus would tear itself to pieces, send flashes of rage through her entire body, and make her bloated, clumsy, lightheaded, and worst of all, weak. No wonder women rarely remained at Sinegard.

She needed to fix this problem.

If only it weren't so deeply embarrassing. She needed help. Venka seemed like someone who would have already begun menstruating. But Rin would have died rather than ask her how she'd managed it. Instead, she mumbled her questions to Kureel one night after she was sure Niang and Venka had gone to sleep.

Kureel laughed out loud in the darkness. "Just wear the girdle to class. You'll be fine. You get used to the cramping."

"But how often do I have to change it? What if it leaks in class? What if it gets on my uniform? What if someone *sees*?"

"Calm down," said Kureel. "The first time is hard, but you'll adapt to it. Keep track of your cycle, then you'll know when it's coming on."

This wasn't what Rin wanted to hear. "There's no way to just stop it forever?"

"Not unless you cut out your womb," Kureel scoffed, then paused at the look on Rin's face. "I was kidding. That's not actually possible."

"It's possible." Arda, who was a Medicine apprentice, interrupted them quietly. "There's a procedure they offer at the infirmary. At your age, it wouldn't even require open surgery. They'll give you a concoction. It'll stop the process pretty much indefinitely."

"Seriously?" Hope flared in Rin's chest. She looked between the two apprentices. "Well, what's stopping you from taking it?"

They both looked at her incredulously.

"It destroys your womb," Arda said finally. "Basically kills one of your inner organs. You won't be able to have children after."

"And it hurts like a bitch," Kureel said. "It's not worth it."

But I don't want children, Rin thought. *I want to stay here.*

If that procedure could stop her menstruating, if it could help her remain at Sinegard, it was worth it.

Once her bleeding stopped, Rin went back to the infirmary and told the physician what she wanted. He did not argue with her; in fact, he seemed pleased.

"I've been trying to convince the girls here to do this for years," he said. "None of them listen. Small wonder so few of you make it past your first year. They should make this mandatory."

He made her wait while he disappeared into the back room, mixing together the requisite medicines. Ten minutes later he returned with a steaming cup.

"Drink this."

Rin took the cup. It was dark porcelain, so she couldn't tell the color of the liquid inside. She wondered if she should feel anything. This was significant, wasn't it? There would be no children for her. No one would agree to marry her after this. Shouldn't that matter?

No. No, of course not. If she'd wanted to grow fat with squealing brats, she would have stayed in Tikany. She had come to Sinegard to escape that future. Why hesitate now?

She searched herself for any twinge of regret. Nothing. She felt absolutely nothing, just as she had felt nothing the day she left Tikany, watching the dusty town recede forever into the distance.

"It'll hurt," the physician warned. "Much worse than it hurt when you were menstruating. Your womb will self-destruct over the next few hours. After this, it will stop fulfilling its function. When your body has matured fully, you can get a surgery to have your womb removed altogether, but this should solve your problem in the interim. You'll be out of class for at least a week after this. But afterward, you'll be free forever. Now, I'm required to ask you one more time if you're certain this is what you want."

"I'm certain." Rin didn't want to think it over any more. She held her breath and lifted the mug to her mouth, wincing at the taste.

The physician had added honey to mask the bitterness, but the sweetness only made it more horrible. It tasted the way that opium smelled. She had to swallow many times before she drained the entire mug. When she finished, her stomach felt numb and weirdly sated, bloated and rubbery. After a few minutes an odd prickling feeling tingled at the base of her torso, like someone was poking her with tiny needles from inside.

"Get back to your room before it starts to hurt," the physician advised. "I'll tell the masters you're ill. The nurse will check on you tonight. You won't want to eat, but I'll have one of your classmates bring you some food just in case."

Rin thanked him and ran with a wobbling gait back to her quarters, clutching her abdomen. The prickling had turned into an acute pain spreading across her lower stomach. She felt as if she had swallowed a knife and it was twisting in a slow circle inside her.

Somehow she made it back to her bed.

Pain is just a message, she told herself. She could choose to ignore it. She could . . . she could . . .

It was terrible. She whimpered aloud.

She did not sleep so much as lie in a fevered daze. She turned deliriously on the sheets, dreaming of unborn, misshapen infants, of Tobi digging his five claws into her stomach.

"Rin. Rin?"

Someone hovered over her. It was Niang, bearing a wooden bowl.

"I brought you some winter melon soup." Niang knelt down beside Rin and held the bowl to her face.

Rin took one whiff of the soup. Her stomach seized painfully.

"I'm good," she said weakly.

"There's also this sedative." Niang pushed a cup toward her. "The physician said it's safe for you to take it now if you want to, but you don't have to."

"Are you joking? Give me that." Rin grabbed the cup and guzzled it down. Immediately her head began to swim. The room became delightfully fuzzy. The stabbing in her abdomen disappeared. Then something rose up in the back of her throat. Rin lunged to the side of the bed and vomited into the basin she had set there. Blood splattered the porcelain.

She glanced down at the basin with a deranged satisfaction. *Better to get the blood out this way,* she thought, *all at once, rather than slowly, every month, for years.*

While she continued to retch, she heard the door to the dormitory open.

Someone walked inside and paused in front of her. "You're insane," said Venka.

Rin glared up at her, blood dripping from her mouth, and smiled.

Rin spent four delirious days in bed before she could return to class. When she did drag herself out of bed, against both Niang's and the physician's recommendations, she found she was hopelessly behind.

She had missed an entire unit on Mugini verb conjugations in Linguistics, the chapter on the demise of the Red Emperor in History, Sunzi's analysis of geographical forecasting in Strategy, and the finer points of setting a splint in Medicine. She expected no lenience from the masters and received none.

The masters treated her like missing class was her fault, and it was. She had no excuses; she could only accept the consequences.

She flubbed questions every time a master called on her. She scored at the bottom of every exam. She didn't complain. For the entire week, she endured the masters' condescension in silence.

Oddly, she didn't feel discouraged, but rather as if a veil had been lifted. Her first few weeks at Sinegard had been like a dream. Dazzled by the magnificence of the city and the Academy, she had allowed herself to drift.

She had now been painfully reminded that her place here was not permanent.

The Keju had meant nothing. The Keju had tested her ability to recite poems like a parrot. Why had she ever imagined that might have prepared her for a school like Sinegard?

But if the Keju had taught her anything, it was that pain was the price of success.

And she hadn't burned herself in a long time.

She had grown content at the Academy. She had grown lazy. She had lost sight of what was at stake. She had needed to be reminded that she was nothing—that she could be sent back home at a moment's notice. That as miserable she was at Sinegard, what awaited her in Tikany was much, much worse.

He looks at you and licks his lips. He brings you to the bed. He forces a hand between your legs. You scream, but no one hears you.

She would stay. She would stay at Sinegard even if it killed her.

She threw herself into her studies. Classes became like warfare, each interaction a battle. With every raised hand and every homework assignment, she competed against Nezha and Venka and every other Sinegardian. She had to prove that she deserved to be kept on, that she merited further training.

She had needed failure to remind her that she wasn't like the Sinegardians—she hadn't grown up speaking casual Hesperian, wasn't familiar with the command structure of the Imperial Militia, didn't know the political relationships between the Twelve Warlords like the back of her hand. The Sinegardians had this knowledge ingrained from childhood. She would have to develop it.

Every waking hour that she didn't spend in class, she spent in the archives. She read the assigned texts out loud to herself; wrapping her tongue around the unfamiliar Sinegardian dialect until she had eradicated all hints of her southern drawl.

She began to burn herself again. She found release in the pain; it was comforting, familiar. It was a trade-off she was well used to. Success required sacrifice. Sacrifice meant pain. Pain meant success.

She stopped sleeping. She sat in the front row so that there was no way she could doze off. Her head ached constantly. She always wanted to vomit. She stopped eating.

She made herself miserable. But then, all of her options led to misery. She could run away. She could get on a boat and escape to another city. She could run drugs for another opium smuggler. She could, if it came down to it, return to Tikany, marry, and hope no one found out that she couldn't have children until it was too late.

But the misery she felt now was a good misery. This misery she reveled in, because she had chosen it for herself.

One month later, Rin tested at the top of one of Jima's frequent Linguistics exams. She beat Nezha's score by two points. When Jima announced the top five scores, Rin jerked upright, happily shocked.

She had spent the entire night cramming Hesperian verb tenses, which were infinitely confusing. Modern Hesperian was a language that followed neither rhyme nor reason. Its rules were close to pure randomness, its pronunciation guides haphazard and riddled with exceptions.

She couldn't reason through Hesperian, so she memorized it, the way she memorized everything she didn't understand.

"Good," Jima said crisply when she handed Rin's exam scroll back to her.

Rin was startled at how good "good" made her feel.

She found that she was fueled by praise from her masters. Praise meant that she had finally, *finally* received validation that she was not nothing. She could be brilliant, could be worth someone's attention. She adored praise—craved it, needed it, and realized she found relief only when she finally had it.

She realized, too, that she felt about praise the way that addicts felt about opium. Each time she received a fresh infusion of flattery, she could think only about how to get more of it. Achievement was a high. Failure was worse than withdrawal. Good test scores brought only momentary relief and temporary pride—she basked in her grace period of several hours before she began to panic about her next test.

She craved praise so deeply that she felt it in her bones. And just like an addict, she did whatever she could to get it.

In the following weeks, Rin clawed her way up from the bottom of the ranks to become one of the top students in each class. She competed regularly with Nezha and Venka for the highest marks in nearly every subject. In Linguistics, she was second now only to Kitay.

She particularly enjoyed Strategy.

Gray-whiskered Master Irjah was the first teacher she'd ever had who didn't rely principally on rote memorization as a learning method. He made the students solve logical syllogisms. He made them define concepts they had taken for granted, concepts like *advantage* and *victory* and *war*. He forced them to be precise and accurate in their answers. He rejected responses that were phrased vaguely or could have multiple interpretations. He stretched their minds, shattered their preconceptions of logic, and then pieced them back together.

He gave praise only sparingly, but when he did, he made sure that everyone in the class heard. Rin craved his approval more than anything.

Now that they had finished analyzing Sunzi's *Principles of War*, Irjah spent the second half of class lobbing hypothetical military situations at them, challenging them to think their way out of various quagmires. Sometimes these simulations involved only questions of logistics ("Calculate how much time and how many supplies you need to move a force of this size across this strait"). Other times he drew up maps for them, indicating with symbols how many troops they had to work with, and forced them to come up with a battle plan.

"You are stuck behind this river," said Irjah. "Your troops stand in a prime position for a ranged assault, but your main column has run out of arrows. What do you do?"

Most of their class suggested raids on the enemy's weapons carriages. Venka wanted to abandon the ranged idea entirely and pursue a direct frontal assault. Nezha suggested they commission the nearby farmers to mass-produce arrows in one night.

"Gather scarecrows from the nearby farmers," said Kitay.

Nezha snorted. "What?"

"Let him talk," said Irjah.

"Dress them in spare uniforms, stick them in a boat, and send them downriver," Kitay continued, ignoring him. "This area is a mountainous region notorious for heavy precipitation. We can assume it has rained recently, so there should be fog. That makes it difficult for the enemy forces to see the river clearly. Their archers will mistake the scarecrows for soldiers, and shoot until they resemble pincushions. We will then send our men downstream and have them collect the arrows. We use our enemy's arrows to kill our enemies."

Kitay won that one.

Another day Irjah presented them with a map of the Wudang mountain region marked with two red crosses to indicate two Federation battalions surrounding the Nikara army from both ends of the valley.

"You're trapped in this valley. The villagers have mostly evacuated, but the Federation general holds a school full of children hostage. He says he will set the children free if your battalion surrenders. You have no guarantee he will honor the terms. How do you respond?"

They stared at the map for many minutes. Their troops had no advantage, no easy way out.

Even Kitay was puzzled. "Try an assault on the left flank?" he suggested. "Evacuate the children while they're preoccupied with a small guerrilla force?"

"They're on higher ground," said Irjah. "They'll shoot you down before you get the chance to draw your weapons."

"Light the valley on fire," Venka tried. "Distract them with the smoke?"

"Good way to burn yourselves to death." Irjah snorted. "Remember, you do not have the high ground."

Rin raised her hand. "Cut around the second army and get onto the dam. Break the dam. Flood the valley. Let everyone inside drown."

Her classmates turned to stare at her in horror.

"Leave the children," she added. "There's no way to save them."

Nezha laughed out loud. "We're trying to *win* this simulation, idiot."

Irjah motioned for Nezha to be silent. "Runin. Please elaborate."

"It's not a victory either way," said Rin. "But if the costs are so high, I would throw all my tiles in. This way they die, and we lose half our troops but no more. Sunzi writes that no battle takes place in isolation. This is just one small move in the grand scheme of the war. The numbers you've given us indicate that these Federation battalions are massive. I'm guessing they constitute a large percentage of the entire Federation army. So if we give up some of our own troops, we lessen their advantage in all subsequent battles."

"You'd rather kill your own people than let the opponent's army walk away?" Irjah asked.

"Killing isn't the same as letting die," Rin objected.

"They're casualties nonetheless."

Rin shook her head. "You don't let an enemy walk away if they'll certainly be a threat to you later. You get rid of them. If they're that far inland, they know the lay of almost the entire country. They have a geographical advantage. This is our one chance to take out the enemy's greatest fighting force."

"Sunzi said to always give the enemy a way out," Irjah said.

Rin privately thought that this was one of Sunzi's stupider principles, but hastily pulled together a counterargument. "But Sunzi didn't mean to *let* them take that way out. The enemy just has to think the situation is less dire than it is, so they don't grow desperate and do stupid and mutually destructive things." Rin pondered for a moment. "I suppose they could try to swim."

"She's talking about decimating entire villages!" Venka protested. "You can't just break a dam like that. Dams take years to rebuild. The entire river delta will flood, not just that valley. You're talking about famine. Dysentery. You'll mess with the agriculture of the entire region, create a whole host of problems that mean decades of suffering down the line—"

"Problems that can be solved," Rin maintained stubbornly. "What was your solution, to let the Federation walk free into the heartland? Fat lot of good the agricultural regions will do you when your whole country's been occupied. You would offer up the whole country to them on a platter."

"Enough, enough." Irjah slammed the table to silence them. "Nobody wins this one. You're dismissed for today. Runin, I want to have a word. My office."

"Where did you come by this solution?" Irjah held up a booklet.

Rin recognized her scrawling handwriting at the top.

Last week Irjah had assigned them to write essay responses to another simulated quagmire—a counterfactual scenario where the Militia had lost popular support for a war of resistance against the Federation. They couldn't rely on peasants to supply soldiers with food or animal feed, could not use peasant homes as lodging without forceful entry. In fact, outbreaks of rebellion in rural areas added several layers of complication to coordinating troop movements.

Rin's solution had been to burn down one of the minor island villages.

The twist was that the island in question belonged to the Empire.

"The first day of Yim's class we talked about how losing Speer ended the Second Poppy War," she said.

Irjah frowned. "You based this essay on the Speerly Massacre?"

She nodded. "Losing Speer during the Second Poppy War pushed Hesperia over the edge—made them uncomfortable enough that they didn't want Mugen expanding farther into the continent. I thought the destruction of another minor island might do the same for the Nikara population, convince them that the real enemy was Mugen. Remind them what the threat was."

"Surely Militia troops attacking a province of the Empire would send the wrong message," Irjah objected.

"They wouldn't *know* it was Militia troops," she said. "We would pose as a Federation squadron. I suppose I should have been clearer about that in the essay. Better still if Mugen just went ahead and attacked the island for us, but you can't leave these things to chance."

He nodded slowly as he perused her essay. "Crude. Crude, but clever. Do you think that's what happened?"

It took her a moment to understand his question. "In this simulation, or during the Poppy Wars?"

"The Poppy Wars." Irjah tilted his head, watching her carefully.

"I'm not entirely sure that's not what happened," Rin said. "There's some evidence that the attack on Speer was allowed to succeed."

Irjah's expression betrayed nothing, but his fingers tapped thoughtfully against his wooden desk. "Explain."

"I find it very difficult to believe that the strongest fighting force in the Militia could have been annihilated so easily. That, and the island was suspiciously poorly defended."

"What are you suggesting?"

"Well, I'm not certain, but it seems as if—I mean, maybe someone on the inside—a Nikara general, or someone else who was privy to certain information—knew about the attack on Speer but didn't alert anyone."

"Now why would we have wanted to lose Speer?" Irjah asked quietly.

She took a moment to formulate a coherent argument. "Maybe they knew Hesperia wouldn't stand for it. Maybe they wanted to generate popular support to distract from the Red Junk movement. Maybe because we needed a sacrifice, and Speer was expendable in a way other regions weren't. We couldn't let any Nikara die. But Speerlies? Why not?"

She had been grasping at straws when she had started to speak, but the moment she said it, her answer sounded startlingly plausible to her.

Irjah looked deeply uncomfortable. "You must understand that this is a very awkward part of Nikan's history," he said. "The way that the Speerlies were treated was . . . regrettable. They were used and exploited by the Empire for centuries. Their warriors were regarded as little more than vicious dogs. Savages. Until Altan came to study at Sinegard, I don't believe anyone really thought the Speerlies were capable of sophisticated thought. Nikan does not like to speak of Speer, and for good reason."

"Yes, sir. It was just a theory."

"Anyhow." Irjah leaned back in his chair. "That isn't all I wanted to discuss. Your strategy in the valley worked for the purposes of the exercise, but no competent ruler would ever give those orders. Do you know why?"

She contemplated in silence for a minute. "I confused tactics with grand strategy," she said finally.

Irjah nodded. "Elaborate."

"The *tactic* would have worked. We might have even won the war. But no ruler would have chosen that option, because the country would have fallen apart afterward. My tactic doesn't grant the possibility of peace."

"Why is that?" Irjah pressed.

"Venka was right about destroying the agricultural heartland. Nikan would suffer famine for years. Rebellions like the Red Junk Opera would spring up everywhere. People would think it was the Empress's fault that they were starving. If we used my strategy, what would happen next is probably a civil war."

"Good," said Irjah. He raised his eyebrows. "Very good. You know, you are astoundingly bright."

Rin tried to conceal her delight, though she felt a flutter of warmth spread across her body.

"Should you perform well in the Trials," Irjah continued, "you might do well as a Strategy apprentice."

Under any other circumstances his words would have thrilled her. Rin managed a resigned smile. "I'm not sure I'll make it that far, sir."

His brow crinkled. "Why's that?"

"Master Jun kicked me out of his class. I probably won't pass the Trials."

"How on earth did that happen?" Irjah demanded.

She recounted her last, disastrous class with Jun without bothering to edit the story. "He let Nezha off with a suspension, but told me not to come back."

"Ah." Irjah frowned. "Jun didn't punish you because you were brawling. Tobi and Altan did far worse than that their first year. He punished you because he's a purist about the school—he thinks any student who isn't descended from a Warlord isn't worth his time. But never mind what Jun thinks. You're clever, you'll pick up whatever techniques they covered this month without much trouble."

Rin shook her head. "It won't make much difference. He's not letting me back in."

"*What?*" Irjah looked outraged. "That's absurd. Does Jima know?"

"Jima can't intervene in a Combat matter. Or won't. I've asked." Rin stood up. "Thanks for your time, sir. If I make it past the Trials, I'd be honored to study with you."

"You'll find a way," Irjah said. His eyes twinkled. "Sunzi would."

Rin hadn't been completely forthcoming with Irjah. He was right— she *would* find a way.

Starting with the fact that she hadn't given up on martial arts.

Jun had banned her from his class, but he hadn't banned her from the library. The stacks at Sinegard contained a wealth of martial arts instruction tomes, the largest collection in all the Empire. Rin had within reach the secrets of most inherited arts, excepting those tightly guarded techniques like the House of Yin's.

In the course of her research Rin discovered that existing martial arts literature was hugely comprehensive and dauntingly complex. She learned that martial arts revolved largely around lineage: different forms belonged to different families, similar techniques taught and improved upon by pupils who had shared the same master. More often than not, schools became torn by rivalries or schisms, so techniques splintered and developed independently of others.

The history was deeply enjoyable, almost more entertaining than novels. But practicing the techniques turned out to be devilishly hard. Most tomes were too dense to serve as useful manuals. A majority assumed that the student was reading the book along with a master who could demonstrate the techniques in real life. Others expounded for pages about a certain school's breathing techniques and philosophy of fighting, but only sporadically mentioned things like kicking and punching.

"I don't want to read about the balance in the universe," Rin grumbled, tossing aside what seemed like the hundredth text she'd tried. "I want to know how to beat people up."

She attempted asking the apprentices for help.

"Sorry," Kureel said without meeting her eyes. "Jun said that teaching first-years outside of the practice rooms was against the rules."

Rin doubted this was a real rule, but she should have known better than to ask one of Jun's apprentices.

Asking Arda was also not an option; she spent all her time in the infirmary with Enro and never returned to the bunks before midnight.

Rin was going to have to teach herself.

A month and a half in, she finally found a gold mine of information in the texts of Ha Seejin, quartermaster under the Red Emperor. Seejin's manuals were wonderfully illustrated, filled with detailed descriptions and clearly labeled diagrams.

Rin perused the pages gleefully. This was it. This was what she needed.

"You can't take this one out," said the apprentice at the front desk.

"Why not?"

"It's from the restricted shelves," said the apprentice, as if this were obvious. "First-years don't get access to those."

"Oh. Sorry. I'll take it back."

Rin walked to the back end of the library. She glanced furtively about to make sure no one was watching. She stuffed the tome down her shirt. Then she turned around and walked back out.

Alone in the courtyard, book in hand, Rin learned. She learned to shape the air with her fists, to imagine a great spinning ball in her arms to guide the shape of her movements. She learned to root her legs against the ground so she couldn't be tipped over, not even by opponents twice her weight. She learned to form fists with her thumb on the outside, to always keep her guard up around her face, and to shift her balance quickly and smoothly.

She became very good at punching stationary objects.

She attended the matches at the rings regularly. She arrived in the basement early and secured a place by the railing so that she didn't miss a single kick or throw. She hoped that by watching the apprentices fight, she could absorb their techniques.

This actually helped—to some extent. By closely examining the apprentices' movements, Rin learned to identify the right place and time for various techniques. When to kick, when to dodge, when to roll madly on the floor to avoid—wait, no, that was an accident, Jeeha had simply tripped. Rin didn't have muscle memory of sparring against another person, so she had to hold these contingencies in her head. But vicarious sparring was better than nothing.

She also attended the matches to watch Altan.

She would have been lying to herself if she didn't admit that she derived great aesthetic pleasure from staring at him. With his lithe, muscled form and chiseled jawline, Altan was undeniably handsome.

But he was also the paragon of good technique. Altan did everything that the Seejin text recommended. He never let his guard down, never allowed an opening, never let his attention slip. He never telegraphed his next move, didn't bounce erratically or go flat on his heels to advertise to his opponent when he was going to kick. He always attacked from angles, never from the front.

Rin had initially conceived of Altan as simply a good, strong fighter. Now she could see that he was, in every sense, a genius. His fighting technique was a study in trigonometry, a beautiful composition of trajectories and rebounded forces. He won consistently because he had perfect control of distance and torque. He had the mathematics of fighting down to a science.

He fought more often than not. Throughout the semester his challengers only grew in number—it seemed every single one of Jun's apprentices wanted to have a go at him.

Rin watched Altan fight twenty-three matches before the end of the fall. He never lost.

CHAPTER 6

Winter descended on Sinegard with a vengeance. The students enjoyed one last pleasant day of autumn sun, and woke the next morning to find that a cold sheet of snow had fallen over the Academy. The snow was lovely to observe for all of two serene minutes. Then it became nothing but a pain in the ass.

The entire campus turned into a risk zone for broken limbs—the streams froze over; the stairways became slushy and treacherous. Outdoor classes moved indoors. The first-years were assigned to scatter salt across the stone walkways at regular intervals to melt the snow, but the slippery paths sent a regular stream of students to the infirmary regardless.

As far as Lore went, the icy weather was the last straw for most of the class, who had been intermittently frequenting the garden in hopes that Jiang might make an appearance. But waiting around in a drug garden for a never-present teacher was one thing; waiting in freezing cold temperatures was another.

In the months since the semester began, Jiang hadn't shown up once to class. Students occasionally spotted him around campus doing inexcusably rude things. He had in turn flipped Nezha's lunch tray out of his hands and walked away whistling, petted

Kitay on the head while making a pigeon-like cooing noise, and tried to snip Venka's hair off with garden shears.

Whenever a student managed to pin him down to ask about his course, Jiang made a loud farting noise with his mouth and elbow and skirted away.

Rin alone continued to frequent the Lore garden, but only because it was a convenient place to train. Now that first-years avoided the garden out of spite, it was the one place where she was guaranteed to be alone.

She was grateful that no one could see her fumbling through the Seejin text. She had picked up the fundamentals with little trouble, but discovered that even just the second form was devilishly hard to put together.

Seejin was fond of rapidly twisting footwork. Here the diagrams failed her. The models' feet in the drawings were positioned in completely different angles from picture to picture. Seejin wrote that if a fighter could extricate himself from any awkward placement, no matter how close he was to falling, he would have achieved perfect balance and therefore the advantage in most combat positions.

It sounded good in theory. In practice, it meant a lot of falling over.

Seejin recommended pupils practice the first form on an elevated surface, preferably a thick tree branch or the top of a wall. Against her better judgment, Rin climbed to the middle of the large willow tree overhanging the garden and positioned her feet hesitantly against the bark.

Despite Jiang's absence throughout the semester, the garden remained impeccably well kept. It was a kaleidoscope of garishly bright colors, similar in color scheme to the decorations outside Tikany's whorehouses. Despite the cold, the violet and scarlet poppy flowers had remained in full blossom, their leaves trimmed in tidy rows. The cacti, which were twice the size they had been at the start of term, had been moved into a new set of clay pots painted in eerie patterns of black and burnt orange. Underneath the shelves, the luminescent mushrooms still pulsed with a faintly disturbing glow, like tiny fairy lamps.

Rin imagined that an opium addict could pass entire days in here. She wondered if that was what Jiang did.

Poised precariously on the willow tree, struggling to stand up straight against the harsh wind, Rin held the book in one hand, mumbling instructions out loud while she positioned her feet accordingly.

"Right foot out, pointing straight forward. Left foot back, perpendicular to the straight line of the right foot. Shift weight forward, lift left foot . . ."

She could see why Seejin thought this might be good balance practice. She also saw why Seejin strongly recommended against attempting the exercise alone. She wobbled perilously several times, and regained her balance only after a few heart-stopping seconds of frantic windmilling. *Calm down. Focus. Right foot up, bring it around . . .*

Master Jiang walked around the corner, loudly whistling "The Gatekeeper's Touches."

Rin's right foot slid out from beneath her. She teetered off the edge of the branch, dropped the book, and would have plummeted to the stone floor if her left ankle hadn't snagged in the crook of two dividing branches.

She jolted to a halt with her face inches from the ground and gasped out loud in relief.

Jiang stared down silently at her. She gazed back, head thundering while the blood rushed down into her temples. The last notes of his song dwindled and faded away in the howling wind.

"Hello there," he said finally. His voice matched his demeanor: placid, disengaged, and idyllically curious. In any other context, it might have been soothing.

Rin struggled ungracefully to haul herself upward.

"Are you all right?" he asked.

"I'm stuck," she mumbled.

"Mmm. Appears so."

He clearly wasn't going to help her down. Rin wriggled her ankle out of the branch, tumbled to the floor, and landed in a painful heap at Jiang's feet. Cheeks burning, she clambered to her feet and brushed the snow off her uniform.

"Elegant," Jiang remarked.

He tilted his head very far to the left, studying her intently as if she were a particularly fascinating specimen. Up close, Jiang looked even more bizarre than Rin had first thought. His face was a riddle; it was neither lined with age nor flushed with youth but rather invulnerable to time, like a smooth stone. His eyes were a pale blue color she had never seen on anyone in the Empire.

"Bit daring, aren't you?" He sounded like he was suppressing laughter. "Do you often dangle from trees?"

"You startled me, sir."

"Hmmph." He puffed air through his cheeks like a little child. "You're Irjah's pet pupil, aren't you?"

Her cheeks flushed. "I—I mean, I don't . . ."

"You *are*." He scratched his chin and scooped her book off the ground, riffling through its pages with a mild curiosity. "Dusky little peasant prodigy, you. He can't stop raving about you."

She shuffled her feet, wondering where this was going. Had that been a compliment? Was she supposed to thank him? She tucked a lock of hair back behind her ear. "Um."

"Oh, don't pretend to be bashful. You love it." Jiang glanced casually down at the book and gazed back up at her. "What are you doing with a Seejin text?"

"I found it in the archives."

"Oh. I take that back. You're not daring. You're just stupid."

When Rin looked confused, Jiang explained: "Jun explicitly forbade Seejin until at least your second year."

She hadn't heard this rule. No wonder the apprentice hadn't let her sign the book out of the archives. "Jun expelled me from his class. I wasn't informed."

"Jun expelled you," Jiang repeated slowly. She couldn't tell if he was amused or not. "What on earth did you do to him?"

"Um. Tackled another student during sparring, sort of. He started it," she added quickly. "The other student, I mean."

Jiang looked impressed. "Stupid *and* hotheaded."

His eyes wandered over to the plants on the shelf behind her. He walked around her, lifted a poppy flower up to his nose, and sniffed experimentally. He made a face. He dug around in the deep pockets of his robes, fished out a pair of shears, then clipped the stem and tossed the broken end into a pile in the corner of a garden.

Rin began to inch toward the gate. Perhaps if she left now, Jiang would forget about the book. "I'm sorry if I shouldn't be in here—"

"Oh, you're not sorry. You're just annoyed I interrupted your training session, and you're hoping I'll leave without mentioning your stolen book." Jiang snipped another stem off the poppy plant. "You're a plucky one, you know that? Got banned from Jun's class, so you thought you'd teach yourself *Seejin*."

He made several syncopated wheezing noises. It took Rin a moment to realize he was laughing.

"What's so funny?" she demanded. "Sir, if you're going to report me, I just want to say—"

"Oh, I'm not going to *report* you. What fun would that be?" He was still chuckling. "Were you really trying to learn Seejin from a book? Do you have a death wish?"

"It's not that hard," she said defensively. "I just followed the pictures."

He turned back toward her; his expression was one of amused disbelief. He opened the book, riffled through the pages with a practiced hand, and then stopped on the page detailing the first form. He brandished the book at her. "That one. Do that."

Rin obliged.

It was a tricky form, full of shifting movements and ball change steps. She squeezed her eyes shut as she moved. She couldn't concentrate in full sight of those luminous mushrooms, those bizarrely pulsing cacti.

When she opened her eyes, Jiang had stopped laughing.

"You're nowhere near ready for Seejin," he said. He slammed the book shut with one hand. "Jun was right. At your level you shouldn't even be *touching* this text."

Rin fought a wave of panic. If she couldn't even use the Seejin text, she might as well leave for Tikany right now. She had found no other books that were half as useful or as clear.

"You might benefit from some animal-based fundamentals," Jiang continued. "Yinmen's work. He was Seejin's predecessor. Have you heard of him?"

She glanced up at him in confusion. "I've looked for those. Those scrolls are incomplete."

"Of course you won't be learning from *scrolls*," Jiang said impatiently. "We'll discuss this in class tomorrow."

"Class? You haven't been here all semester!"

Jiang shrugged. "I find it difficult to bother myself with first-years I don't find particularly interesting."

Rin thought this was just irresponsible teaching, but she wanted to keep Jiang talking. Here he was in a rare moment of lucidity, offering to teach her martial arts that she couldn't learn by herself. She was half-afraid that if she said the wrong thing, she would send him running off like a startled hare.

"So am I interesting?" she asked slowly.

"You're a walking disaster," Jiang said bluntly. "You're training with arcane techniques at a rate that will lead to inevitable injury, and not the kind you recover from. You've misinterpreted Seejin's texts so badly that I believe you've come up with a new art form all by yourself."

Rin scowled. "Then why are you helping me?"

"To spite Jun, mostly." Jiang scratched his chin. "I hate the man. Did you know he petitioned to have me fired last week?"

Rin was mostly surprised that Jun hadn't tried that sooner.

"Also, anyone this obstinate deserves some attention, if only to make sure you don't become a walking hazard to everyone around you," Jiang continued. "You know, your footwork is remarkable."

She flushed. "Really?"

"Placement is perfect. Beautiful angles." He cocked his head. "Of course, everything you're doing is useless."

She scowled. "Well, if you're not going to teach me, then—"

"I didn't say that. You've done a good job working only with the text," Jiang acknowledged. "A better job than many apprentices would have done. It's your upper body strength that's the problem. Namely, you have none." He grabbed for her wrist and pulled her arm up as if he were examining a mannequin. "So skinny. Weren't you a farmhand or something?"

"Not everyone from the south is a farmer," she snapped. "I was a shopgirl."

"Hm. No heavy labor, then. Pampered. You're useless."

She crossed her arms against her chest. "I wasn't *pampered*—"

"Yeah, yeah." He held up a hand to cut her off. "It doesn't matter. Here's the thing: all the technique in the world won't do you any good if you don't have the strength to back it up. You don't need Seejin, kid. You need *ki*. You need muscle."

"So what do you want me to do? Calisthenics?"

He stood still, contemplative, for a long moment. Then he beamed. "No. I have a better idea. Be at the campus gates for class tomorrow."

Before she could respond, he strolled out of the garden.

"Wow." Raban set down his chopsticks. "He must really like you."

"He called me stupid and hotheaded," Rin said. "And then he told me to be on time for class."

"He *definitely* likes you," Raban said. "Jiang's never uttered anything nice to anyone in my year. He mostly yells at us to stay away from his daffodils. He told Kureel that her braids made her look like snakes were growing out the back of her head."

"I heard he got drunk on rice wine last week and pissed into Jun's window," Kitay chipped in. "He sounds *awesome*."

"How long has Jiang been here?" Rin asked. The Lore Master seemed amazingly young, at most half of Jun's age. She couldn't believe the other masters would put up with such aggravating behavior from someone who was clearly their junior.

"Not sure. He was here when I was a first-year, but that doesn't mean much. I heard he came from the Night Castle twenty years ago."

"Jiang was *Cike*?"

Among the divisions of the Militia, only the Cike bore an ill reputation. They were a division of soldiers holed up in the Night Castle, far up the Wudang mountain range, whose sole task was to carry out assassinations for the Empress. The Cike fought without honor. They respected no rules of combat, and they were notorious for their brutality. They operated in the darkness; they did the Empress's dirty work and received no recognition afterward. Most apprentices would have quit the service rather than join the Cike.

Rin had a hard time reconciling her image of the whimsical Lore Master with that of a hardened assassin.

"Well, that's just the rumor. None of the masters will say anything about him. I get the feeling that Jiang's considered a bit of an embarrassment to the school." Raban rubbed the back of his head. "The apprentices love to gossip, though. Every class plays the 'Who is Jiang?' guessing game. My class was convinced that he was the founder of the Red Junk Opera. The truth's been stretched so many times that the only thing certain is that we know absolutely nothing about him."

"Surely he's had apprentices before," said Rin.

"Jiang is the *Lore Master*," Raban said slowly, as if talking to a child. "Nobody pledges Lore."

"Because Jiang won't take any students?"

"Because Lore is a bloody joke," said Raban. "Every other track at Sinegard prepares you for a government position or for command in the Militia. But Lore is . . . I don't know, Lore's odd. I think it was originally meant to be a study of the Hinterlanders, to see if there's any substance to their witch-magic rituals, but everyone lost interest pretty quickly. I know Yim and Sonnen have both petitioned Jima to have the class canceled, but it's still offered every year. I'm not sure why."

"Surely there have been Lore students in the past," said Kitay. "What have they said?"

Raban shrugged. "It's a new discipline—the others have been taught since the Red Emperor founded this school, but Lore's only been around for two decades or so—and no one's stuck with the course all the way through. I hear that a couple years ago some suckers took the bait, but they dropped out of Sinegard and were never heard from again. No one in their right mind now would pledge Lore. Altan was the exception, but nobody ever knows what's going on in Altan's head."

"I thought Altan pledged Strategy," said Kitay.

"Altan could have pledged whatever he wanted. For some reason he was hell-bent on Lore, but then Jiang changed his mind and Altan had to settle for Irjah instead."

This was news to Rin. "Does that happen often—students choosing the master?"

"Very rarely. Most of us are relieved to get one bid; it's an especially impressive student who gets two."

"How many bids did Altan get?"

"Six. Seven if you include Lore, but Jiang withdrew his bid at the last minute." Raban gave her a knowing look. "Why so curious about Altan?"

"Just wondering," Rin said quickly.

"Taken a shine to our crimson-eyed hero, huh? You wouldn't be the first." Raban grinned. "Just be careful. Altan's not too kind to admirers."

"What's he like?" She couldn't help but ask. "As a person, I mean."

Raban shrugged. "We haven't had classes together since our

first year. I don't know him well. I don't think anyone really does. He mostly keeps to himself. He's quiet. Trains alone and doesn't really have friends."

"Sounds like someone we know." Kitay jabbed an elbow at Rin.

She bristled. "Shut up. I have friends."

"You have *a* friend," Kitay said. "Singular."

Rin pushed at Kitay's arm. "But Altan's so *good*," she said. "At everything. Everyone adores him."

Raban shrugged. "Altan's more or less a god on this campus. Doesn't mean he's happy."

Once the conversation had derailed to Altan, Rin forgot half the questions she had meant to ask about Jiang. She and Kitay prodded Raban for anecdotes about Altan until dinner break ended. That night, she tried asking Kureel and Arda, but neither of them could confirm anything substantial.

"I see Jiang in the infirmary sometimes," said Arda. "Enro keeps a walled-off bed just for him. He stays for a day or two every other month and then leaves. Maybe he's sick with something. Or maybe he just really likes the smell of disinfectant, I can't tell. Enro caught him trying to get high off medicine fumes once."

"Jun doesn't like him," said Kureel. "Not hard to see why. What kind of master *acts* like that? Especially at Sinegard?" Her face twisted with disapproval. "I think he's a disgrace to the Academy. Why're you asking?"

"No reason," said Rin. "Just curious."

Kureel shrugged. "Every class falls for it at first. Everyone thinks there's more to Jiang than there is, that Lore is a real subject worth learning. But there's nothing there. Jiang's a joke. You're wasting your time."

But the Lore Master was real. Jiang was a faculty member of the Academy, even if all he did was wander around and annoy the other masters. No one else could have gotten away with provoking Jun like Jiang did on a regular basis. So if Jiang didn't bother teaching, what was he doing at Sinegard?

Rin was slightly amazed when she saw Jiang waiting at the campus gates the next afternoon. She wouldn't have put it past him to simply forget. She opened her mouth to ask where they were going, but he simply waved at her to follow him.

She assumed that she was just going to have to get used to being led around by Jiang with no clear explanation.

They had hardly started down the path before they ran into Jun, returning from city patrol with a group of his apprentices.

"Ah. The lackwit and the peasant." Jun slowed to a stop. His apprentices looked somewhat wary, as if they'd seen this exchange before. "And where are you going on this fine afternoon?"

"None of your business, Loran," Jiang said breezily. He tried to skirt around Jun, but Jun stepped into his path.

"A master leaving the grounds alone with a student. I wonder what they'll say." Jun narrowed his eyes.

"Probably that a master of his rank and standing could do much better than dicking around with female students," Jiang replied cheerfully, looking directly at Jun's apprentices. Kureel looked outraged.

Jun scowled. "She doesn't have permission to leave the grounds. She needs written approval from Jima."

Jiang stretched out his right arm and shoved his sleeve up to the elbow. At first Rin thought that he might punch Jun, but Jiang simply raised his elbow to his mouth and made a loud farting noise.

"That's not written approval." Jun looked unimpressed. Rin suspected he had seen this display many times before.

"I'm Lore Master," Jiang said. "That comes with privileges."

"Privileges like never teaching class?"

Jiang lifted his chin and said self-importantly, "I have taught her class the crushing sensation of disappointment and the even more important lesson that they do not matter as much as they think they do."

"You have taught her class and every class before it that Lore is a joke and the Lore Master is a bumbling idiot."

"Tell Jima to fire me, then." Jiang waggled his eyebrows. "I know you've tried."

Jun raised his eyes to the sky in an expression of eternal suffering. Rin suspected that this was only a small part of an argument that had been going on for years.

"I'm reporting this to Jima," Jun warned.

"Jima has better things to waste her time on. As long as I bring little Runin back in time for dinner, I doubt she'll care. In the meantime, stop blocking the road."

Jiang snapped his fingers and motioned for Rin to follow. Rin clamped her mouth shut and tripped down the path behind him.

"Why does he hate you so much?" Rin asked as they climbed down the mountain pass toward the city.

Jiang shrugged. "They tell me I killed half the men under his command during the Second War. He's still bitter about it."

"Well, did you?" Rin felt like she was obligated to ask.

He shrugged again. "Haven't the faintest clue."

Rin had no idea how to respond to this, and Jiang did not elaborate.

"So tell me about your class," Jiang said after a while. "Same crowd of entitled brats?"

"I don't know them very well," Rin admitted. "They're all . . . I mean . . ."

"Smarter? Better trained? More important than you?"

"Nezha's the son of the Dragon Warlord," Rin blurted out. "How am I supposed to compete with that? Venka's father is the finance minister. Kitay's father is defense minister, or something like that. Niang's family are physicians to the Hare Warlord."

Jiang snorted. "Typical."

"Typical?"

"Sinegard likes to collect the Warlords' broods as much as it can. Keeps them under the Empire's careful watch."

"What for?" she asked.

"Leverage. Indoctrination. This generation of Warlords hate each other too much to coordinate on anything of national importance, and the imperial bureaucracy has too little local authority to force them. Just look at the state of the Imperial Navy."

"We have a navy?" Rin asked.

"Exactly." Jiang snorted. "We used to. Anyhow, Daji's hoping that Sinegard will forge a generation of leaders who like each other—and better, who will obey the throne."

"She really struck gold with me, then," Rin muttered.

Jiang shot her a sideways grin. "What, you're not going to be a good soldier to the Empire?"

"I will," Rin said hastily. "I just don't think most of my classmates like me very much. Or ever will."

"Well, that's because you're a dark little peasant brat who can't pronounce your r's," Jiang said breezily. He made a turn into a narrow corridor. "This way."

He led her into the meatpacking district, where the streets were cramped and crowded and smelled overwhelmingly like blood. Rin gagged and clamped a hand over her nose as they walked. Butcher shops lined the alleyways, built so close they were almost on top of one another in crooked rows like jagged teeth. After twenty minutes of twists and turns, they stopped at a little shack at the end of a block. Jiang rapped thrice on the rickety wooden door.

"*What?*" screeched a voice from within. Rin jumped.

"It's me," Jiang called back, unfazed. "Your favorite person in the whole wide world."

There was the noise of clattering metal from inside. After a moment, a wizened little lady in a purple smock opened the door. She greeted Jiang with a curt nod but squinted suspiciously at Rin.

"This is the Widow Maung," Jiang said. "She sells me things."

"Drugs," clarified the Widow Maung. "I am his drug dealer."

"She means ginseng, and roots and such," Jiang said. "For my health."

The Widow Maung rolled her eyes.

Rin watched the exchange, fascinated.

"The Widow Maung has a problem," Jiang continued cheerfully.

The Widow Maung cleared her throat and spat a thick wad of phlegm into the dirt next to where Jiang stood. "I do not have a problem. You are making up this problem for reasons unbeknownst to me."

"Regardless," Jiang said, maintaining his idyllic smile, "the Widow Maung has graciously allowed you to help her in resolving her problem. Madam, would you bring out the animal?"

The Widow Maung disappeared into the back of the shop. Jiang motioned for Rin to follow him inside. Rin heard a loud squealing sound from behind the wall. Moments later, the Widow Maung returned with a squirming animal clutched in her arms. She plopped it on the counter before them.

"Here's a pig," Jiang said.

"That is a pig," Rin agreed.

The pig in question was a tiny thing, no longer than Rin's forearm. Its skin was spotted black and pink. The way its snout curved up made it look like it was grinning. It was oddly cute.

Rin scratched it behind the ears and it nuzzled her forearm affectionately.

"I named it Sunzi," Jiang said happily.

The Widow Maung looked like she couldn't wait for Jiang to leave.

Jiang hastened to explain. "The Widow Maung needs little Sunzi watered every day. The problem is Sunzi requires a very special sort of water."

"Sunzi could drink sewage water and be fine," the Widow Maung clarified. "You're just making things up for this training exercise."

"Can we just do it like we rehearsed?" Jiang demanded. It was the first time Rin had seen anyone actually get to him. "You're killing the mood."

"Is that something you're often told?" the Widow Maung inquired.

Jiang snorted, amused, and clapped Rin on the back. "Here's the situation. The Widow Maung needs Sunzi to drink this very special sort of water. Fortunately, this fresh, crystal-clear water can be found in a stream at the top of the mountain. The catch is getting Sunzi up the mountain. This is where you come in."

"You're *joking*," Rin said.

Jiang beamed. "Every day you will run into town to visit the Widow Maung. You will lug this adorable piglet up the mountain and let him drink. Then you will bring him back and return to the Academy. Understood?"

"It's a two-hour trip up the mountain and back!"

"It's a two-hour trip *now*," Jiang said cheerfully. "It'll be longer once this little guy starts growing."

"But I have class," she protested.

"Better get up early, then," said Jiang. "It's not like you have Combat in the morning anyway. Remember? Someone got expelled?"

"But—"

"Someone," Jiang drawled, "does not want very much to stay at Sinegard."

The Widow Maung snorted loudly.

Glowering, Rin gathered up Sunzi the piglet in her arms and tried not to wrinkle her nose at the smell.

"Guess I'll be seeing a lot of you," she grumbled.

Sunzi squirmed and nuzzled into the crook of her arm.

Every day over the next four months, Rin rose before the sun came up, ran as fast as she could down the mountain pass and into the meatpacking district to fetch Sunzi, strapped the piglet to her back, and ran back up the mountain. She took the long way up, routing around Sinegard so that none of her classmates would see her running around with a squealing pig.

She was often late to Medicine.

"Where the hell have you been? And why do you smell like *swine*?" Kitay wrinkled his nose as she slid into the seat next to him.

"I've been carrying a pig up a mountain," she said. "Obeying the whims of a madman. Finding a way out."

It was desperate behavior, but she had fallen on desperate times. Rin was now relying on the campus madman to keep her spot at Sinegard. She began to sit in the back of the room so that nobody could smell the traces of Sunzi on her when she returned from the Widow Maung's butcher shop.

From the way everyone kept their distance, she wasn't sure it mattered.

Jiang did more than make her carry the pig. In an astonishing streak of reliability, he stood waiting for her in the garden every day at class time.

"You know, animal-based martial arts weren't developed for combat," he said. "They were first created to promote health and longevity. The Frolics of the Five Animals"—he held up the Yin-men scroll that Rin had spent so long looking for—"is actually a system of exercises to promote blood circulation and delay the inconveniences of old age. It wasn't until later that these forms were adapted for fighting."

"So why am I learning them?"

"Because Jun's curriculum skips the Frolics entirely. Jun teaches a simplified version of watered-down martial arts adapted purely to human biomechanics. But it leaves out far too much. It whittles away centuries of lineage and refinement all for the sake of military efficiency. Jun can teach you how to be a decent soldier. But I can teach you the key to the universe," Jiang said grandly, before bumping his head on a low-hanging branch.

Training with Jiang was nothing like training with Jun. There were obvious hierarchies to Jun's lesson plans, a clear progression from basic techniques to advanced.

But Jiang taught Rin every random thing that came to his deeply unpredictable mind. He would revisit a lesson if he found it particularly interesting; if not, he pretended like it had never happened. Occasionally he would go on long tirades without provocation.

"There are five principal elements present in the universe—get that look off your face, it's not as absurd as it sounds. The masters of old used to believe that all things were made of fire, water, air, earth, and metal. Obviously, modern science has proven that false. Still, it's a useful mnemonic for understanding the different types of energy.

"Fire: the heat in your blood in the midst of a fight, the kinetic energy that makes your heart beat faster." Jiang tapped his chest. "Water: the flowing of force from your muscles to your target, from the earth up through your waist, into your arms. Air: the breath you draw that keeps you alive. Earth: how you stay rooted to the ground, how you derive energy from the way you position yourself against the floor. And metal, for the weapons you wield. A good martial artist will possess all five of these in balance. If you can control each of these with equal skill, you will be unstoppable."

"How do I know if I've got control of them?"

He scratched a spot behind his ears. "Good question. I'm not actually sure."

Asking Jiang for clarification was inevitably infuriating. His answers were always bizarrely worded and absurdly phrased. Some didn't make sense until days later; some never did. If she asked him to explain, he changed the subject. If she let his more absurd comments slide ("Your water element is off balance!"), he poked and prodded about why she wasn't asking more questions.

He spoke oddly, always a little too quickly or a little too slowly, with strange pauses between his words. He laughed in two ways; one laugh was off-kilter—nervous, high-pitched, and obviously forced—the other great and deep and booming. The first kind she heard constantly; the second was rare, and startling when it burst forth. He rarely met her gaze, but rather focused always at a spot on her brow between her eyes.

Jiang moved through the world like he didn't belong there. He acted as if he came from a country of near-humans, people who acted almost exactly like Nikara but not quite, and his behavior was that of a confused visitor who had stopped bothering with trying to imitate those around him. He didn't belong—not simply in Sinegard, but in the very idea of a physical earth. He acted like the rules of nature did not apply to him.

Perhaps they didn't.

One day they went to the highest tier of the Academy, up past the masters' lodges. The single building on this tier was a tall, spiraling pagoda, nine stories stacked elegantly on top of one another. Rin had never been inside.

She recalled from that tour so many months ago that Sinegard Academy had been built on the grounds of an old monastery. The pagoda on the highest tier could have still been a temple. Old stone trenches for burning incense sat outside the pagoda entrance. Guarding either side of the door were two large cylinders mounted on tall rods to let them spin. When she looked closer, Rin saw Old Nikara characters carved into the sides.

"What do these do?" she asked, idly spinning one cylinder.

"They're prayer wheels. But we don't have time to get into that today," Jiang said. He gestured for her to follow him. "In here."

Rin expected that the nine stories of the pagoda would be proper floors connected by flights of stairs, but the interior was merely a winding staircase that led to the very top, an empty cylinder of air in the middle. A solitary beam of sunlight shone in from a square opening in the ceiling, illuminating dust motes floating through the air. A series of musty paintings had been hung on the sides of the staircase. They looked like they hadn't been cleaned in decades.

"This is where the statues to the Four Gods used to stand," said Jiang, pointing up into the dark void.

"Where are they now?"

He shrugged. "The Red Emperor had most religious imagery stripped and looted when he took over Sinegard. Most of it's been melted down into jewelry. But that doesn't matter." He beckoned for Rin to follow him up the staircase.

He lectured as they climbed. "Martial arts came to the Empire by way of a warrior named Bodhidharma from the southeastern continent. When Bodhidharma found the Empire during his travels of the world, he journeyed to a monastery and demanded entry, but the head abbot refused him entrance. So Bodhidharma sat his ass in a nearby cave and faced the wall for nine years, listening to the ants scream."

"Listening to *what*?"

"The ants scream, Runin. Keep up."

She muttered something unrepeatable. Jiang ignored her.

"Legend has it that the intensity of his gaze bored a hole into the cave wall. The monks were either so moved by his religious commitment or so seriously impressed that anyone could be so obstinate that they finally let him into their temple." Jiang paused in front of a painting depicting a dark-skinned warrior and a group of pale men in robes. "That's Bodhidharma there in the center."

"That guy on the left has blood spurting out of a stump," Rin observed.

"Yeah. Legend also has it that one monk was so impressed with his commitment that he cut off his hand in sympathy."

Rin recalled the myth of Mai'rinnen Tearza committing suicide for the sake of Speer's unification with the mainland. Martial arts history seemed to be riddled with people making pointless sacrifices.

"Anyhow. The monks at the temple were interested in what Bodhidharma had to say, but because of their sedentary lives and poor diets, they were weak as shit. Scrawnier than you, even. Kept falling asleep during his lectures. Bodhidharma found this somewhat annoying, so he devised three sets of exercises to improve their health. Now, these monks were in constant physical danger from outlaws and robbers, but were also forbidden by their religious code to carry weapons, so they modified many of the exercises to form a system of weaponless self-defense."

Jiang stopped before another painting. It depicted a row of monks lined up on a wall, frozen in identical stances.

Rin was amazed. "That's—"

"Seejin's first form. Yeah." Jiang nodded in approval. "Bodhidharma warned the monks that martial arts was about the refinement of the individual. Martial arts used well would produce a wise commander, a man who could see clearly through fog and understand the will of the gods. The martial arts in their conception were not meant solely as military tools."

Rin struggled to envision the techniques Jun had taught their class as purely health exercises. "But there had to be an evolution in the arts."

"Correct." Jiang waited for her to ask the question he wanted to hear.

She obliged. "When did the arts become adapted for mass military use?"

Jiang bobbed his head, pleased. "Shortly before the days of the Red Emperor, the Empire was invaded by the horsemen from the Hinterlands to the north. The occupation force introduced a number of repressive measures to control the indigenous population, which included forbidding the Nikara to carry weapons."

Jiang stopped again before a painting depicting a horde of Hinterlander hunters riding upon massive steeds. Their faces were twisted into wild, barbaric scowls. They held bows that were longer than their torsos. At the bottom of the painting, Nikara monks were shown cowering in fear or strewn about in various states of dismemberment.

"The temples that were once havens of nonviolence became instead a sanctuary for anti-Northerner rebels and a center for revolutionary planning and training. Soldiers and sympathizers would don monks' robes and shave their heads, but train for war within the temple grounds. In sacred spaces like these, they plotted the overthrow of their oppressors."

"And health exercises would hardly have helped them," Rin said. "The martial techniques had to be adapted."

Jiang nodded again. "Exactly. The arts then taught in the temple required the progressive mastery of hundreds of long, intricate forms. These could take decades to master. The leaders of the rebellion, thankfully, realized that this approach was unsuitable to the rapid development of a fighting force."

Jiang turned around to face her. They had reached the top of the pagoda. "And so modern martial arts were developed: a system based on human biomechanics rather than the movements of animals. The enormous variety of techniques, some of which were only marginally useful to a soldier, were distilled into an essential core of forms that could be taught to a soldier in five years rather than fifty. This is the basis of what you are taught at Sinegard. This is the common core that is taught to the Imperial Militia. This is what your classmates are learning." He grinned. "I am showing you how to beat it."

Jiang was an effective if unconventional combat instructor. He made her hold her kicks up in the air for long minutes until her leg trembled. He made her duck as he hurled projectiles at her off the weapons rack. He made her do the same exercise blindfolded, and then admitted later that he just thought it would be funny.

"You're a real asshole," she said. "You know that, right?"

Once Jiang was pleased with her fundamentals, they began to spar. They sparred every day, for hours at a time. They sparred bare-fisted and with weapons; sometimes she was bare-fisted while he bore a weapon.

"Your state of mind is just as important as the state of your body," Jiang lectured. "In the confusion of a fight, your mind must be still and steady as a rock. You must be grounded in your center, able to see and control everything. Each of the five elements must be in balance. Too much fire, and you'll lash out recklessly. Too much air and you'll fight skittishly, always on the defensive. Too much earth, and—are you even listening?"

She was not. It was hard to concentrate while Jiang jabbed an unguarded halberd at her, forcing her to dance around to avoid sudden impalement.

By and large, Jiang's metaphors meant little to her, but she learned quickly to avoid injury. And perhaps that was his point. She developed muscle memory. She learned that there were only so many permutations to the way a human body could move, only so many attack combinations that worked, that she could reasonably expect from her opponent. She learned to react automatically to these. She learned to predict Jiang's moves seconds in advance, to read from the tilt of his torso and the flicker of his eyes what he was about to do next.

He pushed her relentlessly. He fought the hardest when she was exhausted. When she fell, he attacked her as soon as she'd gotten back on her feet. She learned to stay constantly on guard, to react to the slightest movements in her peripheral vision.

The day came when she angled her hip against his just so, forced his weight to the side and jammed all her force at an angle that hurled him over her right shoulder.

Jiang skidded across the stone floor and bumped against the garden wall, which shook the shelves so that a potted cactus came perilously close to shattering on the ground.

Jiang lay there for a moment, dazed. Then he looked up, met her eyes, and grinned.

Rin's last day with Sunzi was the hardest.

Sunzi was no longer an adorable piglet but an absurdly fat monster that smelled heinously bad. It wasn't remotely cute. Any affection Rin had felt for those trusting brown eyes was negated by the animal's massive girth.

Carrying Sunzi up the mountain was torture. Sunzi no longer

fit in any sort of sling or basket. Rin had to drape it over her shoulders, grasping it by its two front legs.

She could hardly move as fast as she had when Sunzi could still be cradled in her arms, but she had to, unless she wanted to go without breakfast—or worse, miss class. She rose earlier. She ran faster. She staggered up the mountain, gasping for air with every step. Sunzi lay against her back with its snout resting over one of her shoulders, basking in the morning sun while Rin's muscles screamed with resentment. When she reached Sunzi's drinking area, she let the pig drop to the ground and collapsed.

"Drink, you glutton," she grumbled as Sunzi frolicked in the stream. "I can't wait until the day they carve you up and eat you."

On her way down the mountain, the sun began to beat down in earnest, eliciting rivulets of sweat all over Rin's body despite the winter cold. She limped through the meatpacking district to the Widow Maung's cottage and deposited Sunzi gracelessly on the floor.

It rolled over, squealed loudly and ran in a circle, chasing its own tail.

The Widow Maung came out to the front carrying a bucket of slops.

"I'll be back tomorrow," Rin panted.

The Widow Maung shook her head. "There won't be a tomorrow. Not for this one, anyway." She rubbed Sunzi's snout. "This one's going to the butcher tonight."

Rin blinked. "What? So soon?"

"Sunzi's already reached his peak weight." The Widow Maung slapped Sunzi's sides. "Look at that girth. None of my pigs have ever grown so heavy. Perhaps your crazy teacher was right about the mountain water. Maybe I should send all my pigs up there."

Rin rather hoped that she didn't. Chest still heaving, she bowed low to the widow. "Thank you for letting me carry your pig."

The Widow Maung harrumphed. "Academy freaks," she muttered under her breath, and began to lead Sunzi back to the sty. "Come on, you. Let's get you ready for the butcher."

Oink? Sunzi looked imploringly at Rin.

"Don't look at me," Rin said. "It's the end of the road for you."

She couldn't help but feel a stab of guilt; the longer she looked at Sunzi, the more she was reminded of its piglet form. She tore her eyes away from its dull, naive gaze and headed back up the mountain.

"Already?" Jiang looked surprised when Rin reported Sunzi's fate. He was sitting on the far wall of the garden, swinging his legs over the edge like an energetic child. "Ah, I had high hopes for that pig. But in the end, swine are swine. How do you feel?"

"I'm devastated," Rin said. "Sunzi and I were finally starting to understand each other."

"No, you sod. Your *arms*. Your core. Your legs. How do they feel?"

She frowned and swung her arms about. "Sore?"

Jiang jumped off the wall and walked toward her. "I'm going to hit you," he announced.

"Wait, what?"

She dug her heels into the ground and only managed to get her elbows up right before he slammed a fist at her face.

The force of his punch was enormous—harder than he'd ever hit her. She knew she should have deflected the blow at an angle, sent the *ki* dispersing into the air where it would dispel harmlessly. But she was too startled to do anything but block it head-on. She barely remembered to crouch so that the *ki* behind his punch channeled harmlessly through her body and into the ground.

A crack like a thunderbolt echoed beneath her.

Rin jumped back, stunned. The stone under her feet had splintered under the force of the dispelled energy. One long crack ran between her feet to the edge of the stone block.

They both stared down at it. The crack continued to splinter the stone floor, crawling all the way to the far end of the garden, where it stopped at the base of the willow tree.

Jiang threw his head back and laughed.

It was a high, wild laugh. He laughed like his lungs were bellows. He laughed like he was nothing human. He spread his arms out and windmilled them in the air, and danced with giddy abandon.

"You darling child," he said, spinning toward her. "You brilliant child."

Rin's face split into a grin.

Fuck it, she thought, and leaped up to embrace him.

He picked her up and swung her through the air, around and around among the kaleidoscopically colorful mushrooms.

They sat together under the willow tree, staring serenely at the poppy plants. The wind was still today. Snow continued to fall lightly over the garden, but the first inklings of spring had arrived. The furious winter winds had gone to blow elsewhere; the air felt settled, for once. Peaceful.

"No more training today," Jiang said. "You rest. Sometimes you must loose the string to let the arrow fly."

Rin rolled her eyes.

"You have to pledge Lore," Jiang continued excitedly. "No one—*no one*, not even Altan, picked things up this fast."

Rin suddenly felt very awkward. How was she to tell him the only reason she wanted to learn combat was so she could get through the Trials and study with Irjah?

Jiang hated lies. Rin decided she might as well be straightforward. "I'd been thinking about pledging Strategy," she said hesitantly. "Irjah said he might bid for me."

He waved his hand. "Irjah can't teach you anything you couldn't learn by yourself. Strategy's a limited subject. Spend enough time in the field with Sunzi's *Principles* by your bed, and you'll pick up everything you need to win a campaign."

"But . . ."

"Who are the gods? Where do they reside? Why do they do what they do? These are the fundamental questions of Lore. I can teach you more than *ki* manipulation. I can show you the pathway to the gods. I can make you a shaman."

Gods and shamans? It was often difficult to tell when Jiang was joking and when he wasn't, but he seemed genuinely convinced that he could talk to heavenly powers.

She swallowed. "Sir . . ."

"This is *important*," Jiang insisted. "Please, Rin. This is a dying art. The Red Emperor almost succeeded in killing it. If you don't learn it, if no one learns it, then it disappears for good."

The sudden desperation in his voice made her intensely uncomfortable.

She twisted a blade of grass between her fingers. Certainly she was curious about Lore, but she knew better than to throw away four years of training under Irjah to chase a subject that the other masters had long ago lost faith in. She hadn't come to Sinegard to pursue stories on a whim, especially stories that were disdained by everyone else in the capital.

She was admittedly fascinated by myths and legends, and the way that Jiang made them sound almost real. But she was more interested in making it past the Trials. And an apprenticeship with Irjah opened doors at the Militia. It all but guaranteed an officer position *and* her choice of division. Irjah had contacts with each of the Twelve Warlords, and his protégées always found esteemed placements.

She could lead troops of her own within a year of graduating. She could be a nationally renowned commander within five. She couldn't throw that away on a mere fancy.

"Sir, I just want to learn to be a good soldier," she said.

Jiang's face fell.

"You and the rest of this school," he said.

CHAPTER 7

Jiang did not appear in the garden the next day, or the day after. Rin went to the garden faithfully in the hope that he would return, but she knew, deep down, that Jiang was done with teaching her.

One week later she saw him in the mess hall. She abruptly put her bowl down and made a beeline toward him. She had no clue what she might say, but knew that she needed to at least talk to him. She would apologize, promise to study with him even if she became Irjah's apprentice, or say *something* . . .

Before she could corner him he upended his tray over a startled apprentice's head and dashed out the kitchen door.

"Great Tortoise," said Kitay. "What did you *do* to him?"

"I don't know," she said.

Jiang was unpredictable and fragile, like an easily startled wild animal, and she hadn't realized how precious his attention was until she had scared him away.

After that, he acted as if he didn't even know her. She continued to see brief glimpses of him around campus, just as everyone did, but he refused to acknowledge her.

She should have tried harder to patch things up with him. She should have actively sought him out and admitted her mistake, nebulous though it was.

But she found it less and less of a priority as the term came to an end, and the competition between the first-years reached a frenzied peak.

Throughout the year, the possibility of being culled from Sinegard had hung like a sword over their heads. Now that threat was imminent. In two weeks they would undergo the series of exams that constituted the Trials.

Raban relayed the rules to them. The Trials would be administered and observed by the entire faculty. Depending on their performance, the masters would submit bids for apprenticeship. If a student received no bids, he or she would leave the Academy in disgrace.

Enro exempted all students who were not intent on pledging Medicine from her exam, but the other subjects—Linguistics, History, Strategy, Combat, and Weaponry—were mandatory. There was, of course, no scheduled exam for Lore.

"Irjah, Jima, Yim, and Sonnen give oral exams," said Raban. "You'll be questioned in front of a panel of the masters. They'll take turns interrogating you, and if you mess up, that's the end of your session for that subject. The more questions you answer, the more you get to prove how much you know. So study hard—and speak carefully."

Jun did not conduct an oral exam. The Combat exam consisted of the Tournament.

This would take course over the two days of exams. The first-years would duel in the rings using the same rules that the apprentices used in their matches. They would compete in three preliminary rounds determined by random draws, and based on their win-loss ratios, eight would advance to elimination rounds. Those eight would be placed in a randomized bracket and fight one another until the final round.

Reaching the eliminations in the Tournament was no guarantee of gaining a sponsor, and losing early was not a guarantee of expulsion. But those students who advanced further in the tournament had more chances to show the masters how well they fought. And the winner of the Tournament always received a bid.

"Altan won his year," Raban said. "Kureel won hers. You'll notice they both landed the two most prestigious apprenticeships at Sinegard. There's no actual prize for winning, but the masters like placing bets. Get your ass kicked, and no master will want to take you on."

"I want to pledge Medicine, but we've got to memorize so many extra texts on top of the readings we've done so far, and if I do I won't have time study for History . . . Do you think I should pledge History? Do you think Yim likes me enough?" Niang flapped her hands in the air, agitated. "My brother said I shouldn't rely on getting a Medicine apprenticeship; there are four of us taking Enro's exam and she only ever picks three, so maybe I won't get it . . ."

"Enough, Niang," Venka snapped. "You've been talking about this for days."

"What do you want to pledge?" Niang persisted.

"Combat. And that's the last time we're talking about it," Venka said shrilly. Rin suspected that if Niang said another word, Venka might scream.

But Rin couldn't blame Niang. Or Venka, really. The first-years gossiped obsessively about apprenticeships, and it was both understandable *and* grating. Rin had learned about the hierarchy of masters through eavesdropping on conversations in the mess hall: bids from Jun and Irjah were ideal for apprentices who wanted command positions in the Militia, Jima rarely chose apprentices unless they were nobility destined to become court diplomats, and Enro's bid mattered only to the few of them who wanted to be military physicians.

"Training under Irjah would be nice," said Kitay. "Of course, Jun's apprentices have their pick of divisions, but Irjah can get me into the Second."

"The Rat Province's division?" Rin wrinkled her nose. "Why?"

Kitay shrugged. "They're Army Intelligence. I would *love* to serve in Army Intelligence."

Jun was out of the question for Rin, though she too hoped Irjah might take her. But she knew Irjah wouldn't place a bid unless she proved she had the martial arts to back up her Strategy prowess. A strategist who couldn't fight had no place in the Militia. How could she draw up battle plans if she'd never been on the front lines? If she didn't know what real combat was like?

For her, it all came down to the Tournament.

As for the apprentices, it was apparently the most exciting thing to happen on campus all year. They began speculating wildly about who might win and who would beat whom—and they didn't try very hard to keep the betting books secret from the first-years. Word spread quickly about who the front-runners were.

Most of the money backed the Sinegardians. Venka and Han were solid contenders for the semifinals. Nohai, a massive kid from a fishing island in Snake Province, was widely backed to reach the quarterfinals. Kitay had his fair share of supporters, although this was largely because he had demonstrated a talent for dodging so well that most of his sparring opponents grew frustrated and got sloppy after several long minutes.

Oddly, a number of apprentices put decent money on Rin. Once word got out that she had been training privately with Jiang, the apprentices took an inordinate degree of interest in her. It helped that she was nipping at Kitay's heels in every other one of their classes.

The clear front-runner in their year, however, was Nezha.

"Jun says he's the best to come through his class since Altan," Kitay said, jabbing vehemently at his food. "Won't shut up about him. You should have seen him take out Nohai yesterday. He's a *menace*."

Nezha, who had been a pretty, slender child at the start of the year, had since packed on an absurd amount of muscle. He'd cut short his stupidly long hair in favor of a clipped military cut similar to Altan's. Unlike the rest of them, he already looked like he belonged in a Militia uniform.

He had also garnered a reputation for striking first and thinking later. He had injured eight sparring partners over the course of the term, all in increasingly severe "accidents."

But of course Jun had never punished him—not as severely as he deserved, anyhow. Why would something so mundane as rules apply to the son of the Dragon Warlord?

As the date of the exams loomed closer, the library became oppressively silent. The only sound among the stacks was the furious scribbling of brushes on paper as the first-years tried to commit an entire year's lessons to memory. Most study groups had disbanded, since any advantage given to a study partner was potentially a lost spot in the ranks.

But Kitay, who didn't need to study, obliged Rin purely out of boredom.

"Sunzi's Eighteenth Mandate." Kitay didn't bother looking at the texts. He had memorized the entirety of *Principles of War* on his first read-through. Rin would have killed for that talent.

Rin squinted her eyes in concentration. She knew she looked stupid, but her head was swimming again, and squinting was the only way to make it stop. She felt very cold and hot all at once. She hadn't slept in three days. All she wanted was to collapse on her bunk, but another hour of cramming was worth more than an hour of sleep.

"It's not one of the Seven Considerations . . . wait, is it? No, okay: always modify plans according to circumstances . . . ?"

Kitay shook his head. "That's the Seventeenth Mandate."

Rin cursed out loud and rubbed her fists against her forehead.

"I wonder how you people do it," Kitay mused. "You know, actually having to try to remember things. Your lives sound so difficult."

"I will murder you with this ink brush," Rin grumbled.

"Sunzi's appendix is all about why soft ends make for bad weapons. Didn't you do the extra reading?"

"Quiet!" Venka snapped from the opposite desk.

Kitay dipped his head out of Venka's sight and cracked a grin at Rin. "Here's a hint," he whispered. "Menda in the temple."

Rin gritted her teeth and squeezed her eyes shut. *Oh. Of course.* "All warfare is based on deception."

In preparation for the Tournament, their entire class had taken Sunzi's Eighteenth Mandate to heart. The pupils stopped using the open practice rooms during common hours. Anyone with an inherited art suddenly stopped bragging about it. Even Nezha had ceased to hold his nightly performances in the studio.

"This happens every year," Raban had said. "It's a bit silly, to be honest. As if martial artists your age ever have anything worth stealing."

Silly or not, their class freaked out in earnest. Everyone was accused of having a hidden weapon up his or her sleeve; whoever had never displayed an inherited art was alleged to be harboring one in secret.

Niang confided to Rin one night that Kitay was actually the heir to the long-forgotten Fist of the North Wind, an art that allowed the user to incapacitate opponents by touching a few choice pressure points.

"I might have had a hand in spreading that story," Kitay admitted when Rin asked him about it. "Sunzi would call it psychological warfare."

She snorted. "Sunzi would call it horseshit."

The first-years weren't allowed to train after curfew, so the preparation period turned into a contest of who could find the most creative way of sneaking past the masters. The apprentices, of course, began vigilantly patrolling the campus after curfew to catch students who had stolen outside to train. Nohai reported that he'd stumbled across a sheet detailing points for such captures in the boys' dormitory.

"It's almost like they're enjoying this," Rin muttered.

"Of course they enjoy it," said Kitay. "They get to watch us suffer through the same things they did. This time next year we'll be equally obnoxious."

Displaying a stunning lack of sympathy, the apprentices had also taken advantage of the first-years' anxiety to establish a flourishing market in "study aids." Rin laughed when Niang returned to the dormitory with what Niang thought was willow bark aged a hundred years.

"That's a ginger root," Rin said with a snicker. She weighed the wrinkled root in her hand. "I mean, I suppose it's good in tea."

"How do you know?" Niang looked dismayed. "I paid twenty coppers for that!"

"We dug up ginger roots all the time in our garden back at home," Rin said. "Put them in the sun and you can sell them to old men looking for a virility cure. Does absolutely nothing, but it makes them feel better. We'd also sell wheat flour and call it rhino's horn. I'll bet you the apprentices have been selling barley flour, too."

Venka, whom Rin had seen stowing a vial of powder under her pillow a few nights before, coughed and looked away.

The apprentices also sold information to first-years. Most sold bogus test answers; others offered lists of purported exam questions that seemed highly plausible but obviously wouldn't be confirmed until after the Trials. Worst, though, were the apprentices who posed as sellers to root out the first-years who were willing to cheat.

Menda, a boy from the Horse Province, had agreed to meet with an apprentice after hours in the temple on the fourth tier to purchase a list of Jima's exam questions. Rin didn't know how the apprentice had managed the timing, but Jima had been meditating in said temple that very night.

Menda was noticeably absent from campus the next day.

Meals became silent and reserved affairs. Everyone ate with a book held before his or her nose. If any students ventured to strike up a conversation, the rest of the table quickly and violently shushed them. In short, they made themselves miserable.

"Sometimes I think this is as bad as the Speer Massacre," Kitay said cheerfully. "And then I think—nah. Nothing is as bad as the casual genocide of an entire race! But this is pretty bad."

"Kitay, *please* shut up."

Rin continued to train alone in the garden. She never saw Jiang anymore, but that was just as well; masters were banned from training the students for the Tournament, although Rin suspected Nezha was still receiving instruction from Jun.

One day she heard footsteps as she approached the garden gate. Someone was inside.

At first she hoped it might be Jiang, but when she opened the door she saw a lean, graceful figure with indigo-black hair.

It took her a moment to process what she'd stumbled upon.

Altan. She'd interrupted Altan Trengsin in his practice.

He wielded a three-pronged trident—no, he didn't just *wield* it, he held it intimately, curved it through the air like a ribbon. It was both an extension of his arm and a dance partner.

She should have turned to go, found somewhere else to train, but she couldn't help her curiosity. She couldn't look away. From a distance, he was extraordinarily beautiful. Up close, he was hypnotizing.

He turned at the sound of her footsteps, saw her, and stopped.

"I'm so sorry," she stammered. "I didn't know you were—"

"It's a school garden," he said neutrally. "Don't leave on my account."

His voice was more somber than she had anticipated. She had imagined a harsh, barking tone to match his brutal movements in the ring, but Altan's voice was surprisingly melodious, soft and deep.

His pupils were oddly constricted. Rin couldn't tell if it was simply the light in the garden, but his eyes didn't seem red then. Rather, they looked brown, like hers.

"I've never seen that form before," Rin uttered.

Altan raised an eyebrow. She immediately regretted opening

her mouth. Why had she said that? Why did she *exist*? She wanted to crumble into ashes and scatter away into the air.

But Altan just looked surprised, not irritated. "Stick around Jiang long enough, and you'll learn plenty of arcane forms." He shifted his weight to his back leg and brought his arms in a flowing motion around to the other side of his torso.

Rin's cheeks burned. She felt very clumsy and vast, like she was taking up space that belonged to Altan, even though she was on the other end of the garden. "Master Jiang didn't say anyone else liked to come here."

"Jiang likes to forget about a lot of things." He tilted his head at her. "You must be quite the student, if Jiang's taken an interest in you."

Was that bitterness in his voice, or was she imagining things?

She remembered then that Jiang had withdrawn his bid for Altan, right after Altan had declared he wanted to pledge Lore. She wondered what had happened, and if it still bothered Altan. She wondered if she'd annoyed him by bringing Jiang up.

"I stole a book from the library," she managed. "He thought that was funny."

Why was she still talking? Why was she still here?

The corner of Altan's mouth quirked up in a terribly attractive grin, which set her heart beating erratically. "What a rebel."

She flushed, but Altan just turned away and completed the form.

"Don't let me stop you from training," he said.

"No, I—I came here to think. But if you're here—"

"I'm sorry. I can leave."

"No, it's okay." She didn't know what she was saying. "I was going to—I mean, I'll just . . . bye."

She quickly backed out of the garden. Altan didn't say anything else.

Once she had closed the garden gates behind her, Rin buried her face in her hands and groaned.

*   *   *

"Is there ever a place for meekness in battle?" Irjah asked. This was the seventh question he had posed to her.

Rin was on a streak. Seven was the maximum number of questions any master could ask, and if she nailed this one, she would ace Irjah's exam. And she knew the answer—it was lifted directly from Sunzi's Twenty-Second Mandate.

She lifted her chin and responded in a loud, clear voice. "Yes, but only for the purposes of deception. Sunzi writes that if your opponent is of choleric temper, you should seek to irritate him. Pretend to be weak so that he grows arrogant. The good tactician plays with his enemy like a cat plays with a mouse. Feign weakness and immobility, and then pounce on him."

The seven masters each marked small notes into their scrolls. Rin bounced slightly on her heels, waiting for them to continue.

"Good. No further questions." Irjah nodded and gestured at his colleagues. "Master Yim?"

Yim pushed his chair back and rose slowly. He consulted his scroll for a moment, and then gazed at Rin over the top of his spectacles. "Why did we win the Second Poppy War?"

Rin sucked in a breath. She had not prepared for this question. It was so basic she'd thought she didn't need to. Yim had asked it on the first day of class, and the answer was a logical fallacy. There was no "why," because Nikan hadn't won the Second Poppy War. The Republic of Hesperia had, and Nikan had simply ridden the foreigners' coattails to a victory treaty.

She considered answering the question directly, but then thought she might try a more original response. She had only one shot at an answer. She wanted to impress the masters.

"Because we gave up Speer," she said.

Irjah jerked his head up from his scroll.

Yim raised an eyebrow. "Do you mean because we *lost* Speer?"

"No. I mean it was a strategic decision to sacrifice the island so that the Hesperian parliament might decide to intervene. I think the command in Sinegard knew the attack was going to happen and didn't warn the Speerlies."

"I was *at* Speer," Jun interrupted. "This is amusing historiography at best, slander at worst."

"No, you weren't," Rin said before she could stop herself.

Jun looked amazed. "Excuse me?"

All seven masters were watching her intently now. Rin remembered too late that Irjah had disliked this theory. And that Jun *hated* her.

But it was too late to stop. She weighed the costs in her head. The masters rewarded bravery and creativity. If she backed off, it would be a sign of uncertainty. She had begun digging this hole for herself. She might as well finish.

She took a deep breath. "You can't have been at Speer. I read the reports. None of the regular Militia were there the night the island was attacked. The first troops didn't arrive until sunrise, after the Federation had left. After the Speerlies had all been killed."

Jun's face darkened to the color of an overripe plum. "You dare accuse—"

"She's not accusing anyone of anything," Jiang interrupted serenely. It was the first time he'd spoken since the start of her exam. Rin glanced at him in surprise, but Jiang just scratched his ear, not even looking at her. "She's merely attempting a clever answer to an otherwise inane question. Honestly, Yim, this one has gotten pretty old."

Yim shrugged. "Fair enough. No further questions. Master Jiang?"

All the masters twitched in irritation. From what Rin understood, Jiang was present only as a formality. He never gave an exam; he mostly just made fun of the students when they tripped over their answers.

Jiang gazed levelly into Rin's eyes.

She swallowed, feeling the unsettling sensation of his searching gaze. It was like she was as transparent as a puddle of rainwater.

"Who is imprisoned in the Chuluu Korikh?" he asked.

She blinked. Not once in the four months that he had trained her had Jiang ever mentioned the Chuluu Korikh. Neither had

Master Yim or Irjah, or even Jima. *Chuluu Korikh* wasn't medical terminology, wasn't a reference to a famous battle, wasn't some linguistic term of art. It could be a deeply loaded phrase. It could also be gibberish.

Either Jiang was posing a riddle, or he just wanted to throw her off.

But she didn't want to admit defeat. She didn't want to look clueless in front of Irjah. Jiang had asked her a question, and Jiang never asked questions during the Trials. The masters were expecting an interesting answer now; she couldn't disappoint them.

What was the cleverest way to say *I don't know*?

The Chuluu Korikh. She'd studied Old Nikara with Jima for long enough now that she could gloss this as *stone mountain* in the ancient dialect, but that didn't give her any clues. None of Nikan's major prisons were built under mountains; they were either out in the Baghra Desert or in the dungeons of the Empress's palace.

And Jiang hadn't asked what the Chuluu Korikh *was*. He'd asked who was imprisoned there.

What kind of prisoner couldn't be held in the Baghra Desert?

She pondered this until she had an unsatisfying answer to an unsatisfying question.

"Unnatural criminals," she said slowly, "who have committed unnatural crimes?"

Jun snorted audibly. Jima and Yim looked uncomfortable.

Jiang gave a minuscule shrug.

"Fine," he said. "That's all I have."

Oral exams concluded by midmorning on the third day. The pupils were sent to lunch, which no one ate, and then herded to the rings for the commencement of the Tournament.

Rin drew Han for her first opponent.

When it was her turn to fight she climbed down the rope ladder and looked up. The masters stood in a row before the rails. Irjah gave her a slight nod, a tiny gesture that filled her with determination. Jun folded his arms over his chest. Jiang picked at his finger-nails.

Rin had not fought any of her classmates since her expulsion from Combat. She had not even watched them fight. The only person she had ever sparred against was Jiang, and she had no clue if he was a good approximation of how her classmates might fight.

She was entering this Tournament blind.

She squared her shoulders and took a deep breath, willing herself to at least appear calm.

Han, on the other hand, looked very disconcerted. His eyes darted across her body and then back up to her face as if she were some wild animal he had never seen before, as if he didn't know quite what to make of her.

He's scared, she realized.

He must have heard the rumors that she had studied with Jiang. He didn't know what to believe about her. Didn't know what to expect.

What was more, Rin was the underdog in this match. No one expected her to fight well. But Han had trained with Jun all year. Han was a Sinegardian. Han *had* to win, or he wouldn't be able to face his peers after.

Sunzi wrote that one must always identify and exploit the enemy's weaknesses. Han's weakness was psychological. The stakes were much, much higher for him, and that made him insecure. That made him beatable.

"What, you've never seen a girl before?" Rin asked.

Han blushed furiously.

Good. She made him nervous. She grinned widely, baring teeth. "Lucky you," she said. "You get to be my first."

"You don't have a chance," Han blustered. "You don't know any martial arts."

She merely smiled and slouched back into Seejin's fourth opening stance. She bent her back leg, preparing herself to spring, and raised her fists to guard her face.

"Don't I?"

Han's face clouded with doubt. He had recognized her posture as deliberate and practiced—not at all the stance of someone who had no martial arts training.

Rin rushed him as soon as Sonnen signaled them to begin.

Han played defensive from the start. He made the mistake of giving her the forward momentum, and he never recovered. From the outset, Rin controlled every part of the bout. She attacked, he reacted. She led him in the dance, she decided when to let him parry, and she decided where they would go. She fought methodically, purely from muscle memory. She was efficient. She played his moves against him and confused him.

And Han's attacks fell into such predictable patterns—if one of his kicks missed, he would back up and attempt it again, and again, until she forced him to change direction.

Finally he let his guard down, let her get in close. She jammed her elbow hard into his nose. She felt a satisfying crack. Han dropped to the floor like a puppet whose strings had been cut.

Rin knew she hadn't hurt him that badly. Jiang had punched her in the nose at least twice. Han was more stunned than injured. He could have gotten up. He didn't.

"Break," ordered Sonnen.

Rin wiped the sweat off her forehead and glanced up at the railing.

There was silence above the ring. Her classmates looked like they had on the first day of class—startled and bewildered. Nezha looked dumbfounded.

Then Kitay began to clap. He was the only one.

She fought two more matches that day. They were both variations on her match with Han—pattern recognition, confusion, finishing blow. She won both of them.

Over the span of a day Rin went from the underdog to a leading contender. All those months spent lugging that stupid pig around had given her better endurance than her classmates. Those long, frustrating hours with the Seejin forms had given her impeccable footwork.

The rest of the class had learned their fundamentals from Jun. They moved the same way, sank into the same default patterns when nervous. But Rin didn't. Her best advantage was her unpredictability. She fought like nothing they had been expecting, she threw them off rhythm, and so she continued to win.

At the end of the first day, Rin and six others, including Nezha and Venka, advanced undefeated into elimination rounds. Kitay had ended the first day with a 2–1 record but advanced on good technique.

The quarterfinals were scheduled for the second day. Sonnen drew up a randomized bracket and hung it on a scroll outside the main hall for all to see. The pairings placed Rin against Venka first thing in the morning.

Venka had trained in martial arts for years, and it showed. She was all rapid strikes and slick, impeccable footwork. She fought with a savage viciousness. Her technique was precise to the centimeter, her timing perfect. She was just as fast as Rin, perhaps faster.

The one advantage Rin had was that Venka had never fought with an injury.

"She's sparred plenty of times," said Kitay. "But nobody is actually willing to hit her. Everyone's always stopped before the punch lands. Even Nezha. I'll bet you none of her home tutors were willing to hit her, either. They would have been fired immediately, if not thrown in jail."

"You're kidding," Rin said.

"I know *I've* never hit her."

Rin rubbed a fist into her palm. "Maybe it'll be good for her, then."

Still, injuring Venka was no easy task. More by sheer luck than anything, Rin managed to land a blow early on in the match. Venka, underestimating Rin's speed, had brought her guard back up too slowly after an attempted left hook. Rin took the opening and whipped a backhand through at Venka's nose.

Bone broke under Rin's fist with an audible crack.

Venka immediately retreated. One hand flew to her face, groping around her swelling nose. She glanced down at her blood-covered fingers and then back up at Rin. Her nostrils flared. Her cheeks turned a ghastly white.

"Problem?" Rin asked.

The look Venka gave her was pure murder.

"You shouldn't even be here," she snarled.

"Tell that to your nose," Rin said.

Venka was visibly unhinged. Her pretty sneer was gone, her hair messy, her face bloodied, her eyes wild and unfocused. She was on edge, off rhythm. She attempted several more wild blows until Rin caught her with a solid roundhouse kick to the side of her head.

Venka sprawled to the side and stayed on the ground. Her chest heaved rapidly up and down. Rin couldn't tell if she was crying or panting.

She didn't really care.

The applause as Rin emerged from the ring was scattered at best. The audience had been rooting for Venka. Venka was supposed to be in the finals.

Rin didn't care about that, either. She was used to this by now.

And Venka wasn't the victory she wanted.

Nezha tore his way through the other side of the bracket with ruthless efficiency. His fights were always scheduled in the other ring concurrently with Rin's, and they invariably ended earlier. Rin never saw Nezha in action. She only saw his opponents carried out on stretchers.

Alone among Nezha's opponents, Kitay emerged from his bout unharmed. He had lasted a minute and a half before surrendering.

There were rumors Nezha would be disqualified for intentional maiming, but Rin knew better than to hope. The faculty wanted to see the heir to the House of Yin in the finals. As far as Rin knew, Nezha could kill someone without repercussion. Jun, certainly, would allow it.

No one was surprised when Rin and Nezha both won their semifinals rounds. Finals were postponed until after dinner so that the apprentices could also come and watch.

Nezha disappeared somewhere halfway through dinner. He was likely getting private coaching from Jun. Rin briefly considered reporting it to get Nezha disqualified, but knew that would be a hollow victory. She wanted to see this through to the finish.

She picked at her food. She knew she needed energy, but the thought of eating made her want to vomit.

Halfway through the break, Raban approached her table. He was sweating hard, as if he had just run all the way up from the lower tier.

She thought he was going to congratulate her on making it to finals, but all he said was "You should surrender."

"You're joking," Rin responded. "I'm going to win this thing."

"Look, Rin—you haven't seen any of Nezha's fights."

"I've been a little preoccupied with my own."

"Then you don't know what he's capable of. I just dealt with his semifinals opponent in the infirmary. Nohai." Raban looked deeply rattled. "They're not sure if he's going to be able to walk again. Nezha shattered his kneecap."

"Seems like Nohai's problem." Rin didn't want to hear about Nezha's victories. She was feeling queasy enough as it was. The only way she could go through with the finals was if she convinced herself that Nezha was beatable.

"I know he hates you," Raban continued. "He could cripple you for life."

"He's just a kid." Rin scoffed with a confidence she didn't feel.

"*You're* just a kid!" Raban sounded agitated. "I don't care how good you think you are. Nezha's got six inches and twenty pounds of muscle on you, and I swear he wants to kill you."

"He has weaknesses," she said stubbornly. That had to be true. Didn't it?

"Does it matter? What does this Tournament mean to you anyway?" Raban asked. "There's no way you're getting culled now. Every master is going to submit a bid for you. Why do you have to win?"

Raban was right. At this point Irjah would have no qualms about bidding for her. Rin's position at Sinegard was safe.

But it wasn't about bids now, it was about pride. It was about power. If she surrendered to Nezha, he would hold it over her for the rest of their time at the Academy. No—he'd hold it over her for life.

"Because I can," she said. "Because he thought he could get rid of me. Because I want to break his stupid face."

The basement hall was silent as Rin and Nezha climbed into the ring. The air was thick with anticipation, a voyeuristic bloodlust. Months of hateful rivalry were coming to a head, and everyone wanted to watch the fallout of their collision.

Both Jun and Irjah wore deliberately neutral expressions, giving nothing away. Jiang was absent.

Nezha and Rin bowed shortly, never taking their eyes off each other, and both immediately backed away.

Nezha kept his gaze trained intently on Rin's, almond eyes narrowed in a tight focus. His lips were pressed in concentration. There were no jeers, no taunts. Not even a snarl.

Nezha was taking her seriously, Rin realized. He took her as an equal.

For some reason, this made her fiercely proud. They stared at each other, daring each other to break eye contact first.

"Begin," said Sonnen.

She leaped at him immediately. Her right leg lashed out again and again, forcing him back in retreat.

Kitay had spent all of lunch helping her strategize. She knew Nezha could be blindingly fast. Once he got momentum, he wouldn't stop until his opponent was incapacitated or dead.

Rin needed to overwhelm him from the beginning. She needed to constantly put him on the defensive, because to be on the defensive against Nezha was certain defeat.

The problem was that he was terribly strong. He didn't possess the brute force of Kobin, or even Kureel, but he was so precise in his movements that it didn't matter. He channeled his *ki* with a brilliant precision, built it up and then released it through the smallest pressure point to create the maximum impact.

Unlike Venka, Nezha could absorb losses and continue. She bruised him once or twice. He adapted and hit her back. And his blows *hurt*.

They were two minutes in. Rin had now lasted longer than any of Nezha's previous opponents, and something had become clear to her: He *wasn't* invincible. The techniques that had seemed impossibly difficult to her before now were transparently beatable. When Nezha kicked, his movements were wide and obvious like a boar's. His kicks held terrifying power, but only if they landed.

Rin made sure they never landed.

There was no way she would let him maim her. But she was not here merely to survive. She was here to win.

Exploding Dragon. Crouching Tiger. Extended Crane. She cycled through the movements in Seejin's Frolics as they were needed. The movements she'd practiced so many times before, linked together one after another in that damned form, snapped automatically into play.

But if Nezha was baffled by Rin's fighting style, he didn't show it. He remained calm and concentrated, attacking with methodical efficiency.

They were now four minutes in. Rin felt her lungs seizing, trying to pump oxygen into her fatigued body. But she knew that if she was tired, so was Nezha.

"He gets desperate when he's tired," Kitay had said. "And he's the most dangerous when he's desperate."

Nezha was getting desperate.

There was no control to his *ki* anymore. He threw punch after punch in her direction. He didn't care about the maiming rule. If he got her on the ground, he would kill her.

Nezha swept a low kick at the back of her knees. Rin made a frantic call and let him connect, sinking backward, pretending she'd lost her balance. He moved in immediately, looming over her. She grounded herself against the floor and kicked up.

She nailed him directly in his solar plexus with more force than she'd ever kicked with before—she could *feel* the air forced out of his lungs. She flipped up off the ground, and was astonished to find Nezha still reeling backward, gasping for air.

She flung herself forward and punched wildly at his head.

He dropped to the floor.

Shocked murmurs swept through the audience.

Rin circled Nezha, hoping he wouldn't get up, but knowing he would. She wanted to end it. Slam her heel into the back of his head. But the masters cared about honor. If she hit Nezha while he was down, she'd be sent packing from Sinegard in minutes.

Never mind that if he did the same, she doubted anyone would bat an eye.

Four seconds passed. Nezha raised a shaking hand and slammed it into the ground. He dragged himself forward. His forehead was bleeding, dripping scarlet into his eyes. He blinked it away and glared up at her.

His eyes screamed murder.

"Continue," said Sonnen.

Rin circled Nezha warily. He crouched like an animal, like a wounded wolf rising on its haunches.

The next time she threw a punch he grabbed her arm and pulled her in close. Her breath hitched. He raked his nails across her face and down to her collarbone.

She jerked her arm out of his grasp and cycled backward in rapid retreat. She felt a sharp sting under her left eye, across her neck. Nezha had drawn blood.

"Watch yourself, Yin," Sonnen warned.

Both of them ignored him. *Like a warning would make any difference*, Rin thought. The next time Nezha lunged at her she pulled him to the floor with her. They rolled around in the dirt, each attempting to pin the other and failing.

He punched madly in the air, flinging blows haphazardly at her face.

She dodged the first one. He swung his fist back in reverse and caught her with a backhand that left her gasping. The lower half of her face went numb.

He'd slapped her.

He'd *slapped* her.

A kick she could take. A knife hand strike she could absorb. But that slap had a savage intimacy. An undertone of superiority.

Something in Rin broke.

She couldn't breathe. Black tinged the edges of her vision— black, and then scarlet. An awful rage filled her, consumed her thoughts entirely. She needed revenge like she needed to breathe. She wanted Nezha to *hurt*. She wanted Nezha *punished*.

She lashed back, fingers curled into claws. He let go of her to jump back, but she followed him, redoubling her frenzied attacks. She wasn't as fast as he was. He retaliated, and she was too slow to block, and he hit her on the thigh, on the arm, but her body wouldn't register the damage. Pain was a message she was ignoring, to be felt later.

No—pain led to success.

He struck her face one, twice, thrice. He beat her like an animal and yet she kept fighting.

"What is *wrong* with you?" he hissed.

More important was what was wrong with *him*. Fear. She could see it in his eyes.

He had her backed against the wall, hands around her neck, but she grabbed his shoulders, jammed her knee up into his rib cage, and rammed an elbow into the back of his head. He collapsed forward to the ground, wheezing. She flung herself down and ground her elbow into his lower back. Nezha cried out, arched his back in agony.

Rin pinned Nezha's left arm to the floor with her foot and held his neck down with her right elbow. When he struggled, she slammed her fist into the back of his head and ground his face against the dirt until it was clear that he wouldn't get up.

"Break," said Sonnen, but she barely heard him. Blood thundered in her ears to a rhythm like war drums. Her vision was filtered through a red lens that registered only enemy targets.

She grasped a handful of Nezha's hair in her hand and yanked his head up again to slam into the floor.

"Break!"

Sonnen's arms were around her neck, restraining her, dragging her off Nezha's limp form.

She staggered away from Sonnen. Her body was burning up, feverish. She reeled, suddenly dizzy. She felt full to bursting with heat; she had to dispel it, force it out somewhere or she'd surely die, but the only place to put it was in the bodies of everyone else around her—

Something deep inside her rational mind screamed.

Raban reached for her as she climbed up out of the ring. "Rin, what—"

She shoved his hand away.

"Move," she panted. "Move."

But the masters crowded around her, a hubbub of voices— hands reaching, mouths moving. Their presence was suffocating. She felt if she screamed she could disintegrate them entirely, *wanted* to disintegrate them—but the very small part of her that was still rational reined it in, sent her reeling for the exit instead.

Miraculously they cleared a path for her. She pushed her way through the crowd of apprentices and ran to the stairwell. She barreled up the stairs, burst out the door of the main hall into the cold open air, and sucked in a great breath.

It wasn't enough. She was still burning.

Ignoring the shouts of the masters behind her, she set off at a run.

Jiang was in the first place she looked, the Lore garden. He was sitting cross-legged, eyes closed, still as the stone he sat upon.

She lurched through the garden gates, gripping at the doorpost. The world swirled sideways. Everything looked red: the trees, the stones, Jiang most of all. He flared in front of her like a torch.

He opened his eyes to the sound of her crashing through the gate. "Rin?"

She had forgotten how to speak. The flames within her licked out toward Jiang, sensed his presence like a fire sensed kindling and *yearned* to consume him.

She became convinced that if she didn't kill him, she might explode.

She moved to attack him. He scrambled to his feet, dodged her outstretched hands, and then upended her with a deft throw. She landed on her back. He pinned her to the ground with his arms.

"You're burning," he said in amazement.

"Help me," she gasped. "*Help.*"

He leaned forward and cupped her head in his hands.

"Look at me."

She obeyed with great difficulty. His face swam before her.

"Great Tortoise," he murmured, and let go of her.

His eyes rolled up in the back of his head and he began uttering indecipherable noises, syllables that didn't resemble any language she knew.

He opened his eyes and pressed the palm of his hand to her forehead.

His hand felt like ice. The searing cold flooded from his palm to her forehead and into the rest of her body, through the same rivulets the flame was coursing through; arresting the fire, stilling it in her veins. She felt as if she'd been doused in a freezing bath.

She writhed on the floor, breathing in shock, trembling as the fire left her blood.

Then everything was still.

Jiang's face was the first thing she saw when she regained consciousness. His clothes looked rumpled. There were deep circles under his eyes, as if he hadn't slept in days. How long had she been asleep? Had he been here the entire time?

She raised her head. She was lying in a bunk in the infirmary, but she wasn't injured, as far as she could tell.

"How do you feel?" Jiang asked quietly.

"Bruised, but okay." She sat up slowly and winced. Her mouth felt like it was filled with cotton. She coughed and rubbed at her throat, frowning. "What happened?"

Jiang offered her a cup of water that had been sitting beside her bunk. She took it gratefully. The water sluiced down her dry throat with the most wonderful sensation.

"Congratulations," Jiang said. "You're this year's champion."

His tone did not sound congratulatory at all.

Rin felt none of the exhilaration that she should have, anyway. She couldn't even relish her victory over Nezha. She didn't feel the least bit proud, just scared and confused.

"What did I do?" she whispered.

"You have stumbled upon something that you're not ready for," said Jiang. He sounded agitated. "I never should have taught you the Five Frolics. From this point forward you're just going to be a danger to yourself and everyone around you."

"Not if you help me," she said. "Not if you teach me otherwise."

"I thought you just wanted to be a good soldier."

"I do," she said.

But more than that, she wanted power.

She had no idea what had happened in the ring; she would be foolish not to feel terrified by it, and yet she had never felt power like it. In that instant, she had felt as if she could defeat anyone. Kill anything.

She wanted that power again. She wanted what Jiang could teach her.

"I was ungrateful that day in the garden," she said, choosing her words carefully. If she spoke too obsequiously then it would scare Jiang off. But if she didn't apologize, then Jiang might think that she hadn't learned anything since they'd last spoken. "I wasn't thinking. I apologize."

She watched his eyes apprehensively, looking for that telltale distant expression that indicated that she had lost him.

Jiang's features did not soften, but neither did he get up to leave. "No. It was my fault. I didn't realize how much like Altan you are."

Rin jerked her head up at the mention of Altan.

"He won in his year, you know," Jiang said flatly. "He fought Tobi in the finals. It was a grudge match, just like your match with Nezha. Altan *hated* Tobi. Tobi made some jabs about Speer their first week of school, and Altan never forgave him. But he wasn't like you; he didn't squabble with Tobi throughout the year like a pecking hen. Altan swallowed his anger and concealed it under a mask of indifference until, at the very end, in front of an audience that included six Warlords and the Empress herself, he unleashed a power so potent that it took Sonnen, Jun, and myself to restrain him. By the time the smoke cleared, Tobi was so badly injured that Enro didn't sleep for five days while she watched over him."

"I'm not like that," she said. She hadn't beaten Nezha that badly. Had she? It was hard to remember through that fog of anger. "I'm not—I'm not like Altan."

"You are precisely the same." Jiang shook his head. "You're too reckless. You hold grudges, you cultivate your rage and let it explode, and you're careless about what you're taught. Training you would be a mistake."

Rin's gut plummeted. She was suddenly afraid that she might go mad; she had been given a tantalizing taste of incredible power, but was this the end of the road?

"So that's why you withdrew your bid for Altan?" she asked. "Why you refused to teach him?"

Jiang looked puzzled.

"I didn't withdraw my bid," he said. "I *insisted* they put him under my watch. Altan was a Speerly, already predisposed to rage and disaster. I knew I was the only one who could help him."

"But the apprentices said—"

"The apprentices don't know shit," Jiang snapped. "I asked Jima to let me train him. But the Empress intervened. She knew the military value of a Speerly warrior, she was so *excited* . . . in the end, national interests superseded the sanity of one boy. They put him under Irjah's tutelage, and honed his rage like a weapon, instead of teaching him to control it. You've seen him in the ring. You know what he's like."

Jiang leaned forward. "But *you*. The Empress doesn't know about you." He muttered to himself more than he spoke to her. "You're not safe, but you will be . . . They won't intervene, not this time . . ."

She watched Jiang's face, not daring to hope. "So does that mean—"

He stood up. "I will take you on as an apprentice. I hope I will not come to regret it."

He extended a hand toward her. She reached up and grasped it.

Of the original fifty students who matriculated at Sinegard at the start of the term, thirty-five received bids for apprenticeship. The masters sent their scrolls to the office in the main hall to be picked up by the students.

Those students who received no scrolls were asked to hand in their uniforms and make arrangements to leave the Academy immediately.

Most students received one scroll only. Niang, to her delight, joined two other students in the Medicine track. Nezha and Venka pledged Combat.

Kitay, convinced he'd lost his bids the moment he surrendered to Nezha, tugged at his hair so frantically the entire way to the front office that Rin was half-afraid he'd go bald.

"It was a stupid thing," Kitay said. "Cowardly. No one's surrendered uninjured in the last two decades. Nobody's going to want to sponsor me now."

Up until the Tournament he'd been expecting bids from Jima, Jun, and Irjah. But only one scroll was waiting for him at the registrar.

Kitay unfurled it. His face split into a grin. "Irjah thinks surrendering was brilliant. I'm pledging Strategy!"

The registrar handed two scrolls to Rin. Without opening them, she knew they were from Irjah and Jiang. She could choose between Strategy and Lore.

She pledged Lore.

CHAPTER 8

Sinegard Academy gave students four days off from studies to celebrate the Summer Festival. The next term would begin as soon as they returned.

Most students took this as a chance to visit their families. But Rin didn't have time to travel all the way back to Tikany, nor did she want to. She had planned on spending the break at the Academy, until Kitay invited her to stay at his estate.

"Unless you don't want to," Kitay said nervously. "I mean, if you already have plans—"

"I have no plans," Rin said. "I'd love to."

She packed for her excursion into the city the next morning. This took mere seconds—she had very few personal belongings. She carefully folded two sets of school tunics into her old travel satchel, and hoped Kitay would not find it rude if she wore her uniform during the festival. She had no other clothing; she'd gotten rid of her old southerner's tunics the first chance she got.

"I'll get a rickshaw," Rin offered as she met Kitay at the school gates.

Kitay looked puzzled. "Why do we need a rickshaw?"

Rin frowned. "Then how are we getting there?"

Kitay opened his mouth to reply just as a massive horse-drawn carriage pulled up by the gates. The driver, a portly man in robes of rich gold and burgundy, hopped off the coachman's seat and bowed deeply in Kitay's direction. "Master Chen."

He blinked at Rin, as if trying to decide whether to bow to her as well, and then managed a perfunctory head dip.

"Thanks, Merchi." Kitay handed their bags to the servant and helped Rin into the carriage.

"Comfortable?"

"Very."

From their vantage point in the carriage, they could see almost all the city nested in the valley below: the spiraling pagodas of the administrative district rising through a faint blanket of mist, white houses built into the valley slopes with curved tiled roofs, and the winding stone walls of the alleyways leading downtown.

From the shaded interior of the carriage, Rin felt insulated from the dirty city streets. She felt clean. For the first time since she had arrived in Sinegard, she felt as if she belonged here. She leaned against the side and enjoyed the warm summer breeze against her face. She had not rested like this in a long time.

"We will discuss what happened to you in detail when you return," Jiang had told her. "But your mind has just suffered a very particular trauma. The best thing you can do for yourself now is rest. Let the experience germinate. Let your mind heal."

Kitay, tactfully, did not ask her what had happened. Rin was grateful for it.

Merchi drove them at a brisk pace down the mountain pass. They continued on the main city road for an hour and then turned left onto the isolated road that led into the Jade District.

When Rin had arrived in Sinegard a year ago, she and Tutor Feyrik had traveled through the working-class district, where the inns were cheap and gambling houses stood around every corner. Her daily trips to see the Widow Maung had led her through the loudest, dirtiest, and smelliest parts of the city. What she'd seen of Sinegard so far was no different from Tikany—it was just noisier and more cramped.

Now, riding in the Chen family's carriage, she saw how splendid Sinegard could be. The roads of the Jade District were freshly paved, and glistened like they had been scrubbed clean that very morning. Rin saw no wooden shacks, no evident dumping grounds for chamber pots. She saw no grumpy housewives steaming breads and dumplings on outdoor grills, too poor to afford indoor stoves. She saw no beggars.

She found the stillness unsettling. Tikany was always bustling with activity—drifters collecting trash to repackage and sell; old men sitting on stoops outside, smoking or playing mahjong; little children wearing jumpers that exposed their butt cheeks, wandering around the streets followed by squatting grandparents ready to catch them when they toppled over.

She saw none of that here. The Jade District was composed of pristine barriers and walled-off gardens. Aside from their carriage, the roads were empty.

Merchi stopped the carriage before the gates of a massive compound. They swung ponderously open, revealing four long rectangular buildings arranged in a square, enclosing an enormous garden pavilion. Several dogs rushed them at the entrance, tiny white things whose paws were as immaculately clean as the tiled path they walked on.

Kitay gave a shout, climbed out of the carriage, and knelt down. His dogs leaped on him, tails wagging with delirious delight.

"This one's the Dragon Emperor." He tickled a dog under its chin. "They're all named after the great rulers."

"Which one's the Red Emperor?" Rin asked.

"The one that's going to pee on your foot if you don't move."

The estate's housekeeper was a short, plump woman with freckled, leathery skin named Lan. She spoke with a friendly, girlish voice that was at odds with her wrinkled face. Her Sinegardian accent was so strong that even after several months' practice with the heavily accented Widow Maung, Rin still could only barely decipher it.

"What do you want to eat? I'll cook you anything you want. I know the culinary styles of all twelve provinces. Except the Monkey Province. Too spicy. It's not good for you. I also don't do stinky tofu. My only constraint is what's on the market, but I can get just about anything at the import store. Any favorite recipes? Lobster? Or water chestnuts? You name it, I'll cook it."

Rin, who was accustomed to eating the uninspired slop of the Academy canteen, was at a loss for a response. How was she to explain she simply didn't have the repertoire of meals that Lan demanded? Back in Tikany, the Fangs were fond of a dish named "whatever," which was quite literally made of whatever scraps were left at the shop—usually fried eggs and glass noodles.

"I want Seven Treasure Soup," Kitay intervened, leaving Rin to wonder what on earth that was. "And Lion's Head."

Rin blinked. "What?"

Kitay looked amused. "Oh, you'll see."

"You could act less like a dazed peasant, you know," Kitay said as Lan laid out a spread of quail, quail eggs, shark fin soup served in turtle's shell, and pig's intestines before them. "It's just food."

But "just food" was rice porridge. Maybe some vegetables. A piece of fish, pork, or chicken whenever they could get it.

Nothing on the table was "just" anything.

Seven Treasure Soup turned out to be a deliciously sweet congee-based concoction of red dates, honeyed chestnuts, lotus seeds, and four other ingredients that Rin could not identify. Lion's Head, she discovered with some relief, was not actually a lion's head, but rather a ball of meat mixed with flour and boiled amid strips of white tofu.

"Kitay, I *am* a dazed peasant." Rin tried fruitlessly to pick up a quail egg with her chopsticks. Finally she gave up and used her fingers. "You eat like this? All the time?"

Kitay blushed. "You get used to it. I had a hard time our first week at school. The Academy canteen was *awful*."

It was hard not to feel jealous of Kitay. His private washroom was bigger than the cramped bedroom Rin had shared with Kesegi. His estate's library rivaled the stacks at Sinegard. Everything Kitay owned was replaceable; if he got mud on his shoes, he threw them away. If his shirt ripped, he got a new one—a newly *made* shirt, tailored to his precise height and girth.

Kitay had spent his childhood in luxurious comfort, with nothing better to do than study for the Keju. For him, testing into Sinegard had been a pleasant surprise; a confirmation of something he'd always known was his destiny.

"Where's your father?" Rin asked. Kitay's father was the defense minister to the Empress herself. She was privately relieved she wouldn't have to converse with him yet—the thought itself was terrifying—but she couldn't help feeling curious about the man. Would he be an older version of Kitay—wiry-haired, just as brilliant, and exponentially more powerful?

Kitay made a face. "Defense meetings. You wouldn't know it, but the whole city is on high security alert. The entire City Guard will be on duty all this week. We don't need another Opera incident."

"I thought the Red Junk Opera was dead," said Rin.

"*Mostly* dead. You can't kill a movement. Somewhere out there, some religious lunatics are intent on killing the Empress." Kitay speared a chunk of tofu. "Father's going to be at the palace until the parade is over. He's directly responsible for the Empress's safety. If anything goes wrong, Father's head is on the line."

"Isn't he worried?"

"Not really. He's done this for decades; he'll be all right. Besides, the Empress is a martial artist herself; she's hardly an easy target." Kitay launched into a series of anecdotes his father had told him about serving in the palace, about hilarious encounters with the Empress and the Twelve Warlords, about court gossip and provincial politics.

Rin listened in amazement. What was it like to grow up knowing that your father served at the right hand of the Empress? What a difference an accident of birth made. In another world she might have grown up at an estate like this, with all of her desires within reach. In another world, she might have been born into power.

Rin spent the night in a massive suite she had all to herself. She hadn't slept so long or so well since she came to Sinegard. It was as if her body had shut down after weeks of abuse. She awoke feeling better and clearer-minded than she had in months.

After a lackadaisical breakfast of sweet congee and spiced goose eggs, Kitay and Rin wandered downtown to the market-place.

Rin hadn't set foot downtown since arriving to Sinegard with Tutor Feyrik a year prior. The Widow Maung lived on the other side of the city, and her strict academic schedule had left her with no time to explore Sinegard on her own.

She had thought the market was overwhelming last year. Now, at peak activity during the Summer Festival, it seemed like the city had exploded. Pop-up vendor carts were parked everywhere, crammed into the alleyways so tightly that shoppers had to navigate the market in a cramped, single-file line. But the *sights*. Oh, the sights. Rin saw rows upon rows of pearl necklaces and jade bracelets. Stands of smooth egg-sized rocks that displayed characters, sometimes entire poems, only if you dipped them in water. Stations where calligraphy masters wrote names on giant, lovely fans, wielding their black ink brushes with the care and bravado of swordsmen.

"What do these do?" Rin stopped in front of a rack bearing tiny wooden statues of fat little boys. The boys' tunics were yanked down, exposing their penises. She couldn't believe anything this obscene was on sale.

"Oh, those are my favorite," Kitay said.

By way of explanation, the vendor picked up a teapot and poured water over the statues. The clay darkened as the statues turned wet. Water began spurting out of the penises like sprays of urine.

Rin laughed. "How much are these?"

"Four silvers for one. I'll give you two for seven."

Rin blanched. All she had was a single string of imperial silvers and a handful of copper coins left over from the money Tutor Feyrik had helped her exchange. She had never had to spend money at the Academy, and hadn't considered how expensive things might be in Sinegard when she wasn't living on the Academy's coin.

"Do you want it?" Kitay asked.

Rin waved her hands wildly. "No, I'm good, I can't really . . ."

Understanding dawned on Kitay's face. "My gift." He handed a string of silvers to the merchant. "One urinating statue for my easily entertained friend."

Rin blushed. "Kitay, I can't."

"It costs nothing."

"It costs a lot to me," she said.

Kitay placed the statue in her hand. "If you say one more thing about money, I'm leaving you to get lost."

The market was so massive that Rin was reluctant to stray too far from the entrance; if she became lost in those winding pathways, how would she ever find her way out? But Kitay navigated the market with the ease of a seasoned connoisseur, pointing out which shops he liked and which he didn't.

Kitay's Sinegard was full of wonders, completely accessible, and crammed with things that belonged to him. Kitay's Sinegard wasn't terrifying, because Kitay had money. If he tripped, half the shop owners on the street would help him up, hoping for a handsome tip. If his pocket were cut, he'd go home and get another purse. Kitay could afford to be victimized by the city because he had room to fail.

Rin couldn't. She had to remind herself that, despite Kitay's absurd generosity, none of this was hers. Her only ticket into this city was through the Academy, and she'd have to work hard to keep it.

At night the marketplace lit up with lanterns, one for each vendor. Together the lanterns looked like a horde of fireflies, casting unnatural shadows on everything their light touched.

"Have you ever seen shadow puppetry?" Kitay stopped in front of a large canvas tent. A line of children stood at the entrance doling out copper shells for entrance. "I mean, it's for little kids, but . . ."

"Great Tortoise." Rin's eyes widened. In Tikany, they told *stories* about shadow puppetry. She fished the change out of her pocket. "I got this."

The tent was packed with rows of children. Kitay and Rin filed into the back, trying to pretend they weren't at least five years older than the rest of the audience. At the front, a massive silk screen hung from the top of the tent, illuminated from behind with soft yellow light.

"I tell you now about the rebirth of this nation."

The puppeteer spoke from a box beside the screen, so that even his silhouette was invisible. His voice filled the cramped tent, deep and smooth and resonant. "This is the tale of the salvation and reunion of Nikan. This is the story of the Trifecta, the three warriors of legend."

The light behind the screen dimmed and then flared a bright scarlet hue.

"The Warrior." The first shadow appeared on the screen: the silhouette of a man with a massive sword almost as tall as he was. He was heavily armored, with spiked pads protruding out from his shoulders. The plume on his helmet furled into the air above him.

"The Vipress." The slender form of a woman appeared next to the Warrior. Her head tilted coquettishly to one side; her left arm bent as if she wielded something behind her back. A fan, perhaps. Or a dagger.

"And the Gatekeeper." The Gatekeeper was the thinnest of the three, a stooped figure wrapped in robes. By his side crawled a large tortoise.

The scarlet hue of the screen faded away to a soft yellow that pulsed slowly like a heartbeat. The shadows of the Trifecta grew larger and then disappeared. A silhouette of a mountainous land appeared in their place. And the puppeteer began his story in earnest.

"Sixty-five years ago, in the wake of the First Poppy War, the people of Nikan suffered under the weight of their Federation oppressors. Nikan lay sick, feverish under the clouds of the poppy drug." Translucent ribbons drifted up from the profile of the countryside, giving the illusion of smoke. "The people starved. Mothers sold their infants for a pound of meat, for a bolt of cloth. Fathers killed their children rather than watch them suffer. Yes, that's right. Children just like you!

"The Nikara thought the gods had abandoned them, for how else could the barbarians from the east have wreaked such destruction upon them?"

The screen turned the same sickly yellow pallor as the cheeks of poppy addicts. A line of Nikara peasants knelt with their heads bent to the floor, as if weeping.

"The people found no protection in the Warlords. The rulers of the Twelve Provinces, once powerful, were now weak and disorganized. Preoccupied with ancient grudges, they wasted time and soldiers fighting against each other rather than uniting to drive out the invaders from Mugen. They squandered gold on drink and women. They breathed the poppy drug like air. They taxed their provinces at exorbitant rates, and gave nothing back. Even when the Federation destroyed their villages and raped their women, the Warlords did nothing. They could do nothing.

"The people prayed for heroes. They prayed for twenty years. And finally, the gods sent them."

A silhouette of three children, hand in hand, appeared on the lower left corner of the screen. The child in the center stood taller than the rest. The one on his right had long, flowing hair. The third child, standing a little removed from the other two, had his profile turned away toward the end of the screen, as if he was looking at something the other two could not see.

"The gods did not send these heroes from the skies. Rather they chose three children—war orphans, peasants whose parents had been killed in village raids. They were born of the humblest origins. But they were meant to walk with the gods."

The child in the center strode purposefully to the middle of the screen. The other two followed him at a distance, like he was their leader. The limbs of the shadows moved so smoothly there might have been little men in costume behind the screen, not puppets made of paper and string. Rin marveled at the technique involved, even as she was further absorbed into the story.

"When their village burned, the three children formed a pact to seek revenge against the Federation and liberate their country from the invaders, so that no more children would suffer as they had.

"They trained for many years with the monks of the Wudang temple. By the time they matured, their martial arts skills were prodigious, and they rivaled in skill fully grown men who had been training for decades. At the end of their apprenticeship, they journeyed to the top of the highest peak in all of the land: Mount Tianshan."

A massive mountain came into view. It took up almost the entire screen; the shadows of the three heroes were minuscule beside it. But as they walked toward the mountain, the peak grew smaller and smaller, flatter and flatter, until the heroes stood on flat ground at the very top.

"There are seven thousand steps that lead up to the peak of Mount Tianshan. And at the very top, far up so high that the strongest eagle could not circle the peak, lies a temple. From that temple, the three heroes walked into the heavens and entered the Pantheon, the home of the gods."

The three heroes now approached a gate similar to those that guarded the entrance to the Academy. The doors were twice the heroes' height, decorated with intricately curling patterns of butterflies and tigers, and guarded by a great tortoise that bowed its head low as it let them pass.

"The first hero, strongest among his companions, was summoned by the Dragon Lord. The hero stood a head taller than his friends. His back was broad, his arms like tree trunks. He had been deemed by the gods to be the leader of the three.

"'If I am to command the armies of Nikan, I must have a great blade,' he said, and knelt at the feet of the Dragon Lord. The Dragon Lord bade him stand, and bestowed upon him a massive sword. Thus he became the Warrior."

The Warrior's figure swung the huge sword in a great arc above his head and brought it smashing downward. Sparks of red and gold light emitted from the ground where the sword struck.

"The second hero was a girl among the two men. She walked past the Dragon Lord, the Tiger Lord, and the Lion Lord, for they were gods of war and therefore gods of men. She said: 'I am a woman, and women need different weapons than men. The woman's place is not in the thick of battle. The woman's battle-field is in deception and seduction.' And she knelt before the plinth of the Snail Goddess Nüwa. The Goddess Nüwa was pleased by her words, and made the second hero as deadly as a serpent, as bewitching as the most hypnotic of snakes. Thus was born the Vipress."

A great serpent slithered out from under the Vipress's dress and undulated about her body, coiling upward to rest on her shoulders. The audience applauded the graceful trick of puppetry.

"The third hero was the humblest among his peers. Weak and sickly, he had never been able to train to the extent of his two friends. But he was loyal and unswerving in his devotion to the gods. He did not beg a favor from any deity in the Pantheon, for he knew he was not worthy. Instead he knelt before the humble tortoise who had let them in.

"'I ask only for the strength to protect my friends and the courage to protect my country,' he said. The tortoise replied, 'You will be given this and more. Take the chain of keys from around my neck. From this day forth you are the Gatekeeper. You have the means to unlock the menagerie of the gods, inside which are kept beasts of every kind, both creatures of beauty and monsters vanquished by heroes long past. You will command them as you see fit.'"

The Gatekeeper's shadow raised his robed hands slowly, and from his back unfurled many shadows of different shapes and sizes. Dragons. Demons. Beasts. They enveloped the Gatekeeper like a shroud of darkness.

"When they came back down the mountain, the monks who had once trained them realized the three had surpassed in skill even the oldest master at the temple. Word spread, and martial artists across the land bowed down to the prodigious skill of the three heroes. The Trifecta's reputation grew. Now that their names were known in all of the Twelve Provinces, the Trifecta sent out word to each of the Warlords to invite them to a great banquet at the base of Mount Tianshan."

Twelve figures, each representing a different province, appeared on the screen. Each wore a helmet with a plume shaped like the province he hailed from: Rooster, Ox, Hare, Monkey, and on and on.

"The Warlords, who were full of pride, were each furious that the other eleven had been invited. Each had thought that he alone had been summoned by the Trifecta. Plotting was what the Warlords did best, and immediately they set about planning to get revenge on the Trifecta."

The screen beamed an eerie, misty purple. The shadows of the Warlords dipped their heads toward one another over their bowls as if conducting nefarious negotiations.

"But halfway through their meal, they found they could not move. The Vipress had poisoned their drinks with a numbing agent, and the Warlords had drunk many bowls of the sorghum wine. As they lay incapacitated in their seats, the Warrior stood on the table before them. He announced: 'Today I declare myself the Emperor of Nikan. If you oppose me, I will cut you down and your lands will become mine. But if you pledge to serve me as an ally, to fight as a general under my banner, I will reward you with status and power. Never again will you fight to defend your borders from another Warlord. Never again will you struggle for domination. All will be equal under me, and I will be the greatest leader this kingdom has seen since the Red Emperor.'"

The shadow of the Warrior raised his sword to the sky. Lightning erupted from the sword point, a symbol of a blessing from the heavens themselves.

"When the Warlords regained control of their limbs, each and every one of them agreed to serve the new Dragon Emperor. And so Nikan was united without the shedding of a single drop of blood. For the first time in centuries, the Warlords fought under the same banner, rallying to the Trifecta. And for the first time in recent history, Nikan presented a united front against the Federation invaders. At long last, we drove out the oppressors. And the Empire, again, became free."

The mountainous silhouette of the country returned again, only this time the land was filled with spiraling pagodas, with temples and many villages. It was a country freed from invaders. It was a country blessed by the gods.

"Today we celebrate the unity of the Twelve Provinces," said the puppeteer. "We celebrate the Trifecta. And we pay homage to the gods who have gifted them."

The children burst into applause.

Kitay was frowning when they exited the tent. "I never realized how horrible that story was," he said quietly. "When you're little, you think the Trifecta were being so clever, but really this is just a story of poison and coercion. Nikara politics as usual."

"I don't know anything about Nikara politics," said Rin.

"I do." Kitay made a face. "Father's told me everything that happens at the palace. It's just the same as the puppeteer said. The Warlords are always at each other's throats, vying for the Empress's attention. It's pathetic."

"What do you mean?"

Kitay looked anxious. "You know how the Warlords were so busy fighting each other that they let Mugen wreck the country during the Poppy Wars? Father's convinced that's happening again. Remember what Yim said the first day of class? He was right. Mugen isn't just sitting quietly on that island. My father thinks it's only a matter of time before they attack again, and he's worried the Warlords aren't taking the threat seriously enough."

The Empire's fragmentation seemed to be a concern of every master at the Academy. Although the Militia was technically under the Empress's control, its twelve divisions drew soldiers largely from their home provinces and lay under the direct command of the provincial Warlords. And provincial relations had never been good—Rin had not realized how deep-seated northern contempt for the south was until she arrived in Sinegard.

But Rin didn't want to talk about politics. This break was the first time in a long time that she was able to let herself relax, and she didn't want to dwell on matters like some impending war that she could do nothing to stop. She was still dazed by the visual spectacle of the shadow puppetry, and she wished Kitay would leave the serious matters be.

"I liked the part about the Pantheon," she said after a while.

"Of course you did. It's the only part that's pure fiction."

"Is it, though?" Rin asked. "Who's to say the Trifecta weren't shamans?"

"The Trifecta were martial artists. Politicians. Immensely talented soldiers, sure, but the part about shamanism is just exaggeration," said Kitay. "The Nikara love embellishing war stories, you know that."

"But where did the stories come from?" Rin persisted. "The Trifecta's powers are terribly specific for a kid's tale. If their powers were only myth, then how come that myth is always the same? We heard about the Trifecta all the way in Tikany. Across the provinces, the story has never changed. They're always the Gatekeeper, the Warrior, and the Vipress."

Kitay shrugged. "Some poet got creative, and those characters caught on. It's not that hard to believe. More credible than the existence of shamans, anyhow."

"But there have been shamans before," said Rin. "Back before the Red Emperor conquered Nikan."

"There's no conclusive proof. There are just anecdotes."

"The Red Emperor's scribes kept track of foreign imports down to the last banana cluster," Rin objected. "They were hardly likely to exaggerate about their enemies."

Kitay looked skeptical. "Sure, but none of that means the Trifecta were actually shamans. The Dragon Emperor's dead, and no one's seen or heard of the Gatekeeper since the Second Poppy War."

"Maybe he's just in hiding. Maybe he's still out there, waiting for the next invasion. Or—maybe—what if the Cike are shamans?" The idea had just occurred to Rin. "That's why we don't know anything about them. Maybe they're the only shamans left—"

"The Cike are just killers," Kitay scoffed. "They stab, kill, and poison. They don't call down gods."

"As far as you know," Rin said.

"You're really hung up on this idea of shamans, aren't you?" Kitay asked. "It's just a kid's story, Rin."

"The Red Emperor's scribes wouldn't have kept extensive documentation of a kid's story."

Kitay sighed. "Is that why you pledged Lore? You think you can become a shaman? You think you can summon gods?"

"I don't believe in gods," said Rin. "But I believe in power. And I believe the shamans had some source of power that the rest of us don't know how to access, and I believe it's still possible to learn."

Kitay shook his head. "I'll tell you what shamans are. At some point in time some martial artists were really powerful, and the more battles they won, the more stories spread. They probably encouraged those stories, too, thinking it'd scare their enemies. I wouldn't be surprised if the Empress made up those stories about the Trifecta being shamans herself. It'd certainly help her hold on power. She needs it now, more than ever. The Warlords are getting restless—I bet we're barely years from a coup. But if she's really the Vipress, then how come she hasn't just summoned giant snakes to subdue the Warlords to her will?"

Rin couldn't think of a glaring counterargument to this theory, so she conceded with silence. Debating with Kitay became pointless after a while. He was so convinced of his own rationality, of his encyclopedic knowledge of most things, that he had difficulty conceiving of gaps in his understanding.

"I notice the puppeteer glossed over how we actually *won* the Second Poppy War," Rin said after a while. "You know. Speer. Butchery. Thousands dead in a single night."

"Well, it was a kid's story after all," said Kitay. "And genocide is a little depressing."

Rin and Kitay spent the next two days lazing around, indulging in every act of sloth they hadn't been able to at the Academy. They played chess. They lounged in the garden, stared idly at the clouds, and gossiped about their classmates.

"Niang's pretty cute," Kitay said. "So is Venka."

"Venka's been obsessed with Nezha since we got there," Rin said. "Even I could see that."

Kitay waggled his eyebrows. "One might say *you've* been obsessed with Nezha."

"Don't be disgusting."

"You *are*. You're always asking me about him."

"Because I'm curious," Rin said. "Sunzi says to know your enemy."

"Fuck Sunzi. You just think he's pretty."

Rin tossed the chessboard at his head.

At Kitay's insistence, Lan cooked them spicy peppercorn hot pot, and delicious though it was, Rin had the singular experience of weeping while eating. She spent most of the next day squatting over the toilet with a burning rectum.

"You think this is how the Speerlies felt?" Kitay asked. "What if burning diarrhea is the price of lifelong devotion to the Phoenix?"

"The Phoenix is a vengeful god," Rin groaned.

They sampled all the wines in Kitay's father's liquor closet and got wonderfully, dizzyingly drunk.

"Nezha and I spent most of our childhood raiding this closet. Try this one." Kitay passed her a small ceramic bottle. "White sorghum wine. Fifty percent alcohol."

Rin swallowed hard. It slid down her throat with a marvelous burn.

"This is liquid fire," she said. "This is the sun in a bottle. This is the drink of a Speerly."

Kitay snickered.

"You wanna know how they brew this?" he asked. "The secret ingredient is urine."

She spat the wine out.

Kitay laughed. "They just use alkaline powder now. But the tale goes that a disgruntled official pissed all over one of the Red Emperor's distilleries. Probably the best accidental discovery of the Red Emperor's era."

Rin rolled over onto her stomach to look sideways at him. "Why aren't you at Yuelu Mountain? You should be a scholar. A sage. You know so much about everything."

Kitay could expound for hours on any given subject, and yet showed little interest in their studies. He had breezed through the Trials because his eidetic memory made studying unnecessary, but he had surrendered to Nezha the moment the Tournament took a dangerous turn. Kitay was brilliant, but he didn't belong at Sinegard.

"I wanted to," Kitay admitted. "But I'm my father's only son. And my father's the defense minister. So what choice do I have?"

She fiddled with the bottle. "You're an only child, then?"

Kitay shook his head. "Older sister. Kinata. She's at Yuelu now—studying geomancy, or something like that."

"*Geomancy*?"

"The artful placement of buildings and things." Kitay waved his hands in the air. "It's all aesthetics. Supposedly it's important, if your greatest aspiration is to marry someone important."

"You haven't read every book about it?"

"I only read about the interesting things." Kitay rolled over onto his stomach. "You? Any siblings?"

"None," she said. Then she frowned. "Yes, actually. I don't know why I said that. I have a brother—well, foster brother. Kesegi. He's ten. *Was*. He's eleven now, I guess."

"Do you miss him?"

Rin hugged her knees to her chest. She didn't like the way her stomach suddenly felt. "No. I mean—I don't know. He was so little when I left. I used to take care of him. I guess I'm glad that I don't have to do that anymore."

Kitay raised an eyebrow. "Have you written to him?"

"No." She hesitated. "I don't know why. I guess I assumed the Fangs didn't want to hear from me. Or maybe that he'd be better off if he just forgot about me."

She had wanted to at least write Tutor Feyrik in the beginning, but things had been so awful at the Academy that she couldn't bear to tell him about it. Then, as time passed, and as her schoolwork became more exhausting, it had become so painful to think about home that she'd just stopped.

"You didn't like it at home, huh?" Kitay asked.

"I don't like thinking about it," she mumbled.

She never wanted to think about Tikany. She wanted to pretend that she'd never lived there—no, that it had never existed. Because if she could just erase her past, then she could write herself into whoever she wanted to be in the present. Student. Scholar. Soldier. Anything except who she used to be.

The Summer Festival culminated in a parade in Sinegard's city center.

Rin arrived at the grounds with the members of the House of Chen—Kitay's father and willowy mother, his two uncles and their wives, and his older sister. Rin had forgotten how important Kitay's father actually was until she saw the entire clan decked out in their house colors of burgundy and gold.

Kitay suddenly grabbed Rin's elbow. "Don't look to your left. Pretend like you're talking to me."

"But I *am* talking to you." Rin immediately looked to her left.

And saw Nezha, standing in a crowd of people wearing gowns of silver and cerulean. A massive dragon was embroidered across the back of his robe, the emblem of the House of Yin.

"Oh." She jerked her head away. "Can we go stand over there?"

"Yes, let's."

Once they were safely ensconced behind Kitay's rotund second uncle, Rin peered out to gawk at the members of the House of Yin. She found herself staring at two older versions of Nezha, one male and one female. Both were well into their twenties and unfairly attractive. Nezha's entire family, in fact, looked like they belonged on wall paintings—they appeared more like idealized versions of humans than actual people.

"Nezha's father isn't there," said Kitay. "That's interesting."

"Why?"

"He's the Dragon Warlord," said Kitay. "One of the Twelve."

"Maybe he's sick," said Rin. "Maybe he hates parades as much as you do."

"I'm here, though, aren't I?" Kitay fussed with his sleeves. "You don't just *miss* the Summer Parade. It's a display of unity of all the Twelve Provinces. One year my father broke his leg the day before and he still made it, doped up on sedatives the entire time. If the head of the House of Yin hasn't come, that means something."

"Maybe he's embarrassed," Rin said. "Furious that his son lost the Tournament. He's too ashamed to show his face."

Kitay cracked a smile.

A bugle sounded through the thin morning air, followed by a servant shouting for all members of the procession to fall into order.

Kitay turned to Rin. "So, I don't know if you can . . ."

"No, it's fine," she said. Of course she wouldn't be riding with the House of Chen. Rin was not in Kitay's family; she had no business being in the procession. She spared him the embarrassment of bringing it up. "I'll watch you from the marketplace."

After a good deal of squeezing and elbowing, Rin escaped the crowd and found a spot on top of a fruit stand where she could get a good view of the parade without being crushed to death in the horde of Sinegardians who had gathered downtown. As long as the thatched straw roof did not suddenly cave in, the fruit stand owner need never know.

The parade began with an homage to the Heavenly Menagerie, the roster of mythical creatures that were held by legend to exist in the era of the Red Emperor. Giant dragons and lions snaked through the crowd, undulating up and down on poles controlled by dancers hidden within. Firecrackers popped in rhythm as they moved, like coordinated bursts of thunder. Next came a massive scarlet effigy on tall poles that had been set carefully aflame: the Vermilion Phoenix of the South.

Rin watched the Phoenix curiously. According to her history books, this was the god whom the Speerlies had venerated above all others. In fact, Speer had never worshipped the massive pantheon of gods that the Nikara did. The Speerlies had only ever worshipped their Phoenix.

The creature following the Phoenix resembled nothing Rin had ever seen before. It bore the head of a lion, antlers like a deer's, and the body of a four-legged creature; a tiger, perhaps, but its feet ended in hooves. It wove quietly through the parade; its puppeteers beat no drums, sang no chants, rang no bells to announce its coming.

Rin puzzled over the creature until she matched it with a description she had heard in stories told in Tikany. It was a kirin, the noblest of earthly beasts. Kirins walked the lands of Nikan only when a great leader had passed away, and then only in times of great peril.

Then the procession turned to the illustrious houses, and Rin quickly lost interest. Aside from seeing Kitay's moping face, there was nothing fun about watching palanquin after palanquin of important people dressed in their house colors.

The sun shone at full force overhead. Sweat dripped down Rin's temples. She wished she had something to drink. She shielded her face with her sleeve, waiting for the parade to end so she could find Kitay.

Then the crowd around her began screaming, and Rin realized with a start that borne on a palanquin of golden silk, surrounded by a platoon of both musicians and bodyguards, the Empress had arrived.

The Empress was flawed in many ways.

Her face was not perfectly symmetrical. Her eyebrows were finely arched, one slightly above the other, which gave her an expression of constant disdain. Even her mouth was uneven; one side of her mouth curved higher than the other.

And yet she was without question the most beautiful woman Rin had ever seen.

It was not enough to describe her hair, which was darker than the night and glossier than butterfly wings. Or her skin, which was paler and smoother than any Sinegardian could have wished for. Or her lips, which were the color of blood, as if she had just been sucking at a cherry. All of these things could have applied to normal women in the abstract, might even have been remarkable on their own. But on the Empress they were simple inevitabilities, casual truths.

Venka would have paled in comparison.

Youth, Rin thought, was an amplification of beauty. It was a filter; it could mask what one was lacking, enhance even the most average features. But beauty without youth was dangerous. The Empress's beauty did not require the soft fullness of young lips, the rosy red of young cheeks, the tenderness of young skin. This beauty cut deep, like a sharpened crystal. This beauty was immortal.

Afterward, Rin could not have described what the Empress

had been wearing. She could not recall whether or not the Empress spoke, or if the Empress waved in her direction. She could not remember anything the Empress did at all.

She would only remember those eyes, deep pools of black, eyes that made her feel as if she were suffocating, just like Master Jiang's did, but if this was drowning then Rin didn't want air, didn't need it so long as she could keep gazing into those glittering obsidian wells.

She couldn't look away. She couldn't even *imagine* looking away.

As the Empress's palanquin moved out of sight, Rin felt an odd pang in her heart.

She would have torn apart kingdoms for this woman. She would have followed her to the gates of hell and back. This was her ruler. This was whom she was meant to serve.

CHAPTER 9

"Fang Runin of Tikany, Rooster Province," Rin said. "Second-year apprentice."

The office clerk stamped the Academy's crest in the space next to her name on the registration scroll, and then handed her three sets of black apprentice tunics. "What track?"

"Lore," Rin said. "Under Master Jiang Ziya."

The clerk consulted the scroll again. "You sure?"

"Pretty sure," Rin said, though her pulse quickened. Had something happened?

"I'll be right back," the clerk said, and disappeared into the back office.

Rin waited by the desk, growing more and more anxious as the minutes passed. Had Jiang left the Academy? Been fired? Suffered a nervous breakdown? Been arrested for opium possession off campus? For opium possession *on* campus?

She thought suddenly of the day she had enrolled for Sinegard, when the proctors had tried to detain her for cheating. Had Nezha's family filed a complaint against her for costing their heir the championship? Was that even possible?

Finally the clerk returned with a sheepish look on his face.

"I'm sorry," he said. "But it's been so long since anyone's

pledged Lore. We're not sure what color your armband is supposed to be."

In the end they took leftover cloth from the first-years' uniforms and fashioned her a white armband.

Classes began the next day. After pledging, Rin still spent half her time with the other masters. As she was the only one in her track, she studied Strategy and Linguistics along with Irjah's apprentices. She found to her dismay that though she hadn't pledged Medicine, second-years still had to suffer a mandatory emergency triage class under Enro. History had been replaced with Foreign Relations under Master Yim. Jun still wouldn't allow her to train under him, but she was eligible to study weapons-based combat with Sonnen.

Finally her morning classes ended, and Rin was left with half the day to spend with Jiang. She ran up the steps toward the Lore garden. Time to meet with her master. Time to get answers.

"Describe to me what we are studying," said Jiang. "What is Lore?"

Rin blinked. She'd rather been hoping that he would tell her.

Rin had tried many times over the break to rationalize to herself why she'd chosen to study Lore, only to find herself uttering vague, circular truisms.

It came down to an intuition. A truth she knew for herself but couldn't prove to anyone else. She was studying Lore because she knew Jiang had tapped into some other source of power, something real and mystifying. Because she had tapped into that same source the day of the Tournament. Because she had been consumed by fire, had seen the world turned red, had lost control of herself and been saved by the man whom everyone else at the school deemed insane.

She had seen the other side of the veil, and now her curiosity was so great she would go mad unless she understood what had happened.

That didn't mean she had the faintest inkling of what she was doing.

"Weird things," she said. "We're studying very weird things."

Jiang raised an eyebrow. "How articulate."

"I don't know," she said. "I'm just here because I wanted to study with you. Because of what happened during the Trials. I don't actually know what I'm getting into."

"Oh, you do." Jiang lifted his index finger and touched the tip to a spot on her forehead precisely between her eyes, the spot from which he'd stilled the fire inside her. "Deep in your subconscious mind, you know the truth of things."

"I wanted to—"

"You want to know what happened to you during the Tournament." Jiang cocked his head to the side. "Here is what happened: you called a god, and the god answered."

Rin made a face. Again with the gods? She had been hoping for answers throughout the entire break, had thought that Jiang might make things clear once she returned, but she was now more confused than ever.

Jiang lifted a hand before she could protest. "You don't know what any of this means yet. You don't know if you'll ever replicate what happened in the ring. But you do know that if you don't get answers now, the hunger will consume you and your mind will crack. You've glimpsed the other side and you can't rest until you fill in the blanks. Yes?"

"Yes."

"What happened to you was common in the era before the Red Emperor, back when Nikara shamans didn't know what they were doing. If this had continued, you would have gone mad. But I am here to make sure that doesn't happen. I'm going to keep you sane."

Rin wondered how someone who regularly strolled through campus without clothes on could say that with a straight face.

And she wondered what it said about her that she trusted him.

* * *

Understanding came, like all things with Jiang, in infuriatingly small increments. As Rin had learned before the Trials, Jiang's preferred method of instruction was to do first and explain later, if ever. She learned early on that if she asked the wrong question, she wouldn't get the answer she wanted. "The fact that you're asking," Jiang would say, "is evidence that you're not ready to know."

She learned to shut up and simply follow his lead.

He carefully laid out a foundation for her, though at first his demands seemed menial and pointless. He made her transcribe her history textbook into Old Nikara and back. He made her spend a chilly fall afternoon squatting over the stream catching minnows with her bare hands. He demanded she complete all assignments for every class using her nondominant left hand, so that her essays took twice as long to finish and looked like a child had written them. He made her live by twenty-five-hour days for an entire month. He made her go nocturnal for an entire two weeks, so that all she ever saw was the night sky and an eerily quiet Sinegard, and he was wholly unsympathetic when she complained about missing her other classes. He made her see how long she could go without sleeping. He made her see how long she could go without waking up.

She swallowed her skepticism, took a leap of faith, and chose to follow his instructions, hoping that enlightenment might be on the other side. Yet she did not leap blindly, because she knew what was at the other end. Daily, she saw the proof of enlightenment before her.

Because Jiang did things that no human should be able to do.

The first time, he made the leaves at his feet spin without moving a muscle.

She thought it was a trick of the wind.

And then he did it again, and then a third time, just to prove he had utter control over it.

"Shit," she said, and then repeated, "Shit. Shit. Shit. How. How?"

"Easily," he said.

She gaped at him. "This is—this isn't martial arts, it's . . ."

"It's what?" he pressed.

"It's supernatural."

He looked smug. "Supernatural is a word for anything that doesn't fit your present understanding of the world. I need you to suspend your disbelief. I need you to simply accept that these things are possible."

"I'm supposed to take it as true that you're a *god*?"

"Don't be silly. I am not a god," he said. "I am a mortal who has woken up, and there is power in awareness."

He made the wind howl at his command. He made trees rustle by pointing at them. He made water ripple without touching it, and could cause shadows to twist and screech with a whispered word.

She realized that Jiang showed her these things because she would not have believed them if he'd merely told her they were possible. He was building up a background of possibilities for her, a web of new concepts. How did you explain to a child the idea of gravity, until they knew what it meant to fall?

Some truths could be learned through memorization, like history textbooks or grammar lessons. Some had to be ingrained slowly, had to become true because they were an inevitable part of the pattern of all things.

Power dictates acceptability, Kitay had once told her. Did the same apply to the fabric of the natural world?

Jiang reconfigured Rin's perception of what was real. Through demonstrations of impossible acts, he recalibrated the way she approached the material universe.

It was easier because she was so willing to believe. She fit these challenges to her conceptions of reality into her mind without too much trauma from adjustment. The traumatic event had already occurred. She had felt herself consumed by fire. She had known what it meant to burn. She hadn't imagined it. It had happened.

She learned to resist denying what Jiang showed her because it didn't square with her previous notions of how things worked. She learned to stop being shocked.

Her experience during the Tournament had torn a great, jagged hole through her understanding of the world, and she waited for Jiang to fill it in for her.

Sometimes, if she bordered on asking the right question, he sent her to the library to find the answer herself.

When she asked him where Lore had been practiced before, he sent her on a wild goose chase after all that was odd and cryptic. He made her read texts on the ancient dream walkers of the southern islands and their plant spirit healing practices. He made her write detailed reports about village shamans of the Hinterlands to the north, about how they fell into trances and journeyed as spirits in the bodies of eagles. He had her pore over decades of testimony from southern Nikara villagers who claimed to be clairvoyant.

"How would you describe all of these people?" he inquired.

"Oddities. People with abilities, or people who were pretending to have abilities." Other than that, Rin saw no way that these groups of people were linked. "How would you describe them?"

"I would call them shamans," he said. "Those who commune with the gods."

When she asked him what he meant by the gods, he made her study religion. Not just Nikara religion—all religions of the world, every religion that had been practiced since the dawn of time.

"What does anyone mean by gods?" he asked. "Why do we have gods? What purpose does a god serve in a society? Vex these issues. Find these answers for me."

In a week, she produced what she thought was a brilliant report on the difference between Nikara and Hesperian religious traditions. She proudly recounted her conclusions to Jiang in the Lore garden.

The Hesperians had only one church. They believed in one divine entity: a Holy Maker, separate from and above all mortal affairs, wrought in the image of a man. Rin argued that this god, this Maker, was a means by which Hesperia's government maintained order. The priests of the Order of the Holy Maker held no political office but exerted more cultural control than the Hesperian central government did. Since Hesperia was a large country without warlords who had absolute power over each of its states, rule of law had to be enforced by propagation of the myth of moral codes.

The Empire, in contrast, was a country of what Rin labeled superstitious atheists. Of course, Nikan had its gods in abundance. But like the Fangs, the majority of Nikara were religious only when it suited them. The Empire's wandering monks constituted a small minority of the population, mere curators of the past, rather than part of any institution with real power.

Gods in Nikan were the heroes of myths, tokens of culture, icons to be acknowledged during important life events like weddings, births, or deaths. They were personifications of emotions that the Nikara themselves felt. But no one actually believed that you would have bad luck for the rest of the year if you forgot to light incense to the Azure Dragon. No one really thought that you could keep your loved ones safe by praying to the Great Tortoise.

The Nikara practiced these rituals regardless, went through the motions because there was comfort in doing so, because it was a way for them to express their anxieties about the ebbs and flows of their fortunes.

"And so religion is merely a social construct in both the east and west," Rin concluded. "The difference lies in its utility."

Jiang had been listening attentively throughout her presentation. When she finished, he blew air out of his cheeks like a child and rubbed at his temples. "So you think Nikara religion is simply superstition?"

"Nikara religion is too haphazard to hold any degree of truth," Rin said. "You have the four cardinal gods—the Dragon, the Tiger, the Tortoise, and the Phoenix. Then you have local household gods, village guardian gods, animal gods, gods of rivers, gods of mountains . . ." She counted them off on her fingers.

"How could all of them exist in the same space? How could the spiritual realm be, with all these gods vying for dominance? The best explanation is that when we say 'god' in Nikan, we mean a story. Nothing more."

"So you have no faith in the gods?" Jiang asked.

"I believe in the gods as much as the next Nikara does," she replied. "I believe in gods as a cultural reference. As metaphors. As things we refer to keep us safe because we can't do anything else, as manifestations of our neuroses. But not as things that I truly trust are real. Not as things that hold actual consequence for the universe."

She said this with a straight face, but she was exaggerating.

Because she knew that something was real. She knew that on some level, there was more to the cosmos than what she encountered in the material world. She was not truly such a skeptic as she pretended to be.

But the best way to get Jiang to explain anything was by taking radical positions, because when she argued from the extremes, he made his best arguments in response.

He hadn't yet taken the bait, so she continued: "If there is a divine creator, some ultimate moral authority, then why do bad things happen to good people? And why would this deity create people at all, since people are such imperfect beings?"

"But if nothing is divine, why do we ascribe godlike status to mythological figures?" Jiang countered. "Why bow to the Great Tortoise? The Snail Goddess Nüwa? Why burn incense to the heavenly pantheon? Believing in any religion involves sacrifice. Why would any poor, penniless Nikara farmer knowingly make sacrifices to entities he knew were just myths? Who does that benefit? How did these practices originate?"

"I don't know," admitted Rin.

"Then find out. Find out the nature of the cosmos."

Rin thought it was somewhat unreasonable to ask her to puzzle out what philosophers and theologians had been trying to answer for millennia, but she returned to the library.

And came back with more questions still. "But how does the existence or nonexistence of the gods affect me? Why does it matter how the universe came to be?"

"Because you're part of it. Because you exist. And unless you want to only ever be a tiny modicum of existence that doesn't understand its relation to the grander web of things, you will explore."

"Why should I?"

"Because I know you want power." He tapped her forehead again. "But how can you borrow power from the gods when you don't understand what they are?"

Under Jiang's orders, Rin spent more time in the library than most fifth-year apprentices. He assigned her to write essays on a daily basis, the prompt always derived from a topic they had arrived at after hours of conversation. He made her draw connections between texts of different disciplines, texts that were written centuries apart, and texts written in different languages.

"How do Seejin's theories of transmitting *ki* through human air passages relate to the Speerly practice of inhaling the ash of the deceased?"

"How has the roster of Nikara gods changed over time, and how did this reflect the eminence of different Warlords at different points in history?"

"When did the Federation begin worshipping their sovereign as a divine entity, and why?"

"How does the doctrine of separation of church and state affect Hesperian politics? Why is this doctrine ironic?"

He tore apart her mind and pieced it back together, decided he didn't like the order, tore it apart again. He strained her mental capacity just as Irjah did. But Irjah stretched Rin's mind within known parameters. His assignments simply made Rin more nimble within the spaces she was already familiar with. Jiang forced her mind to expand outward into entirely new dimensions.

He did, in essence, the mental equivalent of making her carry a pig up a mountain.

She obeyed on every count, and wondered what alternative worldview he was trying to make her piece together. She wondered what he was trying to teach her, other than that none of her notions of how the world worked were true.

Meditation was the worst.

Jiang announced in the third month of the term that henceforth Rin would spend an hour each day meditating with him. Rin half hoped he would forget this stipulation, the same way he occasionally forgot what year it was, or what his name was.

But of all the rules Jiang imposed on her, he chose this one to observe faithfully.

"You will sit still for one hour, every morning, in the garden, without exception."

She did. She hated it.

"Press your tongue against the roof of your mouth. Feel your spine elongate. Feel the spaces between your vertebrae. *Wake up!*"

Rin inhaled sharply and jerked out of her slump. Jiang's voice, always so quiet and soothing, had been putting her to sleep.

The spot above her left eyebrow twitched. She fidgeted. Jiang would scold her if she scratched it. She raised her brow as high as it could go instead. The itching intensified.

"Sit still," Jiang said.

"My back hurts," Rin complained.

"That's because you're not sitting up straight."

"I think it's cramped from sparring."

"I think you're full of shit."

Five minutes passed in silence. Rin twisted her back to one side, then the other. Something popped. She winced.

She was painfully bored. She counted her teeth with her tongue. She counted again starting from the opposite direction. She shifted her weight from one butt cheek to the other. She felt an intense urge to get up, move, jump around, anything.

She peeked one eye open and found Master Jiang staring directly back at her.

"Sit. *Still.*"

She swallowed her protest and obeyed.

Meditation felt like a massive waste of time to Rin, who was used to years of stress and constant studying. It felt wrong to be sitting so still, to have nothing occupying her mind. She could barely stand three minutes of this torture, let alone sixty. She was so terrified of the thought of not thinking that she wasn't able to accomplish it because she kept thinking about not thinking.

Jiang, on the other hand, could meditate indefinitely. He became like a statue, serene and tranquil. He seemed like air, like he might fade away if she didn't concentrate enough on him. He seemed like he'd simply left his body behind and gone somewhere else.

A fly settled on her nose. Rin sneezed violently.

"Start the time over," Jiang said placidly.

"Damn it!"

When spring returned to Sinegard, when the weather was warm enough that Rin could stop bundling up in her thick winter robes, Jiang took her on a hiking trip into the nearby Wudang mountain range. They walked for two hours in silence, until noon, when Jiang chose to stop at a sunny alcove that overlooked the entire valley below.

"The subject of today's lesson will be plants." He sat down, pulled off his satchel, and emptied the contents onto the grass. Out spilled an assortment of plants and powders, the severed arm of a cactus, several bright red poppy flowers with pods still attached, and a handful of sun-dried mushrooms.

"Are we getting high?" Rin said. "Oh, wow. We're getting high, aren't we?"

"*I'm* getting high," said Jiang. "You're watching."

He lectured as he crushed the poppy seeds in a small stone bowl with a pestle. "None of these plants are native to Sinegard. These mushrooms were cultivated in the forests of the Hare Province. You won't find them anywhere else; they do well only in tropical climates. This cactus grows best in the Baghra Desert between our northern border and the Hinterlands. This powder is derived from a bush found only in the rain forests of the southern hemisphere. The bush grows small orange fruit that are tasteless and sticky. But the drug is made from the dried, shredded root of the plant."

"And possession of all of these in Sinegard is a capital offense," Rin said, because she felt one of them might as well mention that.

"Ah. The law." Jiang sniffed at an unidentified leaf and then tossed it away. "So inconvenient. So irrelevant." He looked suddenly at her. "Why does Nikan frown upon drug use?"

He did this often: hurled questions at her that she hadn't prepared answers to. If she spoke too quickly or made a hasty generalization, he challenged it, backed her up into an argumentative corner until she spelled out exactly what she meant and justified it rigorously.

Rin had enough practice by now to reason carefully before uttering a response. "Because use of psychedelics is associated with blown minds, wasted potential, and social chaos. Because drug addicts can give very little to society. Because it is an ongoing plague on our country left by the dear Federation."

Jiang nodded slowly. "Well put. Do you agree?"

Rin shrugged. She had seen enough of the opium dens of Tikany to know the effects of addiction. She understood why the laws were so harsh. "I agree now," she said carefully. "But I suppose I'll change my mind after you've had your say."

Jiang's mouth quirked into a lopsided grin. "It is the nature of all things to have a dual purpose," he said. "You've seen what poppy does to the common man. And given what you know of addiction, your conclusions are reasonable. Opium makes wise men stupid. It destroys local economies and weakens entire countries."

He weighed another handful of poppy seeds in his palm. "But something so destructive inherently and simultaneously has marvelous potential. The poppy flower, more than anything, displays the duality of hallucinogens. You know poppy by three names. In its most common form, as opium nuggets smoked from a pipe, poppy makes you useless. It numbs you and closes you off to the world. Then there is the madly addictive heroin, which is extracted as a powder from the sap of the flower. But the seeds? These seeds are a shaman's dream. These seeds, used with the proper mental preparation, give you access to the entire universe contained within your mind."

He put the poppy seeds down and gestured to the array of psychedelics before him. "Shamans across continents have used plants to alter their states of consciousness for centuries. The medicine men of the Hinterlands used this flower to fly upward like an arrow to enter into communion with the gods. This one will put you into a trance where you might enter the Pantheon."

Rin's eyes widened. Here it was. Slowly the lines began to connect. She was finally beginning to understand the purpose of the last six months of research and meditation. So far she had been pursuing two separate lines of inquiry—the shamans and their abilities; the gods and the nature of the universe.

Now, with the introduction of psychedelic plants, Jiang drew these threads into one unified theory, a theory of spiritual connection through psychedelics to the dream world where the gods might reside.

The separate concepts in her mind flung connections at one another, like a web suddenly grown overnight. The formative background Jiang had been laying suddenly made total, utter sense.

She had an outline, but the picture hadn't fully developed. Something didn't square.

"Contained within my mind?" Rin repeated carefully.

Jiang glanced sideways at her. "Do you know what the word *entheogen* means?"

She shook her head.

"It means the generation of the god within," he said. He reached out and tapped her forehead in that same place. "The merging of god and person."

"But we aren't gods," she said. She had spent the past week in the library trying to trace Nikara theology to its roots. Nikara religious mythology was full of encounters between the mortal and divine, but nowhere in her research had anyone mentioned anything about god-creation. "Shamans communicate with gods. They don't create gods."

"What's the difference between a god within and a god outside? What is the difference between the universe contained in your mind and the universe external?" Jiang tapped both of her temples. "Wasn't that the basis of your criticism of Hesperia's theological hierarchy? That the idea of a divine creator separate from us and ruling over us made no sense?"

"Yes, but . . ." She trailed off, trying to make sense of what she wanted to say. "I didn't mean that we are gods, I meant that . . ." She wasn't sure what she meant. She looked at Jiang in supplication.

For once, he gave her the easy answer. "You must conflate these concepts. The god outside you. The god within. Once you understand that these are one and the same, once you can hold both concepts in your head and know them to be true, you'll be a shaman."

"But it can't be so simple," Rin stammered. Her mind was still reeling. She struggled to formulate her thoughts. "If this is . . . then . . . then why doesn't everyone do this? Why doesn't anyone in the opium houses stumble upon the gods?"

"Because they don't know what they're looking for. The Nikara don't believe in their deities, remember?"

"Fine," Rin said, refusing to rise to the bait of having her own words thrown in her face. "But why not?" She had thought the Nikara religious skepticism was reasonable, but not when people like Jiang could do the things they did. "Why aren't there more believers?"

"Once there were," Jiang said, and she was surprised at how bitter he sounded. "Once there were monasteries upon monasteries. Then the Red Emperor in his quest for unification came and burned them down. Shamans lost their power. The monks—the ones with real power, anyhow—died or disappeared."

"Where are they now?"

"Hidden," he said. "Forgotten. In recent history, only the nomadic clans of the Hinterlands and the tribes of Speer had anyone who could commune with the gods. This is no coincidence. The national quest to modernize and mobilize entails a faith in one's ability to control world order, and when that happens, you lose your connection with the gods. When man begins to think that he is responsible for writing the script of the world, he forgets the forces that dream up our reality. Once, this academy was a monastery. Now it is a military training ground. You'll find this same pattern has repeated itself in all the great powers of this world that have entered a so-called civilized age. Mugen doesn't have shamans. Hesperia doesn't have shamans. They worship men whom they believe are gods, not gods themselves."

"What about Nikara superstition?" Rin asked. "I mean—in Sinegard, obviously, where people are educated, religion's defunct, but what about the little villages? What about folk religion?"

"The Nikara believe in icons, not gods," said Jiang. "They don't understand what they're worshipping. They've prioritized ritual over theology. Sixty-four gods of equal standing? How convenient, and how absurd. Religion cannot be packaged so cleanly. The gods are not so neatly organized."

"But I don't understand," she said. "Why have the shamans disappeared? Wouldn't the Red Emperor be all the more powerful for having shamans in his army?"

"No. In fact, the opposite is true. The creation of empire requires conformity and uniform obedience. It requires teachings that can be mass-produced across the entire country. The Militia is a bureaucratic entity that is purely interested in results. What I teach is impossible to duplicate to a class of fifty, much less a division of thousands. The Militia is composed almost entirely of people like Jun, who think that things matter only if they are getting results *immediately*, results that can be duplicated and reused. But shamanism is and always has been an imprecise art. How could it be anything else? It is about the most fundamental truths about each and every one of us, how we relate to the phenomenon of existence. Of course it is imprecise. If we understood it completely, then we would be gods."

Rin was unconvinced. "But surely *some* teachings could be spread."

"You overestimate the Empire. Think of martial arts. Why were you able to defeat your classmates in the trial? Because they learned a version that is watered down, distilled and packaged for convenience. The same is true of their religion."

"But they can't have forgotten completely," Rin said. "This class still exists."

"This class is a joke," said Jiang.

"I don't think it's a joke."

"You, and no one else," said Jiang. "Even Jima doubts the value of this course, but she can't bring herself to abolish it. On some level, Nikara has never given up hope that it can find its shamans again."

"But it has them," she said. "I'll bring shamanism back to this world."

She glanced hopefully toward him, but Jiang sat frozen, staring over the edge of the cliff as if his mind were somewhere far away. He looked very sad then.

"The age of the gods is over," he said finally. "The Nikara may speak of shamans in their legends, but they cannot abide the prospect of the supernatural. To them, we are madmen." He swallowed. "We are not madmen. But how can we convince anyone of this, when the rest of the world believes it so? Once an empire has become convinced of its worldview, anything that evidences the contrary must be erased. The Hinterlanders were banished to the north, cursed and suspected of witchcraft. The Speerlies were marginalized, enslaved, thrown into battle like wild dogs, and ultimately sacrificed."

"Then we'll teach them," she said. "We'll make them remember."

"No one else would have the patience to learn what I have taught you. It's merely our job to remember. I have searched for years for an apprentice, and only you have ever understood the truth of the world."

Rin felt a pang of disappointment at those words; not for herself but for the Empire. It was difficult to know that she lived in a world where humans had once freely spoken to the gods but no longer did.

How could an entire nation simply forget about gods that might grant unimaginable power?

Easily, that's how.

The world was simpler when all that existed was what you could perceive in front of you. Easier to forget the underlying forces that constructed the dream. Easier to believe that reality existed only on one plane. Rin had believed that up until this very moment, and her mind still struggled to readjust.

But she knew the truth now, and that gave her power.

Rin stared silently out over the valley below, still grappling to absorb the magnitude of what she had just learned. Meanwhile Jiang packed the powders into a pipe, lit it up, and took a long, deep draught.

His eyes fluttered closed. A serene smile spread over his face.

"Up we go," he said.

The thing about watching someone get high was that if you weren't getting high yourself, things got very boring very soon. Rin prodded Jiang after a few minutes, and when he didn't stir, she went back down the mountain by herself.

If Rin had thought Jiang might let her start using hallucinogens to meditate, she was wrong. He made her help out in the garden, had her watering the cacti and cultivating the mushrooms, but forbade her to try any plants until he gave her permission.

"Without the right mental preparation, psychedelics won't do anything for you," he said. "You'll just become terribly annoying for a while."

Rin had accepted this initially, but it had now been weeks. "When am I going to be mentally prepared, then?"

"When you can sit still for five minutes without opening your eyes," he said.

"I can sit still! I've been sitting still for nearly a year! That's all I've been doing!"

Jiang brandished his garden shears at her. "Don't take that tone with me."

She slammed her tray of cacti clippings on the shelf. "I know there are things you're not teaching me. I know you're keeping me behind on purpose. I just don't understand why."

"Because you worry me," said Jiang said. "You have an aptitude for Lore like no one I've ever met, not even Altan. But you're impatient. You're careless. And you skimp on meditating."

She *had* been skimping on meditating. She was supposed to keep a meditation log, to document each time she made it to the end of an hour successfully. But as coursework from her other classes piled up, Rin had neglected her daily requisite period of doing nothing.

"I don't see the point," she said. "If it's focus that you want, I can give you focus. I can concentrate on anything. But to empty my mind? To be devoid of all thought? All sense of self? What good does that serve?"

"It serves to sever you from the material world," Jiang answered. "How do you expect to reach the spirit realm when you're obsessing over the things in front of you? I know why it's hard for you. You like beating your classmates. You like harboring your old grudges. It feels good to hate, doesn't it? Up until now you've been storing your anger up and using it as fuel. But unless you learn to let it go, you are never going to find your way to the gods."

"So give me a psychedelic," she suggested. "*Make* me let it go."

"Now you're being rash. I'm not letting you meddle in things that you barely understand yet. It's too dangerous."

"How dangerous could it be to just sit still?"

Jiang stood up straight. The hand holding the shears dropped to his side. "This isn't some fairy story where you wave your hand and ask the gods for three wishes. We are not fucking around here. These are forces that could break you."

"Nothing's going to happen to me," she snapped. "Nothing's been happening to me for months. You keep going on about seeing the gods, but all that happens when I meditate is that I get bored, my nose itches, and every second takes an eternity."

She reached for the poppy flowers.

He slapped her hand away. "You're not ready. You're not even *close* to ready."

Rin flushed. "They're just *drugs*—"

"Just drugs? Just *drugs*?" Jiang's voice rose in pitch. "I'm going to issue you a warning. And I'm only going to do it once. You're not the first student to pledge Lore, you know. Oh, Sinegard's been trying to produce a shaman for years. But you want to know why no one takes this class seriously?"

"Because you keep farting in faculty meetings?"

He didn't even laugh at that, which meant this was more serious than she'd thought.

Jiang, in fact, looked pained.

"We've tried," he said. "Ten years ago. I had four students just as brilliant as you, without Altan's rage or your impatience. I taught them to meditate, I taught them about the Pantheon, but those apprentices only had one thing on their minds, which was to call on the gods and siphon their power. Do you know what happened to them?"

"They called the gods and became great warriors?" Rin said hopefully.

Jiang fixed her with his pale, suffocating gaze. "They all went mad. Every single one. Two were calm enough to be locked in an asylum for the rest of their lives. The other two were a danger to themselves and others around them. The Empress had them sent to Baghra."

She stared at him. She had no idea what to say to that.

"I have met spirits unable to find their bodies again," said

Jiang. He looked very old then. "I have met men who are only halfway to the spirit realm, caught between our world and the next. What does that mean? It means don't. Fuck. Around." He tapped her forehead with each word. "If you don't want that brilliant little mind of yours to shatter, you'll do as I say."

The only time Rin felt fully grounded was during her other classes. These were proceeding at twice the rate as they had her first year, and though Rin barely managed to keep up given the absurd course load Jiang had already assigned her, it was nice to study things that made sense for a change.

Rin had always felt like an outsider among her classmates, but as the year carried on, she began to feel as if she inhabited an entirely separate world from them. She was steadily growing further and further away from the world where things functioned as they should, where reality was not constantly in flux, where she thought she knew the shape and nature of things instead of being constantly reminded that really she knew nothing at all.

"Seriously," Kitay asked over lunch one day. "What are you learning?"

Kitay, like everyone else in her class, thought that Lore was a course in religious history, a smorgasbord of anthropology and folk mythology. She hadn't bothered to correct them. Easier to spread a believable lie than to convince them of the truth.

"That none of my beliefs about the world were true," Rin answered dreamily. "That reality is malleable. That hidden connections exist in every living object. That the whole of the world is merely a thought, a butterfly's dream."

"Rin?"

"Yes?"

"Your elbow is in my porridge."

She blinked. "Oh. Sorry."

Kitay slid his bowl farther away from her arm. "They talk about you, you know. The other apprentices."

Rin folded her arms. "And what do they say?"

He paused. "You can probably catch the drift. It's not, uh, good."

Had she expected anything else? She rolled her eyes. "They don't like me. Big surprise."

"It's not that," Kitay said. "They're *scared* of you."

"Because I won the Tournament?"

"Because you stormed in here from a rural township no one's ever heard of, then threw away one of the school's most prestigious bids to study with the academy madman. They can't figure you out. They don't know what you're trying to do." Kitay cocked his head at her. "What *are* you trying to do?"

She hesitated. She knew that look on Kitay's face. He'd been wearing it more often of late, as her own studies grew more and more distant from topics that she could easily explain to a layman. Kitay hated not having full access to information, and she hated keeping things from him. But how was she supposed to articulate the point of studying Lore to him, when often she could barely justify it to herself?

"Something happened to me that day in the ring," she said finally. "I'm trying to figure out what."

She'd braced herself to deal with Kitay's clinical skepticism, but he only nodded. "And you think Jiang has the answers?"

She exhaled. "If he doesn't, nobody does."

"You've heard the rumors, though—"

"The madmen. The dropouts. The prisoners at Baghra," she said. Everyone had their own horror story about Jiang's previous apprentices. "I know. Trust me, I know."

Kitay gave her a long, searching look. Finally he nodded toward her untouched bowl of porridge. She'd been cramming for one of Jima's exams; she'd forgotten to eat.

"Just take care of yourself," he said.

Second-years were granted eligibility to fight in the ring.

Now that Altan had graduated, the star of the matches turned out to be Nezha, who was rapidly becoming an even more formidable fighter under Jun's brutal training. Within a month he was challenging students two or three years his senior; by their second spring he was the undefeated champion of the rings.

Rin had been eager to enter the matches, but one conversation with Jiang had put an end to her aspirations.

"You don't fight," he said one day as they were balancing on posts above the stream.

She immediately splashed into the water.

"*What?*" she sputtered once she climbed out.

"The matches are only for apprentices whose masters have consented."

"Then consent!"

Jiang dipped a toe into the water and pulled it back out gingerly. "Nah."

"But I *want* to fight!"

"Interesting, but irrelevant."

"But—"

"No buts. I'm your master. You don't question my orders, you obey them."

"I'll obey orders that make sense to me," she retorted as she teetered wildly on a post.

Jiang snorted. "The matches aren't about winning, they're about demonstrating new techniques. What are you going to do, light up in front of the entire student body?"

She didn't push the point further.

Aside from the matches, which Rin attended regularly, she rarely saw her roommates; Niang was always working overtime with Enro, and Venka spent her waking hours either on patrol with the City Guard or training with Nezha.

Kitay began studying with her in the women's dormitory, but only because it was the one place on campus always guaranteed to be empty. The newest class of first-years had no women, and Kureel and Arda had left the Academy at the end of Rin's first year. Both had been offered prestigious positions as junior officers, in the Third and Eighth Divisions respectively.

Altan, too, was gone. But no one knew which division he had joined. Rin had expected it to be the talk of campus. But Altan had vanished as if he'd never been at Sinegard. The legend of Altan Trengsin had already begun to fade within their class, and when the next group of first-years came to Sinegard, none of them even knew who Altan was.

As the months passed, Rin found that one unexpected benefit of being the only apprentice who had pledged Lore was that she was no longer in direct competition with the rest of her classmates.

By no means did they become friendly. But Rin stopped hearing jokes about her accent, Venka stopped wrinkling her nose every time they were both in the women's dormitory, and one by one the other Sinegardians grew accustomed to, if not enthusiastic about, her presence.

Nezha was the sole exception.

They shared every class except Combat and Lore. They each did their best to utterly ignore the other's existence. Many of their advanced classes were so small that this often became incredibly awkward, but Rin supposed cold disengagement was better than active bullying.

Still, she paid attention to Nezha. How could she not? He was clearly the star of the class—inferior to Kitay perhaps in only Strategy and Linguistics, but otherwise Nezha had essentially become the new Altan of the school. The masters adored him; the incoming class of pupils thought he was a god.

"He's not that special," she grumbled to Kitay. "He didn't even win his year's Tournament. Do any of them know that?"

"Sure they do." Kitay, not looking up from his language homework, spoke with the patient exasperation of someone who'd had this conversation many times before.

"Then why don't they worship *me*?" Rin complained.

"Because you don't fight in the ring." Kitay filled in a final blank on his chart of Hesperian verb conjugations. "And also because you're weird and not as pretty."

In general, however, the childish infighting within their class had disappeared. It was partly because they were simply getting older, partly because the stress of the Trials had disappeared—apprentices were secure in their enrollment so long as they kept their grades up—and partly because their coursework had gotten so difficult they couldn't be bothered with petty rivalries.

But near the end of their second year, the class began to split again—this time along provincial and political lines.

The proximate cause was a diplomatic crisis with Federation troops on the border of Horse Province. An outpost brawl between Mugenese traders and Nikara laborers had turned deadly. The Mugenese had sent in armed policemen to kill the instigators. The border patrol of the Horse Province responded in kind.

Master Irjah was summoned immediately to the Empress's diplomatic party, which meant Strategy was canceled for two weeks. The students didn't know that, though, until they found the hastily scrawled note Irjah had left behind.

"'Don't know when I'll be back. Open fire from both sides. Four civilians dead.'" Niang read Irjah's note aloud. "Gods. That's war, isn't it?"

"Not necessarily." Kitay was the only one who seemed utterly calm. "There are skirmishes all the time."

"But there were casualties—"

"There are always casualties," said Kitay. "This has been going on for nearly two decades. We hate them, they hate us, a handful of people die because of it."

"Nikara citizens are dead!" Niang exclaimed.

"Sure, but the Empress isn't going to do anything about it."

"There's nothing she *can* do," Han interrupted. "Horse Province doesn't have enough troops to hold a front—our population's too small, there's no one to recruit from. The real problem is that some Warlords don't know how to put national interest first."

"You don't know what you're talking about," Nezha said.

"What I know is that my father's men are dying on the border," said Han. The sudden venom in his voice surprised Rin. "Meanwhile, your father's sitting pretty in his little palace, turning a blind eye because he's kept nice and safe between two buffer provinces."

Before anyone could move, Nezha's hand shot toward the back of Han's neck and slammed his face into the desk.

The classroom fell silent.

Han looked up, too stunned to retaliate. His nose had broken with an audible crack; blood streamed freely down his chin.

Nezha released Han's neck. "Shut up about my father."

Han spat out something that looked like a fragment of a tooth. "Your father's a fucking coward."

"I said *shut up*—"

"You have the biggest surplus of troops in the Empire and you won't deploy them," Han said. "Why, Nezha? Planning to use them for something else?"

Nezha's eyes flashed. "You want me to break your neck?"

"The Mugenese aren't going to invade," Kitay interrupted quickly. "They'll make noise on the Horse Province border, sure, but they won't commit ground troops. They don't want to make Hesperia angry—"

"The Hesperians don't give a shit," said Han. "They haven't bothered with the eastern hemisphere for years. No ambassadors, no diplomats—"

"Because of the armistice," Kitay said. "They think they don't need to. But if the Federation tips the balance, they'll have to intervene. And Mugen's leadership knows that."

"They also know we have no coordinated frontier defense and no navy," Han snapped. "Don't be delusional."

"A ground invasion is not rational for them," Kitay insisted. "The armistice benefits them. They don't want to bleed thousands of men in the Empire's heartland. There will be no war."

"Sure." Han crossed his arms. "What are we training for, then?"

The second crisis came two months later. Several border cities in Horse Province had begun to boycott Mugenese goods. The Mugenese governor-generals responded by methodically closing, looting, then burning down any Nikara businesses located on the Mugenese side of the border.

When the news broke, Han abruptly departed the Academy to join his father's battalion. Jima threatened permanent expulsion if he left without permission; Han responded by tossing his armband onto her desk.

The third crisis was the death of the Federation's emperor. Nikara spies reported that the crown prince Ryohai was lined up to succeed to the throne, news that deeply unsettled every master at the academy. Prince Ryohai—young, hotheaded, and violently nationalist—was a leading member of Mugen's war party.

"He's been calling for a ground invasion for years," Irjah explained to the class. "Now he has his chance to actually do it."

The next six weeks were terribly tense. Even Kitay had stopped arguing that Mugen would do nothing. Several students, most from the outer north, put in requests for a home leave. They were denied without exception. A few left regardless, but most obeyed Jima's command—if it came down to a war, then some affiliation with Sinegard was better than none.

The new Emperor Ryohai did not declare a ground invasion. The Empress sent a diplomatic party to the longbow island, and by all accounts was politely received by Mugen's new administration. The crisis passed. But a cloud of anxiety hung over the academy still—and nothing could not erase the growing fear that their class might be the first to graduate into a war.

The one person seemingly uninterested in news of Federation politics was Jiang. If asked about Mugen, he grimaced and waved the subject away; if pressed, he squeezed his eyes shut, shook his head, and sang out loud like a little child.

"But you *fought* the Federation!" Rin exclaimed. "How can you not care?"

"I don't remember that," Jiang said.

"How can you not remember that?" she demanded. "You were in the Second Poppy War—all of you were!"

"That's what they tell me," Jiang said.

"So then—"

"So I don't remember," Jiang said loudly, and his voice took on a fragile, tremulous tone that made Rin realize she had better drop the subject or risk sending him on a weeklong spell of absence or erratic behavior.

But as long as she didn't bring up the Federation, Jiang continued to conduct their lessons in the same meandering, lackadaisical manner. It had taken Rin until the end of her first year of apprenticeship to learn to meditate for an hour without moving; once she could do that, Jiang had demanded that she meditate for five. This took her nearly another year. When she finally managed it, Jiang gave her a small opaque flask, the kind used to store sorghum wine, and instructed her to take it to the top of the mountain.

"There's a cave near the peak. You'll know it when you see it. Drink down that flask, then start meditating."

"What's in it?"

Jiang examined his fingernails. "Bits and things."

"For how long?"

"As long as it takes. Days. Weeks. Months. I can't tell you before you start."

Rin told her other masters that she would be absent from class for an indefinite period of time. By now they had resigned themselves to Jiang's nonsense; they waved her off and told her to try not to be gone for more than a year. She hoped they were joking.

Jiang did not accompany her to the top. He bade her farewell from the highest tier of the campus. "Here's a cloak in case you get cold. There's not much up there in terms of rain shelter. I'll see you on the other side."

It rained the entire morning. Rin hiked miserably, wiping mud off her shoes every few steps. When she reached the cave, she was shivering so hard that she almost dropped the flask.

She glanced around the muddy interior. She wanted to build a fire to warm herself, but couldn't find any material for kindling that wasn't soaked through. She huddled into the far end of the cave, as far away from the rain as she could get, and assumed a cross-legged stance. Then she closed her eyes.

She thought of the warrior Bodhidharma, meditating for years while listening to the ants scream. She suspected that the ants wouldn't be the only ones screaming when she was done.

The contents of the flask turned out to be a slightly bitter tea. She thought it might be a hallucinogen distilled in liquid, but hours passed and her mind was as clear as ever.

Night fell. She meditated in darkness.

At first it was horribly difficult.

She couldn't sit still. She was hungry after six hours. All she thought about was her stomach. But after a while the hunger was so overwhelming that she couldn't think about it anymore, because she couldn't remember a time when she hadn't been this hungry.

On the second day she felt dizzy. She was woozy with hunger, so starved that she couldn't feel her stomach. Did she even have a stomach? What was a stomach?

On the third day her head was delightfully light. She was just air, just breath, just a breathing organ. A fan. A flute. In, out, in, out, and on and on.

On the fifth day things moved too fast, too slow, or not at all. She felt infuriated by the slow passage of time. Her brain was racing in a way that wouldn't calm; she felt as if her heartbeat must now be faster than a hummingbird's. How had she not dissolved? How had she not vibrated into nothingness?

On the seventh day she tipped into the void. Her body became very still; so still that she forgot she had one. Her left finger itched and she was amazed at the sensation. She didn't scratch it, but observed the itch as if from the outside and marveled that after a very long time, it went away by itself.

She learned how breath moved through her body as if through an empty house. Learned how to stack her vertebrae one by one on top of each other so her spine formed a perfectly straight line, an unobstructed channel.

But her still body became heavy, and as it became heavy it became easier and easier to discard it, and to drift upward, weightless, into that place she could glimpse only from behind closed eyelids.

On the ninth day she suffered a geometric assault of lines and shapes without form or color, without regard to any aesthetic value except randomness.

You stupid shapes, she thought over and over again like a mantra. *You stupid fucking shapes.*

On the thirteenth day she had a horrible sensation of being trapped, as if buried within stone, as if covered in mud. She was so light, so weightless, but she had nowhere to go; she rebounded around inside this bizarre vessel called a body like a caught firefly.

On the fifteenth day she became convinced that her consciousness had expanded to encompass the totality of life on the planet—the germination of the smallest flower to the eventual death of the largest tree. She saw an endless process of energy transfer, growing and dying, and she was part of every stage of it.

She saw bursts of color and animals that probably didn't exist. She did not see visions, precisely, because visions would have been far more vivid and concrete. But nor were the apparitions merely thoughts. They were like dreams, an uncertain plane of realness somewhere in between, and it was only by washing out every other thought from her mind that she could perceive them clearly.

She stopped counting the days. She had traveled somewhere beyond time; a place where a year and a minute felt the same. What was the difference between finite and infinite? There was being and nonbeing and that was it. Time was not real.

The apparitions became solid. Either she was dreaming, or she had transcended somewhere, but when she took a step forward, her foot touched cold stone. She looked around and saw that she stood in a tiled room no larger than a washroom. There were no doors.

A form appeared before her, dressed in strange garb. At first she thought it was Altan, but the figure's face was softer, its crimson eyes rounder and kinder.

"They said you'd come," said the figure. The voice was a woman's, deep and sad. "The gods have known you'd come."

Rin was at a loss for words. Something about the Woman was deeply familiar, and it wasn't just her resemblance to Altan. The shape of her face, the clothes she wore . . . they sparked memories Rin didn't know she had, of sands and water and open skies.

"You will be asked to do what I refused to do," said the Woman. "You will be offered power beyond your imagination. But I warn you, little warrior. The price of power is pain. The Pantheon controls the fabric of the universe. To deviate from their premeditated order you must give them something in return. And for the gifts of the Phoenix, you will pay the most. The Phoenix wants suffering. The Phoenix wants blood."

"I have blood in abundance," Rin answered. She had no idea what possessed her to say it, but she continued. "I can give the Phoenix what it desires, if the Phoenix gives me power."

The Woman's tone grew agitated. "The Phoenix doesn't *give*. Not permanently. The Phoenix takes, and takes, and takes . . . Fire is insatiable, alone among the elements . . . it will devour you until you are nothing . . ."

"I'm not afraid of fire," said Rin.

"*You* should *be*," hissed the Woman. She glided slowly toward Rin; she didn't move her legs, didn't quite walk, but simply appeared larger and closer with every passing moment—

Rin couldn't breathe. She didn't feel the least bit calm; this was nothing like the peace she was supposed to have achieved, this was terrible . . . She suddenly heard a cacophony of screams echoing around her ears, and then the Woman was screaming and shrieking, writhing in the air like a tortured dancer, even as she reached out and seized Rin's arm . . .

. . . Images spun around Rin, brown-skinned bodies dancing around a campfire, mouths open in grotesque leers, shouting words in a language that sounded like something she'd heard in a dream she no longer remembered . . . The campfire flared and the bodies fell back, burned, charred, disintegrating to nothing but glistening white bones, and Rin thought that was the end of it—death ended things—but the bones jumped back up and continued to dance . . . One of the skeletons looked at her with its bare, toothy smile, and beckoned with a fleshless hand:

"From ashes we came and to ashes we return . . ."

The Woman's grip around Rin's shoulders tightened; she leaned forward and whispered fiercely in Rin's ear: "Go back."

But Rin was enticed by the fire . . . she looked past the bones into the flames, which were furling upward like something alive, taking the shape of a living god, an animal, a bird . . .

The bird lowered its head at them.

The Woman burst into flame.

Then Rin was floating upward again, flying like an arrow at the sky to the realm of the gods.

When she opened her eyes, Jiang was crouched in front of her, watching her intently with his pale eyes. "What did you see?"

She took a deep breath. Tried to orient herself to possessing a body again. She felt so clumsy and heavy, like a puppet formed badly out of wet clay.

"A great circular room," she said hesitantly, squinting to remember her final vision. She did not know if she was having trouble finding the words, or if it was simply her mouth that refused to obey. Every order she gave her body seemed to happen only after a delay. "It was arranged like a set of trigrams, but with thirty-two points splitting into sixty-four. And creatures on pedestals all around the circle."

"Plinths," Jiang corrected.

"You're right. Plinths."

"You saw the Pantheon," he said. "You found the gods."

"I suppose." Her voice trailed off. She felt somewhat confused. *Had* she found the gods? Or had she only imagined those sixty-four deities, spinning about her like glass beads?

"You seem skeptical," he said.

"I was tired," she answered. "I don't know if it was real, or . . . I mean, I could have just been dreaming." How were her visions any different from her imagination? Had she seen those things only because she wanted to?

"Dreaming?" Jiang tilted his head. "Have you ever seen anything like the Pantheon before? In a diagram? Or a painting?"

She frowned. "No, but—"

"The plinths. Were you expecting those?"

"No," she said, "but I've seen plinths before, and the Pantheon wouldn't have been too difficult to conjure from my imagination."

"But why that particular dream? Why would your sleeping mind have chosen to extract those images from your memory compared to any other images? Why not a horse, or a field of jasmine flowers, or Master Jun riding buck naked on the back of a tiger?"

Rin blinked. "Is that something you dream about?"

"Answer the question," he said.

"I don't know," she said, frustrated. "Why do people dream what they dream?"

But he was smiling, as if that was precisely what he'd wanted to hear. "Why indeed?"

She had no response to that. She stared blankly out at the mouth of the cave, mulling these thoughts in her mind, and realized that she had awoken in more ways than one.

Her map of the world, her understanding of reality, had shifted. She could see the outlines, even if she didn't know how to fill in the blanks. She knew the gods existed and that they spoke, and that was enough.

It had taken a long time, but she finally had a vocabulary for what they were learning now. Shamans: those who communed with the gods. The gods: forces of nature, entities as real and yet ephemeral as wind and fire themselves, things inherent to the existence of the universe.

When Hesperians wrote of "God," they wrote of the supernatural.

When Jiang talked of "gods," he talked of the eminently natural.

To commune with the gods was to walk the dream world, the world of spirit. It was to relinquish that which she was and become one with the fundamental state of things. The space in limbo where matter and actions were not yet determined, the fluctuating darkness where the physical world had not yet been dreamed into existence.

The gods were simply those beings that inhabited that space, forces of creation and destruction, love and hatred, nurturing and neglect, light and dark, cold and warm . . . they opposed one another and complemented one another; they were fundamental truths.

They were the elements that constituted the universe itself.

She saw now that reality was a facade; a dream conjured by the undulating forces beneath a thin surface. And by meditating, by ingesting the hallucinogen, by forgetting her connection to the material world, she was able to wake up.

"I understand the truth of things," she murmured. "I know what it means to exist."

He smiled. "It's wonderful, isn't it?"

She understood, then, that Jiang was very far from mad.

He might, in fact, be the sanest person she had ever met.

A thought occurred to her. "So what happens when we die?"

Jiang raised an eyebrow. "I think you can answer that."

She mulled over this for a moment. "We go back to the world of spirit. We—we leave the illusion. We wake up."

Jiang nodded. "We don't *die* so much as we return to the void. We dissolve. We lose our ego. We change from being just one thing to becoming everything. Most of us, at least."

She opened her mouth to ask what he meant by that, but Jiang reached out and poked her in the forehead. "How do you feel?"

"Incredible," she said. She felt more clearheaded than she had in months, as if all this time she'd been trying to peer through a fog and it had suddenly disappeared. She was ecstatic; she'd solved the puzzle, she knew the source of her power, and now all that remained was to learn to siphon it out at will. "So what now?"

"Now we've solved your problem," said Jiang. "Now you know how you are connected to a greater web of cosmological forces. Sometimes martial artists who are particularly attuned to the world will find themselves overwhelmed by one of those forces. They suffer an imbalance—an affinity to one god over the others. This happened to you in the ring. But now you know where that flame came from, and when it happens to you again, you can journey to the Pantheon to find its balance. Now you're cured."

Rin jerked her head toward her master.

Cured?

Cured?

Jiang looked pleased, relieved, and serene, but Rin only felt confused. She hadn't studied Lore so that she could still the flames. Yes, the fire had felt awful, but it had also felt powerful. *She* had felt *powerful.*

She wanted to learn to channel it, not to suppress it.

"Problem?" Jiang asked.

"I . . . I don't . . ." She bit down on her lip before the words tumbled out of her mouth. Jiang was violently averse to any discussion of warfare; if she kept asking about military use, then he might drop her again the way he had before the Trials. He already thought she was too impulsive, too reckless and impatient; she knew how easily she might scare him off.

Never mind. If Jiang wasn't going to teach her to call the power, then she'd figure it out for herself.

"So what's the point of this?" she asked. "Just to feel good?"

"The point? What point? You're enlightened. You have a better understanding of the cosmos than most theologians alive!" Jiang waved his hands around his head. "Do you have any idea what you can do with this knowledge? The Hinterlanders have been interpreting the future for years, reading the cracks in a tortoise shell to divine events to come. They can fix illnesses of the body by healing the spirit. They can speak to plants, cure diseases of the mind . . ."

Rin wondered why the Hinterlanders would achieve all of this and not militarize their abilities, but she held her tongue. "So how long will that take?"

"It makes no sense to speak of this in measurements of years," said Jiang. "The Hinterlanders don't allow interpretation of divinations until one has been training for at least five. Shamanic training is a process that lasts across your lifetime."

She couldn't accept that, though. She wanted power, and she wanted it now—especially if they were on the verge of a war with the Mugenese.

Jiang was watching her curiously.

Be careful, she reminded herself. She still had too much to learn from Jiang. She'd have to play along.

"Anything else?" he asked after a while.

She thought of the Speerly Woman's admonitions. She thought of the Phoenix, and of fire and pain.

"No," she said. "Nothing else."

PART II

CHAPTER 10

The *Emperor Ryohai* had now patrolled the eastern Nikara border in the Nariin Sea for twelve nights. The *Ryohai* was a lightly built ship, an elegant Federation model designed for slicing quickly through choppy waters. It carried few soldiers; its deck wasn't large enough to hold a battalion. It wasn't doing reconnaissance. No courier birds circled the flagless masthead; no spies left the ship under the cover of the ocean mist.

The only thing the *Ryohai* did was flit fretfully around the shoreline, pacing back and forth over still waters like an anxious housewife. Waiting for something. Someone.

The crew spent their days in silence. The *Ryohai* carried only a skeleton crew: the captain, a few deckhands, and a small contingent from the Federation Armed Forces. It bore one esteemed guest: General Gin Seiryu, grand marshal of the Armed Forces and esteemed adviser to Emperor Ryohai himself. And it bore one visitor, one Nikara who had lurked in the shadows of the hold since the *Ryohai* had crossed into the waters of the Nariin Sea.

Cike commander Tyr was good at being invisible. In this state, he did not need to eat or sleep. Absorbed in the shadow, shrouded in darkness, he hardly needed to breathe.

He found the passing days irksome only due to boredom, but he had maintained longer vigils than this one. He had waited a week in the bedroom closet of the Dragon Warlord. He had spent an entire month ensconced under the floorboards beneath the feet of the leaders of the Republic of Hesperia.

Now he waited for the men aboard the *Ryohai* to reveal their purpose.

Tyr had been surprised when he received orders from Sinegard to infiltrate a Federation ship. For years the Cike had operated only within the Empire, killing off dissidents the Empress found particularly troublesome. The Empress did not send the Cike overseas— not since her disastrous attempt to assassinate the young Emperor Ryohai, which had ended with two dead operatives and another driven so mad he had to be carted off, screaming, to a plinth in the stone prison.

But Tyr's duty was not to question but to obey. He crouched inside the shadow, unperceived by all. He waited.

It was a still, windless night. It was a night heavy with secrets.

It had been a night like this one, so many decades ago, when the moon was full and resplendent in the sky, that Tyr's master had first taken him deep into the underground tunnels where light would never touch. His master had guided him around one winding turn after another, spinning him about in the darkness so that he could not keep a map in his head of the underground labyrinth.

When they'd reached the heart of the spider's web, Tyr's master had abandoned him within. *Find your way out*, he had ordered Tyr. *If the goddess takes you, she will guide you. If she does not, you will perish.*

Tyr had never resented his master for leaving him in the darkness. Such was how things must be. Still, his fear had been real and urgent. He had lingered in the airless tunnels for days in a panic. First had come the thirst. Then the hunger. When he tripped over objects in the darkness, objects that clattered and echoed about him, he knew they were bones.

How many apprentices had been sent into the same underground maze? How many had emerged?

Only one in Tyr's generation. Tyr's shamanic line remained pure and strong through the proven ability of its successors, and only a survivor could be instilled with the gifts of the goddess to pass down to the next generation. The fact that Tyr was given this chance meant that every apprentice before him had tried and failed, and died.

Tyr had been so scared then.

He was not scared now.

Now, aboard the ship, the darkness took him once more, just as it had thirty years ago. Tyr was swathed in it, an unborn infant in his mother's womb. To pray to his goddess was to regress to that primordial state before infancy, when the world was quiet. Nothing could see him. Nothing could harm him.

The schooner made its way across the midnight sea, sailing skittishly, like a little child doing something that it shouldn't. The tiny boat wasn't a part of the Nikara fleet. All identifying marks had been clumsily chipped off its hull.

But it sailed from the direction of the Nikara shore. Either the schooner had taken a very long and convoluted route to meet with the *Ryohai* in order to fool an assassin that the *Ryohai* didn't know it had on board, or it was a Nikara vessel.

Tyr crouched behind the masthead, spyglass trained on the schooner's deck.

When he stepped out of the darkness, he experienced a sudden vertigo. This happened more and more often now, whenever he had waited in shadows for too long. It became harder to walk in the world of the material, to detach himself from his goddess.

Careful, he warned himself, *or you won't be able to come back.*

He knew what would happen then. He would become a spouting, unstoppable conduit for the gods, a gate to the spirit realm without a lock. He would be a foaming, useless, seizing vessel, and someone would cart him off to the Chuluu Korikh, where he couldn't do any harm. Someone would register his name in the Wheels and watch him sink into the stone prison the way he'd imprisoned so many of his own subordinates.

He remembered his first visit to the Chuluu Korikh, when he had immured his own master in the mountain. Stood before him, face-to-face, as the stone walls closed around his master's mien: Eyes closed. Sleeping but not dead.

The day would come soon when he would go mad if he left, and madder still if he didn't. But that was the fate that awaited the men and women of the Cike. To be an Empress's assassin meant early death or madness, or both.

Tyr had thought he might still have one or two more decades, as his master had before he'd relinquished the goddess to Tyr. He thought he still had a solid period of time to train an initiate and teach them to walk the void. But he was following his goddess's timeline, and he had no say in when she would ultimately call him back.

I should have chosen an apprentice. I should have chosen one of my people.

Five years ago he'd thought he might choose the Seer of the Cike, that thin child from the Hinterlands. But Chaghan was so frail and bizarre, even for his people. Chaghan would have commanded like a demon. He would have achieved utter obedience from his underlings, but only because he would have taken away their free will. Chaghan would have shattered minds.

Tyr's new lieutenant, the boy sent to him from the Academy, made a far better candidate. The boy was already slated to command the Cike when the time came that Tyr was no longer fit to lead.

But the boy already had a god of his own. And the gods were selfish.

The schooner halted under the *Ryohai*'s shadow. A solitary cloaked figure climbed into a rowboat and crossed the narrow distance between the two ships.

The *Ryohai*'s captain ordered ropes to be lowered. He and half the crew stood on the main deck, waiting for the Nikara contingent to come aboard.

Two deckhands helped the cloaked figure onto the deck.

She pulled the dark hood off her head and shook out a mass of long, shimmering hair. Hair like obsidian. Skin of a mineral whiteness that shone like the moon itself. Lips like freshly spilled blood.

The Empress Su Daji was on this ship.

Tyr was so surprised he nearly stumbled out of the shadows.

Why was she here? His first thought was absurdly petty—did she not trust him to take care of this on his own?

Something had to have gone wrong. Was she here of her own volition? Had the Federation compelled her to come?

Or had his own orders changed?

Tyr's mind raced frantically, wondering how to react. He could act now, kill the soldiers before they could hurt the Empress. But Daji knew he was here—she would have signaled him if she wanted the Federation men dead.

He was to wait, then—wait and watch what Daji's play was.

"Your Highness." General Gin Seiryu was a massive soldier, a giant among men. He towered over the Empress. "You have been long in coming. The Emperor Ryohai grows impatient with you."

"I am not Ryohai's dog to command." Daji's voice resounded across the ship—cool and clear as ice, sharp as knives.

A circle of soldiers formed around Daji, closing her in with the general. But Daji stood tall, chin raised, betraying no fear.

"But you *will* be summoned," the general said harshly. "The Emperor Ryohai grows irritated with your dallying. Your advantages are dwindling. You hold precious few cards, and this you know. You should be glad the Emperor has deigned to speak to you at all."

Daji's lip curled. "His Excellency is certainly gracious."

"Enough of this banter. Speak your piece."

"All in due time," Daji said calmly. "But first, another matter to attend to."

And she looked directly into the shadows where Tyr stood. "Good. You're here."

Tyr took that for his signal.

Knives raised, he rushed from the shadows—only to stumble to his knees as Daji arrested him with her gaze.

He choked, unable to speak. His limbs were numb, frozen; it was all he could do to remain upright. Daji had the power of hypnosis, he knew, but never had she used it on *him*.

All thoughts were pushed from his mind. All he could think about were her eyes. They were at first large, luminous and black; and then they were yellow like a snake's, with narrow pupils that drew him in like a mother grasping at her baby, like a cruel imitation of his own goddess.

And like his goddess, she was so beautiful. So very beautiful.

Transfixed, Tyr lowered his knives.

Visions danced before him. Her great yellow eyes pulsed in his gaze; suddenly gigantic, they filled his entire field of sight to the periphery, drew him into her world.

He saw shapes without names. He saw colors beyond description. He saw faceless women dancing through vermilion and cobalt, bodies curved like the silk ribbons they spun in their hands. Then, as her prey was entranced, the Vipress slammed down into him with her fangs and flooded him with poison.

The psychospiritual assault was devastating and immediate.

She shattered Tyr's world like glass, like he existed in a mirror and she had dashed it against a sharp corner, and he was arrested in the moment of breaking so that it was not over in seconds but took place over eons. Somewhere a shriek began and grew higher and higher in pitch, and did not stop. The Vipress's eyes turned a colorless white that bored into his vision and turned everything into pain. Tyr sought refuge in the shadows, but his goddess was nowhere, and those hypnotic eyes were everywhere. Everywhere he turned, the eyes looked upon him; the great Snake hissed, her gaze trained on him, boring into him, paralyzing him—

Tyr called out for his goddess again, but still she was silent, she had been driven away by a power that was infinitely stronger than darkness itself.

Su Daji had channeled something older than the Empire. Something as old as time.

Tyr's world ceased to spin. He and the Empress drifted alone together in the eye of the hurricane of colors, stabilized only by her generosity. He took a form again, and so did she; no longer a viper but a goddess in the shape of Su Daji, the woman.

"Do not resent me for this. There are forces at play you could not possibly understand, against which your life is irrelevant." Although she appeared mortal, her voice came from everywhere, originated within him, vibrated in his bones. It was the only thing that existed, until she relented and let him speak.

"Why are you doing this?" Tyr whispered.

"Prey do not question the motives of the predator," hissed the thing that was not Su Daji. "The dead do not question the living. Mortals do not challenge the gods."

"I killed for you," Tyr said. "I would have done anything for you."

"I know," she said, and stroked his face. She spoke with a casual sorrow, and for an instant she sounded like the Empress again. The colors dimmed. "You were fools."

She pushed him off the ship.

The pain of drowning, Tyr realized, came in the struggle. But he could not struggle. He was every part of him paralyzed, unable to blink even to shut his eyes against the stinging assault of salt water.

Tyr could do nothing then but die.

He sank back into the darkness. Back into the deep, where sounds could not be heard, sights could not be seen, where nothing could be felt, where nothing lived.

Back into the soft stillness of the womb.

Back to his mother. Back to his goddess.

The death of a shaman did not go unnoticed in the world of spirit. The shattering of Tyr sent a psychospiritual shock wave across the realm of things unknown.

It was felt far away in the peaks of the Wudang Mountains, where the Night Castle stood hidden from the world. It was felt by the Seer of the Bizarre Children, the lost son of the last true khan of the Hinterlands.

The pale Seer traversed the spirit plane as easily as passing through a door, and when he looked for his commander he saw only darkness and the shattered outline of what had once been human. He saw, on the horizon of things yet to come, a land covered in smoke and fire. He saw a battalion of ships crossing the narrow strait. He saw the beginning of a war.

"What do you see?" asked Altan Trengsin.

The white-haired Seer tilted his head to the sky, exposing long, jagged scars running down the sides of his pale neck. He uttered a harsh, cackling laugh.

"He's gone," he said. "He's really gone."

Altan's fingers tightened on the Seer's shoulder.

The Seer's eyes flew open. Behind thin eyelids there was nothing but white. No pupils, no irises, no spot of color. Only a pale mountain landscape, like freshly fallen snow, like nothingness itself. "There has been a Hexagram."

"*Tell me*," Altan said.

The Seer turned to face him. "I see the truth of three things. One: we stand on the verge of war."

"This we've known," Altan said, but the Seer cut him off.

"Two: we have an enemy whom we love."

Altan stiffened.

"Three: Tyr is lost."

Altan swallowed hard. "What does that mean?"

The Seer took his hand. Brought it to his lips and kissed it.

"I have seen the end of things," he said. "The shape of the world has changed. The gods now walk in men as they have not for a long, long time. Tyr will not return. The Bizarre Children answer to you now, and you alone."

Altan exhaled slowly. He felt a tremendous sense of both grief and relief. He had no commander. No. He *was* the commander.

Tyr cannot stop me now, he thought.

Tyr's death was felt by the Gatekeeper himself, who had lingered all these years, not quite dead but not quite alive, ensconced in the shell of a mortal but not mortal himself.

The Gatekeeper was broken and confused, and he had forgotten much of who he was, but one thing he would never forget was the stain of the Vipress's venom.

The Gatekeeper felt her ancient power dissipate into the void that both separated them and brought them together. And he raised his head to the sky and knew that an enemy had returned.

It was felt by the young apprentice at Sinegard who meditated alone when her classmates slept. Who frowned at the disturbance she felt acutely but did not understand.

Who wondered, as she constantly did, what would happen if she disobeyed her master, swallowed the poppy seed, and traversed to commune again with the gods.

If she did more than commune. If she pulled one back down with her.

For although she was forbidden from calling the Phoenix, that did not stop the Phoenix from calling upon her.

Soon, whispered the Phoenix in her sleep. *Soon you will call on me for my power, and when the time comes, you will not be able to resist. Soon you will ignore the warnings of the Woman and the Gatekeeper and fall into my fiery embrace.*

I can make you great. I can make you a legend.

228   R. F. KUANG

She tried to resist.

She tried to empty her mind, like Jiang had taught her; she tried to clear the anger and the fire from her head.

She found that she couldn't.

She found that she didn't want to.

On the first day of the seventh month, another border skirmish erupted, between the Eighteenth Battalion of the Federation Armed Forces and the Nikara patrol in Horse Province bordering the Hinterlands to the north. After six hours of combat, the parties reached a cease-fire. They passed the night in an uneasy truce.

On the second day, a Federation soldier did not report for morning patrol. After a thorough search of the camp, the Federation general at the border city of Muriden demanded the Nikara general open the gates of his camp to be searched.

The Nikara general refused.

On the third day, Emperor Ryohai of the Federation of Mugen issued by courier pigeon a formal demand to the Empress Su Daji for the return of his soldier at Muriden.

The Empress called the Twelve Warlords to her throne at Sinegard and deliberated for seventy-two hours.

On the sixth day, the Empress formally replied that Ryohai could go fuck himself.

On the seventh day, the Federation of Mugen declared war on the Empire of Nikan. Across the longbow island, women wept tears of joy and purchased likenesses of Emperor Ryohai to hang in their homes, men enlisted to serve in the reserve forces, and children ran in the streets screaming with the celebratory bloodlust of a nation at war.

On the eighth day, a battalion of Federation soldiers landed at the port of Muriden and decimated the city. When resisted by province Militia, they ordered that all the males in Muriden, children and babies included, be rounded up and shot.

The women were spared only by the Federation army's haste to move inland. The battalion looted the villages as it went, seized grain and transport animals for their own. What they could not take with them, they killed. They needed no supply lines. They took from the land as they traveled. They marched across the heartland on a warpath to the capital.

On the thirteenth day, a courier eagle reached the office of Jima Lain at the Academy. It read simply:

Horse Province has fallen. Mugen comes for Sinegard.

"It's sort of exciting, really," Kitay said.

"Yes," said Rin. "We're about to be invaded by our centuries-old enemy after they breached a peace treaty that has maintained a fragile geopolitical stability for two decades. So very exciting."

"At least now we know we have job security," said Kitay. "Everyone wants more soldiers."

"Could you be a little less glib about this?"

"Could you be less depressing?"

"Could we move a bit faster?" asked the magistrate.

Rin and Kitay glanced at each other.

Both of them would rather have been doing anything other than aiding the civilian evacuation effort. Since Sinegard was too far north for comfort, the Empire's bureaucracy was moving to a wartime capital in the city of Golyn Niis to the south.

By the time the Federation battalion arrived, Sinegard would be nothing but a ghost city. A city of soldiers. In theory, this meant that Rin and Kitay had the incredibly important job of ensuring that the central leadership of the Empire survived even if the capital didn't.

In practice, this meant dealing with very fat, very annoying city bureaucrats.

Kitay tried to hoist the last crate up into the wagon and promptly staggered under the weight. "What's in this?" he demanded, wobbling as he tried to balance the crate on his hip.

Rin hastily reached down and helped Kitay ease the crate up onto the wagon, which was already teetering from the weight of the magistrate's many possessions.

"My teapots," said the magistrate. "See how I marked the side? Careful not to let it tilt."

"Your teapots," Kitay repeated incredulously. "Your *teapots* are a priority right now."

"They *were* a gift to my father from the Dragon Emperor, may his soul rest in peace." The magistrate surveyed the top-heavy wagon. "Oh, that reminds me—don't forget the vase on the patio."

He looked imploringly at Rin.

She was dazed from the afternoon heat, exhausted from hours of packing the magistrate's entire estate into several ill-prepared moving vehicles. She noticed in her stupor that the magistrate's jowls quivered hilariously when he spoke. Under different circumstances she might have pointed that out to Kitay. Under different circumstances, Kitay might have laughed.

The magistrate gestured again to the vase. "Be careful with that, will you? It's as old as the Red Emperor. You might want to strap it down to the back of the wagon."

Rin stared at him in disbelief.

"Sir?" Kitay asked.

The magistrate turned to look at him. "What?"

With a grunt, Kitay raised the crate over his head and flung it to the ground. It landed on the dirt with a hard thud, not the tremendous crash Rin had rather been hoping for. The wooden lid of the crate popped off. Out rolled several very nice porcelain teapots, glazed with a lovely flower pattern. Despite their tumble, they looked unbroken.

Then Kitay took to them with a slab of wood.

When he was done smashing them, he pushed his wiry curls out of his face and whirled on the sweating magistrate, who cringed in his seat as if afraid Kitay might start smashing at him, too.

"We are at *war*," Kitay said. "And you are being evacuated because for *gods know what reason*, you've been deemed important to this country's survival. So do your job. Reassure your people. Help us maintain order. *Do not pack your fucking teapots.*"

* * *

Within days, the Academy was transformed from a campus to a military encampment. The grounds were overrun with green-clad soldiers from the Eighth Division of the nearby Ram Province, and the students were absorbed into their number.

The Militia soldiers were a stoic, curt crowd. They took on the Academy students begrudgingly, all the while making it very clear that they thought the students had no place in the war.

"It's a superiority issue," Kitay speculated later. "Most of the soldiers were never at Sinegard. It's like being told to work with someone who in three years would have been your superior officer, even though you have a decade of combat experience on them."

"They don't have combat experience, either," said Rin. "We've fought no wars in the last two decades. They know less of what they're doing than we do."

Kitay couldn't argue with that.

At least the arrival of the Eighth Division meant the return of Raban, who was tasked with evacuating the first-year students out of the city, along with the civilians.

"But I want to fight!" protested a student who barely came up to Rin's shoulder.

"Fat lot of good you'll do," Raban answered.

The first-year stuck out his chin. "Sinegard is my home. I'll defend it. I'm not a little kid, I don't have to be herded out like all those terrified women and children."

"You *are* defending Sinegard. You're protecting its inhabitants. All those women and children? You're in charge of their safety. Your job is to make sure they get to the mountain pass. That's quite a serious task." Raban caught Rin's eye as he shepherded the first-years out of the main gate.

"I'm scared some of the younger ones are going to sneak back in," he told her quietly.

"You've got to admire them," said Rin. "Their city's about to be invaded and their first thought is to defend it."

"They're being stupid," said Raban. He spoke with none of

his usual patience. He looked exhausted. "This is not the time for heroism. This is war. If they stay, they're dead."

Escape plans were made for the students. In case the city fell, they were to flee down the little-known ravine on the other side of the valley to join the rest of the civilians in a mountain hideout where they couldn't be reached by the Federation battalions. This plan did not include the masters.

"Jima doesn't think we can win," said Kitay. "She and the faculty are going to go down with the school."

"Jima's just being cautious," said Raban, trying to lift their spirits. "Sunzi said to plan for every contingency, right?"

"Sunzi also said that when you cross a river, you should burn the bridges so that your army can't entertain thoughts of retreating," said Kitay. "This sounds a lot like retreating to me."

"Prudence is different from cowardice," said Raban. "And besides, Sunzi also wrote that you should never attack a cornered foe. They'll fight harder than any man thinks possible. Because a cornered enemy has nothing to lose."

The days seemed to both stretch for an eternity and disappear before anything could get done. Rin had the uncomfortable sense that they were just waiting around for the enemy to land on their front porch. At the same time she felt frantically underprepared, as if battle preparations were not being done quickly enough.

"I wonder what a Federation soldier looks like," Kitay said as they descended the mountain to pick up sharpened weapons from the armory.

"They have arms and legs, I'm guessing. Maybe even a head."

"No, I mean, what do they *look* like?" Kitay asked. "Like Nikara? All of the Federation came from the eastern continent. They're not like Hesperians, so they must look *somewhat* normal."

Rin couldn't see why this was relevant. "Does it matter?"

"Don't you want to see the face of the enemy?" Kitay asked.

"No, I don't," she said. "Because then I might think they're human. And they're not human. We're talking about the people who gave opium to toddlers the last time they invaded. The people who massacred Speer."

"Maybe they're more human than we realize," said Kitay. "Has anyone ever stopped to ask what the Federation want? Why is it that they must fight us?"

"Because they're crammed on that tiny island and they think Nikan should be *theirs*. Because they fought us before and they almost won," Rin said curtly. "What does it matter? They're coming, and we're staying, and at the end of the day whoever is alive is the side that wins. War doesn't determine who's right. War determines who remains."

All classes at Sinegard ceased to meet. The masters resumed positions they had retired from decades ago. Irjah took over strategic command of the Sinegardian Reserve Forces. Enro and her apprentices returned to the city's central hospital to set up a triage center. Jima assumed martial command over the city, a position she shared with the Ram Warlord. This involved, in parts, shouting at city officials and at obstinate squadron leaders.

The outlook was grim. The Eighth Division was three thousand men strong, hardly enough to take on the reported invading force of ten thousand. The Ram Warlord had sent for reinforcements from the Third Division, which was returning from patrol up north by the Hinterlands, but the Third was unlikely to arrive before the Federation did.

Jiang was rarely available. He was always either in Jima's office going over contingency plans with Irjah, or not on campus at all. When Rin finally managed to track him down, he seemed harried and impatient. She had to run to keep up with him on his way down the steps.

"We're putting lessons on hiatus," he said. "I'm sure you've noticed there's no time for that now. I can't devote the time to train you properly."

He made to brush past her, but she grabbed his sleeve. "Master,

I wanted to ask—what if we called the gods? I mean, against the Federation?"

"What are you *talking* about?" He seemed faintly aghast. "Now is hardly the time for this."

"Surely there are battle applications to what we've been studying," she pressed.

"We've been studying how to consult the gods," he said. "Not how to bring them back down to earth."

"But they could help us fight!"

"What? No. *No*." He flapped his hands, growing visibly agitated as he spoke. "Have you not listened to a word I've said these past two years? I *told* you, the gods are not weapons you can just dust off and use. The gods won't be summoned into battle."

"That's not true," she said. "I've read the reports from the Red Emperor's crusades. I know the monks summoned gods against him. And the tribes of the Hinterlands—"

"The Hinterlanders consult the gods for healing. They seek guidance and enlightenment," Jiang interrupted. "They do not call the gods down onto earth, because they know better. Every war we've fought with the aid of the gods, we've won at a terrible consequence. There is a price. There is always a price."

"Then what's the *point*?" she snapped. "Why learn Lore at all?"

His expression then was terrible. He looked as he had that day Sunzi the pig was slaughtered, when she told him she wanted to pledge Strategy. He looked wounded. Betrayed.

"The point of every lesson does not have to be to destroy," he said. "I taught you Lore to help you find balance. I taught you so that you would understand how the universe is more than what we perceive. I didn't teach you so that you could weaponize it."

"The gods—"

"The gods will not be used at our beck and call. The gods are so far out of our realm of understanding that any attempt to weaponize them can only end in disaster."

"What about the Phoenix?"

Jiang stopped walking. "Oh, no. Oh, no, no, no."

"The god of the Speerlies," said Rin. "Each time it has been called, it has answered. If we could just . . ."

Jiang looked pained. "You know what happened to the Speerlies."

"But they were channeling fire long before the Second Poppy War! They practiced shamanism for centuries! The *power*—"

"The power would consume you," Jiang said harshly. "That's what fire *does*. Why do you think the Speerlies never won back their freedom? You'd think a race like that wouldn't have remained subordinate for long. They would have conquered all of Nikan, if their power were sustainable. How come they never revolted against the Empire? The fire *killed* them, Rin, just as it empowered them. It drove them mad, it robbed them of their ability to think for themselves, until all they knew to do was fight and destroy as they had been ordered. The Speerlies were obsessed with their own power, and as long as the Emperor gave them free license to run rampant with their bloodlust, there was very little they cared about. The Speerlies were collectively deluded. They called the fire, yes, but they are hardly worth emulating. The Red Emperor was cruel and ruthless, but even he had the good sense never to train shamans in his Militia, outside of the Speerlies. Treating the gods as weapons only ever spells death."

"We're at *war*! We might die anyway. So maybe calling the gods gives us a fighting chance. What's the worst that could happen?"

"You're so young," he said softly. "You have no idea."

After that, Rin saw neither hide nor hair of Jiang on campus at all. Rin knew he was deliberately avoiding her, as he had before her Trials, as he did whenever he didn't want to have a conversation. She found this incredibly frustrating.

You're so young.

That was even more frustrating.

She wasn't so young that she didn't know her country was at war. Not so young that she hadn't been tasked to defend it.

Children ceased to be children when you put a sword in their hands. When you taught them to fight a war, then you armed them and put them on the front lines, they were not children anymore. They were soldiers.

Sinegard's time was running out. Scouts reported daily that the Federation force was almost on their doorstep.

Rin couldn't sleep, though she desperately needed to. Each time she closed her eyes, anxiety crushed her like an avalanche. During the day her head swam with exhaustion and her eyes burned, yet she could not calm herself enough to rest. She tried meditating, but terror plagued her mind; her heart raced and her breath contracted with fear.

At night, when she lay alone in the darkness, she heard over and over the call of the Phoenix. It plagued her dreams, whispered seductively to her from the other realm. The temptation was so great that it nearly drove her mad.

I will keep you sane, Jiang had promised.

But he had not kept her sane. He had shown her a great power, a tantalizingly wonderful power strong enough to protect her city and country, and then he had forbidden her from accessing it.

Rin obeyed, because he was her master, and the allegiance between master and apprentice still meant something, even in times of war.

But that didn't stop her from going into his garden when she knew he was not on campus, and shoving several handfuls of poppy seeds in her front pocket.

CHAPTER 11

When the main column of the Federation Armed Forces marched on Sinegard, they did not attempt to conceal their arrival. They did not need to. Sinegard knew already that they were coming, and the terror the Federation inflicted gave them a far greater strategic advantage than the element of surprise. They advanced in three columns, marching from every direction but the west, where Sinegard was backed by the Wudang Mountains. They forged forward with massive crimson banners flying overhead, illuminated by raised torches.

For Ryohai, the banners read. *For the Emperor.*

In his *Principles of War*, the great military theorist Sunzi had warned against attacking an enemy that occupied the higher ground. The target above held the advantage of surveillance and would not need to tire out their troops by climbing uphill.

The Federation invasion strategy was a giant *fuck you* to Sunzi.

To storm Sinegard from higher ground would have required a detour up the Wudang Mountains, which would have delayed the Federation assault by almost an entire week. The Federation would not give Sinegard a week. The Federation had the weapons and the numbers to take Sinegard from below.

From her vantage point high on the southern city wall, Rin watched the Federation force approach like a great fiery snake winding its way through the valley, encircling Sinegard to crush and swallow it. She saw it coming, and she trembled.

I want to hide. I want someone to tell me I'm going to be safe, that this is just a joke, a bad dream.

In that moment she realized that all this time she had been playing at being a soldier, playing at bravery.

But now, on the eve of the battle, she could not pretend anymore.

Fear bubbled in the back of her throat, so thick and tangible that she almost choked on it. Fear made her fingers tremble violently so that she almost dropped her sword. Fear made her forget how to breathe. She had to force air into her lungs, close her eyes, and count to herself as she inhaled and exhaled. Fear made her dizzy and nauseated, made her want to vomit over the side of the wall.

It's just a physiological reaction, she told herself. *It's just in your mind. You can control it. You can make it go away.*

They had gone over this in training. They had been warned about this feeling. They were taught to control their fear, turn it to their advantage; use their adrenaline to remain alert, to ward off fatigue.

But a few days of training could not negate what her body instinctively felt, which was the imminent truth that she was going to bleed, she was going to hurt, and she was most likely going to die.

When had she last been this scared? Had she felt this paralysis, this numbing dread before she stepped into the ring with Nezha two years ago? No, she had been angry then, and proud. She had thought she was invincible. She had been looking forward to the fight, anticipating the bloodlust.

That felt stupid now. *So,* so stupid. War was not a game, where one fought for honor and admiration, where masters would keep her from sustaining any real harm.

War was a nightmare.

She wanted to cry. She wanted to scream and hide behind some-one, behind one of the soldiers, wanted to whimper, *I am scared, I want to wake up from this dream, please save me.*

But no one was coming for her. No one was going to save her. There was no waking up.

"Are you all right?" Kitay asked.

"No," she said, trembling. Her voice was a frightened squeak. "I'm scared. Kitay, we're going to die."

"No, we're not," Kitay said fiercely. "We're going to win, and we are going to *live.*"

"You've done the math, too." They were outnumbered three to one. "Victory is not possible."

"You have to believe it is." Kitay's fingers were clenched so tightly around his sword hilt that they had turned white. "The Third will get here in time. You have to tell yourself that's true."

Rin swallowed hard and nodded. *You were not trained to snivel and cower*, she told herself. The girl from Tikany, the es-caped bride who had never seen a city, would have been scared. The girl from Tikany was gone. She was a third-year apprentice of the Academy at Sinegard, she was a soldier of the Eighth Division, and she was trained to fight.

And she was not alone. She had poppy seeds in her pocket. She had a god on her side.

"Tell me when," Kitay said. He was poised with his sword over the rope that constrained a booby trap they had set to defend the outer perimeter. Kitay had designed this trap; he would unleash it just as soon as the enemy was within range.

They were so close she could see the firelight flickering over their faces.

Kitay's hand trembled.

"Not yet," she whispered.

The first of the Federation battalion crossed the boundary.

"Now."

Kitay slashed at the rope.

A rolling avalanche of logs was freed from its breaking point, pulled down by gravity to bowl straight through the main advancing force. The logs rolled chaotically, shattered limbs and crushed bone with a noise like thunder that went on and on. For a moment the rumbling of carnage was so great Rin thought they might have won the battle before it started, might have seriously crippled the advancing force. Kitay whooped hysterically over the clamor, clutching Rin to keep from falling over as the gates themselves shook.

But when the roar of the logs died down, the invaders continued to advance into Sinegard to the steady beat of war drums.

A tier above Rin and Kitay, standing at the highest precipices of the South Gate, the archers loosed a round of arrows. Most clattered uselessly against raised shields. Some found their way through the cracks, embedded their heads in the unguarded fleshy parts of soldiers' necks. But the heavily armored Federation soldiers simply marched over the bodies of their fallen comrades, continuing their relentless assault toward the city gates.

The squadron leader shouted for another round of arrows.

It was close to pointless. There were far more soldiers than there were arrows. Sinegard's outer defense was flimsy at best. Each of Kitay's booby traps had been sprung, and though all but one went off beautifully, they were not enough to even dent the enemy ranks.

There was nothing to do but wait. Wait until the gate was broken, until there was a tremendous crash. Then the signal gongs were ringing, screaming to all who didn't already know that the Federation had breached the walls. The Federation was in Sinegard.

They marched to the cacophony of cannon fire and rockets, bombarding Sinegard's outer defenses with their siege breakers.

The gate buckled and broke under the strain.

They poured through like a swarm of ants, like a cloud of hornets; unstoppable and infinite, overwhelming in number.

We can't win. Rin stood in a daze of despair, sword hanging by her side. What difference would it make if she fought back? It might stay her death sentence by a few seconds, maybe minutes, but at the end of the night she would be dead, her body broken and bloody on the ground, and nothing would matter . . .

This battle wasn't like the ones in the legends, where numbers didn't matter, where a handful of warriors like the Trifecta could flatten an entire legion. It didn't matter how good their techniques were, it mattered how the numbers balanced.

And the Sinegardians were so badly outnumbered.

Rin's heart sank as she watched the armored troops advance into the city, rows and columns stretching into infinity.

I'm going to die here, she realized. *They're going to slaughter all of us.*

"*Rin!*"

Kitay shoved her hard; she stumbled against stones as an axe embedded itself in the wall where her head had been.

Its wielder jerked the axe out of the wall and swung it again toward them, but this time Rin blocked it with her sword. The impact sent adrenaline coursing through her blood.

Fear was impossible to eradicate. But so was the will to survive.

Rin ducked under the soldier's arm and jammed her sword up through the soft groove beneath his chin, unprotected by the helmet. She cut through fat and sinew, felt the tip of her sword pierce directly through his tongue and move up past his nose to where his brain was. His carotid artery exploded over the length of steel. Blood wet her hand to the elbow. He jerked a little and fell toward her.

He's dead, she thought numbly. *I've killed him.*

For all her combat training, Rin had never thought about what it would be like to actually take someone's life. To sever an artery, not just feign doing so. To break a body so badly that all functions ceased, that the animation was stilled forever.

They were taught to incapacitate at the Academy. They were trained to fight against their friends. They operated within the masters' strict rules, monitored closely to avoid injury. For all their talk and theory, they had not been trained to truly kill.

Rin thought she might feel the life leave her victim's body. She thought she might register his death with thoughts more significant than *One down, ten thousand to go.* She thought she'd feel *something.*

She registered nothing. Just a temporary shock, then the grim realization that she needed do this again, and again, and again.

She extricated her weapon from the soldier's jaw just as another swung a sword over her head. She rammed her sword up, blocked the blow. And parried. And thrust. And spilled blood again.

It wasn't any easier the second time.

It seemed as if the world were filled with Federation soldiers. They all looked the same—identical helmets, identical armor. *Cut one down and here comes another.*

Within the melee Rin didn't have time to think. She fought by reflex. Every action demanded a reaction. She couldn't see Kitay anymore; he had disappeared into the sea of bodies, an ocean of clashing metal and torches.

Fighting the Federation was wholly different from fighting in the ring. She didn't have melee practice. The enemy came from every angle, not just one, and defeating one opponent didn't bring you any closer to winning the battle.

The Federation did not have martial arts. Their movements were blocky, studied. Their patterns were predictable. But they had practice with formations, with group combat. They moved as if they had a hive mind; coordinated actions produced by years of drilling. They were better trained. They were better equipped.

The Federation didn't fight a graceful fight. They fought a brutal one. And they didn't fear death. If they were hurt, they fell, and their comrades advanced over their dead bodies. They were relentless. There were *so many of them.*

I am going to die.

Unless. Unless.

The poppy seeds in her pocket screamed for her to swallow them. She could take them now. She could go to the Pantheon and call a god down. What did Jiang's warnings matter, when they were all going to die regardless?

She had seen the face of the Phoenix. She knew what power was at her fingertips, if only she asked.

I can make you fearless. I can make you a legend.

She did not want to be a legend, but she wanted to stay alive. She wanted more than anything to live, consequences be damned, and if calling the Phoenix would do that for her, then so be it. Jiang's warning meant nothing to her now, not while her countrymen and classmates were hacked to pieces beside her, not while she didn't know if each second was going to be her last. If she was going to die, she would not die like this—small, weak, and helpless.

She had a link to a god.

She would die a shaman.

Heart hammering, she ducked behind a gated corner; for the few seconds in which nobody saw her, she jammed her hand into her pocket and dug the seeds out. She brought them to her mouth.

She hesitated.

If she swallowed the seeds but it didn't work, she would certainly die. She could not fight drugged, dazed, and hallucinating.

A horn blasted through the air. She jerked her head up. It was a distress signal, coming from the East Gate.

But the South Gate had no troops to spare. Everywhere was a crisis zone. They were outnumbered three to one; if they lost half their troops to the East Gate, then they may as well let the Federation stroll into the city unchecked.

But Rin's squadron had been ordered to rally if they heard the distress call. She froze, uncertain, seeds uneaten in her palm. Well, she couldn't swallow them *now*—the drug needed time to take effect, and then she would be in limbo indefinitely while she probed her way to the Pantheon. And even if she could still her thoughts long enough to call the gods, she didn't know that they would answer.

Should she stay here, hidden, and try to call a god, or should she go to the aid of her comrades?

"Go!" Her squadron leader shouted to her over the din of battle. "Go to the gate!"

She ran.

The South Gate had been a melee. But the East Gate was a slaughter zone.

The Nikara soldiers were down. Rin raced toward their posts, but her hope died the closer she got. She couldn't see anyone in Nikara armor still fighting. The Federation soldiers were just pouring through the gate, completely unopposed.

It was obvious now that the Federation forces had made the East Gate their main target. They had stationed three times as many troops there, had set up sophisticated siege weaponry outside the city walls. Trebuchets launched flaming pieces of debris into the unresponsive sentry towers.

She saw Niang slumped in a corner, crouched over a limp body in a Militia uniform. As Rin passed, Niang lifted her face, streaked with tears and blood. The body was Raban's.

Rin felt as if she'd been stabbed in the gut. *No—not Raban, no . . .*

Something slammed against her back. She whipped around. Two Federation soldiers had crept up behind her. The first raised his sword again and slashed down. She ducked around the path of his blade and lashed out with her sword.

Metal met sinew. She was blinded by the blood streaming into her eyes; she couldn't see what she was cutting, only felt a great tension and then release, and then the Federation soldier was at her knees howling in pain.

She stabbed downward without thinking. The howling stopped.

Then his comrade slammed his shield into her sword arm. Rin cried out and dropped her sword. The soldier kicked it away and smashed his shield at Rin's rib cage, then pulled his sword back to deliver the finishing blow while she was down.

His sword arm faltered, then dropped. The soldier made a startled gurgling noise as he stared in disbelief at the blade protruding from his stomach.

He fell forward and lay still.

Nezha met Rin's eyes, and then wrenched his sword out of the soldier's back. With his other hand he flung a spare weapon at her.

She pulled it from the air. Her fingers closed with familiarity around the hilt. A wave of relief shot through her. She had a weapon.

"Thanks," she said.

"On your left," he responded.

Without thinking they sank into a formation; back to back, fighting while covering each other's blind spots. They made a startlingly good team. Rin covered for Nezha's overstretched attacks; Nezha guarded Rin's lower corners. They were each intimately familiar with the other's weaknesses: Rin knew Nezha was slow to bring his guard back up after missed blows; Nezha parried from above while Rin ducked in low for close-quarters attacks.

It wasn't as if she could read his mind. She had simply spent so much time observing him that she knew exactly how he was going to attack. They were like a well-oiled machine. They were a spontaneously coordinated dance. They weren't two parts of a whole, not quite, but they came close.

If they hadn't spent so much time hating each other, Rin thought, they might have trained together.

Backs to each other, swords at the enemy, they fought with savage desperation. They fought better than men twice their age. They drew on each other's strengths; as long as Nezha was fighting, wasn't flagging, Rin didn't feel fatigued, either. Because she wasn't just fighting to keep herself alive now, she was fighting with a partner. They fought so well that they half-convinced themselves they might emerge intact. The onslaught was, in fact, thinning.

"They're retreating," Nezha said in disbelief.

Rin's chest flooded with hope for one short, blissful moment, until she realized that Nezha was wrong. The soldiers weren't backing away from them. They were making way for their general.

The general stood a head taller than the tallest man Rin had ever seen. His limbs were like tree trunks, his armor made of enough metal to coat three smaller men. He sat astride a warhorse as massive as he was; a monstrous creature, decked in steel. His face was hidden behind a metal helmet that covered all but his eyes.

"What is this?" His voice sounded with an unnatural reverberation, as if the very ground shook when he spoke. "Why have you stopped? "

He brought his warhorse to a halt before Rin and Nezha.

"Two puppies," he said, his voice low in amusement. "Two Nikara puppies, holding an entire gate by themselves. Has Sinegard fallen so low that the city must be defended by children?"

Nezha was trembling. Rin was too scared to tremble.

"Watch closely," the general said to his soldiers. "This is how we deal with Nikara scum."

Rin reached out and grasped Nezha's wrist.

Nezha nodded curtly in response to her unspoken question.

Together?

Together.

The general reared his monstrous horse back and charged them.

There was nothing they could do now. In that moment, Rin could only squeeze her eyes shut and wait for the end.

It didn't come.

A deafening *clang* shattered the air—the sound of metal against metal. The air itself shook with the unnatural vibration of a great force stopped in its tracks.

When Rin realized she hadn't been cut in half or trampled to death, she opened her eyes.

"What the fuck," Nezha said.

Jiang stood before them, his white hair hanging still in the air as if he had been struck by lightning. His feet did not touch the ground. Both his arms were flung out, blocking the tremendous force of the general's halberd with his own iron staff.

The general tried to force Jiang's staff out of the way, and his arms trembled with a mighty pressure, but Jiang did not look like he was exerting any force at all. The air crackled unnaturally, like a prolonged rumble of thunder. The Federation soldiers fell back, as if they could sense an impending explosion.

"Jiang Ziya," said the general. "So you live after all."

"Do I know you?" Jiang asked.

The general responded with another massive swing of his halberd. Jiang waved his staff and blocked the blow as effortlessly as if he were swatting away a fly. He dispelled the force of the blow into the air and the ground below them. The paving stones shuddered from the impact, nearly knocking Rin and Nezha off their feet.

"Call off your men."

Though Jiang spoke calmly, his voice echoed as if he had shouted. He appeared to have grown taller; not larger, but extended somehow, just as his shadow was extended against the wall behind them. No longer willowy and fidgety, Jiang seemed an entirely different person—someone younger, someone infinitely more powerful.

Rin stared at him in awe. The man before her was not the doddering, eccentric embarrassment of the Academy. This man was a soldier.

This man was a shaman.

When Jiang spoke again, his voice contained the echo of itself; he spoke in two pitches, one normal and one far lower, as if his shadow shouted back everything he said at double the volume. "Call off your men, or I will summon into existence things that should not be in this world."

Nezha grabbed at Rin's arm. His eyes were wide. "*Look.*"

The air behind Jiang was warping, shimmering, turning darker than the night itself. Jiang's eyes had rolled up into the back of his head. He chanted loudly, singing in that unfamiliar language that Rin had heard him use only once before.

"You are *Sealed*!" the general bellowed. But he backed rapidly away from the void and clutched his halberd close.

"Am I now?" Jiang spread his arms.

Behind him sounded a keening wail, too high-pitched for any beast known to man.

Something was coming through the darkness.

Beyond the void, Rin saw silhouettes that should exist only in puppetry, outlines of beasts that belonged to story. A three-headed lion. A nine-tailed vixen. A mass of serpents tangled into one another, its multitude of heads snapping and biting in every direction.

"Rin. Nezha." Jiang didn't turn around to look at them. "*Run*."

Then Rin understood. Whatever was being summoned, Jiang couldn't control them. *The gods will not be called willingly into battle. The gods will always demand something in return.* He was doing precisely what he had forbidden her to do.

Nezha pulled Rin to her feet. Her left leg felt as if white-hot knives had been jammed into her kneecap. She cried out and staggered against him.

He steadied her. His eyes were wide with terror. There was no time to run.

Jiang convulsed in the air before them, and then lost control altogether. The void burst outward, ripping the fabric of the world, collapsing the gated wall around them. He slammed his staff into the air. A wave of force emitted from the site of contact and exploded outward in a visible ring. For a moment everything was still.

And then the east wall came down.

Rin moaned and rolled onto her side. She could barely see, barely feel. None of her senses worked; she was wrapped in a cocoon of darkness penetrated only by shards of pain. Her leg rubbed against something soft and human, and she reached for it. It was Nezha.

She groaned and forced her eyes open. Nezha lay slumped

against her, bleeding profusely from a cut on his forehead. His eyes were closed.

Rin sat up, wincing, and shook his shoulder. "Nezha?"

He stirred faintly. Relief washed over her.

"We have to get up—Nezha, come on, we have to—"

A shower of debris erupted in the far corner by the gate.

Something was buried there under the rubble. Something was alive.

She clung to Nezha's hand and watched the shifting rubble, hoping wildly it would be Jiang, that he would have survived whatever terror he had called and that he was all right, and he would be himself again, and he would save the—

The hand that clawed out from beneath the rubble was bloody, massive, and heavily armored.

Rin should have killed the general before he pulled himself out of the rubble. She should have taken Nezha and run. She should have done *something*.

But her limbs would not obey the commands that her brain sent; her nerves could not register anything but that same fear and despair. She lay paralyzed on the ground, heart slamming against her ribs.

The general staggered to his feet, took one lopsided step forward and then another. His helmet was gone. When he turned toward them, Rin's breath caught. Half of his face had been scraped away in the explosion, revealing an awful skeletal smile underneath peeling skin.

"Nikara *scum*," he snarled as he advanced. His foot caught against the limp form of one of his own soldiers. Without looking, he kicked it aside in disgust. His furious gaze remained fixed on Rin and Nezha. "I will *bury* you."

Nezha gave a low moan of terror.

Rin's arms were finally responding to her commands. She tried to haul Nezha up, but her own legs were weak with fear and she could not stand.

The general loomed over them. He raised his halberd.

Half-crazed with panic, Rin swung her sword upward in a great, wild arc. Her blade clattered uselessly against the general's armored torso.

The general closed his gauntleted fingers around her thin blade and wrenched it out of her hands. His fingers bent grooves into the steel.

Trembling, she let go of her sword. He dragged her up by the collar and flung her at what was left of the wall. Her head cracked against stone; her vision erupted in black, then spots of light, then a fuzzy nothing. She blinked slowly, and whatever vision was restored showed the general raising his halberd slowly over Nezha's limp form.

Rin opened her mouth to scream just as the general jammed the bladed tip into Nezha's stomach. Nezha made a high, keening noise. A second thrust silenced him.

Sobbing with fear, Rin scrabbled in her pocket for the poppy seeds. She seized a handful and brought them to her mouth, choked them down just as the general noticed she was still moving.

"No, you don't," he snarled, hauling her back up by the front of her robes. He dragged her close to his face, leering down at her with his horrific half-smile. "No more of that Nikara witchcraft. Even the gods won't inhabit dead vessels."

Rin shook madly in his grasp, tears leaking down her face as she choked for air. Her head throbbed where he'd slammed it against the stone. She felt as if she were floating, swimming in darkness, whether from the poppy seeds or her head injury, she didn't know. She was either dying or going to see the gods. Maybe both.

Please, she prayed. *Please come to me. I'll do anything.*

Then she tipped forward into the void; she was in that tunnel to the heavens again, spirited upward, hurtling at a tremendous speed to a place unknown. The edges of her vision turned black and then a familiar red, a sheet of crimson that spread across her entire field of vision like a glass lens.

In her mind's eye she saw the Woman appear before her. The Woman reached a hand toward her, but—

"*Get out of my way!*" Rin screamed. She didn't have time for a guardian, she didn't have time for warnings—she needed the gods, she needed *her* god.

To her shock, the Woman obeyed.

And then she was through the barrier, she was hurtling upward again, and she was in the throne room of the gods, the Pantheon.

All the plinths were empty except one.

She saw it then in all of its glorious fire. A great and terrible voice echoed in her mind. It echoed throughout the universe.

I can give you the power you seek.

She struggled wildly to breathe, but the general's grip only tightened around her neck.

I can give you the strength to topple empires. To burn your enemies until their bones are nothing but ash. All this I will give you and more. You know the trade. You know the terms.

"Anything," Rin whispered. "Anything at all."

Everything.

Something like a gust of wind blew through the chamber. She thought she heard something cackling.

Rin opened her eyes. She was not light-headed anymore. She reached up and clasped the general's wrists. She was deathly weak; her grasp should have been like a feather's touch. But the general howled. He dropped her, and when he raised his arms to strike her, she saw that both his wrists were a mottled, bubbling red.

She crouched, raised her elbows over her head to form a pathetic shield.

And a great sheet of flame erupted before her. The heat of it hit her in the face. The general stumbled backward.

"No . . ." His mouth opened wide in disbelief. He looked at her like he was seeing someone else. "Not you."

Rin struggled to her feet. Flames continued to pour out before her, flames she had no control over.

"You're *dead*!" the general shouted. "I killed you!"

She rose slowly, flames streaming from her hands, rivulets that ensconced them, gave no escape. The general howled in pain as the fire licked at his open wounds, the gaping holes on his face, all across his body.

"I watched you burn! I watched you all burn!"

"Not me," she whispered, and opened her hands toward him.

The fire billowed outward with a vengeance. She felt a tearing sensation, as if it were being ripped from her gut, from somewhere inside her. It coursed through her, not harming her but immobilizing her. It used her as a conduit. She controlled the flame no more than the wick of a candle might; it rallied to her and enveloped her.

In her mind's eye she saw the Phoenix, undulating from its plinth in the Pantheon. Watching. Laughing.

She couldn't see the general through the flame, only a silhouette, an outline of armor collapsing and folding in on itself, a kneeling pile of something that was less a man than it was a chunk of charred flesh, carbon, and metal.

"Stop," she whispered. *Please, make it stop.*

But the fire kept burning. The lump that had been the general staggered back and crumpled, a ball of flame that grew smaller and smaller and then was extinguished.

Her lips were dry, cracked; when she moved them, they bled. "Please, stop."

The fire roared louder and louder. She couldn't hear; she couldn't breathe through the heat. She sank to her knees, eyes squeezed shut, grabbing her face with her hands.

I'm begging you.

In her mind's eye she saw the Phoenix recoil, as if irritated. It opened its wings in a huge, fiery expanse and then folded them.

The way to the Pantheon shut.

Rin swayed and fell.

Time ceased to hold meaning. There was a battle around her and then there wasn't. Rin was enveloped in a silo of nothing, insulated from anything that happened around her. Nothing else existed, until it did.

"She's burning," she heard Niang say. "Feverish . . . I checked for poison in her wounds, but there's nothing."

It's not a fever, Rin wanted to say, *it's a god*. The water that Niang dripped on her forehead did nothing to quench the flames still coursing inside her.

She tried to ask for Jiang, but her mouth would not obey. She couldn't speak. She couldn't move.

She thought she could see, but she didn't know if she was dreaming, because when she opened her eyes next she saw a face so lovely she almost cried.

Arched eyebrows, a porcelain smoothness. Lips like blood.

The Empress?

But the Empress was far away, with the Third Division, still marching in from the north. They could not have arrived so soon, before daybreak.

Was it daybreak already? She thought she could see the first rays of the rising sun, the break of dawn on this long, horrible night.

"What do they call her?" the Empress demanded.

"Her"? Is the Empress talking about me?

"Runin." Irjah's voice. "Fang Runin."

"Runin," the Empress repeated. Her voice was like a plucked string on a table harp, sharp and penetrating and beautiful all at once. "Runin, look at me."

Rin felt the Empress's fingers on her cheeks. They were cool, like snow, like a winter breeze. She opened her eyes to the Empress, looked into those lovely eyes. How could anyone possess such beautiful eyes? They were nothing like a viper's eyes. They were not the eyes of a snake; they were wild and dark and strange, but beautiful, like a deer's.

And the *visions* . . . she saw a cloud of butterflies, silk sheets of ribbon fluttering in the wind. She saw a world that consisted only of beauty and color and rhythm. She would have done anything to stay trapped within that gaze.

The Empress inhaled sharply, and the visions fell away.

Her grasp on Rin's face tightened.

"I watched you burn," she said. "I thought I watched you die."

"I'm not dead," Rin tried to say, but her tongue was too heavy in her mouth and all she made was a gagging noise.

"Shhh." The Empress held an icy finger against her lips. "Don't speak. It's all right. I know what you are."

Then there was a cool press of lips against her forehead, the same coolness that Jiang had forced into her during her Trials, and the fire inside her died.

CHAPTER 12

When Rin was released from Enro's supervision, she was moved to the basement of the main hall, where the matches used to be held. She should have found this odd, but she was too dazed to think much about anything. She slept an inordinate amount. There was no clock in the basement, but often she dozed off to find that the sun had gone down. She had trouble staying awake for more than a few minutes. Food was brought to her, and each time she ate, she fell asleep again almost immediately.

Once, as she slept, she heard voices above her.

"This is inelegant," said the Empress.

"This is *inhumane*," said Irjah. "You're treating her like a common criminal. This girl might have won the battle for us."

"And she might yet burn down this city," said Jun. "We don't know what she's capable of."

"She's just a girl," said Irjah. "She'll be scared. Someone needs to tell her what's happening to her."

"We don't *know* what's happening to her," said Jun.

"It's obvious," the Empress said. "She's another Altan."

"So we'll let Tyr deal with her when he's here," said Jun.

"Tyr's coming all the way from the Night Castle," said Irjah. "You're going to keep her sedated for an entire week?"

"I'm certainly not going to let her wander the city," Jun answered. "You *saw* what the Gatekeeper did to the east wall. His Seal is breaking, Daji. He's a bigger threat than the Federation."

"Not anymore," the Empress said coolly. "The Gatekeeper's been dealt with."

When Rin ventured to open her eyes, she saw no one standing over her, and she only half remembered what had been said. After another indefinite spell of dreamless sleep she wasn't sure whether she had imagined the entire thing.

Eventually she came to her senses. But when she tried to leave the basement, she was forcibly restrained by three Third Division soldiers stationed outside the door.

"What's happening?" she demanded. She was still a bit dazed, but conscious enough to know this wasn't normal. "Why can't I go?"

"It's for your safety," one of them responded.

"What are you talking about? Who authorized this?"

"Our orders are to keep you here," the soldier said tersely. "If you try to force your way out, we will have to hurt you."

The soldier nearest her was already reaching for his weapon. Rin backed up. She understood there was no arguing her way out of this.

So she reverted to the most primitive of methods. She opened her mouth and screamed. She writhed on the floor. She beat at the soldiers with her fists and spat in their faces. She threatened to urinate in front of them. She shouted obscenities about their mothers. She shouted obscenities about their grandmothers.

This continued for hours.

Finally they acquiesced to her demand to see someone in charge.

Unfortunately, they sent Master Jun.

"This isn't necessary," she said sulkily when he arrived. She had hastily rearranged her clothes so that it didn't look like she had just been rolling around in the dirt. "I'm not going to harm anyone."

Jun looked like the last thing he would do was believe her.

"You've just demonstrated an ability to spontaneously combust. You set fire to the eastern half of the city. Do you understand why we might not want you running around camp?"

Rin thought the combustion had been more deliberate than spontaneous, but she didn't think explaining *how* she'd done it would make her seem like any less of a threat.

"I want to see Jiang," she said.

Jun's expression was unreadable. He left without replying.

Once Rin got over the indignation of being locked up, she decided the best thing to do was wait. She was loyal to the Empress. She was a good soldier. The other masters at Sinegard would vouch for her, even if Jun wouldn't. So long as she kept her head, she had nothing to fear. She mused, absurdly, that if she was going to get in trouble for anything, it might be opium possession.

At least she wasn't being kept in isolation. Rin discovered that visitors could enter the basement freely. She just couldn't leave.

Niang visited often, but she wasn't much for conversation. When Niang smiled, it was forced. She moved listlessly. She didn't laugh when Rin tried to cheer her up. They passed hours sitting beside each other in silence, listening to each other breathe. Niang was stunned with grief, and Rin didn't know how to comfort her.

"I miss Raban too," she tried once, but that only made Niang tear up and leave.

Kitay, on the other hand, she grilled mercilessly for news. He visited as often as he could, but was constantly being called away for relief operations.

In bits and pieces, she learned what had happened in the aftermath of the battle.

The Federation had been on the verge of taking Sinegard when she had killed their general. That, combined with the timely arrival of the Empress and the Third Division, had turned the battle in their favor. The Federation had retreated in the interim. Kitay doubted they would soon return.

"Things ended pretty quick once the Third got here," he said. He cradled his arm in a sling, but assured Rin that it was only a minor sprain. "It had a lot to do with . . . well, you know. The Federation was spooked. I think they were afraid that we had more than one Speerly."

She sat up. "What?"

Kitay looked confused. "Well, isn't that what you are?"

A Speerly? *Her?*

"That's what they've been saying all over the city," said Kitay. Rin could sense his discomfort. Kitay's mind worked at twice the speed of a normal person's; his curiosity was insatiable. He needed to know what she had done, what she was, and why she hadn't told him.

But she didn't know what to tell him. She didn't know herself.

"What are they saying?" she asked.

"That you fell into a frenzied bloodlust. That you fought like you'd been possessed by a horde of demons. That the general cut you down over and over and stabbed you eighteen times and still you kept moving."

She held out her arms. "No stab wounds. That was just Nezha."

Kitay didn't laugh. "Is it true? You're locked down here, so it *must* be."

So Kitay didn't know about the fire. Rin considered telling him, but hesitated.

How would she explain shamanism to Kitay, who was so convinced of his own rationality? Kitay was the paragon of the modernist thought that Jiang despised. Kitay was an atheist, a skeptic, who couldn't accept challenges to his worldview. He would think her mad. And she was too exhausted to argue.

"I don't know what happened," she said. "It was all just a blur. And I don't know what I am. I was a war orphan. I could be from anywhere. I could be anyone."

Kitay looked unsatisfied. "Jun's convinced you're a Speerly."

But how could that be? Rin would have been an infant when Speer was attacked, and there was no way she would have survived if no one else had.

"But the Federation massacred the Speerlies," she said. "They left no survivors."

"Altan survived," Kitay said. "You survived."

The Academy students had suffered a far higher proportion of casualties than the soldiers of the Eighth Division. Barely half of their class had made it through, most of them with minor injuries. Fifteen of their classmates were dead. Five more were in critical condition in Enro's triage center, their lives hanging perilously in balance.

Nezha was among them.

"He's going through a third round of operations today," said Kitay. "They don't know if he's going to live. Even if he does, he might never fight again. They say the halberd pierced his torso all the way through. They say his spine is severed."

Rin had simply been relieved that Nezha wasn't dead. She hadn't considered that the alternative might be worse.

"I hope he dies," Kitay said suddenly.

She whirled on him, shocked, but Kitay continued, "If it's death or a lifetime as a cripple, I hope he gets off easy. Nezha couldn't live with himself if he couldn't fight."

Rin didn't know how to respond to that.

The Nikara's victory had bought them time, but it had not guaranteed them the city. Intelligence from the Second Division reported that Federation reinforcements were being sent across the narrow sea while the main invading forces waited for their rendezvous.

When the Federation attacked for a second time, the Nikara wouldn't be able to hold the city. Sinegard was being fully evacuated. The Imperial bureaucracy had been moved completely to the wartime capital of Golyn Niis, which meant Sinegard's security had been deprioritized.

"They're liquidating the Academy," Kitay said. "We've all been drafted into the Divisions. Niang's been sent to the Eleventh,

Venka to the Sixth in Golyn Niis. They're not sending Nezha any-where until he . . . well, you know." He paused. "I got my orders for the Second yesterday. Junior officer."

It was the division Kitay had always dreamed of joining. Under different circumstances congratulations would have been in order. But now, celebration simply felt wrong. Rin tried anyway. "That's great. That's what you wanted, right?"

He shrugged. "They're desperate for soldiers. It's not a matter of prestige anymore; they've started drafting people right out of the countryside. But it'll be good to serve under Irjah. I'm shipping out tomorrow."

She placed a hand on his shoulder. "Take care of yourself."

"You too." Kitay sat back on his hands. "Any idea when they're going to let you out of here?"

"You know more than I do."

"No one's come in to talk to you?"

She shook her head. "Not since Jun. Have they found Jiang yet?"

Kitay gave her a sympathetic look, and she knew the answer before he spoke. It was the same answer he had given her for days.

Jiang was gone. Not dead—disappeared. No one had heard or seen anything since the end of the battle. The rubble of the east wall had been thoroughly searched for survivors, yet there was no sign of the Lore Master. There was no proof that he was dead, but nothing that gave hope that he was alive. He seemed to have vanished into the very void that he had called into being.

Once Kitay left with the Second Division for Golyn Niis, there was no one to keep Rin company. She passed her time sleeping. She wanted to sleep all the time now, especially after meals, and when she did it was a heavy and dreamless sleep. She wondered if her food and drink were drugged. Somehow, she was almost grateful for this. It was worse to be alone with her thoughts.

She wasn't safe, now that she had succeeded in calling a god. She didn't feel powerful. She was locked in a basement. Her own commanders didn't trust her. Half her friends were dying or dead, her master was lost to the void, and she was being contained for her own safety and the safety of everyone around her.

If this was what it meant to be a Speerly—if she even *was* a Speerly—Rin didn't know if it was worth it.

She slept, and when she couldn't force herself to sleep anymore, she curled into the corner and cried.

On the sixth day of her containment, Rin had just awoken when the door to the main hall opened. Irjah looked inside, checked to see that she was awake, and then quickly shut the door behind him.

"Master Irjah." Rin smoothed her rumpled tunic and stood.

"I'm General Irjah now," he said. He didn't seem particularly happy about it. "Casualties lead to promotions."

"General," she amended. "Apologies."

He shrugged and motioned for her to sit back down. "It hardly matters at this point. How are you doing?"

"Tired, sir," she said. She assumed a cross-legged position on the floor, because there were no stools in the basement.

After a moment's hesitation, Irjah sat on the floor as well.

"So." He placed his hands on his knees. "They're saying you're a Speerly."

"How much do you know?" she asked in a small voice. Did Irjah know she had called the fire? Did Irjah know what Jiang had taught her?

"I raised Altan after the Second War," said Irjah. "I know."

Rin felt a deep sense of relief. If Irjah knew what Altan was like, what Speerlies were capable of, then surely he could vouch for her, persuade the Militia that she wasn't dangerous—at least not to them.

"They've come to a decision about you," Irjah said.

"I didn't know I was up for debate," she answered, just to be difficult.

Irjah gave her a tired smile that did not reach his eyes. "You're going to get your transfer orders soon."

"Really?" She straightened up, suddenly excited. They were letting her out. *Finally.* "Sir, I was hoping I could join the Second with Kitay—"

Irjah cut her off. "You're not joining the Second. You're not joining any of the Twelve Divisions."

Her elation was replaced immediately by dread. She was suddenly aware of a faint buzzing noise in the air. "What do you mean?"

Irjah fiddled uncomfortably with his thumbs, and then said: "The Warlords have decided it best to send you to join the Cike."

For a moment she sat there looking dumbly at him.

The Cike? That infamous thirteenth division, the Empress's squad of assassins? The killers with no honor, no reputation, and no glory? The fighting force so vile, so nefarious, that the Militia preferred to pretend it didn't exist?

"Rin? Do you understand what I'm telling you?"

"The *Cike*?" Rin repeated.

"Yes."

"You're sending me to the freak squad?" Her voice cracked. She had a sudden urge to burst into tears. "The Bizarre Children?"

"The Cike is a division of the Militia just like the others," Irjah said hastily. His tone was artificially soothing. "They are a perfectly respectable contingent."

"They are losers and rejects! They—"

"They serve the Empress just as the army does."

"But I—" Rin swallowed hard. "I thought I was a good soldier."

Irjah's expression softened. "Oh, Rin. You *are*. You are an incredible soldier."

"So why can't I be in a real division?" She was acutely aware of how childish she sounded. But under the circumstances, she thought she deserved to act like a child.

"You know why," Irjah said quietly. "Speerlies have not fought with the Twelve Provinces since the last Poppy War. And before that, when they did, the cooperation was always . . . difficult."

Rin knew her history. She knew what Irjah alluded to. The last time the Speerlies had fought alongside the Militia, they had been regarded as barbaric oddities, much as the Cike was regarded now. The Speerlies raged and fought in their own camps; they were a walking hazard to everyone in their vicinity, friends and foe alike. They followed orders, but only vaguely; they were given targets and objectives, but good luck to the officer who tried any sophisticated maneuvers. "The Militia hates Speerlies."

"The Militia is afraid of Speerlies," Irjah corrected. "The Nikara have never been good at dealing with what they don't understand, and Speer has always made the Nikara uncomfortable. I expect you now know why."

"Yes, sir."

"*I* recommended you to the Cike. And I did it for you, child." Irjah fixed her with a level gaze. "The rivalry between the Warlords has never completely disappeared, even since their alliance under the Dragon Emperor. Though their soldiers might hate you, the Twelve Warlords would be very eager to get their hands on a Speerly. Whatever division you joined would gain an unfair advantage. And whatever division you didn't join might not like the shift in the balance of power. If I sent you to any one of the twelve divisions, you would be in very grave danger from the other eleven."

"I . . ." She hadn't considered this. "But there's already a Speerly in the Militia," she said. "What about Altan?"

Irjah's beard twitched. "Would you like to meet your commander?"

"*What?*" She blinked, not comprehending.

Irjah turned and called to someone behind the door, "Well, come on in."

The door opened. The man who walked through was tall and lithe; he did not wear a Militia uniform but a black tunic without any insignia. He carried a silver trident strapped across his back.

Rin swallowed, fighting a ridiculous urge to sweep her hair

behind her ears. She felt a familiar flush, a heat starting at the tops of her ears.

He had gained several scars since she'd last seen him, including two on his forearm and one that ran ragged across his face, from the lower right corner of his left eye down to his right jaw. His hair was no longer cropped tidily as it had been at school, but had grown unruly and wild, like he hadn't bothered with it in months.

"Hi," said Altan Trengsin. "What was that about losers and rejects?"

"How on earth did you survive the firebombs?"

Rin opened her mouth, but no words came out.

Altan. *Altan Trengsin*. She tried to form a coherent response, but all she could process was that her childhood hero was standing before her.

He knelt down in front of her.

"How do you exist?" he asked quietly. "I thought I was the only one left."

She finally found her voice. "I don't know. They never told me what happened to my parents. My foster parents didn't know."

"And you never suspected what you were?"

She shook her head. "Not until I . . . I mean, when I . . ."

She choked suddenly. The memories she had been suppressing flooded up in front of her: the shrieking Woman, the cackling Phoenix, the terrible heat ripping through her body, the way the general's armor bent and liquefied under the heat of the fire . . .

She lifted her hands to her face and found that they were trembling.

She hadn't been able to control it. She hadn't been able to turn it off. The flames had just kept pouring out of her without end; she might have burned Nezha, she might have burned Kitay, she might have turned all of Sinegard to ashes if the Phoenix hadn't heeded her prayer. And even when the flames did stop, the fire coursing inside her hadn't, not until the Empress kissed her forehead and made them die away.

I'm going crazy, she thought. *I have become everything that Jiang warned me against.*

"Hey. *Hey.*"

Cool fingers wrapped around her wrists. Gently, Altan pulled her hands away from her face.

She looked up and met his eyes. They were a shade of crimson brighter than poppy petals.

"It's okay," he said. "I know. I know what it's like. I'm going to help you."

"The Cike aren't so bad once you get to know them," he said as he led her out of the basement. "I mean, we kill people on orders, but on the whole we're quite nice."

"Are you all shamans?" she asked. She felt dizzy.

Altan shook his head. "Not all. We've got two who don't mess with the gods—a munitions expert and a physician. But the rest are. Tyr had the most training out of all of us before he came to the Cike—he grew up with a sect of monks that worshipped a goddess of darkness. The others were like you: dripping in power and shamanic potential, but confused. We take them to the Night Castle, train them, and set them loose on the Empress's enemies. Everybody wins."

Rin tried to find this reassuring. "Where do they come from?"

"All over. You'd be surprised how many places the old religions are still alive," said Altan. "Lots of hidden cults from across the provinces. Some contribute an initiate to the Cike every year in exchange for the Empress leaving them alone. It's not easy to find shamans in this country, not in this age, but the Empress procures them wherever she can. A lot of them come from the prison at Baghra—the Cike is their second chance."

"But you're not really Militia."

"No. We're assassins. In wartime, though, we function as the Thirteenth Division."

Rin wondered how many people Altan had killed. *Whom* he had killed. "What do you do in peacetime?"

"Peacetime?" He gave her a wry look. "There's no peacetime for the Cike. There's never a shortage of people the Empress wants dead."

Altan instructed her to pack her things and meet him at the gate. They were scheduled to march out that afternoon with the squadron of Officer Yenjen of the Fifth Division to the war front, where the rest of the Cike had gone a week prior.

All of Rin's belongings had been confiscated after the battle. She barely had time to pick up a new set of weapons from the armory before making her way across the city. The Fifth Division soldiers bore light traveling packs and two sets of weapons each. Rin had only a sword with a slightly dull blade and its accompanying sheath. She looked and felt woefully unprepared. She did not even have a second set of clothing. She suspected she would begin to smell very bad very soon.

"Where are we headed?" she asked as they began descending the mountain path.

"Khurdalain," Altan said. "Tiger Province. It'll be two weeks' march south until we get to the Western Murui River, and then we'll catch a ride down to the port."

Despite everything, Rin felt a thrill of excitement. Khurdalain was a coastal port city by the eastern Nariin Sea, a thriving center of international trade. It was the only city in the Empire that regularly dealt with foreigners; the Hesperians and Bolonians had established embassies there centuries ago. Even Federation merchants had once occupied the docks, until Khurdalain became a central theater of the Poppy Wars.

Khurdalain was a city that had seen two decades of warfare and survived. And now the Empress had established a front in Khurdalain once again to draw the Federation invaders into eastern and central Nikan.

Altan relayed the Empress's defense strategy to Rin as they marched.

Khurdalain was an ideal location to establish the initial front.

The Federation armored columns would have enjoyed a crushing advantage in the wide-open plains of northern Nikan, but Khurdalain abounded in rivers and creeks, which favored defensive operations.

Routing the Federation into Khurdalain would force them onto their weakest ground. The attack on Sinegard had been a bold attempt to separate the northern provinces from the southern. If the Federation generals could choose, they would almost certainly have cut directly into the Nikara heartland by marching directly south. But if Khurdalain was well defended, the Federation would be forced to change the north-to-south direction of their offensive to east-to-west. And Nikan would have room in the southwest to retreat and regroup should Khurdalain fall.

Ideally, the Militia would have attempted a pincer maneuver to squeeze the Federation from both sides, cutting them off from both their escape routes and supply lines. But the Militia was nowhere near competent or large enough for such an attempt. The Twelve Warlords had barely coordinated in time to rally to Sinegard's defense; now each was too preoccupied defending his own province independently to genuinely attempt joint military action.

"Why can't they just unite like they did during the Second War?" Rin asked.

"Because the Dragon Emperor is dead," said Altan. "He can't rally the Warlords to him this time, and the Empress can't command the same allegiance that he did. Oh, the Warlords will kowtow to Sinegard and swear vows of loyalty to the Empress's face, but when it comes to it, they'll put their own provinces first."

Holding Khurdalain would not be easy. The recent offensive at Sinegard had proven the Federation had clear military superiority in terms of mobility and weaponry. And Mugen held the advantage on the northern coastline; their troops were easily reinforced over the narrow sea; fresh troops and supplies were just a ship's journey away.

Khurdalain had little advantage in the way of defense structures.

It was an open port city, designed as an enclave for foreigners prior to the Poppy Wars. Nikan's best defense structures had been built along the lower river delta of the Western Murui, far south of Khurdalain. Compared to the heavily garrisoned wartime capital at Golyn Niis, Khurdalain was a sitting duck, arms flung open to welcome invaders.

But Khurdalain had to be defended. If Mugen advanced down the heartland and managed to take Golyn Niis, they could then easily turn east, chasing whatever remnants of the Militia were left onto the coast. And if they were trapped by the sea, the pitifully small Nikara fleet could not save them. So Khurdalain was the vital crux on which the fate of the rest of the country lay.

"We're the final front," said Altan. "If we fail, this country's lost." He clapped her on the shoulder. "Excited?"

CHAPTER 13

Clang.

Rin barely got her sword up in time to stop Altan's trident from slicing her face in half. She did her best to ground herself, to dispel the *ki* of the blow evenly across her body and into the dirt, but even so, her legs trembled from the impact.

She and Altan had been at this for hours, it seemed. Her arms ached; her lungs seized for air.

But Altan wasn't done. He shifted the trident, caught the blade of her sword between two prongs, and twisted hard. The pressure wrenched the sword out of Rin's hands and sent it clattering against the ground. Altan pressed the tip of his trident to her throat. She raised her arms hastily in surrender.

"You're reacting based on fear," Altan said. "You're not controlling this fight. You need to clear your mind and concentrate. Concentrate on *me*. Not my weapon."

"It's a bit hard when you're trying to jab my eyes out," she muttered, pushing his trident away from her face.

Altan lowered his weapon. "You're still hedging. You're resisting. You've got to let the Phoenix in. When you've called the god, when the god is walking in you, that's a state of ecstasy. It's a *ki* amplifier. You don't get tired. You're capable of extraordinary exertion. You don't feel pain. You have to sink into that state."

Rin could recall vividly the state of mind he wanted her to embrace. The burning feeling in her veins, the red lenses that shielded her vision. How other people became not people but targets. How she didn't need rest, only pain, pain to fuel the fire.

The only times Rin had consciously been in this state were during the Trials, and then again at Sinegard. Both times she had been furious, desperate.

She hadn't been able to rekindle the same state of mind since. She hadn't been that angry since. She had only been confused, agitated, and, like right now, exhausted.

"Learn to tame it," Altan said. "Learn to sink in and out of it. If you're focused only on your enemy's weapon, you'll always be on the defensive. Look past the weapon to your target. Focus on what you want to kill."

Altan was a much better teacher than Jiang. Jiang was frustratingly vague, absentminded, and deliberately obtuse. Jiang liked to dance around the answers, liked to make her circle around the truth like a starving vulture before he would give her a gratifying morsel of understanding.

But Altan wasted no time. He cut straight to the chase, gave her precisely the answers that she wanted. He understood her fears, and he knew what she was capable of.

Training with Altan was like training with an older brother. It was so bizarre for someone to tell her that they were the *same*— that his joints hyperextended like hers did, so she should turn out her foot in such a way. To have similarities with someone else, similarities that lay deep in their genes, was an overwhelmingly wonderful sensation.

With Altan she felt as if she *belonged*—not just to the same division or army, but to something deeper and older. She felt situated within an ancient web of lineage. She had a place. She was not a nameless war orphan; she was a Speerly.

At least, everyone seemed to think so. But despite everything, she couldn't shake the feeling that something was amiss. She couldn't call the god as easily as Altan could. Couldn't move with the same grace as he could. Was that heritage, or training?

"Were you always like this?" she asked.

Altan appeared to tense. "Like what?"

"Like . . . *you*." She gestured vaguely at him. "You're—you're not like the other students. Other soldiers. Could you always summon the fire? Could you always fight like you do?"

Altan's expression was unreadable. "I trained at Sinegard for a long time."

"But so did I!"

"You weren't trained like a Speerly. But you're a warrior, too. It's in your blood. I'll beat your heritage into you soon enough." Altan gestured to her with his trident. "Weapons up."

"Why a trident?" she asked when he finally let her take a break. "Why not a sword?" She hadn't seen any other soldier who didn't wield the standard Militia halberd and sword.

"Longer reach," he said. "Opponents don't come in close quarters when you're fighting inside a silo of fire."

She touched the prongs. The ends had been sharpened many times over; they were not shiny or smooth, but etched with the evidence of multiple battles. "Is that Speerly-made?"

It had to be. The trident was metal all the way through, not like Nikara weapons, which had wooden hilts. The trident was heavier, true, but Altan needed a weapon that wouldn't burn through when he touched it.

"It came from the island," he said. He poked her with the blunt end and gestured for her to pick up her sword. "Stop stalling. Come on, get up. Again."

She threw her arms down in exhaustion. "Can't we just get high?" she asked. She didn't see how relentless physical training got her any closer to calling the Phoenix at all.

"No, we can't just get high," Altan said. He poked her again. "Lazy. That kind of thinking is a rookie mistake. Anyone can swallow some seeds and reach the Pantheon. That part's easy. But forming a link with the god, channeling its power to your will and calling it back down—that takes discipline. Unless you've had practice honing your mind, it's too easy for you to lose control. Think of it as a dam. The gods are sources of potential energy, like water flowing downhill. The drug is like the gate—it opens the way to let the gods through. But if your gate is too large, or flimsily constructed, then power rushes through unobstructed. The god ignores your will. Chaos ensues. Unless you want to burn down your own allies, you have to remember why you called the Phoenix. You've got to direct its power."

"It's like a prayer," she said.

Altan nodded. "It's exactly like a prayer. All prayer is simply repetition—a imposition of your demands upon the gods. The difference between shamans and everyone else is that our prayers actually work. Didn't Jiang teach you this?"

Jiang had taught her the opposite of that. Jiang had asked her to clear her mind in meditation, to forget her own ego; to forget that she was a being separate from the universe. Jiang had taught her to erase her own will. Altan was asking her to impose her will on the gods.

"He only ever taught me to access the gods. Not to pull them back to our world."

Altan looked amazed. "Then how did you call the Phoenix at Sinegard?"

"I wasn't supposed to," she said. "Jiang warned me not to. He said the gods weren't meant to be weaponized. Only consulted. He was teaching me to calm myself, to find my connection to the larger cosmos and correct my imbalance, or . . . or whatever," she finished lamely.

It was becoming apparent how little Jiang had really taught her. He hadn't prepared her for this war at all. He had only tried to restrain her from wielding the power that she now knew she could access.

"That's useless." Altan looked disdainful. "Jiang was a scholar.

I am a soldier. He was concerned with theology; I am concerned with how to destroy." He opened his fist, turned it outward, and a small ring of fire danced over the lines of his palm. With his other hand he extended his trident. The flame raced from the ends of his fingers, danced across his shoulders, and licked all the way out to the trident's three prongs.

She marveled at the utter command Altan held over the fire, the way he shaped it like a sculptor might shape clay, how he bent it to his will with the slightest movement of his fingers. When she had summoned the Phoenix, the fire had poured out of her in an uncontrolled flood. But Altan controlled it like an extension of his own self.

"Jiang was right to be cautious," he said. "The gods are unpredictable. The gods are dangerous. And there's no one who understands them, not fully. But we at the Night Castle have practiced the weaponization of the gods to an art. We have come closer to understanding the gods than the old monks ever did. We have developed the power to rewrite the fabric of this world. If we don't use it, then what's the point?"

After two weeks of hard marching, four days of sailing, and another three days' march, they reached Khurdalain's city gates shortly before nightfall. When they emerged from the tree line toward the main road, Rin glimpsed the ocean for the first time.

She stopped walking.

Sinegard and Tikany were both landlocked regions. Rin had seen rivers and lakes, but never such a large body of water as this. She gaped openmouthed at that great expanse of blue, stretching on farther than she could see, farther than she could imagine.

Altan halted beside her. He glanced down at her dumbfounded expression, and he smiled. "Never seen the ocean before?"

She couldn't look away. She felt like she had the first day she had glimpsed Sinegard in all of its splendor, like she had been dropped into a fantastical world where the stories she'd heard were somehow true.

"I saw paintings," she said. "I read descriptions. In Tikany the merchants would ride up from the coast and tell us about their adventures at sea. But this—I never dreamed *anything* could look like this."

Altan took her hand and pointed it out toward the ocean. "The Federation of Mugen lies just across the narrow strait. If you climb the Kukhoni range, you can just glimpse it. And if you take a ship south of there, down close by Golyn Niis and into Snake Province, you'll get to Speer."

She couldn't possibly see it from where they stood, but still she stared out over the shimmering water, imagining a small, lonely island in the South Nikan Sea. Speer had spent decades in isolation before the great continental powers tore the island apart in the struggle between them.

"What's it like?"

"Speer? Speer was beautiful." Altan's voice was soft, wistful. "They call it the Dead Island now, but all I can remember of it is green. On one side of the island you could see the shore of the Nikara Empire; on the other was boundless water, a limitless horizon. We would take boats out and sail into that ocean without knowing what we would find; journeys into the endless dark to seek out the other side of the world. The Speerlies divided the night sky into sixty-four houses of constellations, one for each god. And as long as you could find the southern star of the Phoenix, you could always find your way back to Speer."

Rin wondered what the Dead Island was like now. When Mugen destroyed Speer, had they destroyed the villages as well? Or did the huts and lodges still stand, ghost towns waiting for inhabitants who would never return?

"Why did you leave?" she asked.

She realized then that she knew very little about Altan. His survival was a mystery to her, just as her very existence was a mystery to everyone else.

He must have been very young when he came to Nikan, a refugee of the war that killed his people. He couldn't have been older than four or five. Who had spirited him off that island? Why only him?

And why her?

But Altan didn't answer. He stared silently at the darkening sky for a long moment and then turned back toward the path.

"Come on," he said, and reached for her arm. "We're going to fall behind."

Officer Yenjen raised a Nikara flag outside the city walls, and then ordered his squadron to take cover behind the trees until they received a response. After a half hour's wait, a slight girl, dressed head to toe in black, peeked out from the city gate. She motioned frantically for the party to hurry up and get inside, then quickly shut the gate once they were through.

"Your division is waiting in the old fishing district. That's north of here. Follow the main road," she instructed Officer Yenjen. Then she turned and saluted her commander. "Trengsin."

"Qara."

"That's our Speerly?"

"That's her."

Qara tilted her head as she sized Rin up. She was a tiny woman—girl, really—reaching only to Rin's shoulder. Her hair hung past her waist in a thick, dark braid. Her features were oddly elongated, not quite Nikara but not quite anything that Rin could put her finger on.

A massive hunting falcon sat perched on her left shoulder, tilting its head at Rin with a disdainful expression. Its eyes and Qara's were an identical shade of gold.

"How are our people?"

"Fine," said Qara. "Well. Mostly fine."

"When's your brother back?"

Qara's falcon stretched its head up and then hunched back down, feathers raised as if unsettled. Qara reached up and stroked the bird's neck.

"When he's back," she said.

Yenjen and his squadron had already disappeared down the winding alleys of the city. Qara motioned for Rin and Altan to follow her up a set of stairs adjacent to the city walls.

"Where is she from?" Rin muttered to Altan.

"She's a Hinterlander," Altan said, and grabbed her arm just as she stumbled against the rickety stairs. "Don't trip."

Qara led them up a high walkway that spanned over the first few blocks of Khurdalain. Once at the top, Rin turned and got her first good look at the port city.

Khurdalain could have been a foreign city uprooted at the foundations and dropped straight onto the other side of the world. It was a chimera of multiple architectural styles, a bizarre amalgamation of building types from different countries spanning continents. Rin saw churches of the kind she'd seen only sketches of in history textbooks, the proof of former Bolonian occupation. She saw buildings with spiraling columns, buildings with elegant monochrome towers with deep grooves etched in their sides instead of the sloping pagodas native to Sinegard. Sinegard was the beacon of the Nikara Empire, but Khurdalain was Nikan's window to the rest of the world.

Qara led them across the walkway and onto a flat rooftop. They covered another block by running over the level-topped houses, built in the style of old Hesperia, and then dropped down to walk on the street when the buildings became too far apart. Between the gaps of the buildings, Rin could see the dying sun reflected in the ocean.

"This used to be a Hesperian settlement," said Qara, pointing out over the wharf. The long strip was a waterfront boulevard, ringed with blocky storefronts. The walkway was built of thick wooden planks soggy from seawater. Everything in Khurdalain smelled faintly of the sea; the breeze itself was laced with a salty ocean tang. "That ring of buildings over there—the ones with those terraced roofs—those used to be the Bolonian consulates."

"What happened?" Rin asked.

"The Dragon Emperor happened," said Qara. "Don't you know your history?"

The Dragon Emperor had expelled the foreigners from Nikan in the days of turmoil following the Second Poppy War, but Rin knew that a scattering of Hesperians still remained—missionaries intent on spreading the word of their Holy Maker.

"Are there still any Hesperians in the city?" she asked hopefully. She had never seen a Hesperian. Foreigners in Nikan were not permitted to travel as far north as Sinegard; they were restricted to trading at a handful of port cities, of which Khurdalain was the largest. She wondered if Hesperians were really pale-skinned and covered with fur, if their hair was really carrot red.

"A couple hundred," Altan said, but Qara shook her head.

"Not anymore. They've cleared out since the attack on Sinegard. Their government sent a ship for them. Nearly tipped over, they were trying to cram so many people in. There are one or two of their missionaries left, and a few foreign ministers. They're documenting what they see, sending it to their governments back at home. But that's it."

Rin remembered what Kitay had said about calling on Hesperia for aid, and snorted. "They think that's helping?"

"They're Hesperians," said Qara. "They always think they're helping."

The old section of Khurdalain—the Nikara quarter—was set in low-rise buildings embedded inside a grid of alleyways, intersected by a webbed system of canals, so narrow that even a cart would have a hard time getting through. It made sense that the Nikara army had set up base in this part of the city. Even if the Federation knew vaguely where they were, their overwhelming numbers would be no advantage in these crooked, tunneling streets.

Architecture aside, Rin imagined that under normal circumstances, Khurdalain might be a louder, dirtier version of Sinegard. Before occupation, this place must have been a bustling hub of exchange, more exciting even than the Sinegardian downtown markets. But Khurdalain under siege was quiet and muted, almost sullenly so. She saw no civilians as they walked; they either had already evacuated or were heeding the warnings of the Militia, keeping their heads down and staying away from where Federation soldiers might see them.

Qara briefed them on the combat situation as they walked. "We've been under siege for almost a month now. We've got Federation encampments on three sides, all except the one you came from. Worst is that they've been steadily encroaching into urban areas. Khurdalain has high walls, but they have trebuchets."

"How much of the city have they taken?" Altan asked.

"Only a narrow strip of beach by the sea, and half of the foreign quarter. We could take back the Bolonian embassies, but the Fifth Division won't cooperate."

"Won't cooperate?"

Qara scowled. "We're having some, ah, difficulties with integration. That new general of theirs doesn't help. Jun Loran."

Altan looked as dismayed as Rin felt. "Jun's here?"

"Shipped in three days ago."

Rin shuddered. At least she wasn't serving directly under him. "Isn't the Fifth from Tiger Province? Why isn't the Tiger Warlord in command?"

"The Tiger Warlord is a three-year-old kid whose steward is a politician with no military experience. Jun has resumed command of his province's army. The Ram and Ox Warlords are here too, with their provincial divisions, but they've been squabbling with each other over supplies more than they've been fighting the Federation. And no one can figure out an attack plan that doesn't put civilian areas in the line of fire."

"What are the civilians still doing here?" Rin asked. It seemed to her that the Militia's job would be a lot easier if civilian protection were not a priority. "Why haven't they evacuated, like the Sinegardians?"

"Because Khurdalain is not a city that you can easily leave," said Qara. "Most of the people here make their living from fishing or in the factories. There's no agriculture out here. If they move further inland, they have nothing. Most of the peasants moved here to escape rural squalor in the first place. If we ask them to leave, they'll starve. The people are determined to stay, and we'll just have to make sure they stay alive."

Qara's falcon cocked its head suddenly, as if it heard something. When she walked forward several paces Rin could hear it, too: raised voices coming from behind the general's compound.

"Cike!"

Rin cringed. She would recognize that voice anywhere.

General Jun Loran stormed down the alley toward them, purple-faced with fury.

"Ow-*ow*!"

By his side, Jun dragged a scrawny boy by the ear, jerking him along with brutal tugs. The boy wore an eyepatch over his left eye, and his right eye watered in pain as he tottered along behind Jun.

Altan stopped short. "Tiger's tits."

"Ramsa," Qara swore under her breath. Rin couldn't tell if it was a name or a curse in Qara's language.

"You." Jun stopped in front of Qara. "Where is your commander?"

Altan stepped forward. "That'd be me."

"*Trengsin?*" Jun regarded Altan with open disbelief. "You're joking. Where's Tyr?"

A spasm of irritation flickered across Altan's face. "Tyr is dead."

"*What?*"

Altan crossed his arms. "No one bothered to tell you?"

Jun ignored the jibe. "He's dead? How?"

"Occupational hazard," Altan said, which Rin suspected meant that he didn't have a clue.

"So they put the Cike in the hands of a child," Jun muttered. "Incredible."

Altan looked between Jun and the boy, who was still bent over by Jun's side, whimpering in pain. "What's this about?"

"My men caught him elbows-deep in their munitions stores," Jun said. "Third time this week."

"I thought it was *our* munitions wagon!" the boy protested.

"You don't have a munitions wagon," Jun snapped. "We established that the first two times."

Qara sighed and rubbed her forehead with the palm of her hand.

"I wouldn't have to steal if they'd just *share*," the boy said plaintively, appealing to Altan. His voice was thin and reedy, and his good eye was huge in his thin face. "I can't do my job if I don't have fire powder."

"If your men are lacking equipment, you might have thought to bring it from the Night Castle."

"We used up all ours at the embassy," the boy grumbled. "Remember?"

Jun jerked the boy's ear downward, and the boy howled in pain.

Altan reached behind his back for his trident. "Let go, Jun."

Jun glanced at the trident, and the side of his mouth quirked up. "Are you threatening me?"

Altan did not extend his weapon—to point his blade at a commander of another division would be the highest treason—but he didn't take his hand off the shaft. Rin thought she saw fire flicker momentarily across his fingertips. "I'm making a request."

Jun took one step back, but did not let go of the boy. "Your men do not have access to Fifth Division supplies."

"And disciplining him is my prerogative, not yours," said Altan. "Unhand him. *Now*, Jun."

Jun made a disgusted noise and let go of the boy, who skirted away quickly and scampered over to Altan's side, rubbing the side of his head with a rueful expression.

"Last time they hung me up by my ankles in the town square," the boy complained. He sounded like a child tattling on a classmate to a teacher.

Altan looked outraged.

"Would you treat the First or Eighth like this?" he demanded.

"The First and Eighth have better sense than to root around in the Fifth's equipment," Jun snapped. "Your men have been causing nothing but trouble since they got here."

"We've been doing our damn job!" the boy burst out. "*You're* the ones hiding behind walls like bloody cowards."

"Quiet, Ramsa," Altan snapped.

Jun barked out a short, derisive laugh. "You are a squad of ten. Do not overestimate your value to this Militia."

"Be that as it may, we serve the Empress just as you do," Altan said. "We left the Night Castle to be your reinforcements. So you'll treat my men with respect, or the Empress will hear of it."

"Of course. You're the Empress's special brats," Jun drawled. "*Reinforcements.* What a *joke.*"

He shot a last disdainful look at Altan and stalked off. He pretended not to see Rin.

"So that's been the last week," Qara said with a sigh.

"I thought you said everything was fine," Altan said.

"I exaggerated."

Ramsa peered up at his commander. "Hi, Trengsin," he said cheerfully. "Glad you're back."

Altan pressed his hands against his face and then tilted his head up, inhaling deeply. His arms dropped. He sighed. "Where's my office?"

"Down that alley to the left," said Ramsa. "Cleared out the old customs office. You'll like it. We brought your maps."

"Thanks," Altan said. "Where are the Warlords stationed?"

"The old government complex around the corner. They've been holding councils on the regular. They don't really invite us, on account of, well. You know." Ramsa trailed off, suddenly looking very guilty.

Altan shot Qara a questioning look.

"Ramsa blew up half the foreign quarter at the docks," she reported. "Didn't give the Warlords advance warning."

"I blew up *one building*."

"It was a big building," Qara said flatly. "The Fifth still had two men inside."

"Well, did they survive?" Altan asked.

Qara stared at him in disbelief. "*Ramsa detonated a building on them.*"

"I take it you lot have done nothing useful while I've been gone, then," Altan said.

"We set up fortifications!" Ramsa said.

"Of the defense line?" Altan asked hopefully.

"No, just around your office. And our barracks. Warlords won't let us near the defense line anymore."

Altan looked deeply aggravated. "I need to go get that squared up. The government complex is down that way?"

"Yeah."

"Fine." Altan cast a distracted look at Rin. "Qara, she'll need equipment. Get her geared up and moved in. Ramsa, come with me."

"Are you Altan's lieutenant?" Rin asked as Qara led her down another winding set of alleyways.

"Not me. My brother," Qara said. She quickened her pace, ducked under a round gate embedded in a wall, and waited for Rin to follow her through. "I'm filling in until he's back. You'll stay here with me."

She pulled Rin down yet another stairwell that led to a damp underground room. It was a tiny chamber, barely the size of the Academy outhouse. A draft blew in from the cellar opening. Rin rubbed her arms and shivered.

"We get the women's barracks all to ourselves," Qara said. "Lucky us."

Rin glanced about the room. The walls were packed dirt, not brick, which meant no insulation. A single mat had been unfurled in the corner, surrounded by a bundle of Qara's things. Rin supposed she'd have to get her own blanket unless she wanted to sleep among the cockroaches. "There aren't any women in the divisions?"

"We don't share barracks with the divisions." Qara fumbled in a bag near her mat, pulled out a bundle of clothing, and tossed it at Rin. "You should probably change out of that Academy uniform. I'll take your old things. Enki wants old linens for bandages."

Rin quickly wriggled out of her travel-worn Academy tunic, pulled on the uniform, then handed her old clothes to Qara. Her new uniform was a nondescript black tunic. Unlike the Militia uniforms, it bore no insignia of the Red Emperor over her left breast. The Cike uniforms were designed to have no identifying marks at all.

"Armband, too." Qara's hand was outstretched, expectant.

Rin touched her white armband, feeling self-conscious. She hadn't taken it off since the battle, even though she was no longer officially Jiang's apprentice. "Do I have to?" She'd seen plenty of academy armbands among the soldiers in Yenjen's squadron, even though they looked well past academy age. Officers from Sinegard often wore those armbands for years after they graduated as a mark of pride.

Qara folded her arms. "This isn't the Academy. Your apprentice affiliation doesn't matter here."

"I know that—" Rin began to say, but Qara cut her off.

"You don't understand. This is not the Militia, this is the Cike. We were all sent here because we were deemed fit to kill, but unfit for a division. Most of us didn't go to Sinegard, and the ones who did don't have great memories of the place. Nobody here cares who your master was, and advertising it won't earn you any goodwill. Forget about approval or rankings or glory, or whatever bullshit you were angling for at Sinegard. You are *Cike*. By default, you don't get a good reputation."

"I don't care about my reputation—" Rin protested, but again Qara cut her off.

"No, you listen to me. You're not at school anymore. You aren't competing with anyone; you're not trying to get good marks. You live with us, you fight with us, you die with us. From now on, your utmost loyalty is to the Cike and the Empire. You want an illustrious career, you should have joined the divisions. But you didn't, which means something's wrong with you, which means you're stuck with us. Understand?"

"I didn't ask to come here," Rin snapped defensively. "I didn't have a choice."

"None of us did," Qara said curtly. "Try to keep up."

Rin tried to keep a map of the base in her head as they walked, a mental picture of the labyrinth that was Khurdalain, but she gave up after the fifteenth turn. She half suspected Qara was taking a deliberately convoluted route to wherever they were going.

"How do you guys get anywhere?" she asked.

"Memorize the routes," Qara responded. "The harder we are to find, the better. And if you want to find Enki, just follow the whining."

Rin was about to ask what this meant when she heard another set of raised voices from around the corner.

"Please," begged a male voice. "Please, it hurts so much."

"Look, I sympathize, I really do," said a second, much deeper voice. "But frankly it's not my problem, so I don't care."

"It's just a few seeds!"

Rin and Qara rounded the corner. The voices belonged to a slight, dark-skinned man and a hapless-looking soldier with an insignia that marked him as a private of the Fifth. The soldier's right arm ended in a bloody stub at the elbow.

Rin cringed at the sight; she could almost see the gangrene through the poor bandaging. No wonder he was begging for poppy.

"It's just a few seeds to you, and the next poor chap who asks, and the next after that," said Enki. "Eventually I'm all out of seeds, and my division hasn't got anything to fight with. Then the next time *your* division's backed up in a corner, *my* division can't do their jobs and save your sorry asses. They are a priority. You are not. Understand?"

The soldier spat on Enki's doorstep. "*Freaks.*"

He brushed past Enki and backed out into the alleyway, casting dark glances at Rin and Qara as he passed them.

"I need to move shop," Enki complained to Qara as she shut the door behind her. Inside was a small, crowded room filled with the bitter smell of medicinal herbs. "This is no condition to store materials in. I need somewhere dry."

"Move closer to the division barracks and you'll have a thousand soldiers on your doorstep demanding a quick fix," said Qara.

"Hm. You think Altan would let me move into the back closet?"

"I think Altan likes having his closet to himself."

"You're probably right. Who's this?" Enki examined Rin from head to toe, as if looking for signs of injury. His voice was truly lovely, rich and velvety. Simply listening to him made Rin feel sleepy. "What's ailing you?"

"She's the Speerly, Enki."

"Oh! I'd forgotten." Enki rubbed the back of his shaved head. "How did *you* slip through Mugen's fingers?"

"I don't know," said Rin. "I only just found out myself."

Enki nodded slowly, still studying Rin as if she were a particularly fascinating specimen. He wore a carefully neutral expression that gave nothing away. "But of course. You had no idea."

"She'll need equipment," said Qara.

"Sure, no problem." Enki disappeared into a closet built into the back of the room. They listened to him bustling around for a moment, and then he reappeared with a tray of dried plants. "Any of these work for you?"

Rin had never seen so many different kinds of psychedelics in one place. There were more drug varieties here than in Jiang's entire garden. Jiang would have been delighted.

She brushed her fingers along the opium pods, the shriveled mushrooms, and the muddy white powders.

"What difference does it make?" she asked.

"It's really a matter of preference," said Enki. "These drugs will all get you nice and tripped up, but the key is to find a mixture that lets you summon the gods without getting so stoned that you can't wield your weapon. The stronger hallucinogens will shoot you right up to the Pantheon, but you'll lose all perception of the material world. Fat lot of good summoning a god will do you if you can't see an arrow right in front of your face. The weaker drugs require a bit more focus to get in the right mind state, but they leave you with more of your bodily faculties. If you've had meditation training, then I'd stick with more moderate strains if you can."

Rin didn't think that a siege was a great time to experiment, so she decided to settle for the familiar. She found the poppy seed variety that she had stolen from Jiang's garden among Enki's collection. She reached out to grab a handful, but Enki pulled the tray back out of her reach.

"No you don't." Enki brought a scale out from under the counter and began measuring precise amounts into little pouches. "You come to me for doses, which I will document. The amount you receive is calibrated to your body weight. You're not big; you definitely won't need as much as the others. Use it sparingly, and only when ordered. A shaman who's addicted is better off dead."

Rin hadn't considered that. "Does that happen often?"

"In this line of work?" Enki said. "It's almost inevitable."

The Militia's food rations made the Academy canteen look like a veritable restaurant in comparison. Rin stood in line for half an hour and received a measly bowl of rice gruel. She swirled her spoon around the gray, watery soup, and several uncooked lumps drifted up to the surface.

She looked around the mess hall for black uniforms, and found a few of her contingent clustered at one long table at the end of the hall. They sat far away from the other soldiers. The two tables closest to them were empty.

"This is our Speerly," Qara announced when Rin sat down.

The Cike looked up at Rin with a mixture of apprehension and wary interest. Qara, Ramsa, and Enki sat with a man she didn't recognize, all four of them garbed in pitch-black uniforms without any insignia or armband. Rin was struck by how young they all were. None looked older than Enki, and even he didn't look like he'd seen a full four zodiac cycles. Most appeared to be in their late twenties. Ramsa barely looked fifteen.

It was no surprise that they had no problem with a commander of Altan's age, or that they were called the Bizarre Children. Rin wondered if they were recruited young, or if they simply died before they had the chance to grow older.

"Welcome to the freak squad," said the man next to her. "I'm Baji."

Baji was a thickly built mercenary type with a loud booming voice. Despite his considerable girth he was somewhat handsome, in a coarse, dark sort of way. He looked like one of the Fangs' opium smugglers. Strapped to his back was a huge nine-pointed rake. It looked amazingly heavy. Rin wondered at the strength it took to wield it.

"Admiring this?" Baji patted the rake. The pointed ends were crusted over with something suspiciously brown. "Nine prongs. One of a kind. You won't find its make anywhere else."

Because no smithy would create a weapon so outlandish, Rin thought. *And because farmers have no use for lethally sharp rakes.* "Seems impractical."

"That's what *I* said," Ramsa butted in. "What are you, a potato farmer?"

Baji directed his spoon at the boy. "Shut your mouth or I swear to heaven I will put nine perfectly spaced holes in the side of your head."

Rin lifted a spoonful of rice gruel to her mouth and tried not to picture what Baji had just described. Her eyes landed on a barrel placed right behind Baji's seat. The water inside was oddly clouded, and the surface erupted in occasional ripples, as if a fish were swimming around inside.

"What's that in the barrel?" she asked.

"That's the Friar." Baji twisted around in his seat and rapped his knuckles against the wooden rim. "Hey, Aratsha! Come say hello to the Speerly!"

For a second the barrel did nothing. Rin wondered whether Baji was entirely in his right mind. She had heard rumors that Cike operatives were crazy, that they had been sent to the Night Castle when they lost their sanity.

Then the water began rising out of the barrel, as if falling in reverse, and solidified into a shape that looked vaguely like a man. Two bulbous orbs that might have been eyes widened as they swiveled in Rin's direction. Something that looked vaguely like a mouth moved. "Oh! You cut your hair."

Rin was too busy gaping to respond.

Baji made an impatient noise. "No, you dolt, this is the new one. From *Sinegard*," he emphasized.

"Oh, really?" The water blob made a gesture that seemed like a bow. Vibrations rippled through his entire form when he spoke. "Well, you should have said so. Careful, you'll catch a moth in your mouth."

Rin's jaw shut with a click. "What happened to you?" she finally managed.

"What are you talking about?" The watery figure sounded alarmed. He dipped his head, as if examining his torso.

"No, I mean—" Rin stammered. "What—why do you—"

"Aratsha prefers to spend his time in this guise if he can help it," Baji interjected. "You don't want to see his human form. Very grisly."

"Like you're such a visual delight." Aratsha snorted.

"Sometimes we let him out into the river when we need a drinking source poisoned," Baji said.

"I am quite handy with poisons," Aratsha acknowledged.

"Are you? I thought you just fouled things up with your general presence."

"Don't be rude, Baji. You're the one who can't be bothered to clean his weapon."

Baji dipped his rake threateningly over the barrel. "Shall I clean it off in you? What part of you is this, anyway? Your leg? Your—"

Aratsha yelped and collapsed back into the barrel. Within seconds the water was very still. It could have been a barrel of rainwater.

"He's a weird one," Baji said cheerfully, turning back to Rin. "He's an initiate of a minor river god. Far more committed to his religion than the rest of us."

"Which god do you summon?"

"The god of pigs."

"What?"

"I summon the fighting spirit of a very angry boar. Come off it. Not all gods are as glorious as yours, sweetheart. I picked the first one I saw. The masters were disappointed."

The masters? Had Baji gone to Sinegard? Rin remembered Jiang had told her there had been Lore students before her, students who had gone mad, but they were supposed to be in mental asylums or Baghra. They were too unstable, they had been locked up for their own good. "So that means—"

"It means I smash things very well, sweetheart." Baji drained his bowl, tilted his head back, and belched. His expression made it clear he didn't want to discuss it further.

"Will you slide down?" A very slight young man with a whispery goatee walked over to their table with a heaping bowl of lotus root and slid into the seat on the other side of Rin.

"Unegen can turn into a fox," Baji said by way of introduction.

"Turn into—?"

"My god lets me shift shapes," Unegen said. "And yours lets you spit fire. Not a big deal." He spooned a heap of steamed lotus into his mouth, swallowed, grimaced, and then belched. "I don't think the cook's even trying anymore. How are we low on salt? We're next to an ocean."

"You can't just pour seawater on food," interjected Ramsa. "There's a sanitation process."

"How hard can it be? We're soldiers, not barbarians." Unegen leaned down the table, tapping to get Qara's attention. "Where's your other half?"

Qara looked irritated. "Out."

"Well, when's he back?"

"When he's back," Qara said testily. "Chaghan comes and goes on his own schedule. You know that."

"As long as his schedule accommodates the fact that we're, you know, fighting a war," said Baji. "He could at least hurry."

Qara snorted. "You two don't even like Chaghan. What do you want him back for?"

"We've been eating rice gruel for days. It's about time we had some dessert up here." Baji smiled, displaying sharp incisors. "I'm talking sugar."

"I thought Chaghan was getting something for Altan," Rin said, confused.

"Sure," said Unegen. "Doesn't mean he can't stop at a bakery on the way back."

"Is he at least close?" Baji asked.

"I'm not my brother's homing pigeon," Qara grumbled. "We'll know where he is when he's back."

"Can't you two just, you know, do that thing?" Unegen tapped his temples.

Qara made a face. "We're anchor twins, not mirror-wells."

"Oh, you can't do mirror-wells?"

"Nobody can do mirror-wells," Qara snapped. "Not anymore."

Unegen looked at Rin over the table and winked, as if winding Qara up was something he and Baji regularly did for fun.

"Oh, leave Qara alone."

Rin twisted around in her seat to see Altan. He walked up to them, looking over her head. "Someone needs to patrol the outer perimeter. Baji, it's your turn."

"Oh, I can't," Baji said.

"Why not?"

"I'm eating."

Altan rolled his eyes. "*Baji.*"

"Send Ramsa," Baji whined. "He hasn't been out since—"

Bang. The door to the mess hall slammed open. All heads whipped toward the far end of the room, where a figure garbed in the black robes of the Cike was staggering through the doorway. The division soldiers standing by the exit hastily skirted away, clearing a path for the massive stranger.

Only the Cike were unfazed.

"Suni's back," Unegen said. "Took him long enough."

Suni was a giant man with a boyish face. A thick golden dusting of hair covered his arms and legs, more hair than Rin had ever seen on a man. He walked with an odd lope, like an ape's walk, like he'd rather be swinging through a tree instead of moving ponderously over land. His arms were almost thicker than Rin's entire torso; he looked as if he could crush her head in like a walnut if he wanted to.

He made a beeline toward the Cike.

"Great Tortoise," Rin muttered under her breath. "What is he?"

"Suni's mom fucked a monkey," Ramsa said happily.

"Shut up, Ramsa. Suni channels the Monkey God," Unegen reported. "Makes you glad he's on our side, doesn't it?"

Rin wasn't sure that made her any less scared of him, but Suni was already at their table.

"How'd it go?" Unegen asked cheerfully. "Did they see you?"

Suni didn't seem to hear Unegen. He cocked his head, as if sniffing at them. His temples were caked with dried blood. His tousled hair and vacant stare made him appear more animal than human, like some wild beast that couldn't decide whether to attack or flee.

Rin tensed. Something was wrong.

"It's so loud," Suni said. His voice was a low growl, gritty and guttural.

The smile slid off Unegen's face. "What?"

"They keep shouting."

"Who keeps shouting?"

Suni's eyes darted around the table. They were wild and unfocused. Rin tensed a split second before Suni leaped over the table at them. He slammed his arm into Unegen's neck, pinning him to the floor. Unegen choked, batted frantically at Suni's hulking torso.

Rin jumped to the side, lifting up her chair as a weapon just as Qara grabbed for her longbow.

Suni was grappling furiously with Unegen on the floor. There was a popping noise and then a little red fox was where Unegen had been before. It almost slithered out of Suni's grip, but Suni tightened his hold and seized the fox by the throat.

"Altan!" Qara shouted.

Altan hurtled over the fallen table, pushing Rin out of the way. He jumped onto Suni just before Suni could wrench Unegen's neck. Startled, Suni lashed out with his left arm, catching Altan in the shoulder. Altan ignored the blow and slapped Suni hard across the face.

Suni roared and let go of Unegen. The fox wriggled away and scampered toward Qara's feet, where he collapsed, sides heaving for air.

Suni and Altan were now wrestling on the floor, each trying to pin the other. Altan looked tiny against the massive Suni, who had to be twice his weight. Suni got a hold around Altan's shoulders, but Altan gripped Suni's face and squeezed his fingers toward his eyes.

Suni howled and flung Altan away from him. For a moment Altan looked like a limp puppet, tossed in the air, but he landed upright, tensed like a cat, just as Suni charged him again.

The Cike had formed a ring around Suni. Qara held an arrow fitted to her bow, ready to pierce Suni through the forehead. Baji held his rake at the ready, but Suni and Altan were rolling around so wildly he couldn't get a clean blow in. Rin's fingers closed tightly around the hilt of her sword.

Altan landed a solid kick to Suni's sternum. A crack echoed through the room. Suni tottered back, stunned. Altan rose to a low crouch, standing between Suni and the rest of the Cike.

"Get back," Altan said softly.

"They're so loud," Suni said. He didn't sound angry. He sounded scared. "*They're so loud!*"

"I said get *back*!"

Baji and Unegen retreated reluctantly. But Qara remained where she was, keeping her arrow trained at Suni's head.

"They're being so loud," said Suni. "I can't understand what they're saying."

"I can tell you everything you need to know," Altan said quietly. "Just put your arms down, Suni, can you do that for me?"

"I'm scared," Suni whimpered.

"We don't point arrows at our friends," Altan snapped without moving his head.

Qara lowered her longbow. Her arms shook visibly.

Altan walked slowly toward Suni, arms spread out in supplication. "It's me. It's just me."

"Are you going to help me?" Suni asked. His voice didn't match his demeanor. He sounded like a little child—terrified, helpless.

"Only if you let me," Altan answered.

Suni dropped his arms.

Rin's sword trembled in her hands. She was certain that Suni would snap Altan's neck.

"They're so loud," Suni said. "They keep telling me to do things, I don't know who to listen to . . ."

"Listen to me," said Altan. "Just me."

With brisk, short steps, he closed the gap between himself and Suni.

Suni tensed. Qara's hands flew to her longbow again; Rin crouched to spring forward.

Suni's massive hand closed around Altan's. He took a deep breath. Altan touched his forehead gently and brought Suni's forehead down to his own.

"It's okay," he whispered. "You're fine. You're Suni and you belong to the Cike. You don't have to listen to any voices. You just have to listen to me."

Eyes closed, Suni nodded. His heavy breathing subsided. A lopsided grin broke out over his face. When he opened his eyes, the wildness had left them.

"Hi, Trengsin," he said. "Good to have you back."

Altan exhaled slowly, then nodded and clapped Suni on the shoulder.

CHAPTER 14

"So much of a siege is sitting around on your ass," Ramsa complained. "You know how much actual fighting there's been since the Federation started landing on the beach in droves? None. We're just scouting each other out, testing the limits, playing chicken."

Ramsa had recruited Rin to help him fortify the back alleys of the intersection by the wharf.

They were slowly transforming the streets of Khurdalain into defense lines. Each evacuated house became a fort; each intersection became a trap of barbed wire. They had spent the morning methodically knocking holes through walls to link the labyrinth of lanes into a navigable transportation system to which only the Nikara had the map. Now they were filling bags with sand to pad the gaps in the walls against Federation bombardments.

"I thought you blew up an embassy building," said Rin.

"That was one time," Ramsa snapped. "More action than anyone's attempted since we got here, anyhow."

"You mean the Federation hasn't attacked yet?"

"They've launched exploratory parties to sniff out the borders. No major troop movements yet."

"And they've been at it this long? *Why?*"

"Because Khurdalain's better fortified than Sinegard. Khurdalain withstood the first two Poppy Wars, and it sure as hell is going to make it through a third." Ramsa bent down. "Pass me that bag."

She hauled it up, and he hoisted it to the top of the fortification with a grunt.

Rin couldn't help liking the scrawny urchin, who reminded her of a younger Kitay, if Kitay had been a one-eyed pyromaniac with an unfortunate adoration for explosions. She wondered how long he'd had been with the Cike. He looked impossibly young. How did a child end up on the front lines of a war?

"You've got a Sinegardian accent," she noticed.

Ramsa nodded. "Lived there for a while. My family were alchemists for the Militia base in the capital. Oversaw fire powder production."

"So what are you doing here?"

"You mean with the Cike?" Ramsa shrugged. "Long story. Father got wrapped up in some political stuff, ended up turning on the Empress. Extremists, you know. Could have been the Opera, but I'll never be sure. Anyways, he tried to detonate a rocket over the palace and ended up blowing up our factory instead." He pointed to his eyepatch. "Burned my eyeball right out. Daji's guards lopped the heads off everyone remotely involved. Public execution and everything."

Rin blinked, mostly stunned by Ramsa's breezy delivery. "Then what about you?"

"I got off easy. Father never told me much about his plans, so after they realized I didn't know anything, they just tossed me into Baghra. I think they thought killing a kid might make them look bad."

"*Baghra?*"

Ramsa nodded cheerfully. "Worst two years of my life. Near the tail end, the Empress paid me a visit and said she'd let me out if I worked on munitions for the Cike."

"And you just said yes?"

"Do you know what Baghra is like? By then, I was just about ready to do anything," said Ramsa. "Baji was in Baghra, too. Just ask him."

"What was he there for?"

Ramsa shrugged. "Who knows? He won't say. He was only there for a few months, though. But let's face it—even Khurdalain is so much better than a cell in Baghra. And the work here is *awesome*."

Rin gave him a sideways look. Ramsa sounded disturbingly chipper about his situation.

She decided to change the subject. "What was that about in the mess hall?"

"What do you mean?"

"The—uh . . ." She flailed her arms around. "The monkey man."

"Huh? Oh, that's just Suni. Does that maybe every other day. I think he just likes the attention. Altan's pretty good with him; Tyr used to just lock him up for hours until he'd calmed down." Ramsa handed her another bag. "Don't let Suni scare you. He's really pretty nice when he's not being a terror. It's just that god fucking with his head."

"So you're not a shaman?" she asked.

Ramsa shook his head quickly. "I don't mess with that shit. It screws you up. You saw Suni in there. My only god is science. Combine six parts sulfur, six parts saltpeter, and one part birthwort herb, and you've got fire powder. Formulaic. Dependable. Doesn't change. I understand the appeal, I really do, but I like having my mind to myself."

Three days passed before Rin spoke with Altan again. He spent a good deal of his time tied up in meetings with the Warlords, trying to patch up relations with the military leadership before they deteriorated any further. She would see him darting back to his office in between meetings, looking haggard and pissed. Finally, he sent Qara to summon her.

"Hey. I'm about to call a meeting. Wanted to check in on you first." Altan didn't look at her as he spoke; he was busy scrawling something on a map covering his desk. "I'm sorry it couldn't be earlier, I've been dealing with bureaucratic bullshit."

"That's all right." She fidgeted with her hands. He looked exhausted. "What are the Warlords like?"

"They're nearly useless." Altan made a disgusted noise. "The Ox Warlord's a slimy politician, and the Ram Warlord is an insecure fool who'll bend whichever way the wind blows. Jun's got them both by the ear, and the only thing they all agree on is that they hate the Cike. Means we don't get supplies, reinforcements, or intelligence, and they wouldn't let us into the mess hall if they had their way. It's a stupid way to fight a war."

"I'm sorry you have to put up with that."

"It's not your problem." He looked up from his map. "So what do you think of your division?"

"They're weird," she said.

"Oh?"

"None of them seem to realize we're in a war zone," she rephrased. Every regular division soldier she'd encountered was grim-faced, exhausted, but the way the Cike spoke and behaved made them seem like fidgety children—bored rather than scared, off-kilter and out of touch.

"They're killers by profession," Altan said. "They're desensitized to danger—everyone but Unegen, anyway; he's skittish about everything. But the rest can act like they don't understand what everyone's so freaked out about."

"Is that why the Militia hates them?"

"The Militia hates us because we have unlimited access to psychedelics, we can do what they can't, and they don't understand why. It is very difficult to justify how the Cike behave to people who don't believe in shamans," Altan said.

Rin could sympathize with the Militia. Suni's fits of rage were frequent and public. Qara mumbled to her birds in full view of the other soldiers. And once word had gotten out about Enki's veritable apothecary of hallucinogens, it spread like wildfire; the division soldiers couldn't understand why only the Cike should have access to morphine.

"So why don't you just try to tell them?" she asked. "How shamanism works, I mean."

"Because that's such an easy conversation to have? But trust me. They'll see soon enough." Altan tapped his map. "They're treating you all right, though? Made any friends?"

"I like Ramsa," she offered.

"He's a charmer. Like a new puppy. You think he's adorable until he pisses on the furniture."

"Did he?"

"No. But he did take a shit in Baji's pillow once. Don't get on his bad side." Altan grimaced.

"How old is he?" Rin had to ask.

"At least twelve. Probably no older than fifteen." Altan shrugged. "Baji's got this theory that he's actually a forty-year-old who doesn't age, because we've never seen him get any taller, but he's not nearly mature enough."

"And you put him into war zones?"

"Ramsa puts himself into war zones," Altan said. "You just try to stop him. Have you met the rest? No problems?"

"No problems," she said hastily. "Everything's fine, it's just . . ."

"They're not Sinegard graduates," he finished for her. "There's no routine. No discipline. Nothing you're used to. Am I right?"

She nodded.

"You can't think of them as just the Thirteenth Division. You can't command them like ground troops. They're like chess pieces, right? Only they're mismatched and overpowered. Baji's the most competent, and probably should be the commander, but he gets distracted by anything with legs. Unegen's good for intelligence gathering, but he's scared of his own shadow. Bad in open combat. Aratsha's useless unless you're right beside a body of water. You always want Suni in a firefight, but he's got no subtlety, so you can't assign him to anything else. Qara's the best archer I've seen and probably the most useful of the lot, but she's mediocre in hand-to-hand. And Chaghan's a walking psychospiritual bomb, but only when he's here." Altan threw his hands up. "Put that all together and try to formulate a strategy."

Rin glanced down at the markings on his map. "But you've thought of something?"

"I think so." A grin quirked over his face. "Why don't we go call the rest of them?"

Ramsa arrived first. He smelled suspiciously of fire powder, though Rin couldn't imagine where he'd gotten more. Baji and Unegen showed up minutes later, hoisting Aratsha's barrel between them. Qara appeared with Enki, heatedly discussing something in Qara's language. When they saw the others, they quickly fell silent. Suni came in last, and Rin was privately relieved when he took a seat at the opposite end of the room.

Altan's office had only the one chair, so they sat on the floor in a circle like a ring of schoolchildren. Aratsha bobbed conspicuously in the corner, towering over them like some grotesque watery plant.

"Gang's together again," Ramsa said happily.

"Sans Chaghan," said Baji. "When's he back? Qara? Estimated location?"

Qara glowered at him.

"Never mind," said Baji.

"We're all here? Good." Altan walked into the office carrying a rolled-up map in one hand. He unfurled it over his desk, then pinned it up against the far wall. The crucial landmarks of the city had been marked in red and black ink, dotted over with circles of varying size.

"Here's our position in Khurdalain," he said. He pointed to the black circles. "This is us." Then to the red ones. "This is Mugen."

The maps reminded Rin of a game of wikki, the chess variation Irjah had taught them to play in their third-year Strategy class. Wikki play did not involve direct confrontation, but rather dominance through strategic encirclement. Both the Nikara and the Federation had as of yet avoided direct clash, instead filling empty spaces on the complicated network of canals that was Khurdalain to establish a relative advantage. The opposing forces held each other in a fragile equilibrium, gradually raising the stakes as reinforcements flocked to the city from both sides.

"The wharf now stands as the main line of defense. We insulate the civilian quarters against Federation encampments on the beach. They haven't attempted a press farther inland because all three divisions are concentrated right on the mouth of the Sharhap River. But that balance only holds so long as they're uncertain about our numbers. We're not sure how good their intelligence is, but we're guessing they're aware that we'd be pretty evenly matched in an open field. After Sinegard, the Federation forces don't want to risk direct confrontation. They don't want to bleed forces before their inland campaign. They'll only attack when they have the sure numbers advantage."

Altan indicated on the map where he had circled an area to the north of where they were stationed.

"In three days, the Federation will bring in a fleet to supplement the troops at the Sharhap River. Their warship will unload twelve sampans bearing men, supplies, and fire powder off the coast. Qara's birds have seen them sailing over the narrow strait. At their current speed, we predict they will land after sunset of the third day," Altan announced. "I want to sink them."

"And I want to sleep with the Empress." Baji looked around. "Sorry, I thought we were voicing our fantasies."

Altan looked unamused.

"Look at your own map," Baji insisted. "The Sharhap is swarming with Jun's men. You can't attack the Federation without escalation. This forces their hand. And the Warlords won't get on board—they're not ready, they want to wait for the Seventh to get here."

"They're not landing at the Sharhap," Altan responded. "They're docking at the Murui. Far away from the fishing wharf.

The civilians stay away from Murui; the flat shore means that there's a broad intertidal zone and a fast-running tide. Which means there's no fixed coastline. They'll have difficulty unloading. And the terrain beyond the beaches is nonideal for them; it's criss-crossed by rivers and creeks, and there are hardly any good roads."

Baji looked confused. "Then why the hell are they docking there?"

Altan looked smug. "For precisely the same reasons that the First and Eighth are amassing troops by Sharhap. Sharhap's the obvious landing spot. The Federation don't think anyone will be guarding Murui. But they weren't counting on, you know, talking birds."

"Nice one," Unegen said.

"Thank you." Qara looked smug.

"The coast at Murui leads into a tight latticework of irrigation channels by a rice paddy. We will draw the boats as far as possible inland, and Aratsha will ground them by reversing the currents to cut off an escape route."

They looked to Aratsha.

"You can do that?" Baji asked.

The watery blob that was Aratsha's head bobbed from side to side. "A fleet that size? Not easily. I can give you thirty minutes. One hour, tops."

"That's more than enough," said Altan. "If we can get them bunched together, they'll catch fire in seconds. But we need to corral them into the narrow strait. Ramsa. Can you create a diversion?"

Ramsa tossed something round in a sack across the table to Altan.

Altan caught it, opened it, and made a face. "What *is* this?"

"It's the Bone-Burning Fire Oil Magic Bomb," Ramsa said. "New model."

"Cool." Suni leaned toward the bag. "What's in it?"

"Tung oil, sal ammoniac, scallion juice, and feces." Ramsa rattled off the ingredients with relish.

Altan looked faintly alarmed. "*Whose* feces?"

"That's not important," Ramsa said hastily. "This can knock birds out of the sky from fifty feet away. I can plant some bamboo rockets for you, too, but you'll have trouble igniting in this humidity."

Altan raised an eyebrow.

"Right." Ramsa chuckled. "I love Speerlies."

"Aratsha will reverse the currents to trap them," Altan continued. "Suni, Baji, Rin, and I will defend from the shore. They'll have reduced visibility from the combination of smoke and fog, so they'll think we're a larger squad than we are."

"What happens if they try to storm the shore?" Unegen asked.

"They can't," said Altan. "It's marshland. They'll sink into the bog. At nighttime it'll be impossible for them to find solid land. We will defend those crucial points in teams of two. Qara and Unegen will detach supply boats from the back of the van and drag them back to the main channel. Whatever we can't take, we'll burn."

"One problem," Ramsa said. "I'm out of fire powder. The Warlords aren't sharing."

"I'll deal with the Warlords," Altan said. "You just keep making those shit bombs."

The great military strategist Sunzi wrote that fire should be used on a dry night, when flames might spread with the smallest provocation. Fire should be used when one was upwind, so that the wind would carry its brother element, smoke, into the enemy encampment. Fire should be used on a clear night, when there was no chance for rainfall to quench the flames.

Fire should not be used on a night like this, when the humid winds from the beach would prevent it from spreading, when stealth was of utmost importance but any torchlight would give them away.

But tonight they were not using regular fire. They needed nothing so rudimentary as kindling and oil. They didn't need torches. They had Speerlies.

Rin crouched among the reeds beside Altan, eyes fixed on the darkening sky as she awaited Qara's signal. They pressed flat against the mud bank, stomachs on the ground. Water seeped through her thin tunic from the moist mud, and the peat emitted such a rank odor of rotten eggs that breathing through her mouth only made her want to gag.

On the opposite bank she could just see Suni and Baji crawl up against the river and drop down among the reeds. Between them, they held the only two strips of solid land in the paddy; two slender pieces of dry peat that reached into the marsh like fingers.

The thick fog that might have dampened regular kindling now gave them the advantage. It would be a boon to the Federation as they made their amphibious landing, but it would also serve to conceal the Cike and to exaggerate their numbers.

"How did you know there would be a fog?" she whispered to Altan.

"There's a fog every time it rains. This is the wet cycle for the rice paddies. Qara's birds have been keeping track of cloud movements for the past week," Altan said. "We know the marsh inside out."

Altan's attention to detail was remarkable. The Cike operated with a system of signals and cues that Rin would never have been able to decipher had she not been drilled relentlessly the day before. When Qara's falcon flew overhead, that had been the signal for Aratsha to begin his subtle manipulation of the river currents. Half an hour before that, an owl had flown low over the river, signaling Baji and Suni to ingest a handful of colorful fungi. The drug's reaction time was timed precisely to the estimated arrival of the fleet.

Amateurs obsess over strategy, Irjah had once told their class. *Professionals obsess over logistics.*

Rin had choked down a bagful of poppy seeds when she saw Qara's first signal; they stuck thickly to her throat, settled lightly in her stomach. She felt the effects when she stood; she was just high enough that her head felt light but not so woozy that she couldn't wield a sword.

Altan had ingested nothing. Altan, for some reason, did not seem to need any drugs to summon the Phoenix. He called the fire as casually as one might whistle. It was an extension of him that he could manipulate with no concentration at all.

A faint rustle overhead. Rin could barely make out the silhouette of Qara's eagle, passing over for the second time to alert them to the arrival of the Federation. She heard a gentle sloshing noise coming from the channel.

Rin squinted at the river and saw not a fleet of boats but a line of Federation soldiers, implausibly walking in the river that reached up to their shoulders. They carried wooden planks high over their heads.

She realized that they were engineers. They were going to use those planks to create bridges for the incoming fleet to roll supplies onto dry land. *Smart*, she thought. The engineers each held a waterproof lamp high over the murky channel, casting an eerie glow over the canal.

Altan motioned for Suni and Baji to crouch deeper to the ground so they wouldn't be visible over the reeds. The long grass tickled Rin's earlobes, but she didn't move.

Then, far down by the mouth of the channel, Rin saw the dim flicker of a lantern signal. At first she could see only the boat at the fore.

Then the full fleet emerged from the mist.

Rin counted under her breath. The fleet was twelve boats—sleek, well-constructed river sampans—packed with eight men each, sitting in a straight line with trunks of equipment stacked in high piles at the center of each boat.

The fleet paused at a fork in the river. The Federation had two choices; one channel took them to a wide bay where they could unload with relative ease, and the other took them on a detour into the salt marsh labyrinth where the Cike lay in waiting.

The Cike needed to force the fleet to the left.

Altan lifted an arm and flicked his hand out as if releasing a whip. Tendrils of flame licked out from his hands, streaking in either direction like glowing snakes. Rin heard a short sizzling noise as the flame raced through the reeds.

Then, with a high-pitched whistling noise, the first of Ramsa's rockets erupted into the night sky.

Ramsa had rigged the marsh so that each rocket's ignition would light the next sequentially, granting several seconds of delay between explosions. They set the marsh ablaze with a horrifically pungent stink that overwhelmed even the sulfurous odor of the peat.

"Tiger's tits," Altan muttered. "He wasn't joking about the feces."

The explosions continued, a chain reaction of fire powder to simulate the noise and devastation of an army that didn't exist. Bamboo bombs at the far end of the river erupted with what sounded like thunderclaps. A succession of smaller fire rockets exploded with resonant booms and enormous pillars of smoke; these did not catch fire, but served to confuse the Federation soldiers and obstruct their vision, so their boats could not see where they were going.

The explosions goaded the Federation soldiers directly into the dead zone created by Aratsha. When the first flare went up, the Federation boats swerved rapidly away from the source of the explosions. The boats collided with one another, snarled together and crammed in the narrow creek as the fleet moved clumsily forward. The tall rice fields, unharvested since the siege had begun, forced the boats to clump together.

Realizing his mistake, the Federation captain ordered his men to reverse direction, but panicked shouts echoed across the boats as the ships realized they could not move.

The Federation was locked in.

Time for the real attack.

As fire rockets continued to shoot toward the Federation fleet, a series of flaming arrows screamed through the night sky and thudded into the cargo trunks. The volley of arrows came so rapidly that it seemed as if an entire squadron were concealed in the marshes, firing from different directions, but Rin knew that it was only Qara, safely ensconced on the opposite bank, firing with the blinding speed of a trained huntress from the Hinterlands.

Next Qara took out the engineers. She punctured the forehead of every other man, tidily collapsing the man-made bridge with a surreal neatness.

Assaulted from all sides by enemy fire, the Federation fleet began to burn.

The Federation soldiers abandoned their flaming boats in a panic. They leaped for the bank, only to be bogged down in the muddy marsh. Men slipped and fell in paddy water that came up to their waists, filling up their heavy armor. Then, at a whisper from Altan, the reeds along the shore also burst into flame, surrounding the Federation like a death trap.

Even so, some made it to the opposite bank. A throng of soldiers—ten, twenty—clambered onto dry land—only to run into Suni and Baji.

Rin wondered how Suni and Baji intended to hold the entire strip of peat alone. They were only two, and from what she knew of their shamanic abilities, they couldn't control a far-ranging element the way Altan or Aratsha could. Surely they were outnumbered.

She shouldn't have worried.

They barreled through the soldiers like boulders crashing through a wheat field.

In the dim light of Ramsa's flares, Suni and Baji were a flurry of motion that evoked the flashing combat of a shadow puppetry show.

They were so much the opposite of Altan. Altan fought with the practiced grace of a martial artist. Altan moved like a ribbon of smoke, like a dancer. But Baji and Suni were a study in brutality, paragons of sheer and untempered force. They utilized none of the economical forms of Seejin. Their only guiding principle was to smash everything in their vicinity—which they did with abandon, knocking men back off the shore as quickly as they clambered on.

A Sinegard-trained martial artist was worth four Militia men. But Suni and Baji were each worth at least ten.

Baji cut through bodies like a canteen cook chopping through vegetables. His absurd nine-pointed rake, unwieldy in the hands of any other soldier, became a death machine in Baji's grip. He snagged sword blades between the nine prongs, locking three or four blades together before wrenching them out of his opponents' grasps.

His god had given him no apparent transformations, but he fought with a berserker's rage, truly a wild boar in a bloodthirsty frenzy.

Suni fought with no weapon at all. Already massive, he seemed to have grown to the size of a small giant, stretching up to well over ten feet. It shouldn't have been possible for Suni to disarm men with steel swords as he did, but he was simply so terribly strong that his opponents were like children in comparison.

As Rin watched, Suni grasped the heads of the two closest soldiers and smashed them against each other. They burst like ripe cantaloupes. Blood and brain matter splashed out, drenching Suni's entire torso, but he hardly paused to wipe the gore from his face as he turned to smash his fist into another soldier's head.

Fur had sprouted from his arms and back that seemed to serve as an organic shield, repelling metal. A soldier jammed his spear into Suni's back from behind, but the blade simply clattered off to the side. Suni turned around and bent slightly, placed his arms around the soldier's head, and tore it clean off his body with such ease that he might have been twisting the lid off a jar.

When he turned back to the marsh, Rin caught a glimpse of his eyes in the firelight. They were black all the way through.

She shuddered. Those were the eyes of a beast. Whatever was fighting on the shore, that wasn't Suni. That was some ancient entity, malevolent and gleeful, ecstatic to be given free rein to break men's bodies like toys.

"The other bank! Get to the other bank!"

A clump of soldiers broke off from the jammed fleet and approached Altan and Rin's shore in a desperate swarm.

"We're up, kiddo," Altan said, and emerged from the reeds, trident spinning in his grasp.

Rin scampered to her feet, then swayed when the effects of the poppy hit her like a club to the side of the head. She stumbled. She knew she was in a dangerous place. Unless she called the god, the poppy would only make her useless in battle, high and disoriented. But when she reached inside herself for the fire, she grasped nothing.

She tried chanting in the old Speerly language. Altan had taught her the incantation. She didn't understand the words; Altan barely understood them himself, but that didn't matter. What mattered were the harsh sounds, the repetition of incantations that sounded like spitting. The language of Speer was primal, guttural, and savage. It sounded like a curse. It sounded like a condemnation.

Still, it slowed her mind, brought her to the center of her swirling thoughts, and established a direct connection to the Pantheon above.

But she didn't feel herself tipping forward into the void. She heard no whooshing sound in her ears. She was not journeying upward. She reached inside herself, searching for the link to the Phoenix and . . . nothing. She felt nothing.

Something soared through the air and embedded itself in the mud by Rin's feet. She examined it with great difficulty, as if she were looking through a hazy fog. Finally, her drugged mind identified it as an arrow.

The Federation was shooting back.

She was faintly aware of Baji shouting at her from across the channel. She tried to shake away the distractions and direct her mind inward, but panic bubbled up in her chest. She couldn't concentrate. She focused on everything at once: Qara's birds, the incoming soldiers, the bodies getting closer and closer to the shore.

Across the bay she heard an unearthly scream. Suni emitted a series of high-pitched shrieks like a deranged monkey, beat his fists against his chest, and howled up at the night sky.

Beside him Baji threw his head back and boomed out a laugh, and that, too, sounded unnatural. He was too gleeful, more delighted than anyone in the midst of such carnage had the right to be. And Rin realized that this wasn't Baji laughing, this was the god in him that read spilled blood as worship.

Baji lifted his foot and shoved the soldiers squarely into the water, toppling them over like dominoes; he sent them sprawling into the river, where they flailed and struggled against the soggy marsh.

Who controlled whom? Was it the soldier who had called the god, or the god in the body of the soldier?

She didn't want to be possessed. She wanted to remain free.

But the cognitive dissonance clashed in her head. Three sets of countervailing orders competed for priority in her mind—Jiang's mandate to empty her mind, Altan's insistence that she hone her anger as a razor blade, and her own fear of letting the fire rip through her again, because once it began she didn't know how to stop it.

But she couldn't just *stand* there.

Come on, come on . . . She reached for the flames and grasped nothing. She was stuck halfway to the Pantheon and halfway in the material world, unable to fully grasp either. She had lost all sense of balance; she was disoriented, navigating her body as if remotely from very far away.

Something cold and clammy grasped at her ankles. Rin jumped back just as a soldier hauled himself out of the water. He sucked in air with hoarse gasps; he must have held his breath the entire length of the channel.

He saw her, yelled, and fell backward.

All she could register was how *young* he looked. He was not a hardened, trained soldier. This might have been his first combat engagement. He hadn't even thought to draw his weapon.

She advanced on him slowly, walking as if in a dream. Her sword hand felt foreign to her; it was someone else's arm that brought the blade down, it was someone else's foot that kicked the soldier down by his shoulder—

He was faster than she thought; he swept out and kicked her kneecap, knocking her into the mud. Before she could react, he climbed over her, pinning her down with both knees.

She looked up. Their eyes met.

Naked fear was written across his face, round and soft like a child's. He was barely taller than her. He couldn't have been older than Ramsa.

He fumbled with his knife, had to adjust it against his stomach to get a proper grip before he brought it down—

Three metal prongs sprouted from above his collarbone, puncturing the place where his windpipe met his lungs. Blood bubbled from the corners of the soldier's mouth. He splashed backward into the marsh.

"Are you all right?" Altan asked.

Before them the soldier flailed and gurgled pitifully. Altan had aimed two inches above his heart, robbed him of the mercy of an instant death and sentenced him to drown in his own blood.

Rin nodded mutely, scrabbling in the mud for her sword.

"Stay down," he said. "And get back."

He pushed her behind him with more force than necessary. She stumbled against the reeds, then looked up just in time to see Altan light up like a torch.

The effect was like a match struck to oil. Flames burst out of his chest, poured off his bare shoulders and back in streaming rivulets; surrounding him, protecting him. He was a living torch. His fire took the shape of a pair of massive wings that unfurled magnificently about him. Steam rose from the water in a five-foot radius from where Altan stood.

She had to shield her eyes from him.

This was a fully grown Speerly. This was a god in a man.

Altan repelled the soldiers like a wave. They scrambled backward, preferring to take their chances on their burning boats rather than take on this terrifying apparition.

Altan advanced on them, and the flesh sloughed off their bodies.

She could not bear the sight of him and yet she could not tear her eyes away.

Rin wondered if this was how she had burned at Sinegard.

But surely in that moment, with the flames ripping out of every orifice, she had not been so wonderfully graceful. When Altan moved, his fiery wings swirled and dipped as a reflection of him, sweeping indiscriminately across the flotilla and setting things freshly aflame.

It made sense, she thought wildly, that the Cike became living manifestations of their gods.

When Jiang had taught her to access the Pantheon, he had only ever taught her to kneel before the deities.

But the Cike pulled them down with them back into the world of mortals, and when they did, they were destructive and chaotic and terrible. When the shamans of the Cike prayed, they were not requesting that the gods do things for them so much as they were begging the gods to act *through* them; when they opened their minds to the heavens they became vessels for their chosen deities to inhabit.

The more Altan moved, the brighter he burned, as if the Phoenix itself were slowly burning through him to breach the divide between the world of dreaming and the material world. Any arrows that flew in his direction were rendered useless by roiling flames, flung to the side to sizzle dully in the marshy waters.

Rin was half-afraid that Altan would burn away altogether, until there was nothing but the fire.

In that moment she found it impossible to believe that the Speerlies could have been massacred. What a marvel the Speerly army must have been. A full regiment of warriors who burned with the same glory as Altan . . . how had anyone ever killed that race off? One Speerly was a terror; a thousand should have been unstoppable. They should have been able to burn down the world.

Whatever weaponry they had used then, the Federation soldiers were not so powerful now. Their fleet was at every possible disadvantage: trapped on all sides, with fire to their backs, a muddy marsh under their feet, and veritable gods guarding the only strips of solid land in sight.

The jammed boats had begun to burn in earnest; the crates of uniforms, blankets, and medicine smoldered and crackled, emitting thick streams of smoke that cloaked the marsh in an impenetrable shroud. The soldiers on the boats doubled over, choking, and the ones who huddled uncertainly in the shallow water began to scream, for the water had begun to boil under the heat of the blazing inferno.

It was utter carnage. It was beautiful.

Altan's plan had been brilliant in conception. Under normal circumstances, a squad of eight could not hope to stand a chance against such massive odds. But Altan had chosen a battlefield where every single one of the Federation advantages was negated by their surroundings, and the Cike's advantages were amplified.

What it came down to was that the smallest division of the Militia had brought down an entire fleet.

Altan didn't break balance when he strode onto the boat at the fore. He adjusted to the tilting floor so gracefully he might have been walking on solid ground. While the Federation soldiers flailed and reeled away, he flashed his trident out and out again, eliciting blood and silencing cries each time.

They clambered and fell before him like worshippers. He cut them down like reeds.

They splashed into the water, and the screams became louder. Rin saw them boil to death before her very eyes, skin scalded bubbling red like crab shells, and then bursting; cooked inside and out, eyes bulging in their death throes.

She had fought at Sinegard; she had incinerated a general with her own flames, but in that moment she could barely comprehend the casual destruction that Altan wrought. He fought on a scale that should not be human.

Only the captain of the fleet did not scream, did not jump into the water to escape him, but stood as erect and proud as if he were back on his ship, not in the burning wreckage of his fleet.

The captain withdrew his sword slowly and held it out before him.

He could not possibly defeat Altan in combat, but Rin found it strangely honorable that he was going to try.

The captain's lips moved rapidly, as if he was muttering an incantation to the darkness. Rin half wondered whether the captain was a shaman himself, but when she parsed out his frantic Mugini she realized he was praying.

"I am nothing to the glory that is the Emperor. By his favor I am made clean. By his grace I am given purpose. It is an honor to serve. It is an honor to live. It is an honor to die. For Ryohai. For Ryohai. For—"

Altan stepped lightly across the charred helm. Flames licked around his legs, engulfed him, but they could not hurt him.

The captain lifted his sword to his neck.

Altan lunged forward at the last moment, suddenly aware of what the captain meant to do, but he was too far to reach.

The captain drew the blade to the side in a sharp sawing motion. His eyes met Altan's, and a moment before the life dimmed from them, Rin thought she saw a glimmer of victory. Then his corpse slumped into the bog.

When Aratsha's power gave out, the wreckage that drifted back out into the Nariin Sea was a smoldering mess of charred boats, useless supplies, and broken men.

Altan called for a retreat before the Federation soldiers could regroup. Far more soldiers had escaped than they had killed, but their aim had never been to destroy the army. Sinking the supplies was enough.

Not all of the supplies, though. In the confusion of the melee, Unegen and Qara had detached two boats from the rear and hidden them in an inland canal. They boarded these now, and Aratsha spirited them through the narrow canals of Khurdalain into a downtown nook not far from the wharf.

Ramsa ran up to them when they returned.

"Did it work?" he demanded. "Did the flares work?"

"Lit up like a charm. Nice work, kid," Altan said.

Ramsa gave a hoot of victory. Altan clapped him on the shoulder, and Ramsa beamed widely. Rin could read it clearly on Ramsa's face: he adored Altan like an older brother.

It was hard not to feel the same. Altan was so solemnly competent, so casually brilliant, that all she wanted was to please him. He was strict in his command, sparing with his praise, but when he gave it, it felt wonderful. She wanted it, craved it like something tangible.

Next time. Next time she wouldn't be deadweight. She would learn to channel that anger at will, even if she risked losing herself to it.

They celebrated that night with a sack of sugar pillaged from one of the stolen boats. The mess hall was locked and they had nothing to sprinkle the sugar on, so they ate it straight by the spoonful. Once Rin would have found this disgusting; now she shoved great heaps of it into her mouth when the spoon and sack came around to her place in the circle.

Upon Ramsa's insistence, Altan acquiesced to lighting a roaring bonfire for them out in an empty field.

"We're not worried about being seen?" Rin asked.

"We're well behind Nikara lines. It's fine. Just don't throw anything on it," he said. "You can't experiment with pyrotechnics so close to civilians."

Ramsa blew air out of his cheeks. "Whatever you say, Trengsin."

Altan gave him an exasperated look. "I mean it this time."

"You suck the fun out of everything," Ramsa grumbled as Altan stepped away from the fire.

"You're not staying?" Baji asked.

Altan shook his head. "Need to brief the Warlords. I'll be back in a few hours. You go on and celebrate. I'm very pleased with your performance today."

"'*I'm very pleased with your performance today*,'" Baji mimicked when Altan had left. "Someone tell him to get that stick out of his butt."

Ramsa leaned back on his elbows and nudged Rin with his foot. "Was he this insufferable at the Academy?"

"I don't know," she said. "I didn't know him well at Sinegard."

"I bet he's always been like this. Old man in a young man's body. You think he ever smiles?"

"Only once a year," said Baji. "Accidentally, in his sleep."

"Come on," Unegen said, though he was also smiling. "He's a good commander."

"He *is* a good commander," Suni agreed. "Better than Tyr."

Suni's gentle voice surprised Rin. When he was free of his god, Suni was remarkably quiet, almost timid, and he spoke only after ponderous deliberation.

Rin watched him sitting calmly before the fire. His broad features were relaxed and placid; he seemed utterly at ease with himself. She wondered when he would next lose control and fall prey to that screaming voice in his mind. He was so terrifyingly strong—he had broken men apart in his hands like eggs. He killed so well and so efficiently.

He could have killed Altan. Three nights ago in the mess hall Suni could have broken Altan's neck as easily as he would wring a chicken's. The thought made her dry-mouthed with fear.

And she wondered at how Altan had known this and had crossed the distance to Suni anyway, had placed his life completely in the hands of his subordinate.

Baji had somehow extracted a bottle of sorghum spirits from

one of the many warehouses of Khurdalain. They passed it around the circle. They had just scored a major combat victory; they could afford to be off guard for just one night.

"Hey, Rin." Ramsa rolled onto his stomach and propped his chin up on his hands.

"Yeah?"

"Does this mean the Speerlies aren't extinct after all?" he inquired. "Are you and Altan going to make babies and repopulate the Speerly race?"

Qara snorted loudly. Unegen spat out a mouthful of sorghum wine.

Rin turned bright red. "Not likely," she said.

"Why not? You don't like Altan?"

The cheeky little shit. "No, I mean I can't," she said. "I can't have children."

"Why not?" Ramsa pressed.

"I had my womb destroyed at the Academy," she said. She hugged her knees up to her chest. "It was, um, interfering with my training."

Ramsa looked so bewildered then that Rin burst out laughing. Qara snickered into her canteen.

"*What?*" Ramsa asked, indignant.

"I'll tell you one day," Baji promised. He'd imbibed twice as much wine as the rest of them; he was already slurring his words together. "When your balls have dropped."

"My balls *have* dropped."

"When your voice drops, then."

They passed the bottle around in silence for a moment. Now that the frenzy at the marsh was over, the Cike seemed diminished somehow, like they had been animated only by the presence of their gods, and now in the gods' absence they were empty, shells that lacked vitality.

They seemed eminently human—vulnerable and breakable.

"So you're the last of your kind," said Suni after a short silence. "That's sad."

"I guess." Rin poked a stick at the fire. She still didn't feel quite acclimated to her new identity. She had no memories of Speer, no real attachments to it. The only time she felt like being a Speerly meant something was when she was with Altan. "Everything about Speer is sad."

"It's that idiot queen's fault," said Unegen. "They never would have died off if Tearza hadn't stabbed herself."

"She didn't stab herself," said Ramsa. "She burned to death. Imploded from inside. Boom." He spread his fingers in the air.

"Why *did* she kill herself?" Rin asked. "I never understood that story."

"In the version I heard, she was in love with the Red Emperor," said Baji. "He comes to her island, and she's immediately besotted with him. He turns around and threatens to invade the island if Speer doesn't become a tributary state. And she's so distraught at his betrayal that she flees to her temple and kills herself."

Rin wrinkled her nose. Every version she heard of the myth made Tearza seem more and more stupid.

"It is not a love story." Qara spoke up from her corner for the first time. Their eyes flickered toward her with mild surprise.

"That myth is Nikara propaganda," she continued flatly. "The story of Tearza was modeled on the myth of Han Ping, because the story makes for a better telling than the truth."

"And what is the truth?" asked Rin.

"You don't know?" Qara fixed Rin with a somber gaze. "Speerlies especially ought to know."

"Obviously I don't. So how would you tell it?"

"I would tell it not as a love story, but as a story of gods and humans." Qara's voice dropped to such a low volume that the Cike had to lean in to hear her. "They say Tearza could have called the Phoenix and saved the isle. They say that if Tearza had summoned the flames, Nikan never would have been able to annex Speer. They say that if she wanted to, Tearza could have summoned such a power that the Red Emperor and his armies would not have dared set foot on Speer, not for a thousand years."

Qara paused. She did not take her eyes off Rin.

"And then?" Rin pressed.

"Tearza refused," Qara said. "She said the independence of Speer did not warrant the sacrifice the Phoenix demanded. The Phoenix declared that Tearza had broken her vows as the ruler of Speer, and so it punished her for it."

Rin was quiet for a moment. Then she asked, "Do you think she was right?"

Qara shrugged. "I think Tearza was wise. *And* I think that she was a bad ruler. Shamans should know when to resist the power of the gods. That is wisdom. But rulers should do everything in their power to save their country. That is responsibility. If you hold the fate of the country in your hands, if you have accepted your obligation to your people, then your life ceases to be your own. Once you accept the title of ruler, your choices are made for you. In those days, to rule Speer meant serving the Phoenix. Speer used to be a proud race. A free people. When Tearza killed herself, the Speerlies became little more than the Emperor's mad dogs. Tearza has the blood of Speer on her hands. Tearza deserved what she got."

When Altan returned from reporting to the Warlords, most of the Cike had drifted off to sleep. Rin remained awake, staring at the flickering bonfire.

"Hey," he said, and sat down next to her. He smelled of smoke.

She drew her knees up to her chest and tilted her head sideways to look at him. "How'd they take it?"

Altan smiled. It was the first time she'd seen him smile since they came to Khurdalain. "They couldn't believe it. How are you doing?"

"Embarrassed," she said frankly, "and still a little high."

He leaned back and crossed his arms. His smile disappeared. "What happened?"

"Couldn't concentrate," she said. *Got scared. Held off. Did everything you told me not to do.*

Altan looked faintly puzzled, and more than a little disappointed.

"I'm sorry," she said in a small voice.

"No, it's my fault." His voice was carefully neutral. "I threw you into combat before you were ready. At the Night Castle, you would have trained for months before we put you in the field."

This was meant to make her feel better, but Rin only felt ashamed.

"I couldn't clear my mind," she said.

"Then don't," Altan said. "Open-minded meditation is for monks. It only gets you to the Pantheon, it doesn't bring the god back down with you. You don't need to open your mind to all sixty-four deities. You only need our god. You only need the fire."

"But Jiang said that was dangerous."

Though Rin thought she saw a spasm of impatience flicker across Altan's face, his tone remained carefully neutral. "Because Jiang *feared*, and so he held you back. Were you acting under his orders when you called the Phoenix at Sinegard?"

"No," she admitted, "but—"

"Have you *ever* successfully called a god under Jiang's instruction? Did Jiang even teach you how? I'll bet he did the opposite. I'll bet he wanted you to shut them out."

"He was trying to protect me," she protested, though she wasn't sure why. After all, it was precisely what had frustrated her about Jiang. But somehow, after what she'd done at Sinegard, Jiang's caution made more sense. "He warned that I might . . . that the consequences . . ."

"Great danger is always associated with great power. The difference between the great and the mediocre is that the great are willing to take that risk." Altan's face twisted into a scowl. "Jiang was a coward, scared of what he had unlocked. Jiang was a doddering fool who didn't realize what talents he had. What talents *you* have."

"He was still my master," she said, feeling an instinctive urge to defend him.

"He's not your master anymore. You don't have a master. You have a commander." Altan put a hand on her shoulder. "The easiest shortcut to the state is anger. Build on your anger. Don't *ever* let go of that anger. Rage gives you power. Caution does not."

Rin wanted to believe him. She was in awe of the extent of Altan's power. And she knew that, if she allowed it, the same power could be her own.

And yet, Jiang's warnings echoed in the back of her mind.

I have met spirits unable to find their bodies again. I have met men who are only halfway to the spirit realm, caught between our world and the next.

Was that the price of power? For her mind to shatter, like Suni's clearly had? Would she become neurotically paranoid, like Unegen?

But Altan's mind hadn't shattered. Among the Cike, Altan used his abilities most recklessly. Baji and Suni needed hallucinogens to call their gods, but the fire was never more than a whisper away for Altan. He seemed to always be in that state of rage he wanted Rin to cultivate. And yet he never lost control. He gave an incredible illusion of sanity and stability, whatever was going on below his dispassionate mask.

Who is imprisoned in the Chuluu Korikh?

Unnatural criminals, who have committed unnatural crimes.

She suspected she knew now what Jiang's question had meant.

She didn't want to admit that she was scared. Scared of being in a state where she had little control of herself, less still of the fires pouring out of her. Scared of being consumed by the fire, becoming a conduit that demanded more and more sacrifice for her god.

"The last time I did it, I couldn't stop," she said. "I had to beg it. I don't—I don't know how to control myself when I've called the Phoenix."

"Think of it like a candle," he said. "Difficult to light. Only this is even more difficult to extinguish, and if you're not careful, you'll burn yourself."

But that didn't help at all—she'd *tried* lighting the candle, yet nothing had happened. So what would happen if she finally figured that out, only to be unable to extinguish the flames? "Then how do *you* do it? How do you make it stop?"

Altan leaned back away from the flames.

"I don't," he said.

CHAPTER 15

The Ram and Ox Warlords quickly realigned to Altan's side once they realized the Cike had accomplished what the First, Fifth, and Eighth Divisions together had not even attempted. They disseminated the news through the ranks in a way that made it seem that they were jointly responsible for the feat.

Khurdalain's citizens threw a victory parade to raise morale and collect supplies for the soldiers. Civilians donated food and clothing to the barracks. When the Warlords paraded through the streets, they were met with wide applause that they were only too happy to accept.

The civilians assumed the marsh victory had been achieved through a massive joint assault. Altan did nothing to correct them.

"Lying fart-bags," Ramsa complained. "They're stealing your credit."

"Let them," said Altan. "If it means they'll work with me, let them say anything they want."

Altan had needed that victory. In a cohort of generals who had survived the Poppy Wars, Altan was the youngest commander by decades. The battle at the marsh had given him much-needed credibility in the eyes of the Militia, and more important, in the eyes of the Warlords. They treated him now with deference instead of condescension, consulted him in their war councils, and not only listened to Cike intelligence but acted on it.

Only Jun offered no congratulations.

"You've left a thousand starving enemy soldiers in the wetlands with no supplies and no food," Jun said slowly.

"Yes," Altan said. "Isn't that a good thing?"

"You idiot," said Jun. He paced about the office, circled back, then slammed his hands on Altan's desk. "You *idiot*. Do you realize what you've done?"

"Secured a victory," Altan said, "which is more than you've managed in the weeks you've been here. Their supply ship has turned all the way back to the longbow island to restock. We've set their plans back at least two weeks."

"You've invited retaliation," Jun snapped. "Those soldiers are cold, wet, and hungry. Maybe they didn't care much about this war when they crossed the narrow strait, but now they're angry. They're pissed, they're humiliated, and more than anything they desperately need supplies. You've raised the stakes for them."

"The stakes were already high," Altan said.

"Yes, and now you've dragged pride into it. Do you know how much reputation matters to Federation commanders? We needed time for fortifications, but you've doubled their timetables. What, did you think they would just turn tail and go home? You want to know what they'll do next? They're going to come for us."

But when the Federation did come, it was with a white flag and a plea for a cease-fire.

When Qara's birds spotted the incoming Federation delegation, she sent Rin to alert Altan with the news. Thrilled, Rin barged past Jun's aides to force her way into the office of the Ram Warlord.

"Three Federation delegates," she reported. "They brought a wagon."

"Shoot them," Jun suggested immediately.

"They're carrying a white flag," Rin said.

"A strategic gambit. Shoot them," Jun repeated, and his junior officers nodded their assent.

The Ox Warlord held up a hand. He was a tremendously large man, two heads taller than Jun and thrice again his girth. His weapon of choice was a double-bladed battle-axe that was the size of Rin's torso, which he kept on the table in front of him, stroking the blade obsessively. "They could be coming under peace."

"Or they could be coming to poison our water supply, or to assassinate any one of us," Jun snapped. "Do you really think we've won this war so easily?"

"They're bearing a white flag," the Ox Warlord said slowly, as if speaking to a child.

The Ram Warlord said nothing. His wide-set eyes darted nervously between Jun and the Ox Warlord. Rin could see what Ramsa had meant; the Ram Warlord seemed like a child waiting to be told what to do.

"A white flag doesn't mean anything to them," Jun insisted. "This is a ruse. How many false treaties did they sign during the Poppy Wars?"

"Would you take a gamble on peace?" the Ox Warlord challenged.

"I wouldn't gamble with any of these citizens' lives."

"It's not your cease-fire to refuse," the Ram Warlord pointed out.

Jun and the Ox Warlord both glared at him, and the Ram Warlord stammered in his haste to explain. "I mean, we ought to let the boy handle it. The marsh victory was his doing. They're surrendering to him."

All eyes turned to Altan.

Rin was amazed at the subtle interdivisional politics at play. The Ram Warlord was shrewder than she'd guessed. His suggestion was a clever way of absolving responsibility. If negotiations went sour, then blame would fall on Altan's shoulders. And if they went well, then the Ram Warlord still came out on top for his magnanimity.

Altan hesitated, clearly torn between his better judgment and desire to see the full extent of his victory at Khurdalain. Rin could see the hope reflected clearly on his face. If the Federation surrender was genuine, then he would be single-handedly responsible for winning this war. He would be the youngest commander ever to have achieved a military victory on this scale.

"Shoot them," Jun repeated. "We don't need a peace negotiation. Our forces are tied now; if the assault on the wharf goes well, we can push them back indefinitely until the Seventh gets here."

But Altan shook his head. "If we reject their surrender, then this war goes on until one party has decimated the other. Khurdalain can't hold out that long. If there's a chance we can end this war now, we need to take it."

The Federation delegates who met them in the town square bore no weapons and wore no armor. They dressed in light, form-fitting blue uniforms designed to make it clear that they concealed no weapons in their sleeves.

The head delegate, whose uniform stripes indicated his higher rank, stepped forward when he saw them.

"Do you speak our language?" He spoke in a halting and outdated Nikara dialect, complete with a bad approximation of a Sinegardian accent.

The Warlords hesitated, but Altan cut in, "I do."

"Good," the delegate responded in Mugini. "Then we may proceed without misunderstanding."

It was the first time Rin had gotten a good look at the Mugenese outside the chaos of a melee, and she was disappointed by how very similar they looked to the Nikara. The slant of their eyes and the shape of their mouths were nowhere near as pronounced as the textbooks reported. Their hair was the same pitch-black as Nezha's, their skin as pale as any northerner's.

In fact, they looked more like Sinegardians than Rin and Altan did.

Aside from their language, which was more clipped and rapid than Sinegardian Nikara, they were virtually indistinguishable from the Nikara themselves.

It disturbed her that the Federation soldiers so closely resembled her own people. She would have preferred a faceless, monstrous enemy, or one that was entirely foreign, like the pale-haired Hesperians across the sea.

"What are your terms?" Jun asked.

"Our general requests a cease-fire for the next forty-eight hours while we meet to negotiate conditions of surrender," said the head delegate. He indicated the wagon. "We know your city has been unable to import spices since the fighting began. We bring an offering of salt and sugar. A gesture of our goodwill." The delegate placed his hand on the lid of the closest chest. "May I?"

Altan gave a nod of permission. The delegates pulled up the lids, displaying heaps of white and caramel crystals that glistened in the afternoon sun.

"Eat it," suggested Jun.

The delegate cocked his head. "Pardon?"

"Taste the sugar," Jun said. "So we know you're not trying to poison us."

"That would be a terribly inefficient way of conducting warfare," said the delegate.

"Even so."

Shrugging, the delegate obliged Jun's request. His throat bobbed as he swallowed. "Not poison."

Jun licked his finger, stuck it in the chest of sugar, and tipped it into his mouth. He swilled it around in his mouth, and seemed disappointed when he couldn't detect traces of any other material.

"Only sugar," said the delegate.

"Excellent," the Ox Warlord said. "Bring these to the mess hall."

"No," said Altan quickly. "Leave it out here. We'll distribute this in the town square. A small amount for every household."

He met the Ox Warlord's eyes with a level gaze, and Rin realized why he'd said it. If the rations were brought to the mess hall, the divisions would immediately fight over distribution of resources. Altan had tied the Warlords' hands by designating the rations for the people.

In any case, a trickle of Khurdalaini civilians had already begun to gather around the wagon in curiosity. Salt and sugar had been sorely missed since the siege began. Rin suspected that if the Warlords confiscated the trunks for military use, the people would riot.

The Ox Warlord shrugged. "Whatever you say, kid."

Altan looked warily about the square. Given the ranks of Militia soldiers present, a large crowd of civilians had deemed it safe to form around the three delegates. Rin saw such open hostility in their eyes that she didn't doubt they would tear the Mugenese apart if the Militia didn't intervene.

"We will continue this negotiation in a private office," Altan suggested. "Away from the people."

The delegate inclined his head. "As you like."

"The Emperor Ryohai is impressed with the resistance at Khurdalain," said the delegate. His tone was clipped and courteous, despite his words. "Your people have fought well. The Emperor Ryohai would like to extend his compliments to the people of Khurdalain, who have proven themselves a stronger breed than the rest of this land of sniveling cowards."

Jun translated to the Warlords. The Ox Warlord rolled his eyes.

"Let's skip ahead to the part where you surrender," said Altan.

The delegate raised an eyebrow. "Alas, the Emperor Ryohai has no intentions of abandoning his designs on the Nikara continent. Expansion onto the continent is the divine right of the glorious Federation of Mugen. Your provincial government is weak and fragile. Your technology is centuries behind that of the west. Your isolation has set you behind while the rest of the world develops.

Your demise was only a matter of time. This landmass belongs to a country that can propel it into the next century."

"Did you come here just to insult us?" Jun demanded. "Not a wise way to surrender."

The delegate's lip curled. "We came only to *discuss* surrender. The Emperor Ryohai has no desire to punish the people of Khurdalain. He admires their fighting spirit. He says that your resilience has proven worthy of the Federation. He adds also that the people of Khurdalain would make excellent subjects to the Federation crown."

"Ah," said Jun. "This is *that* kind of negotiation."

"We do not want to destroy this town," said the delegate. "This is an important port. A hub of international trade. If Khurdalain lays down its arms, then the Emperor Ryohai will consider this city a territory of the Federation, and we will not lay a finger on a single man, woman, or child. All citizens will be pardoned, on the condition that they swear allegiance to the Emperor Ryohai."

"Pause," said Altan. "You're asking us to surrender to *you*?"

The delegate inclined his head. "These are generous terms. We know how Khurdalain struggles under occupation. Your people are starving. Your supplies will only last you a few more months. When we break the siege, we will take the open battle to the streets, and then your people will die in droves. You can avoid that. Let the Federation fleet through, and the Emperor will reward you. We shall permit you to live."

"Incredible," muttered Jun. "Absolutely incredible."

Altan crossed his arms. "Tell your generals that if you turn your fleets back and evacuate the shore now, we will let *you* live."

The delegate merely regarded him with an idle curiosity. "You must be the Speerly from the marsh."

"I am." Altan said. "And I'll be the one who accepts your surrender."

The corners of the head delegate's mouth turned up. "But of course," he said smoothly. "Only a child would assume a war could end so quickly, or so bloodlessly."

"That child speaks for all of us," Jun cut in, voice steely. He spoke in Nikara. "Take your conditions and tell the Emperor Ryohai that Khurdalain will never bow to the longbow island."

"In that case," said the delegate, "every last man, woman, and child in Khurdalain shall die."

"Tall words from a man who's just had his fleet burned to bits," Jun sneered.

The delegate answered in flat, emotionless Nikara. "The marsh defeat has set us back several weeks. But we have been preparing for this war for two decades. Our training schools far outstrip your pathetic Sinegard Academy. We have studied the western techniques of warfare while you have spent these twenty years indulging in your isolation. The Nikara Empire belongs to the past. We will raze your country to the ground."

The Ox Warlord reached for his axe. "Or I can take your head off right now."

The delegate looked supremely unconcerned. "Kill me if you like. On the longbow island, we are taught that our lives are meaningless. I am only one in a horde of millions. I will die, and I will be reincarnated again in the Emperor Ryohai's service. But for you, heretics who do not bow to the divine throne, death will be final."

Altan stood up. His face had turned pale with fury. "You are trapped on a narrow strip of land. You are outnumbered. We took your supplies. We burned your boats. We sank your munitions. Your men have met the wrath of a Speerly, and they burned."

"Oh, Speerlies are not so difficult to kill," the delegate said. "We managed it once. We'll do it again."

The office doors burst open. Ramsa ran inside, wild-eyed.

"That's saltpeter!" he shrieked. "That's not salt, it's *saltpeter*."

The office fell silent.

The Warlords looked at Ramsa as if they couldn't comprehend what he was saying. Altan's mouth opened in confusion.

Then the delegate threw his head back and laughed with the abandon of a man who knew he was about to die.

"Remember," he said. "You could have saved Khurdalain."

Rin and Altan stood up at the same time.

She had barely reached for her sword when a blast split the air like a thunderbolt.

One moment she was standing behind Altan and the next she was on the floor, dazed, with such a ferocious ringing in her ears that it drowned out any other sound.

She lifted her hand to her face and it came away bloody.

As if to compensate for her hearing, her vision became exceedingly bright; the blurred sights were like images on a shadow puppet screen, occurring both too fast and too slow for her to comprehend. She perceived movements as if from inside a drug-induced fever dream, but this was no dream; her senses simply refused to comply with the perception of what had happened.

She saw the walls of the office shudder and then lean so far to the side she was sure that the building would collapse with them in it, and then right themselves.

She saw Ramsa tackle Altan to the ground.

She saw Altan stagger to his feet, reaching for his trident.

She saw the Ox Warlord swing his axe through the air.

She saw Altan shouting "No, *no!*"—before the Ox Warlord decapitated the delegate.

The delegate's head rolled to a stop by the doorway, eyes open and glassy, and Rin thought she saw it smile.

Strong arms grasped her by the shoulders and hauled her to her feet. Altan spun her around to face him, eyes darting around her form as if checking for injuries.

His mouth moved, but no sound came through. She shook her head frantically and pointed to her ears.

He mouthed the words. *"Are you all right?"*

She examined her body. Somehow all four limbs were working, and she couldn't even feel the pain where she bled from a head wound. She nodded.

Altan let her go and knelt down before Ramsa, who was curled in a ball on the ground, pale and trembling.

On the other side of the room General Jun and the Ram Warlord hauled themselves to their feet. They were both unharmed;
the blast had blown them over but had not injured them. The
Warlords' quarters were far enough from the center of the town
that the explosion only shook them.

Even Ramsa seemed like he would be fine. His eyes were glassy
and he wobbled when Altan pulled him to his feet, but he was
nodding and talking, and looked otherwise uninjured.

Rin exhaled in relief.

They were all right. It hadn't worked. They were all right.

And then she remembered the civilians.

Odd how the rest of her senses were amplified when she couldn't
hear.

Khurdalain looked like the Academy in the first days of winter. She squinted; at first she thought her eyesight had blurred as
well, and then she realized that a fine powder hung in the air. It
clouded everything like some bizarre mix of fog and snowfall, a
blanket of innocence that mixed in with the blood, that obscured
the full extent of the explosion.

The square had been flattened, shop fronts and residential
complexes collapsed, debris strewn out in oddly symmetrical lines
from the radius of the blast, as if they stood inside a giant's footprint.

Farther out from the blast site, the buildings were not flattened
but blown open; they tilted at bizarre angles, entire walls torn
away. There was a strangely intimate perversity to how their insides were revealed, displaying private bedrooms and washrooms
to the outside.

Men and women had been thrown against the walls of buildings. They remained frozen there with a kind of ghastly adhesion,
pinned like preserved butterflies. The intense pressure from the
bombs had torn off their clothes; they hung naked like a grotesque
display of the human form.

The stench of charcoal, blood, and burned flesh was so heavy

that Rin could taste it on her tongue. Even worse was the sickening sweet undercurrent of caramelized sugar wafting through
the air.

She did not know how long she stood there staring. She was in-
cited to movement only when jostled by a pair of soldiers rushing
past her with a stretcher, reminding her that she had a job to do.

Find the survivors. Help the survivors.

She made her way down the street, but her sense of balance
seemed to have disappeared completely along with her hearing.
She lurched from side to side when she tried to walk, and so she
traversed the street by clinging to furniture like a drunkard.

To her left she saw a group of soldiers hauling a pair of children
out from a pile of debris. She couldn't believe they had survived, it
seemed impossible so close to the blast epicenter—but the little boy
they lifted from the wreckage was moving, wailing and struggling
but moving nonetheless. His sister was not so fortunate; her leg
was mangled, crushed by the foundations of the house. She clung
to the soldier's arms, white-faced, too racked with pain to cry.

"Help me! *Help me!*"

A tinny voice made it through the roaring in her ears, like
someone shouting from across a great field, but it was the only
sound she could hear.

She looked up and saw a man clinging desperately to the remains of a wall with one hand.

The floor of the building had been blown out right beneath
him. It was a five-story inn; without its fourth wall it looked like
one of the porcelain dollhouses that Rin had seen in the market,
the kind that swung wide open to reveal its contents.

The floors tilted down toward the gap; the inn's furniture and
its other occupants had already slid out, forming a grotesque pile
of shattered chairs and bodies.

A small crowd had gathered under the teetering inn to watch
the man.

"*Help,*" he moaned. "Someone, help . . ."

Rin felt like a spectator, like this was a show, like the man was the only thing in the world that mattered, yet she couldn't think of anything to do; the building had been blown apart; it looked minutes from collapsing in on itself, and the man was too high up to reach from the rooftops of any surrounding buildings.

All she could do was stand there in awe with her mouth hanging slackly open, watching as the man struggled in vain to hoist himself up.

She felt so utterly, entirely useless. Even if she could call the Phoenix then, summoning fire now would not save this man from dying.

Because all the Cike knew how to do was destroy. For all their powers, for all their gods, they couldn't protect their people. Couldn't reverse time. Couldn't bring back the dead.

They had won that battle on the marsh, but they were powerless in the face of the consequences.

Altan shouted something, and he might have been calling for a sheet to break the man's fall, because moments later Rin saw several soldiers come running back down into the square with a cloth.

But before they could reach the end of the street, the inn teetered perilously. Rin thought it might crash all the way to the ground, flattening the man underneath it, but the wooden planks dipped downward and came to a jarring halt.

The man was now only four floors up. He flung his other hand up at the roof in an attempt to secure a better hold. Perhaps he was emboldened by his closeness to the ground. For a moment Rin thought he might make it—but then his hand slipped against the shattered glass and he fell back, the downward rebound pulling him off the roof entirely.

He seemed to hang in the air for a moment before he fell.

The crowd scrambled backward.

Rin turned away, grateful that she could not hear his body break on the ground.

* * *

The city settled into a tense silence.

Every soldier was dispatched to Khurdalain's defenses in anticipation of a ground assault. Rin held her post on the outer wall for hours, eyes trained on the perimeter. If the Federation was going to attempt to breach the walls, certainly it would be now.

But evening fell, and no attack came.

"They can't possibly be afraid," Rin murmured, then winced. Her hearing had finally come back, though a high-pitched ringing still sounded constantly in her ears.

Ramsa shook his head. "They're playing the long game. They'll keep trying to weaken us. Get us scared, hungry, and tired."

Eventually the defensive line relaxed. If the Federation launched a midnight invasion, the city alarm system would bring the troops back to the walls; in the meantime, there was more pressing work to do.

It felt brutally ironic that civilians had been dancing on this street only hours ago, celebrating what they'd thought would be a Federation surrender. Khurdalain had expected to win this war. Khurdalain had thought that things were going back to normal.

But Khurdalain was resilient. Khurdalain had survived two Poppy Wars. Khurdalain knew how to deal with devastation.

The civilians quietly combed through the wreckage for their loved ones, and when so many hours had passed that the only bodies that were recovered were those of the dead, they built them a funeral bier, lit it on fire, and pushed it out to the sea. They did this with a sad, practiced efficiency.

The medical squads of all three divisions jointly created a triage center in the city center. For the rest of the day civilians straggled in, amateur tourniquets tied clumsily around severed limbs— crushed ankles, hands shattered to the stump.

Rin had a year's worth of instruction in field medicine under Enro, so Enki put her to work tying off new tourniquets for those bleeding in line as they waited for medical attention.

Her first patient was a young woman, not much older than Rin was. She held out her arm, wrapped in what looked like an old dress.

Rin unwrapped the blood-soaked bundle and hissed involuntarily at the damage. She could see bone all the way up to the elbow. That entire hand would have to go.

The girl waited patiently as Rin assessed the damage, eyes glassy, as if she'd long ago resigned herself to her new disability.

Rin pulled a strip of linen out of a pot of boiling water and wrapped it around the upper arm, looped one end around a stick, and twisted to tighten the binding. The girl moaned with pain, but gritted her teeth and glared straight forward.

"They'll probably take the hand off. This will keep you from losing any more blood, and it'll make it easier for them to amputate." Rin fastened the knot and stepped back. "I'm sorry."

"I knew we should have left," the girl said. The way she spoke, Rin wasn't sure that she was talking to her. "I knew we should have left the moment those ships landed on the shore."

"Why didn't you?" Rin asked.

The girl glared at her. Her eyes were hollow, accusatory. "You think we had anywhere to go?"

Rin fixed her eyes on the ground and moved on to the next patient.

CHAPTER 16

Hours later Rin finally received permission to leave the triage center. She stumbled back toward the Cike's quarters, hollow-eyed and light-headed from sleep deprivation. Once she checked in with Altan, she intended to collapse in her bunk and sleep until someone forced her out to report for duty.

"Enki finally let you off?"

She glanced over her shoulder.

Unegen and Baji rounded the corner, coming back from patrol. They joined her as she walked down the eerily empty streets. The Warlords had imposed martial law on the city; civilians had a strict curfew now, no longer allowed to venture beyond their block without Militia permission.

"I'm to be back in six hours," she said. "You?"

"Nonstop patrol until something more interesting happens," said Unegen. "Did Enki get the casualty count?"

"Six hundred dead," she said. "A thousand wounded. Fifty division soldiers. The rest civilians."

"Shit," Unegen muttered.

"Yeah," she said listlessly.

"The Warlords are just sitting on their hands," Baji complained. "The bombs scared the wits out of them. Fucking useless.

Don't they see? We can't just absorb the attack. We've got to strike back."

"Strike back?" Rin repeated. The very idea sounded halfhearted, disrespectful, and pointless. All she wanted to do was curl up in a ball and hold her hands over her ears and pretend nothing was happening. Leave this war to someone else.

"What are we supposed to do?" Unegen was saying. "The Warlords won't attack, and we'll get slaughtered on the open field ourselves."

"We can't just wait for the Seventh, they'll take weeks—"

They approached headquarters just as Qara stepped out of Altan's office. She closed the door delicately behind her, noticed them, and her face froze.

Baji and Unegen stopped walking. The heavy silence that transpired seemed to contain some unspoken message that everyone but Rin understood.

"It's like that, huh?" Unegen asked.

"It's worse," said Qara.

"What's going on?" Rin asked. "Is he in there?"

Qara looked warily at her. For some reason she smelled overwhelmingly of smoke. Her expression was unreadable. Rin might have seen tear tracks glistening on her cheek, or it might have been a trick of the lamplight.

"He's indisposed," Qara said.

The Federation's retaliation did not end with the bombing.

Two days after the downtown explosions, the Federation sent bilingual agents to negotiate with starving fishermen in the town of Zhabei, just south of Khurdalain, and told them the Mugenese would clear their boats from the dock if the fishermen collected all the stray cats and dogs in the town for them.

Only starving civilians would have obeyed such a bizarre order. The fishermen were desperate, and they handed over every last stray animal they could find without question.

The Federation soldiers tied kindling to the animals' tails and lit them on fire. Then they set them loose in Zhabei.

The ensuing flames burned for three days before rainfall finally extinguished them. When the smoke cleared, nothing remained of Zhabei but ashes.

Thousands of civilians were left homeless overnight, and the refugee problem in Khurdalain became unmanageable. The men, women, and children of Zhabei crammed into the shrinking parts of the city that were not yet under Federation occupation. Poor hygiene, lack of clean water, and an outbreak of cholera made the civilian districts a nightmare.

Popular sentiment turned against the Militia. The First, Fifth, and Eighth Divisions attempted to maintain martial rule, only to meet open defiance and riots.

The Warlords, desperately needing a scapegoat, publicly blamed their reversals of fortune on Altan. It helped them that the bombing shattered his credibility as a commander. He had won his first combat victory, only to have it ripped from him and turned into a tragic defeat, an example of the consequences of acting without thinking.

When Altan finally emerged from his office, he seemed to take it in stride. No one made mention of his absence; the Cike seemed to collectively pretend that nothing had happened at all. He showed no signs of insecurity—if anything, his behavior become almost manic.

"So we're back where we started," he said, pacing rapidly about his office. "Fine. We'll fight back. Next time we'll be thorough. Next time we'll win."

He planned far more operations than they could ever feasibly carry out. But the Cike were not historically soldiers, they were assassins. The battle at the marsh had been an unprecedented feat of teamwork for them; they were trained to take out crucial targets, not entire battalions. Yet assassinations did not go far in winning wars. The Federation was not like a snake, to be vanquished by cutting off the head. If a general was killed in his camp, a colonel was immediately promoted in his place. For the Cike to go about their business as usual, conducting one assassination after another, would have been a slow and inefficient way of waging a war.

So Altan used his soldiers like a guerrilla strike force instead. They stole supplies, waged hit-and-run attacks, and caused as much disruption as they could in enemy camps.

"I want the entire intersection sealed off," Altan declared, drawing a large circle on the map. "Sandbags. Barbed wire. We need to minimize all points of entry within the next twenty-four hours. I want this warehouse back."

"We can't do that," Baji said uneasily.

"Why not?" Altan snapped. A vein pulsed in his neck; dark circles ringed his eyes. Rin didn't think he had slept in days.

"Because they've got a thousand men right in that circle. It's impossible."

Altan examined the map. "For normal soldiers, maybe. But we have *gods*. They can't defeat us on an open field."

"They can if there are a thousand of them." Baji stood up, pushing his chair back with a screech. "The confidence is touching, Trengsin, but this is a suicide mission."

"I'm not being—"

"We have *eight soldiers*. Qara and Unegen haven't slept in days, Suni is one bad trip away from the Stone Mountain, and Ramsa still hasn't gotten his wits back from that explosion. Maybe we could do this with Chaghan, but I suppose wherever you've sent him matters more—"

The brush snapped in Altan's hand. "Are you contradicting me?"

"I'm pointing out your delusions." Baji pushed his chair to the side and slung his rake over his back. "You're a good commander, Trengsin, and I'll take the risks I'm asked to take, but I'll only obey commands that make some fucking sense. This doesn't even come close."

He stormed out of the office.

Even the operations that they did execute had a fatalistic, desperate air to them. For every bomb they planted, for every camp they set fire to, Rin suspected they were only annoying disturbances to the Federation. Though Qara and Unegen delivered valuable intelligence, the Fifth refused to act on it. And all the disruption Suni, Baji, and Ramsa together could create was only a drop in a bucket compared to the massive encampment that grew steadily larger as more and more ships unloaded troops on the coast.

The Cike were stretched to their limit, especially Rin. Each moment not spent on an operation was spent on patrol. And when she was off duty, she trained with Altan.

But those sessions had come to a standstill. She made rapid progress with her sword, disarming Altan almost as often as he disarmed her, but she came no closer to calling the Phoenix than she had on the marsh.

"I don't understand," Altan said. "You've done this before. You did this at Sinegard. What's stopping you?"

Rin knew what the problem was, though she couldn't admit it. She was afraid.

Afraid that the power would consume her. Afraid she might rip a hole into the void, like Jiang had, and that she would disappear into the very power that she had called. Despite what Altan had told her, she could not just ignore two years of Jiang's teachings.

And as if she could sense her fear, the Speerly Woman became more and more vivid each time Rin meditated. Rin could see details now she hadn't seen before; cracks in her skin like she had been smashed apart and then put back together, burn scars where piece met piece.

"Don't give in," the Woman said. "You've been so brave . . . but it takes more bravery to resist the power. That boy couldn't do it, and you are so close to giving in . . . but that's what it wants, that's precisely what it's planned."

"Gods don't want anything," said Rin. "They're just forces. Powers to be tapped. How can it be wrong to use what exists in nature?"

"Not this god," said the Woman. "The nature of this god is to destroy. The nature of this god is to be greedy, to never be satisfied with what he has consumed. Be careful . . ."

Light streamed through the cracks in the Speerly Woman, as if she were being illuminated from within. Her face twisted in pain and then she disappeared, shattering the space in the void.

As downtown warfare took a greater toll on civilian life, the city was permeated with an atmosphere of intense suspicion. Two weeks after the saltpeter explosion, six Nikara farmers were sentenced to death by Jun's men for spying on behalf of the Federation. Likely they had been promised safe passage out of the besieged city if they provided valuable snippets of information. That, or they simply needed to feed themselves. Either way, thousands of fishermen, women, and children watched with a mixture of glee and disgust as Jun took their heads off in public, spiked them on poles, and placed them on display along the tall outer walls.

The vigilante justice the civilians inflicted on one another was greater—and more vicious—than anything the Militia could enforce. When rumors abounded that the Federation was planning to poison the central city water supply, armed bands of men with clubs stalked the streets, stopping and searching individuals at random. Anyone with a powdery substance was beaten severely. In the end, division soldiers had to intervene to save a group of merchants delivering herbs to the hospital from being torn apart by a crowd.

As the weeks dragged on, Altan's shoulders became stooped, his face lined and haggard. His eyes were now permanently ringed with shadows. He hardly slept; he stopped working far later than any of them and was up earlier. He took his rest in short, fretful shifts, if at all.

He spent many hours frantically pacing the walled fortifications himself, watching the horizon for any sign of Federation movement, as if willing the next assault to happen so that he could fight the entire Federation army by himself.

Once when Rin walked into his office to submit an intelligence report, she found him asleep on his desk. His cheek had ink on it; it was pressed against war plans that he had been deliberating over for hours. His shoulders were slumped on the wooden surface. In sleep, the tense lines that normally arrested his face were gone, bringing his age down at least five years.

She always forgot how young he was.

He looked so vulnerable.

He smelled like smoke.

She couldn't help herself. She stretched out a hand and touched him tentatively on the shoulder.

He sat up immediately. One hand flew instinctively to a dagger at his waist, the other shot out in front of him, igniting instantaneously. Rin took a quick step backward.

Altan took several panicked breaths before he saw Rin.

"It's just me," she said.

His chest rose and fell, and then his breathing slowed. She thought she had seen fear in his eyes, but then he swallowed and an impassive mask slid over his face.

His pupils were oddly constricted.

"I don't know," he said after a long moment. "I don't know what I'm doing."

Nobody does, she wanted to say, but she was interrupted by the loud ringing of a signal gong.

Someone was at the gates.

Qara was already standing sentry over the west wall when they climbed the stairs.

"They're here," she said simply before Altan could ask.

Rin leaned over the wall to see an army riding slowly up to the gates. It had to be a force of no less than two thousand. She was anxious at first, until she saw that they were clad in Nikara armor. At the front of the column flew a Nikara banner, the symbol of the Red Emperor above the emblems of the Twelve Warlords.

Reinforcements.

Rin refused to allow herself to hope. It couldn't be.

"Possibly it's a trap," said Altan.

But Rin was looking past the flag at a face in the ranks—a boy, a beautiful boy with the palest skin and lovely almond eyes, walking on his own two legs as if his spine had never been severed. As if he had never been impaled on a general's halberd.

As if he could sense her gaze, Nezha looked up.

Their eyes met under the moonlight. Rin's heart leaped.

The Dragon Warlord had responded to the call. The Seventh Division was here.

"That's not a trap," she said.

CHAPTER 17

"You're really all better?"

"Near enough," said Nezha. "They sent me down with the next shipment of soldiers as soon as I could walk."

The Seventh Division had brought with them three thousand fresh troops and wagons of badly needed supplies from farther inland—bandages, medicine, sacks of rice and spices. It was the best thing to happen at Khurdalain in weeks.

"Three months," she marveled. "And Kitay said you were never going to walk again."

"He exaggerated," he said. "I got lucky. The blade went right in between my stomach and my kidney. Didn't puncture anything on its way out. Hurt like hell, but it healed cleanly. Scar's ugly, though. Do you want to see?"

"Keep your shirt on," she said hastily. "Still, three months? That's amazing."

Nezha looked away, gazing over the quiet stretch of city under the wall that they'd been assigned to patrol. He hesitated, as if trying to decide whether or not to say something, but then abruptly changed the subject. "So. Screaming at rocks. Is that, like, normal behavior here?"

"That's just Suni." Rin broke a wheat bun in half and offered a piece to Nezha. They had increased bread rations to twice a week, and it was worth savoring. "Ignore him."

He took it, chewed, and made a face. Even in wartime, Nezha had a way of acting as if he'd expected better luxuries. "It's a little hard to ignore when he's yelling right outside your tent."

"I'll ask Suni to avoid your particular tent."

"Would you?"

Snideness aside, Rin was deeply grateful for Nezha's presence. As much as they had hated each other at the Academy, Rin found comfort in having someone else from her class here on the other side of the country, so far away from Sinegard. It was good to have someone who could sympathize, in some way, with what she was going through.

It helped that Nezha had stopped acting like he had a stick up his ass. War brought out the worst in some people; with Nezha, though, it had transformed him, stripping away his snobby pretensions. It seemed petty now to maintain her old grudge. It was difficult to dislike someone who had saved her life.

And she didn't want to admit it, but Nezha was a welcome relief from Altan, who had taken lately to hurling objects across the room at the slightest hint of disobedience. Rin found herself wondering why they hadn't become friends sooner.

"You know they think your contingent is a freak show, right?" Nezha said.

But then, of course, he would say things like that. Rin bristled. They *were* freaks. But they were *her* freaks. Only the Cike got to speak about the Cike like that. "They're the best damn soldiers in this army."

Nezha raised an eyebrow. "Didn't one of you blow up the foreign embassy?"

"That was an accident."

"And didn't that big hairy one choke out your commander in the mess hall?"

"All right, Suni's pretty weird—but the rest of us are perfectly—"

"Perfectly normal?" Nezha laughed out loud. "Really? Your

people just casually ingest drugs, mumble to animals, and scream through the night?"

"Side effect of battle prowess," she said, forcing levity into her voice.

Nezha looked unconvinced. "Sounds like battle prowess is the side effect of the madness."

Rin didn't want to think about that. It was a horrifying prospect, and she knew it was more than just a rumor. But the more terrified she became, the less likely she'd be able to summon the Phoenix, and the angrier Altan would become.

"Why aren't your eyes red?" Nezha asked abruptly.

"What?"

He reached out and touched a spot on her temple, beside her left eye. "Altan's irises are red. I thought Speerly eyes were red."

"I don't know," she said, suddenly confused. She had never once considered it—Altan had never brought it up. "My eyes have always been brown."

"Maybe you're not a Speerly."

"Maybe."

"But they were red before." Nezha looked puzzled. "At Sinegard. When you killed the general."

"You weren't even conscious," she said. "You had a spear in your stomach."

Nezha arched an eyebrow. "I know what I saw."

Footsteps sounded behind them. Rin jumped, although she had no reason to feel guilty. She was only keeping watch; she wasn't barred from idle small talk.

"There you are," said Enki.

Nezha swiftly stood. "I'll go."

She glanced up at him, confused. "No, you don't have to—"

"He should go," said Enki.

Nezha gave Enki a stiff nod and disappeared briskly around the corner of the wall.

Enki waited a few moments until the sound of Nezha's footsteps pattering down the stairs died away. Then he glanced down at Rin, mouth pressed in a solemn line. "You didn't tell me the Dragon Warlord's brat was a shaman."

Rin frowned. "What are you talking about?"

"The insignia." Enki gestured around to his upper back, where Nezha wore his family crest across his uniform. "That's a dragon mark."

"That's just his crest," said Rin.

"Wasn't he injured at Sinegard?" Enki inquired.

"Yes." Rin wondered how Enki had known. Then again, Nezha was the son of the Dragon Warlord; his personal life was public knowledge among the Militia.

"How badly was he hurt?"

"I don't know," Rin said. "I was half-unconscious myself when it happened. The general stabbed him—twice, stomach wounds, probably—why does that matter?" She was confused by Nezha's rapid recovery herself, but she didn't see why Enki was interrogating her about it. "They missed his vitals," she added, though that sounded implausible as soon as the words left her mouth.

"Two stomach wounds," Enki repeated. "Two wounds from a highly experienced Federation general who was not likely to miss. And he's up and walking in months?"

"You know, considering that one of us literally lives in a *barrel*, Nezha getting lucky is not that absurd."

Enki looked unconvinced. "Your friend is hiding something."

"Ask him yourself, then," Rin said irritably. "Did you need something?"

Enki was frowning, contemplative, but he nodded. "Altan wants to see you. His office. Now."

Altan's office was a mess.

Books and brushes littered the floor. Maps were strewn haphazardly across his desk, city plans tacked up over every inch of wall. They were covered in Altan's jagged, messy scrawl, outlining diagrams of strategies that made no sense to anyone but Altan. He had circled some critical regions so hard that they looked like he had etched them into the wall with a knifepoint.

Altan was sitting alone at his desk when Rin entered. His eyes were ringed with such a prominent indigo that they looked like bruises.

"You summoned me?" she asked.

Altan set his pen down. "You're spending too much time with the Dragon Warlord's brat."

Rin bristled. "What's *that* supposed to mean?"

"It means I won't allow it," said Altan. "Nezha's one of Jun's people. You know better than to trust him."

Rin opened her mouth and then closed it, trying to figure out whether Altan was being serious. Finally she said, "Nezha's not in the Fifth. Jun can't give him orders."

"Jun was his master," Altan said. "I've seen his armband. He pledged Combat. He's loyal to Jun; he'll tell him anything . . ."

Rin stared at him in disbelief. "Nezha's just my *friend*."

"No one is ever your friend. Not when you're Cike. He's spying on us."

"*Spying* on us?" Rin repeated. "Altan, we're in the same army."

Altan stood up and slammed his hands down on the table.

Rin flinched back.

"*We are* not *in the same army*. We are the Cike. We're the Bizarre Children. We're the force that shouldn't exist, and Jun wants us to fail. He wants *me* to fail," he said. "They all do."

"The other divisions aren't our enemy," Rin said quietly.

Altan paced around the room, arms twitching involuntarily, glaring at his maps as if he could will into formation armies that didn't exist. He looked quite deranged.

"Everyone is our enemy," he said. He seemed to be talking to himself more than he was talking to her. "Everyone wants us dead, gone . . . but I won't go out like this . . ."

Rin swallowed. "Altan—"

He jerked his head toward her. "Can you call the fire yet?"

Rin felt a twinge of guilt. Try as she might, she still couldn't access the god, could not call it back like she had in Sinegard.

Before she could respond, though, Altan made a noise of disgust. "Never mind. Of course you can't. You still think you're playing a game. You think you're still at school."

"I do *not*."

He crossed the room toward her, grasped her shoulders, and shook her so hard that she gasped out loud. But he only pulled her closer until they were face-to-face, eye to eye. His irises were a furious crimson.

"How hard could it be?" he demanded. His grip tightened, fingers digging painfully into her collarbone. "Tell me, *why* is this so hard for you? It's not like this is new to you; you've done it before, why can't you do it now?"

"Altan, you're hurting me."

His grip only tightened. "You could at least fucking *try*—"

"I've tried!" she exploded. "It's not easy, all right? I can't just . . . I'm not *you*."

"Are you a toddler?" Altan said, as if curious. He didn't shout, but his voice took on a strangled monotone, carefully controlled and deadly quiet. That was how she knew he was furious. "Or are you, perhaps, an idiot masquerading as a soldier? You said you needed time. I have allotted you months. On Speer, you would have been disowned by now. Your family would have hurled you into the ocean for the sheer *embarrassment*."

"I'm sorry," Rin whispered, then immediately regretted it. Altan didn't want her apology. He wanted her humiliation. He wanted her to burn in shame, to feel so miserable with herself that she couldn't bear it.

And she did. How was it that he could make her feel so small? She felt more useless than she had at Sinegard when Jun had humiliated her before everyone. This was worse. This was a thousand times worse, because unlike Jun, Altan mattered to her. Altan was a Speerly, Altan was her *commander*. She needed his approval like she needed air.

He pushed her violently away from him.

Rin fought the urge to touch her collarbone, where she knew she would soon have two bruises left by Altan's thumbs, perfectly formed dents like teardrops. She swallowed hard, averted her eyes, and said nothing.

"You call yourself a Sinegard-trained soldier?" Altan's voice had sunk to barely more than a whisper, and it was worse than if he were shouting. She *wished* he were shouting. Anything would be better than this cold evisceration. "You're no soldier. You're deadweight. Until you can call the fire, you're fucking *useless* to me. You're here because you're purportedly a Speerly. So far I have seen no proof that you are. Fix this. Prove your worth. Do your fucking job or get out."

She saved her tears for after she was out of the office. Her eyes were still red when she entered the mess hall.

"Have you been *crying*?" Nezha demanded as he sat down across from her.

"Go away," she mumbled.

He didn't go away. "Tell me what happened."

Rin bit her lower lip. She wasn't supposed to speak to Nezha. It would have been a double betrayal to complain to him about Altan.

"Was it Altan? Did he say something?"

She looked away pointedly.

"Wait. What's that?" Nezha reached for her collarbone.

She slapped his hand away and yanked at her uniform.

"You're just going to sit there and take it?" Nezha asked in disbelief. "I remember a girl who punched me in the face for uttering an ill word about her teacher."

"Altan's different," Rin said.

"Not so different that he gets to talk to you like that," Nezha said. His eyes slid over her collarbone. "It *was* Altan. Tiger's tits. They're saying he's gone mad in the Fifth, but I never thought he'd actually resort to *this*."

"You don't get to talk," Rin snapped. Why did Nezha think he could now take on the role of confidant? "You made fun of me for years at Sinegard. You didn't say a kind word to me until Mugen was at our doorstep."

To his credit, Nezha actually looked guilty. "Rin, I'm—"

She cut him off before he could get a word in. "I was the war orphan from the south, and you were the rich kid from Sinegard, and you tormented me. You made Sinegard a living hell, Nezha."

It felt good to say it out loud. It felt good to see Nezha's stricken expression. They had skirted around this since Nezha had arrived, had acted as if they had always been friends at the Academy, because theirs had been such a childish feud compared to the very real battles they were fighting now. But if he wanted to malign her commander, then she would remind him exactly whom he was talking to.

Nezha slammed a hand on the table, just as Altan had, but this time she didn't flinch.

"You weren't the only victim!" he said. "The first day we met you punched me. Then you kicked me in the balls. Then you tackled me in class. In front of Jun. In front of *everyone*. How do you think that felt? How fucking embarrassing do you think that was? Look, I'm sorry, all right? I'm really sorry." The remorse in Nezha's voice sounded genuine. "But I saved your life. Doesn't that make us at least a little square?"

Square? *Square?* She had to laugh. "You almost got me expelled!"

"And you almost killed me," he said.

That shut her up.

"I was scared of you," Nezha continued. "And I lashed out. I was stupid. I was a spoiled brat. I was a real pain in the ass. I thought I was better than you, and I'm not. I'm sorry."

Rin was too stunned to come up with a response, so she turned away. "I'm not supposed to be talking to you," she said stiffly to the wall.

"Fine," Nezha snapped. "Sorry I tried. I'll leave you alone, then."

He grabbed his plate, stood up, and walked briskly away. She let him.

Night watch was lonely and boring without Nezha. All of the Cike had watch duty on rotation, but at that moment Rin was convinced Altan had placed her there as punishment. What was the point of staring down at a coastline where nothing ever happened? If another fleet did show up, Qara's birds would see it days in advance.

Rin twisted her fingers irritably together as she huddled against the wall, trying to warm herself. *Stupid*, she thought, glaring at her hands. Probably she wouldn't feel so cold if she could just summon a bit of flame.

Everything felt awful. The mere thought of both Altan and Nezha made her cringe. She knew vaguely that she'd fucked up, that she'd probably done something that she shouldn't have, but she couldn't reason a way out of this dilemma. She wasn't even sure precisely what the matter *was*, only that both were furious with her.

She heard then a droning noise; so faint at first she thought she was imagining it. But then it increased quickly in volume, like a fast-approaching swarm of bees. The noise reached a peak and clarified into human shouts. She squinted; the commotion wasn't coming from the coastline but from the downtown districts behind her. She jumped down from her perch and ran to look down the other side. A flood of civilians streamed into the alleyways, a frantic stampede of bodies. She searched the crowd and saw Qara and Unegen emerging from their barracks. She scaled down the wall and wove through the flood of bodies, pushing against the crowd to reach them.

"What's going on?" She grabbed Unegen's arm. "Why are they running?"

"No clue," Unegen said. "Find the others."

A civilian—an old woman—tried to push past Rin but stumbled. Rin knelt to help her, but the woman had already picked herself up, scurrying along faster than Rin had ever seen an old person move. Men, women, and children streamed around her, some barefoot, some only half-dressed, wearing identical expressions of terror in their frenzy to flee out the city gates.

"What the hell is going on?" Baji, bleary-eyed and shirtless, pushed through the crowd toward them. "Great Tortoise. Are we evacuating now?"

Something bumped into Rin's knee. She looked down and saw a small child—tiny, half Kesegi's age. He wasn't wearing any pants. He groped blindly at her shin, bawling loudly. He must have lost his parents in the confusion. She reached down and picked him up, the same way she used to hold Kesegi when he cried.

As she searched through the mob for anyone who looked like they were missing a child, she saw three great spouts of flame appear in the air, in the shape of three small dragons flying upward at the sky. It had to be Altan's signal.

Through the noise Rin heard his hoarse yell, "Cike, to me!"

She placed the child in the arms the first civilian she saw and fought her way through the masses to where Altan stood. Jun was there, too, surrounded by about ten of his men. Nezha stood among them. He didn't meet her eyes.

Altan looked more openly furious than she had ever seen him. "I *warned* you not to evacuate without giving notice."

"This isn't me," said Jun. "They're running from something."

"From what?"

"Damned if I know," Jun snapped.

Altan heaved a great sigh of impatience, reached into the horde of bodies, and pulled someone out at random. It was a young woman, a little older than Rin, wearing nothing but a nightgown. She screeched loudly in protest, then clamped her jaw shut when she saw their Militia uniforms.

"What's going on?" Altan demanded. "What are you all running from?"

"A chimei," she said, out of breath and terrified. "There's a chimei downtown, near the town square . . ."

A chimei? The name was vaguely familiar. Rin thought back to where she had last seen it—somewhere in the library, perhaps, in one of the absurd tomes Jiang had made her read when conducting a thorough investigation on every piece of arcane knowledge known to mankind. She thought it might be a beast, some mythological creature with bizarre abilities.

"Really," Jun said skeptically. "How do you know it's a chimei?"

The girl looked him straight in the eyes. "Because it's tearing the faces off corpses," she said in a wavering voice. "I saw the bodies, I saw . . ." She broke off.

"What does it look like?" Altan asked.

The woman shivered. "I didn't get a close look, but I think . . . it looked like a great four-legged beast. Large as a horse, arms like a monkey's."

"A beast," Altan repeated. "Anything else?"

"Its fur was black, and its eyes . . ." She swallowed.

"Its eyes were what?" Jun pressed.

The woman flinched. "Like *his*," she said, and pointed to Altan. "Red like blood. Bright as flame."

Altan released the young woman back into the crowd, and she immediately disappeared into the fleeing mass.

The two commanders faced each other.

"We need to send someone in," Altan said. "Someone has to kill that beast."

"Yes," Jun agreed immediately. "My people are tied up with crowd control, but I can gather a squadron."

"We don't need a squadron. One of my people should be fine. We can't dispatch everyone. Mugen could use this chance to attack our base. This could be a diversion."

"I'll go," Rin volunteered immediately.

Altan frowned at her. "You know how to handle a chimei?"

She didn't know. She'd only just remembered what a chimei *was*—and that was only from Academy readings that she barely remembered. But she was sure that was more than anyone else in the divisions or the Cike knew, because no one else had been

forced to read arcane bestiaries at Sinegard. And she wasn't about
to admit incompetence to Altan in front of Jun. She could handle
this task. She *had* to.

"As well as anyone else does, sir. I've read the bestiaries."

Altan considered for a short moment, then nodded curtly. "Go
against the grain of the crowd. Keep to the alleys."

"I'll go, too," Nezha volunteered.

"That's not necessary," Altan said immediately.

But Jun said, "She should take a Militia man. Just in case."

Altan glared at Jun, and she realized what this was about. Jun
wanted someone to accompany her, just in case she saw something that Altan didn't report to Jun.

Rin couldn't believe that division politics were at play even now.

Altan looked like he wanted to argue. But there was no time.
He shoved past Nezha toward the crowd and seized a torch from
a passing civilian.

"Hey! I need that!"

"Shut up," Altan said, and pushed the civilian away. He handed
the torch to Rin and pulled her into a side alley where she could
avoid the traffic. "*Go.*"

Rin and Nezha couldn't reach downtown by fighting the stampede
of bodies. But the buildings in their district had low, flat roofs that
were easy to climb onto. Rin and Nezha ran across them, their
torches bobbing in the light. When they reached the end of the
block, they dropped down into an alley and crossed another block
in silence.

Finally Nezha asked, "What's a chimei?"

"You heard the woman," Rin said curtly. "Great beast. Red
eyes."

"I've never heard of it."

"Probably shouldn't have come along, then." She turned a
corner.

"I read the bestiaries, too," Nezha said after he had caught up
to her. "Nothing about a chimei."

"You didn't read the old texts. Archive basement," she said. "Red Emperor's era. It only gets a few mentions, but it's there. Sometimes it's depicted as a child with red eyes. Sometimes as a black shadow. It tears the faces off its victims but leaves the rest of the corpse intact."

"Creepy," Nezha said. "What's its deal with faces?"

"I'm not sure," Rin admitted. She searched her memory for anything else she could remember about chimeis. "The bestiaries didn't say. I think it collects them. The books claim that the chimei can imitate just about anyone—people you care about, people you could never hurt."

"Even people it hasn't killed?"

"Probably," she guessed. "It's been collecting faces for thousands of years. With that many facial features, you could approximate anyone."

"So what? How does that make it dangerous?"

She shot him a glance over her shoulder. "You'd be fine stabbing something with your mother's face?"

"I'd know it wasn't real."

"You'd know in the back of your mind it wasn't real. But could you do it in the moment? Look in your mother's eyes, listen to her begging, and put your knife to her throat?"

"If I knew there was no way it could be my mother," Nezha said. "The chimei sounds scary only if it catches you by surprise. But not if you *know*."

"I don't think it's that simple," said Rin. "This thing didn't just frighten one or two people. It scared off half the city. What's more, the bestiaries don't tell us how to kill it. There isn't a defeat of a chimei on record in history. We're fighting this one blind."

The streets in the middle of town were still—doors closed, wagons parked. What should have been a bustling marketplace was dusty and quiet.

But not empty.

Bodies were littered around the streets in various states.

Rin knelt down by the closest one and turned it over. The corpse was unmarked except for the head. The face had been chewed off in the most grotesque manner. The eye sockets were empty, the nose missing, lips torn clean off.

"You weren't kidding," Nezha said. He covered his mouth with a hand. "Tiger's tits. What happens when we find it?"

"Probably I'll kill it," she said. "You can help."

"You are obnoxiously overconfident in your combat abilities," said Nezha.

"I thrashed you at school. I'm frank about my combat abilities," she said. It helped if she talked big. It made the fear go away.

Several feet away, Nezha kicked another body over. It wore the dark blue uniform of the Federation Armed Forces. A five-pointed yellow star on his right breast identified him as an officer of rank.

"Poor guy," he said. "Someone didn't get the message."

Rin walked past Nezha and held her torch out over the bloody walkway. An entire squadron of slain Federation forces was littered across the cobblestones.

"I don't think the Federation sent it," she said slowly.

"Maybe they've kept it locked up all this time," Nezha suggested. "Maybe they didn't know what it could do."

"The Federation doesn't take chances like that," she said. "You saw how cautious they were with the trebuchets at Sinegard. They wouldn't unleash a beast they couldn't control."

"So it just came on its own? A monster that no one's seen in centuries decides to reappear in the one city under siege?"

Rin had a sinking suspicion of where the chimei had come from. She'd seen the monster before. She'd seen it in the illustrations of the Jade Emperor's menagerie.

I will summon into existence beings that should not be in this world.

When Jiang had opened that void at Sinegard, he had ripped a hole in the fabric between their world and the next. And now, with the Gatekeeper gone, demons were climbing through at will.

There is a price. There is always a price.

Now she could see what he meant.

She pushed the thoughts from her mind and knelt down to examine the corpses more closely. None of the soldiers had drawn their weapons. This made no sense. Surely they couldn't all have been caught off guard. If they'd been fighting a monstrous beast, they should have died with their swords drawn. There should be signs of a struggle.

"Where do you think—" she began to ask, but Nezha clamped a cold hand over her mouth.

"Listen," he whispered.

She could hear nothing. But then, across the market square from where they stood, a faint noise came from within an overturned wagon, the sound of something shaking. Then the shaking stilled, giving way to what sounded like high-pitched sobbing.

Rin walked closer with her torch held out to investigate.

"Are you mad?" Nezha grabbed her arm. "That could be the beast itself."

"So what are we going to do, run from it?" She shook him off and continued at a brisk pace toward the wagon.

Nezha hesitated, but she heard him following. When they reached the wagon, he met her eyes over the torchlight, and she nodded. She drew her sword, and together they yanked the cover off the wagon.

"Go away!"

The thing under the cover wasn't a beast. It was a tiny girl, no taller than Nezha's waist, curled up in the back end of the wagon. She wore a flimsy blood-covered dress. She shrieked when she saw them and buried her head in her knees. Her entire body convulsed with violent, terrified sobs. "Get away! Get away from me!"

"Put your sword down, you're scaring her!" Nezha stepped in front of Rin, blocking her from the little girl's view. He shifted his torch to his other hand and put a hand softly on the girl's shoulder. "Hey. Hey, it's okay. We're here to help you."

The girl sniffled. "Horrible monster . . ."

"I know. The monster isn't here. We've, uh, we've scared it away. We're not here to hurt you, I promise. Can you look at me?"

Slowly, the girl lifted her head and met Nezha's gaze. Her eyes were enormous, wide and scared, in her tear-streaked face.

As Rin looked over Nezha's shoulder into those eyes, she was struck with the oddest sensation, a fierce desire to protect the little girl at all costs. She felt it like a physical urge, a foreign maternal desire. She would die before letting any harm come to this innocent child.

"You're not a monster?" the girl whimpered.

Nezha stretched his arms out to her. "We're humans through and through," he said gently.

The girl leaned into his arms, and her sobs subsided.

Rin watched Nezha in amazement. He seemed to know exactly how to act around the child, adjusting his tone and his body language to be as comforting as possible.

Nezha handed Rin his torch with one arm and patted the girl on the head with the other. "Will you let me help you out of this thing?"

She nodded hesitantly and rose to her feet. Nezha grasped her waist, lifted her out of the broken wagon, and set her gently on the ground.

"There. You're all right. Can you walk?"

She nodded again and reached shakily for his hand. Nezha grasped it firmly, wrapped his slender fingers around her tiny hand. "Don't worry, I'm not going anywhere. Do you have a name?"

"Khudali," she whispered.

"Khudali. You're safe now," Nezha promised. "You're with us. And we're monster killers. But we need your help. Can you be brave for me?"

Khudali swallowed and nodded.

"Good girl. Now can you tell me what happened? Anything you remember."

Khudali took a deep breath and began to speak in a halting, trembling voice. "I was with my parents and my sister. We were just riding the wagon back home. The Militia told us not to be out too late so we wanted to get back in time, and then . . ." Khudali began to sob again.

"It's okay," Nezha said quickly. "We know the beast came. I just need you to give me any details you can. Anything that comes to mind."

Khudali nodded. "Everyone was screaming, but none of the soldiers did anything. And when it came near us, the Federation just watched. I hid inside the wagon. I didn't see its face."

"Did you see where it went?" Rin asked sharply.

Khudali flinched and shrank back behind Nezha.

"You're scaring her," Nezha said in a low voice, gesturing again for Rin to stand back. He turned back to Khudali. "Can you show me what direction it ran in?" he asked softly. "Where did it go?"

"I . . . I can't tell you how to get there. But I can take you," she said. "I remember what I saw."

She led them a few steps toward a corner of the alley, then paused.

"That's where it ate my brother," she said. "But then it disappeared."

"Hold on," said Nezha. "You said you came here with your sister."

Khudali looked up at Nezha, again with those wide, imploring eyes.

"I suppose I did," she said.

Then she smiled.

In one instant she was a tiny girl; the next, a long-limbed beast. Except for its face, it was entirely covered in coarse pitch-black fur. Its loping arms could have reached the ground, like Suni's, a monkey's arms. Its head was very small, still the head of Khudali, which made it all the more grotesque. It reached for Nezha with thick fingers and lifted him into the air by his collar.

Rin drew her sword and hacked at its legs, its arms, its torso. But the chimei's bristly fur was like a coat of iron needles, repelling her sword better than any shield could.

"Its face," she yelled. "Aim for the face!"

But Nezha wasn't moving. His hands dangled uselessly at his sides. He gazed into the chimei's tiny face, Khudali's face, entranced.

"What are you doing?" Rin screamed.

Slowly, the chimei turned its head to look down at her. It found her eyes.

Rin reeled and stumbled backward, choking.

When she gazed into those eyes, its entrancing eyes, the chimei's monstrous body melted away in her vision. She couldn't see the black hair, the beast's body, the rough torso matted with blood. Only the face.

It wasn't the face of a beast. It was the face of something beautiful. It was blurry for a moment, like it couldn't decide what it wanted to be, and then it turned into a face she hadn't seen in years.

Soft, mud-colored cheeks. Rumpled black hair. One baby tooth slightly larger than the rest, one baby tooth missing.

"Kesegi?" Rin uttered.

She dropped her torch. Kesegi smiled uncertainly.

"Do you recognize me?" he asked in his sweet little voice. "After all this time?"

Her heart broke. "Of *course* I recognize you."

Kesegi looked at her hopefully. Then he opened his mouth and screeched, and the screech wasn't anything human. The chimei rushed at her—Rin flung her hands up before her face—but something stopped it.

Nezha had broken free of its grasp; now he held on to its back, where he couldn't see its face. Nezha stabbed inward, but his knife clattered uselessly against the chimei's collarbone. He tried again, aiming for its face. Kesegi's face.

"No!" Rin screamed. "Kesegi, no—"

Nezha missed—his blade ricocheted off iron fur. He raised his weapon for a second blow, but Rin dashed forward and shoved her sword between Nezha's blade and the chimei.

She had to protect Kesegi, couldn't let Nezha kill him, not *Kesegi* . . . he was just a kid, so helpless, so little . . .

It had been three years since she'd left him. She had abandoned him with a pair of opium smugglers, while she left for Sinegard without sending so much as a letter for three years, three impossibly long years.

It seemed like so long ago. An entire lifetime.

So why was Kesegi still so small?

She reeled, mind fuzzy. Answering the question was like trying to see through a dense mist. She knew there was some reason why this didn't make sense, but she couldn't quite piece together what it was . . . only that there was something wrong with this Kesegi in front of her.

It wasn't *her* Kesegi.

It wasn't Kesegi at all.

She struggled to come to her senses, blinking rapidly like she was trying to clear away a fog. *It's the chimei, you idiot*, she told herself. *It's playing off your emotions. This is what it does. This is how it kills.*

And now that she remembered, she saw there was something wrong with Kesegi's face . . . his eyes were not soft and brown, but bright red, two glaring lanterns that demanded her gaze . . .

Howling, the chimei finally succeeded in flinging Nezha off its back. Nezha jerked through the air and crashed against the alley wall. His head thudded against the stone. He slid to the ground and did not stir.

The chimei bolted into the shadows and disappeared.

Rin ran toward Nezha's prone form.

"Shit, *shit* . . ." She pressed her hand to the back of his head. It came away sticky. She probed around, feeling for the contours of the cut, and was relieved to find it was fairly shallow—even light head wounds bled heavily. Nezha might be fine.

But where had the chimei gone . . . ?

She heard a rustling noise above her. She turned, too slowly.

The chimei jumped straight down to land on her back, seizing her shoulders with a horrifically strong grip. She wriggled ferociously, stabbing backward with her sword. But she attacked in vain; the chimei's fur was still an impenetrable shield, against which her blade could only scrape uselessly.

With one massive hand the chimei seized the blade and broke it. It made a disdainful noise and flung the pieces into the darkness. Then it encircled Rin's neck with its arms, clinging to her back like a child—a giant, monstrous child. Its arms pressed against her windpipe. Rin's eyes bulged. She couldn't breathe. She fell to her knees and clambered desperately over the dirt toward the dropped torch.

She felt the chimei's breath hot on her neck. It scratched at her face, pulled at her lips and nostrils the way a child might.

"Play with me," it insisted in Kesegi's voice. "Why won't you *play with me*?"

Can't breathe . . .

Rin's fingers found the torch. She seized it and jabbed it blindly upward.

The burning end smashed into the chimei's exposed face with a loud sizzle. The beast screeched and flung itself off Rin. It writhed in the dirt, limbs twitching at bizarre angles as it keened loudly in pain.

Rin screamed, too—her hair had caught fire. She pulled up her hood and rubbed the cloth over her head to smother the flames.

"Sister, please," the chimei gasped. In its agony it somehow managed to sound even more like Kesegi.

She crawled doggedly toward it, pointedly looking away from its eyes. She clutched the torch tightly in her right hand. She had to burn it again. Burning it seemed to be the only way to hurt it.

"*Rin.*"

This time it spoke in Altan's voice.

This time she couldn't stop herself from looking.

At first it only had Altan's face, and then it *was* Altan, lying sprawled on the ground, blood dripping from his temple. It had Altan's eyes. It had Altan's scar.

Raw, smoking, he snarled at her.

Staving off the chimei's attempts to claw off her face, she pinned it against the ground, jamming down its arms with her knees.

She had to burn its face off. The faces were the source of its power. The chimei had collected a mass of likenesses from every person it had killed, every face it had torn off. It sustained itself on human likenesses, and now it tried to obtain hers.

She forced the torch into its face.

The chimei screamed again. *Altan* screamed again.

She had never heard Altan scream, not in reality, but she was certain that it would have sounded like this.

"Please," sobbed Altan, his voice raw. *"Please, don't."*

Rin clenched her teeth and tightened her grip on the torch, pressed it harder against the chimei's head. The smell of burning flesh filled her nostrils. She choked; the smoke made her tear up but she did not stop. She tried to rip her gaze away, but the chimei's eyes were arresting. It held her eyes. It forced her to look.

"You can't kill me," Altan hissed. "You love me."

"I don't love you," Rin said. "And I can kill anything."

It was a terrifying power of the chimei's that the more it burned, the more it looked like Altan. Rin's heart slammed against her rib cage. *Close your mind. Block out your thoughts. Don't think. Don't think. Don't think. Don't . . .*

But she couldn't detach Altan's likeness from the chimei. They were one and the same. She loved it, she loved him, and he was going to kill her. Unless she killed him first.

But no, that didn't make sense . . .

She tried to focus again, to still her terror and regain her rationality, but this time what she concentrated on was not detaching Altan from the chimei but resolving to kill it no matter who she thought it was.

She was killing the chimei. She was killing Altan. Both were true. Both were necessary.

She didn't have the poppy seed, but she didn't need to call the Phoenix in this moment. She had the torch and she had the pain, and that was enough.

She smashed the blunt end of the torch into Altan's face. She smashed again, with a greater force than she knew she was capable of. Bone gave way to wood. His cheek caved in, creating a cavernous hole where flesh and bone should be.

"You're hurting me." Altan sounded shocked.

No, I'm killing you. She smashed it again and again and again. Once her arm started going, she couldn't stop. Altan's face became a mottled mess of fragmented bone and flesh. Brown skin turned bright red. His face lost shape altogether. She beat out those eyes, beat them bloody so she wouldn't have to look into them anymore. When he struggled, she turned the torch around and burned him in the wounds. Then he screamed.

Finally the chimei ceased its struggles beneath her. Its muscles stopped tensing, its legs stopped kicking. Rin lurched forward over its head, breathing heavily. She had burned through its face to the bone. Underneath the charred, smoking skin lay a tiny, pristine white skull.

Rin climbed off the corpse and sucked in a great, heaving breath. Then she vomited.

"I'm sorry," said Nezha when he awoke.

"Don't be," Rin said. She lay slumped against the wall beside him. The entire contents of her stomach were splattered on the sidewalk. "It's not your fault."

"It *is* my fault. You didn't freeze when you saw it."

"I *did* freeze. An entire squadron froze." Rin jerked her thumb back toward the Federation carcasses in the market square. "And you helped me snap out of it. Don't blame yourself."

"I was stupid. I should have known that little girl—"

"Neither of us knew," Rin said curtly.

Nezha said nothing.

"Do you have a sister?" she asked after a while.

"I used to have a brother," Nezha said. "A little brother. He died when we were young."

"Oh." Rin didn't know what to say to that. "Sorry."

Nezha pulled himself to a sitting position. "When the chimei was screaming at me it felt like—like it was my fault again."

Rin swallowed hard. "When I killed it, it felt like murder."

Nezha gave her a long look. "Who was it for you?"

Rin didn't answer that.

They limped back to the base together in silence, occasionally ducking around a dark corner to make sure they weren't being followed. They did so more out of habit than necessity. Rin guessed there wouldn't be any Federation soldiers in that part of the city for a while.

When they reached the junction that split the Cike headquarters and the Seventh Division's base, Nezha stopped and turned to face her.

Her heart skipped a beat.

He was so beautiful then, standing right in the space of the road where a beam of moonlight fell across his face, illuminating one side and casting long shadows on the other.

He looked like glazed porcelain, preserved glass. He was a sculptor's approximation of a person, not human himself. *He can't be real*, she thought. A boy made of flesh and bone could not be so painfully lovely, so free of any blemish or flaw.

"So. About earlier," he said.

Rin folded her arms tightly across her chest. "Not a good time."

Nezha laughed humorlessly. "We're fighting a war. There's never going to be a good time."

"Nezha . . ."

He put his hand on her arm. "I just wanted to say I'm sorry."

"You don't have to—"

"Yes, I do. I've been a real dick to you. And I had no right to talk about your commander like that. I'm sorry."

"I forgive you," she said cautiously, and found that she meant it.

Altan was waiting in his office when she returned to base. He opened the door even before she knocked.

"It's gone?"

"It's gone," Rin confirmed. She swallowed; her heart was still racing. "Sir."

He nodded curtly. "Good."

They regarded each other in silence for a moment. He was hidden in the shadow of the door. Rin couldn't see the expression on his face. She was glad of that. She couldn't face him right now. She couldn't look at him without seeing his face burning, breaking under her hands, dissolving into a pulpy mess of flesh and gore and sinew.

All thoughts of Nezha had been pushed out of her mind. How could that possibly matter right now?

She had just killed Altan.

What was that supposed to mean? What did it say that the chimei had thought she wouldn't be able to kill Altan, and that she had killed him anyway?

If she could do this, what couldn't she do?

Who couldn't she kill?

Maybe that was the kind of anger it took to call the Phoenix easily and regularly the way Altan did. Not just rage, not just fear, but a deep, burning resentment, fanned by a particularly cruel kind of abuse.

Maybe she'd learned something after all.

"Anything else?" Altan asked.

He took a step toward her. She flinched. He must have noticed it, and still he moved closer. "Something you want to tell me?"

"No, sir," she whispered. "There's nothing."

CHAPTER 18

"The riverbanks are clear," Rin said. "Small signs of activity on the northwestern corner, but nothing we haven't seen before. Probably just transporting more supplies to the far end of camp. I doubt they'll try today."

"Good," said Altan. He marked a point on his map, then set the brush down. He rubbed at his temples and paused like he'd forgotten what he was going to say.

Rin fidgeted with her sleeve.

They hadn't trained together in weeks. It was just as well. There was no time for training now. Months into the siege, the Nikara position in Khurdalain was dire. Even with the added reinforcements of the Seventh Division, the port city was perilously close to falling under Federation occupation. Three days before, the Fifth Division had lost a major town in the suburbs of Khurdalain that had served as a transportation center, exposing much of the eastern part of the city to the Federation.

Beyond that, they'd also lost a good deal of their imported supplies, which forced the army onto even poorer rations than they'd been subsisting on. They were surviving on rice gruel and yams now, two things that Baji declared he would never touch again after this war was over. As it was, they were more likely to chew down handfuls of raw rice than receive fully cooked meals from the mess hall.

Jun's frontline units were inching backward, and suffering heavy casualties while doing so. The Federation took stronghold after stronghold on the riverbank. The water of the creek had been red for days, forcing Jun to send out men to bring back barrels of water not contaminated by putrefied corpses.

Apart from downtown Khurdalain, the Nikara still occupied three crucial buildings on the wharf—two warehouses and a former Hesperian trading office—but their increasingly limited manpower was spread too thin to hold the buildings indefinitely.

At least they had shattered fantasies of an early Federation victory. They knew from intercepted missives that Mugen had expected to take Khurdalain within a week. But the siege had now stretched on for months. Rin realized in the abstract that the longer they fended Mugen off at Khurdalain, the more time Golyn Niis had to assemble defenses. They had already bought more time than they could have hoped for.

But that didn't make Khurdalain feel like any less of an utter defeat.

"One more thing," she said.

Altan nodded jerkily for her to continue.

She spoke quickly. "The Fifth wanted a meeting about the beach offensive. They want to move it up before they lose any more troops at the warehouse. The day after tomorrow at the latest."

Altan raised an eyebrow. "Why is the Fifth conveying a request through you?"

The request had actually been conveyed through Nezha, speaking on behalf of his father, the Dragon Warlord, whom Jun had approached because he didn't want to give Altan legitimacy by going to his headquarters. Rin found the interdivisional politics incredibly annoying, but could do nothing about it.

"Because at least one of them likes me. Sir."

Altan blinked. Rin immediately regretted speaking.

Before he could answer, a scream shattered the morning air.

*   *   *

Altan reached the top of the sentry tower first, but Rin was right behind him, her heart pounding furiously. Had there been an attack? But she saw no Federation soldiers in the vicinity, no arrows flying overhead . . .

Qara lay collapsed on the floor of the tower. She was alone. As they watched, she writhed against the stone floor, making low, tortured moans in the back of her throat. Her eyes had rolled back in her head. Her limbs seized uncontrollably.

Rin had never seen anyone react to a wound like this. Had Qara been poisoned? But why would the Federation target a sentry, and no one else? Rin and Altan instinctively crouched low, out of the line of potential fire, but there were no subsequent arrows, if there had even been a first. Except for Qara's twitching, they saw no disturbances at all.

Altan dropped to his knees. He grasped Qara by her shoulders, dragging her to a sitting position. "What's wrong? What's happened?"

"It *hurts* . . ."

Altan shook her hard. "*Answer me.*"

Qara just moaned again. Rin was stunned by how roughly Altan treated her, despite her obvious agony. But, she realized belatedly, Qara had no visible injuries. There was no blood on the ground, or on her clothes.

Altan smacked Qara's face lightly to get her attention. "Is he back?"

Rin looked between them in confusion. Who was he talking about? Qara's brother?

Qara's face twisted in agony, but she managed to nod.

Altan cursed under his breath. "Is he hurt? Where is he?"

Chest heaving, Qara clenched the front of Altan's tunic. Her eyes were squeezed shut, as if she was concentrating on something.

"The east gate," she managed. "He's here."

* * *

By the time Rin had helped Qara down the stairs, Altan had disappeared from sight.

She looked up and saw archers of the Fifth Division standing frozen at the top of the wall, arrows fitted to their bows. Rin could hear clashing steel on the other side, but none of the soldiers were shooting.

Altan had to be on the other side. Were they afraid they might hit him? Or were they just unwilling to help?

She helped Qara to a sitting position by the nearest wall and made a mad dash up to the wall overlooking the east gate.

On the other side of the gate, an entire squadron of Federation soldiers clustered around Altan. He fought astride a horse, slashing his way through in a frenzied effort to get back to the gate. His arms moved faster than Rin's eyes could follow. His trident flashed once, twice in the noon sun, glistening with blood. Each time he wrenched it back out, a Federation soldier collapsed.

The crowd of soldiers thinned as soldier after soldier dropped, and finally Rin saw the reason why Altan had not summoned his flames. A young man was seated in front of him on the horse, sagging back against his arms. His face and chest were covered with blood. His skin had turned the same pallid white as his hair. For a moment Rin thought—*hoped*—that he was Jiang, but this man was shorter, visibly younger, and much thinner.

Altan was taking on the Federation soldiers as best he could, but they had backed him up against the gate.

Down below, Rin saw the Cike had gathered on the other side.

"Open the doors!" Baji shouted. "Let them back through!"

The soldiers exchanged reluctant looks and did nothing.

"What are you waiting for?" Qara shrieked.

"Jun's orders," one of them stammered. "We're not to open it at any cost—"

Rin looked back over the wall and saw another squadron of Federation reinforcements rapidly approaching. She leaned over the wall and waved her hands to get Baji's attention. "There are more coming!"

"Fuck it." Baji kicked one of the soldiers out of his way, jammed the butt of his rake into the stomach of another, and began cranking the gate open himself while Suni fended off the guards behind him.

The heavy doors inched ponderously open.

Standing directly behind the opening crack, Qara whipped arrow after arrow out of her quiver, firing them rapidly one after the next into the crowd of Federation soldiers. Under a hail of arrow fire, the Mugenese fell back long enough for Altan to squeeze through the blockade.

Baji cranked the gates the other way until they slammed shut.

Altan yanked on the reins, forcing his horse to a sudden stop.

Qara ran up to him, shouting in a language Rin didn't understand. Her tirade was interspersed with a variety of colorful Nikara invectives.

Altan held up a hand to silence her. He dismounted in one fluid movement, and then helped the young man down. The man staggered as his legs touched the ground; he slumped against the horse for support. Altan offered him a shoulder, but the man shook him off.

"Is he there?" Altan demanded. "Did you see him?"

Chest heaving, the man nodded.

"Do you have schematics?" Altan asked.

The man nodded again.

What were they talking about? Rin shot Unegen a questioning glance, but Unegen was equally nonplussed.

"Okay," Altan said. "Okay. So. You're an idiot."

Then he and Qara both began yelling at him.

"Are you *stupid*—"

"—could have been killed—"

"—sheer recklessness—"

"—don't care how powerful you think you are, how dare you—"

"Look," said the man, whose cheeks had gone as white as snow. He had begun to tremble. "I'm happy to discuss this, really, but I'm currently leaking life out three different wounds and I think I may pass out. Would you give me a moment?"

Altan, Qara, and the newcomer did not come out of Altan's office for the rest of that afternoon. Rin was sent to fetch Enki for medical attention, but was then told by Altan in no uncertain terms to get lost. She milled around the city, bored and unsettled and without orders. She wanted to ask one of the other operatives for some explanation of what had just happened, but Unegen and Baji were gone on a reconnaissance assignment and did not return until dinner.

"Who was that?" Rin asked as soon as they appeared in the mess hall.

"The man of dramatic entrance? He's Altan's lieutenant," said Unegen. He sat down on the bench across from her. He adopted a contemptuous, proud affectation. "The one and only Chaghan Suren of the Hinterlands."

"Took him long enough," Baji grumbled. "Where's he been, on vacation?"

"That was Qara's brother? Is that why . . ." Rin didn't know how to ask politely about Qara's seizure, but Baji read the puzzled look on her face.

"They're anchor twins. Some sort of . . . ah, some kind of spiritual link," said Baji. "Qara explained it to us once, but I forget the details. Long story short, they're bound together. Cut Chaghan and Qara bleeds. Kill Qara and Chaghan dies. Something like that."

This concept was not wholly new to Rin. She recalled that Jiang had discussed this kind of dependency before. She had read that shamans of the Hinterlands would sometimes anchor themselves to each other to enhance their abilities. But after seeing Qara on the floor like that, Rin didn't think it was an advantage but rather an awful vulnerability.

"Where's he been?"

"All over the place." Baji shrugged. "Altan sent him out of Khurdalain months ago, right around the time we got word they'd invaded Sinegard."

"But *why*? What was he doing?"

"He didn't tell us. Why don't you ask him yourself?" Baji nodded, his eyes fixed over her shoulder.

She turned around and jumped. Chaghan stood directly behind her; she hadn't even heard him approach.

For someone who had been bleeding out that morning, Chaghan looked remarkably well. His left arm was carefully bandaged up to his torso, but otherwise he seemed unhurt. Rin wondered exactly what Enki had done to heal him so quickly.

Up close, Chaghan's resemblance to Qara was obvious. He was taller than his sister, but they possessed the same slight, birdlike frame. His cheeks were high and hollow; his eyes embedded within deep sockets that cast a shadow over his pale gaze.

"May I join you?" he asked. The way he spoke made it sound like an order, not a question.

Unegen immediately shifted to make space. Chaghan circled the table and sat directly opposite Rin. He placed his elbows delicately on the surface, steepled his fingers together, and rested his chin on his fingertips.

"So you're the new Speerly," he said.

He reminded Rin very much of Jiang. It wasn't simply his white hair or his slender frame, but the way he looked at her, as if he saw straight through her, not looking at her at all but a place behind her. When he looked at her, Rin felt the unsettling sensation of being searched, as if he could see straight through her clothing.

She had never seen eyes like his. They were abnormally huge, dominating his otherwise narrow face. He had no pupils or irises.

She forced a facade of calm and picked up her spoon. "That's me."

The corner of his mouth twitched upward. "Altan said you were having performance issues."

Baji choked and coughed into his food.

Rin felt the heat rising in her cheeks. "*Excuse me?*"

Was that what Altan and Chaghan had spent the afternoon discussing? The idea of Altan talking about her shortcomings to this newcomer was deeply humiliating.

"Have you managed to call the Phoenix once since Sinegard?" Chaghan inquired.

I bet I could call it on you right now, you twit. Her fingers tightened around her spoon. "I've been working on it."

"Altan seems to think you're stuck in a rut."

Unegen looked like he dearly wished he were sitting anywhere else.

Rin gritted her teeth. "Well, he thought wrong."

Chaghan shot her a patronizing smile. "I can help, you know. I'm his Seer. This is what I'm good at. I traverse the world of spirit. I speak to the gods. I don't summon deities, but I know my way around the Pantheon better than anyone else. And if you're having issues, I can help you find your way back to your god."

"I'm not *having issues*," she snapped. "I was scared at the marsh. I am not now."

And that was the truth. She suspected she could call the Phoenix now, right in this mess hall, if Altan asked her to. If Altan would deign to talk to her beyond giving her orders. If Altan trusted her enough to give her an assignment above patrolling stretches of the city where nothing ever happened.

Chaghan raised an eyebrow. "Altan isn't so sure."

"Well, maybe Altan should get his head out of his ass," she snapped, then immediately regretted speaking. Disappointing Altan was one thing; complaining about it to his lieutenant was another.

No one at the table was bothering to pretend to eat anymore; Baji and Unegen both fidgeted like they couldn't wait to leave, looking around at everything except Rin and Chaghan.

But Chaghan only looked amused. "Oh, you think he's an asshole?"

Anger flared inside her. Her last remaining shreds of caution fled. "He's impatient, overdemanding, paranoid, and—"

"Look, everyone's on edge," Baji interrupted hastily. "We

shouldn't complain. Chaghan, there's no need to tell—I mean, look . . ."

Chaghan tapped his fingers against the table. "Baji. Unegen. I want a word with Rin."

He spoke so imperiously, so arrogantly, that Rin thought that surely Baji would tell Chaghan where he could shove it, but he and Unegen simply picked up their bowls and left the table. Amazed, she watched them walk to the other end of the room without so much as a word. Not even Altan commanded that kind of unquestioning subordination.

When the others were out of earshot, Chaghan leaned forward. "If you ever speak about Altan like that again," he said pleasantly, "I will have you killed."

Chaghan might have cowed Baji and Unegen, but Rin was too angry to be afraid of him. "Go ahead and try," she snapped. "It's not like we have soldiers to spare."

Chaghan's mouth quirked into a grin. "Altan did say you were difficult."

She gave him a wary look. "Altan's not wrong."

"So you don't respect him."

"I respect him," she said. "I just—he's been . . ." *Different. Paranoid. Not the commander I thought I knew.*

What she didn't want to admit was that Altan was scaring her.

But Chaghan looked surprisingly sympathetic. "You must understand. Altan is new to command. He's trying to figure out what he's doing just as much as you are. He's scared."

He was scared? Rin almost laughed. Altan's attempted operations had grown so much in scale over the past two weeks that it felt as if he were trying to take on the entire Federation by himself. "Altan doesn't know what *scared* means."

"Altan is perhaps the most powerful martial artist in Nikan right now. Maybe the world," said Chaghan. "But for all that, most of his life he was just good at following orders. Tyr's death was a shock to us. Altan wasn't ready to take over. Command is difficult for him. He doesn't know how to make peace with the

Warlords. He's overextended. He's trying to fight an entire war with a squad of ten. And he's going to lose."

"You don't think we can hold Khurdalain?"

"I think we were never meant to hold Khurdalain," said Chaghan. "I think Khurdalain was a sacrifice for time paid in blood. Altan is going to lose because Khurdalain is not winnable, and when he does, it's going to break him."

"Altan won't break," she said. Altan was the strongest fighter she'd ever seen. Altan *couldn't* break.

"Altan is more fragile than you think," said Chaghan. "He's cracking under the weight of command, can't you see? This is new territory for him, and he's flailing, because he's utterly dependent on victory."

Rin rolled her eyes. "The entire country's dependent on our victory."

Chaghan shook his head. "That's not what I mean. Altan is used to *winning*. His entire life he's been put on a pedestal. He was the last Speerly, a national rarity. Best student at the Academy. Tyr's favorite in the Cike. He's been fed a steady stream of constant affirmation for being very good at destroying things, but he won't get any praise here, especially not when his own soldiers are openly insubordinate."

"I'm not being—"

"Oh, come now, Rin. You're being a little bitch, is what you're doing, all because Altan won't pet you on the head and say you're doing a great job."

She stood up and slammed her hands on the table. "Look, asshole, I don't need you to tell me what to do."

"And yet, as your lieutenant, that is precisely my job." Chaghan glanced lazily up at her, and his expression was so smug that Rin trembled from the effort of not smashing his face into the table. "Your duty is to obey. My duty is to see that you stop fucking up. So I would suggest you get your shit together, learn to call the damn fire, and give Altan one less thing to worry about. Am I clear?"

CHAPTER 19

"So who's the newcomer?" Nezha asked casually.

Rin wasn't sure if she could discuss Chaghan without kicking something, which would be bad, especially since they were supposed to be hiding. But they had been staking out the barricade for what seemed like hours, and she was getting bored.

"He's Altan's lieutenant."

"How come I've never seen him before?"

"He's been away," she said.

A hail of arrows whizzed above them. Nezha ducked back below the barricade.

The Seventh Division had launched a joint assault with the Cike against the embassies by the wharf in an attempt to cut the main Federation encampment in two. In theory if they could hold the old Hesperian quarters, they could then divide the enemy forces and cut off their access to the docks. They had sent two regiments: one attacking perpendicular to the river and the other snaking around to the wharf from the direction of the canals.

But they had to move past five heavily defended intersections to get to the wharf, and those had turned into five separate bloodbaths. The Federation hadn't met them out on the open field because they didn't need to; safely ensconced behind the walls of the buildings they held on the wharf, they responded to the Nikara onslaught by embedding themselves on rooftops and shooting from windows on the upper floors of the embassy buildings.

The Seventh Division's only option was to throw their infantry en masse against the Federation's fortified position. They had to gamble that the press of Nikara bodies would be enough to force the Federation out. It had turned into a contest of flesh against steel, and the Militia was determined to break the Federation upon their bodies.

"You mean, you have no clue," Nezha said as a fire rocket exploded over his head.

"I mean, you have no business asking."

She didn't know if Nezha was fishing for information for his father, or if he was just trying to make small talk. She supposed it didn't matter. Chaghan's presence was hardly a secret, especially after Altan's dramatic rescue outside the east gate. Perhaps because of that, though, the Militia seemed even more spooked by him than they were by the rest of the Cike combined.

Several paces down, Suni lit one of Ramsa's specialty bombs and hurled it over the barricade.

They ducked back down and plugged up their ears until a now-familiar acrid, sulfuric smell filled their nostrils.

The arrow fire stopped.

"Is that *shit*?" Nezha demanded.

"Don't ask," Rin said. In the temporary lull granted by Ramsa's dung bomb they moved past the barricade and stormed down the street to reach the next of the five intersections.

"I heard he's creepy," Nezha continued. "I heard he's from the Hinterlands."

"Qara's from the Hinterlands, too. So what?"

"So I've heard he's unnatural," Nezha said.

Rin snorted. "It's the Cike. We're *all* unnatural."

A massive explosion rolled through the air in front of them, followed by a series of bursts of fire.

Altan.

He was leading the charge. His roiling flames, combined with Ramsa's many fire powder spectacles, created a number of large fires that drastically improved their nighttime visibility.

Altan had broken through to the next intersection. The Nikara continued their surge forward.

"But he can do things that Speerlies can't," Nezha said as they pressed on. "They say he can read the future. Shatter minds. My father says that even the Warlords know of him, did you know that? It makes you wonder. If Altan's got a lieutenant who's so powerful that he scares the Warlords, why is he sending him away from Khurdalain? What are they planning?"

"I'm not spying on my own division for you," Rin said.

"I didn't ask you to," Nezha said delicately. "I'm just saying you might want to keep an open mind."

"And you might want to keep your nose out of my division's matters."

But Nezha had stopped listening; he stared over Rin's shoulder at something farther along the wharf, where the first line of Nikara soldiers was pressing. "What is *that*?"

Rin craned her neck to see what he was looking at. Then she squinted in confusion.

An odd greenish-yellow fog had begun wending its way over the blockade toward the two division squadrons in front of them.

As if in a dream, the fighting stopped. The foremost squadron ceased moving, lowering their weapons with an almost hypnotic fascination as the cloud reached the wall, paused, gathered itself like a wave, and then ponderously lapped over into the dugouts.

Then the screaming began.

"Retreat," shouted a squadron officer. "*Retreat!*"

The Militia reversed direction immediately, commencing a disorganized stampede away from the gas. They abandoned their hard-won stations along the wharf in a frenzy to get away from the gas.

Rin coughed and glanced over her shoulder as she ran. Most of the soldiers who hadn't escaped the gas lay gasping and twitching on the ground, clawing at their faces as if their own throats were attacking them. Others lay quite still.

An arrowhead lashed across her cheek and embedded itself in the ground before her. The side of her mouth exploded in pain; she cupped a hand against it and continued running. The Federation soldiers were firing from behind the poisonous fog, they were going to pick them off one by one . . .

The forest line loomed up before her. She would be fine once she could take cover behind the foliage. Rin ducked her head and sprinted for the trees. Only a hundred yards . . . fifty . . . twenty . . .

Behind her she heard a strangled cry. She twisted her head to look and tripped over a rock, just as another arrow whistled over her head. Blood streamed from her cheek into her eyes. Rin wiped it furiously off and rolled over flat against the ground.

The source of the cry was Nezha. He was crawling furiously forward, but the gas had caught up to him. He met her eyes through the fog. He might have lifted one hand toward her.

She watched in horror, mouth open in a silent scream, as the gas enveloped him.

Through the gas, she saw forms advancing. Federation soldiers. They wore bulky contraptions over their heads, masks that concealed their necks and faces. They seemed unaffected by the gas.

One of them lifted a bulky gloved hand and pointed where Nezha lay.

Without thinking, Rin took a deep breath of air and rushed into the fog.

It burned her skin as soon as she touched it.

She clenched her teeth and forged ahead through the pain—but she'd hardly gone ten paces when someone grabbed her by the shoulder and yanked her back out of the gas zone. She struggled furiously to escape their grip.

Altan didn't let go.

"Back off!" She elbowed him in the face. Altan stumbled and grabbed at his nose. Rin tried to duck past him, but Altan wrenched her backward by her wrist.

"What are you doing?" he demanded.

"They've got Nezha!" she screamed.

"I don't care." He pushed her in the direction of the tree line. "Retreat."

"You're leaving one of our men to die!"

"He's not one of our men, he's one of the Seventh's men. *Go*."

"I won't leave my friend behind!"

"You will do as I command."

"But *Nezha*—"

"I'm not sorry about this," Altan said, and jammed a fist into her solar plexus.

Stunned, paralyzed, she sank to her knees.

She heard Altan shout out an order, and then someone picked her up and slung her over their shoulders as if she were a child. She beat and screamed as the soldier began jogging in the direction of the barracks. From the soldier's back, she thought she could see the masked Federation soldiers dragging Nezha away.

The gas attack created the precisely the effect that the Federation intended. The sugar bomb had been devastating—the gas attack was monstrous. Khurdalain erupted into a state of terror. Though the gas itself dissipated within an hour, rumors of it spread quickly. The fog was an invisible enemy, one that killed indiscriminately. There was no hiding from the fumes. Civilians began fleeing the city en masse, no longer confident in the Militia's ability to protect them. Panic enveloped the streets.

Jun's soldiers had shouted themselves hoarse in the alleys, trying to convince civilians they would be safer behind city walls. But the people weren't listening. They felt trapped. The narrow, winding roads of Khurdalain meant certain death in case of another gas attack.

While the city collapsed into chaos, the commanders commenced an emergency meeting in the nearest headquarters. The Cike crammed into the Ram Warlord's office along with the Warlords and their junior officers. Rin leaned against the corner of the wall, listening dully as the commanders argued over their immediate strategy.

Only one of Jun's soldiers on the beach had survived the attack. He had been posted in the back, and had dropped his weapon and run as soon as he saw his comrades choking.

"It was like breathing fire," he reported. "Like red-hot needles were piercing my lungs. I thought I was being strangled by some invisible demon . . . my throat closed up, I couldn't breathe . . ." He shuddered.

Rin listened, and resented him for not being Nezha.

It was only fifty yards. I could have saved him. I could have dragged us both out.

"We need to evacuate downtown right now," Jun said. He was remarkably calm for a man who had just lost more than a hundred men to a poisonous fog. "My men will—"

"Your men will do crowd control. The civilians are going to trample themselves trying to get out of the city, and it'll be easy for Mugen to pick them off if they're not corralled out in an orderly fashion," Altan said.

Amazingly, Jun didn't argue.

"We'll pack up headquarters and move it farther back into the Sihang warehouse," Altan continued. "We can dump the prisoner in the basement."

Rin jerked her head up. "What prisoner?"

She was faintly aware that she should not be talking, that as an unranked soldier of the Cike she was not technically a part of this meeting and was certainly acting out of line. But she was too grief-stricken and exhausted to care.

Unegen leaned down and murmured into her ear, "One of the Federation soldiers got caught in their own gas. Altan took his mask and pulled him out."

Rin blinked in disbelief.

"You went back in?" she asked. Her voice rang very loudly in her ears. "You had a mask?"

Altan shot her an irritated look. "This is not the time," he said.

She clambered to her feet. "You let one of our people die?"

"You and I can discuss this later."

She understood, in the abstract, the strategic boon of taking a Federation prisoner; the last Federation soldiers who had been captured spying across the bank had promptly been torn apart by furious civilians. And yet . . .

"You are *unbelievable*," Rin said.

"We will see to headquarters evacuation," Altan said loudly over her. "We'll regroup in the warehouse."

Jun nodded curtly, then muttered something to his officers. They saluted him and left the headquarters at a run.

At the same time, Altan issued orders to the Cike.

"Qara, Unegen, Ramsa: secure us a safe route to the warehouse and guide Jun's officers there. Baji and Suni, help Enki pack up shop. The rest of you resume positions in case of another gas attack." He paused at the door. "Rin. You stay."

She hung back as the rest of them exited the office. Unegen cast her a nervous look on his way out.

Altan waited until they were alone, and then he closed the door. He crossed the room and stood so that there was very little distance between them.

"You do not contradict me," he said quietly.

Rin crossed her arms. "Ever, or just in front of Jun?"

Altan didn't rise to the bait. "You will answer to me as a soldier to her commander."

"Or what? You'll have Suni drag me out of your office?"

"You're out of line." Altan's voice dropped to a dangerously low volume.

"And you let my friend die," Rin answered. "He was lying there and you *left him there*."

"You couldn't have extracted him."

"Yes, I could have," she seethed. "And even if I couldn't have—you might have, you might have saved my *friend* instead of dragging out some Federation soldier who deserved to die in there—"

"Prisoners of war have greater strategic importance than individual soldiers," Altan said calmly.

"That is such bullshit," she snarled.

Altan didn't answer. He took two steps forward and struck her across the face.

None of her guards were up. She took the full force of his hit with no preparation. His blow was so powerful that her head snapped to the side. The sudden impact made her knees buckle, jerked her to the ground. She raised a hand to her cheek, stunned. Her fingers came away bloody; he'd reopened her arrow wound.

Slowly she looked up at Altan. Her ears rang.

Altan's scarlet gaze met hers, and the naked rage on his face stunned her.

"How *dare* you," he said. His voice was overly loud, distorted through her thundering ears. "You misunderstand the nature of our relationship. I am not your friend. I am not your brother, though kin we may be. I am your commander. You do not argue with my orders. You follow them without question. You obey me, or you leave this Militia."

His voice held the same double timbre that Jiang's voice had held when he opened the void at Sinegard. Altan's eyes burned red—no, they were not red, they were the color of fire itself. Flames blazed behind him, flames whiter and hotter than any fire she'd ever been able to summon. She was immune to her own fire, but not his; it burned in her face, choking her, forcing her backward.

The ringing in her ears reached a crescendo.

He doesn't get to do this to you, said a voice in Rin's head. *He doesn't get to terrorize you.* She had not come this far to crouch like this in fear. Not to Altan. Not to anyone.

She stood up, even as she reached somewhere inside herself—somewhere spiteful and dark and horrible—and opened the channel to the entity she already knew was waiting for her summons. The room pitched forward as if viewed through a long scarlet prism. The familiar burn was back in her veins, the burn that demanded blood and ashes.

Through the red haze she thought she saw Altan's eyes widen in surprise. She squared her shoulders. Flames flared from her shoulders and back, flames that mirrored Altan's.

She took a step toward him.

A loud crackling noise filled the room. She felt an immense pressure. She trembled under the weight of it. She heard a bird's laughter. She heard a god's amused sigh.

You children, murmured the Phoenix. *You absurd, ridiculous children. My children.*

Altan looked stunned.

But just as her flames resisted his, she began to feel uncomfortably hot again, felt his fire begin to burn her. Rin's fire was an incendiary flash, an impulsive flare of anger. Altan's fire drew as its source an unending hate. It was a deep, slow burn. She could almost taste it, the venomous intent, the ancient misery, and it horrified her.

How could one person hate so much?

What had *happened* to him?

She could not maintain her fire anymore. Altan's flames burned hotter than hers. They had fought a contest of wills and she had lost.

She struggled for another moment and then her flames shrank back into her as quickly as they'd sprung out. Altan's fire dimmed a moment after hers did.

This is it, Rin thought. *I've crossed the line. This is the end.*

But Altan didn't look furious. He didn't look like he was about to execute her.

No—he looked *pleased.*

"So that's what it takes," he said.

She felt drained, as if the fire had burned up something inside her. She couldn't even feel anger. She could barely stand.

"Fuck you," she said. "*Fuck you.*"

"Get to your post, soldier," said Altan.

She left his office, slamming the door shut behind her.

Fuck me.

CHAPTER 20

"There you are."

She found Chaghan over the north wall. He stood with his arms crossed, watching as civilians poured out of Khurdalain's dense streets like ants fleeing a collapsed hill. They straggled through the city gates with their worldly possessions packed onto wagons, strapped to the sides of oxen or horses, slung across their shoulders on poles meant for carrying water, or simply dragged along in sacks. They had chosen to take their chances in the open country rather than to stay another day in the doomed city.

The Militia was remaining in Khurdalain—it was still a strategic base that needed to be held—but they would be protecting nothing but empty buildings from here on out.

"Khurdalain's done for," Chaghan said, leaning against the wall. "Militia included. There'll be no supplies after this. No hospital. No food. Soldiers fight battles, but civilians keep armies alive. Lose the resource well, and you've lost the war."

"I need to talk to you," she said.

He turned to face her, and she suppressed a shudder at the sight of those eyes without pupils. His gaze seemed to rest on the scarlet palm print on her cheek. His lips pressed together in a thin line, as if he knew exactly how the mark had gotten there.

"Lovers' spat?" he drawled.

"Difference of opinion."

"Shouldn't have harped on about that boy," he tutted. "Altan doesn't tolerate shit like that. He's not very patient."

"He's not *human*," she said, recalling the horrible anger behind Altan's power. She'd thought she understood Altan. She'd thought she had reached the man behind the command title. But she realized now that she didn't know him at all. The Altan she'd known—at least, the Altan in her mind—would have done anything for his troops. He wouldn't have left someone in the gas to die. "He—I don't know *what* he is."

"But Altan was never allowed to be human," Chaghan said, and his voice was uncharacteristically gentle. "Since childhood, he's been regarded as a Militia asset. Your masters at the Academy fed him opium for attacking his classmates and trained him like a dog for this war. Now he's been shouldered with the most difficult command position that exists in the Militia, and you wonder why he's not going to trouble himself with your little boy toy?"

Rin almost hit Chaghan for that, but she restrained herself with a twitch and set her jaw. "I'm not here to talk about Altan."

"Then why, pray tell, are you here?"

"I need you to show me what you can do," she said.

"I do a lot of things, sweetheart."

She bristled. "I need you to take me to the gods."

Chaghan looked smug. "I thought you didn't have a problem calling the gods."

"I can't do it as easily as Altan can."

"But you *can* do it."

Her fingers curled into fists by her sides. "I want to do what Altan can do."

Chaghan raised an eyebrow.

She took a deep breath. Chaghan didn't need to know what had happened in the office. "I've been trying for months now. I think I've got it, I'm not sure, but there's something . . . someone that's blocking me."

Chaghan assumed a mildly curious expression, tilting his head in a manner painfully reminiscent of Jiang. "You're being haunted?"

"It's a woman."

"Really."

"Come with me," she said. "I'll show you."

"Why now?" He crossed his arms over his chest. "What happened?"

She didn't answer his question. "I need to do what he can do," she said flatly. "I need to call the same power that he can."

"And you didn't bother with me before because . . ."

"You weren't fucking here!"

"And when I returned?"

"I was obeying the warnings of my master."

Chaghan sounded like he was gloating. "Those warnings no longer apply?"

She set her jaw. "I've realized that masters inevitably let you down."

He nodded slowly, though his expression gave nothing away. "And if I can't get rid of this . . . ghost?"

"Then at least you'll understand." She held out her hands. *"Please."*

That supplication was enough. Chaghan gave a slight nod, and then beckoned her to sit down beside him. While she watched, he unpacked his knapsack and spread it out on the stone floor. An impressive supply of psychedelics was packed inside, tucked neatly into more than twenty little pockets.

"This is not derived from the poppy plant," he said as he mixed powders into a glass vial. "This drug is something far more potent. A small overdose will cause blindness. More than that and you will be dead in minutes. Do you trust me?"

"No. But that's irrelevant."

Chuckling softly, Chaghan gave the vial a shake. He dumped the mixture into his palm, licked his index finger, and dipped it lightly in the drug so that the tip of his finger was covered by a light smattering of fine blue dust.

"Open your mouth," he said.

She pushed down a swell of hesitation and obliged.

Chaghan pressed the tip of his finger against her tongue.

She closed her eyes. Felt the psychedelics seep into her saliva.

The onset was immediate and crushing, like a dark wave of ocean water had suddenly slammed on top of her. Her nervous system broke down completely; she lost the ability to sit up and crumpled at Chaghan's feet.

She was at his mercy now, completely and utterly vulnerable before him. *He could kill me right now*, she thought dully. She didn't know why it was the first thought that sprang to her mind. *He could get rid of me now, if he wanted to.*

But Chaghan only knelt down beside her, grasped her face by her cheeks, and pressed his forehead against hers. His eyes were open very, very wide. She stared into them, fascinated; they were a pale expanse, a window into a snowy landscape, and she was traversing through them . . .

And then they were hurtling upward.

She hadn't known what she had expected. Not once in two years of training had Jiang guided her into the spirit realm. It had always been her mind alone, her soul alone in the void, journeying up toward the gods.

With Chaghan, she felt as if a piece of her had been ripped away, was clutched in the palm of his hand, being taken somewhere of his choosing. She was immaterial, without body or form, but Chaghan was not; Chaghan remained as solid and real as before, perhaps even more so. In the material world, he was gaunt and emaciated, but in the realm of spirit he was solid and present . . .

She understood, now, why Chaghan and Qara had to be two halves of a whole. Qara was grounded, material, fully made of earth. To call them anchor twins was a misnomer—*she* alone was the anchor to her ethereal brother, who belonged more in the realm of spirit than he did in a world of flesh and blood.

The route to the Pantheon was familiar by now, and so was the gate. Once again the Woman materialized in front of her. But something was different this time; this time the Woman was less like a ghost and more like a corpse; half her face was torn away, revealing bone underneath, and her warrior's garb had burned away from her body.

The Woman stretched a hand out toward Rin in supplication.

"It'll eat you alive," she said. "The fire will consume you. To find our god is to find hell on earth, little warrior. You will burn and burn and never find peace."

"How curious," said Chaghan. "Who are you?"

The Woman whirled on him.

"You know who I am," she said. "I am the guardian. I am the Traitor and the Damned. I am redemption. I am the girl's last chance for salvation."

"I see," Chaghan murmured. "So this is where you've been hiding."

"What are you talking about?" Rin demanded. "Who is she?"

But Chaghan spoke past her, directly to the woman. "You should have been immured in the Chuluu Korikh."

"The Chuluu Korikh can't hold me," hissed the Woman. "I am a Speerly. My ashes are free." She reached out and stroked Rin's damaged cheek like a mother caressing her child. "You don't want me gone. You need me."

Rin shuddered at her touch. "I need my god. I need power, and I need fire."

"If you call it now, you will bring down hell on earth," the Woman warned.

"Khurdalain is hell on earth," said Rin. She saw Nezha screaming in the fog, and her voice wavered.

"You don't know what true suffering is," the Woman insisted angrily.

Rin curled her fingers into fists at her sides, suddenly pissed off. True suffering? She had seen her friends stabbed with halberds, shot full of arrows, cut down with swords, burned to death in poisonous fog. She had seen Sinegard go up in flames. She had seen Khurdalain occupied by Federation invaders almost overnight.

"I have seen more than my fair share of suffering," she hissed.

"I'm trying to save you, little one. Why can't you see that?"

"What about Altan?" Rin challenged. "Why haven't you ever tried to stop him?"

The Woman tilted her head. "Is that what this is about? Are you jealous of what he can do?"

Rin opened her mouth, but nothing came out. No. Yes. Did it matter? If she had been as strong as Altan, he wouldn't have been able to restrain her.

If she were as strong as Altan, she could have saved Nezha.

"That boy is beyond redemption," said the Woman. "That boy is broken like the rest. But you, *you* are still pure. You can still be saved."

"I don't want to be saved!" Rin shrieked. "I want power! I want Altan's power! I want to be the most powerful shaman there ever was, so that there is no one I can't save!"

"That power can burn down the world," the Woman said sadly. "That power will destroy everything you've ever loved. You will defeat your enemy, and the victory will turn to ashes in your mouth."

Chaghan had finally regained his composure.

"You have no right to remain here," he said. His voice trembled slightly as he spoke, but he raised one thin hand toward the Woman in a banishing gesture. "You belong to the realm of the dead. Return to the dead."

"Do not try," sneered the Woman. "You cannot banish me. In my time I have bested shamans far more powerful than you."

"There are no shamans more powerful than me," said Chaghan, and he began to chant in his own language, the harshly guttural language Jiang had once spoken, the language Rin recognized now as the speech of the Hinterlands.

His eyes glowed golden.

The Woman started to shake, as if standing over an earthquake, and then suddenly she burst into flames. The fire lit her face from within, like a glowing coal, like an ember about to explode.

She shattered.

Chaghan took Rin's wrist and *tugged*. She became immaterial again, rushing headlong into the space where things were not real. She did not choose where they went; she could only concentrate on staying whole, staying *herself*, until Chaghan stopped and she could regain her bearings without losing herself entirely.

This was not the Pantheon.

She glanced around, confused. They were in a dimly lit room the size of Altan's office, with a low, curved ceiling that forced them to crouch where they stood. Everywhere she looked, small tiles had been arranged in mosaics, depicting scenes she did not recognize or understand. A fisherman bearing a net full of armored warriors. A young boy encircled by a dragon. A woman with long hair weeping over a broken sword and two bodies. In the room's center stood a great hexagonal altar, engraved with sixty-four intricate characters of Old Nikara calligraphy.

"Where are we?" Rin asked.

"A safe place of my choosing," Chaghan said. He looked visibly rattled. "She was much stronger than I expected. I took us to the first place I thought of. This is a Divinatory. Here we can ask questions about your Woman. Come to the altar."

She looked about in wonder as she followed him, running her fingers over the carefully designed tiles. "Is this part of the Pantheon?"

"No."

"Then is this place real?"

"It's real in your mind," said Chaghan. "That's as real as anything gets."

"Jiang never taught me about this."

"That's because you Nikara are so *primitive*," said Chaghan. "You still think there's a strict binary between the material world and the Pantheon. You think calling the gods is like summoning a dog from the yard into the house. But you can't conceive of the dream world as a physical place. The gods are painters. Your material world is a canvas. And this Divinatory is an angle from which we can see the colors on the palette. This isn't really a *place*, it's a *perspective*. But you're interpreting it as a room because your human mind can't process anything else."

"What about this altar? The mosaics? Who built them?"

"No one did. You still don't understand. They're mental constructions so that you can comprehend concepts that are already written. To the Talwu, this room looks completely different."

"The Talwu?"

Chaghan tilted his chin toward something in front of them.

"You're back so soon," spoke a cool, alien voice.

In the dim light, Rin had not noticed the creature standing behind the hexagonal altar. It walked around the circle at a steady pace and sank into a deep bow before Chaghan. It looked like nothing Rin had ever seen; it was similar to a tiger, but its hair grew two feet long. It had a woman's face, a lion's feet, a pig's teeth, and a very long tail that might have belonged to a monkey.

"She is a goddess. Guardian of the Hexagrams," Chaghan said to Rin as he sank into an equally deep bow. He pulled her down to the floor with him.

The Talwu dipped her head toward Chaghan. "The time of asking has expired for you. But *you* . . ." She looked at Rin. "You have never asked a question of me. You may proceed."

"What is this place?" Rin asked Chaghan. "What can it— *she*—tell me?"

"The Divinatory keeps the Hexagrams," he answered. "The Hexagrams are sixty-four different combinations of lines broken and unbroken." He indicated the calligraphy at the sides of the altar, and Rin saw that each character indeed was made up of six lines. "Ask the Talwu your question, cast a Hexagram, and it will read the lines for you."

"It can tell me the future?"

"No one can divine the future," said Chaghan. "It is always

shifting, always dependent on individual choices. But the Talwu can tell you the forces at play. The underlying shape of things. The color of events to pass. The future is a pattern dependent on the movements of the present, but the Talwu can read the currents for you, just as a seasoned sailor can read the ocean. You need only present a question."

Rin was beginning to see the reason why Chaghan commanded the fear that he did. He was just like Jiang—unthreatening and eccentric, until one understood what deep power lay behind his frail facade.

How would Jiang pose a question? She contemplated the wording of her inquiry for a moment. Then she stepped toward the Talwu.

"What does the Phoenix want me to know?"

The Talwu almost smiled.

"Cast the coins six times."

Three coins suddenly appeared, stacked on the hexagonal altar. They were not coins of the Nikara Empire; they were too large, cut into a hexagonal shape rather than the round taels and ingots Rin was familiar with. She picked them up and weighed them in her palm. They were heavier than they looked. On the front side of each was etched the unmistakable profile of the Red Emperor; on the back were inscribed characters of Old Nikara that she could not decipher.

"Each throw of the coins will determine one line in the Hexagram," said Chaghan. "These lines are patterns written into the universe. They are ancient combinations, descriptions of shapes that were long before either of us was born. They will not make sense to you. But the Talwu will read them, and I will interpret."

"Why must *you* interpret?"

"Because I am a Seer. This is what I'm trained to do," said Chaghan. "We Hinterlanders do not call the gods down as you do. We go *to* them. Our shamans spend hours in trances, learning the secrets of the cosmos. I have spent more time in the Pantheon than I have in your world. I have deciphered enough Hexagrams now to know how they describe the shape of our world. And if you try to interpret for yourself, you'll just get confused. Let me help you."

"Fine." Rin flung the three coins out onto the hexagonal altar. All three coins landed tails up.

"*The first line, undivided*," read the Talwu. "*One is ready to move, but his footprints run crisscross.*"

"What does that mean?" Rin asked.

Chaghan shook his head. "Any number of things. The lines each assume shades of meaning depending on the others. Finish the Hexagram."

She tossed the coins again. All heads.

"*The second line, divided*," read the Talwu. "*The subject ascends to his place in the sun. There will be supreme good fortune.*"

"That's good, isn't it?" Rin asked.

"Depends on whose fortune it is," said Chaghan. "The subject is not necessarily you."

Her third toss saw one head, two tails.

"*The third line, divided. The end of the day has come. The net has been cast on the setting sun. This spells misfortune.*"

Rin felt a sudden chill. The end of an era, the setting sun on a country . . . she hardly needed Chaghan to interpret that for her.

"We're not going to win this war, are we?" she asked the Talwu.

"I only read the Hexagrams," said the Talwu. "I confirm and deny nothing."

"It's the net I'm concerned about. It's a trap," said Chaghan. "We've missed something. Something's been laid out for us, but we can't see it."

Chaghan's words confused Rin as much as the line itself did, but Chaghan commanded her to throw the coins again. Two tails, one head.

"*The fourth line, undivided*," read the Talwu. "*The subject comes, abrupt with fire, with death, to be rejected by all. As if an exit; as if an entry. As though burning; as though dying; as though discarded.*"

"That one is quite clear," said Chaghan, although Rin had more questions about that line than the others. She opened her mouth, but he shook his head. "Throw the coins again."

The Talwu looked down. "*The fifth line, divided. The subject is with tears flowing in torrents, groaning in sorrow.*"

Chaghan looked stricken. "Truly?"

"The Hexagrams do not lie," the Talwu said. Her voice was devoid of emotion. "The only lies are in the interpretation."

Chaghan's hand shook suddenly. The wooden beads of his bracelet clattered, echoing in the silent room. Rin shot him a concerned look, but he only shook his head and motioned for her to finish. Arms heavy with dread, Rin cast the coins a sixth and final time.

"*A leader abandons their people,*" read the Talwu. "*A ruler begins a campaign. One sees great joy in decapitating enemies. This signifies evil.*"

Chaghan's pale eyes were open very, very wide.

"You have cast the Twenty-Sixth Hexagram. The Net," announced the Talwu. "There is a clinging, and a conflict. Things will come to pass that exist only side by side. Misfortune and victory. Liberation and death."

"But the Phoenix . . . the Woman . . ." Rin had not received any of the answers she wanted. The Talwu hadn't helped her at all; it had only warned of even worse things to come, things she didn't have the power to prevent.

The Talwu lifted a clawed hand. "Your time of asking is up. Return in a lunar month, and you may cast another Hexagram."

Before Rin could speak, Chaghan knelt forward hastily and dragged Rin down beside him.

"Thank you, Enlightened One," he said, and to Rin he murmured, "Say nothing."

The room dissolved as she sank to her knees, and with an icy jolt, like she had been doused in cold water, Rin found herself shoved back into her material body.

She took a deep breath. She opened her eyes.

Beside her, Chaghan drew himself up to a sitting position. His pale eyes were huge, deep in their shadowed sockets. His gaze seemed to be focused still on something very far away, something entirely not in this world. Slowly, he returned to himself, and when he finally registered Rin's presence, his expression became one of deep anxiety.

"We must get Altan," he said.

If Altan was surprised when Chaghan barged into the Sihang warehouse with Rin in tow, he didn't show it. He looked too exhausted for anything to faze him at all.

"Summon the Cike," said Chaghan. "We need to leave this city."

"On what information?" Altan asked.

"There was a Hexagram."

"I thought you didn't get another question for a month."

"It wasn't mine," said Chaghan. "It was hers."

Altan didn't even glance at Rin. "We can't leave Khurdalain. They need us now more than ever. We're about to lose the city. If the Federation gets through us, they enter the heartland. We are the final front."

"You are fighting a battle the Federation does not need to win," said Chaghan. "The Hexagrams spoke of a great victory, and great destruction. Khurdalain has only been a frustration for both sides. There is one other city that Mugen wants right now."

"That's impossible," said Altan. "They cannot march to Golyn Niis so soon from the coast. The Golyn River route is too narrow to move troop columns. They would have to find the mountain pass."

Chaghan raised his eyebrows. "I'll bet you they've found it."

"All right. Fine." Altan stood up. "I believe you. Let's go."

"Just like that?" Rin asked. "No due diligence?"

Altan walked out of the room and headed down the hallway at a brisk stride. They scurried to keep up with him. He descended the steps of the warehouse until he stood before the basement cellar where the Federation prisoner was kept.

"What are you doing?" Rin asked.

"Due diligence," Altan said, and yanked the door open.

The cellar smelled strongly of defecation.

The prisoner had been shackled to a post in the corner of the room, hands and feet bound, a cloth jammed into his mouth. He was unconscious when they entered the room; he didn't stir when Altan slammed the door shut, or when Altan crossed the room to kneel down beside him.

He had been beaten; one eye was swollen a violent shade of purple, and blood was crusted around a broken nose. But the worst damage had been inflicted by the gas: what skin was not purple had blistered into an angry red rash, so that his face did not look human at all but rather like a frightening combobulation of colors. Rin found a savage satisfaction in seeing the prisoners' features as burned and disfigured as they were.

Altan touched two fingers to an open wound on the prisoner's cheek and gave a small, sharp jab.

"Wake up," he said in fluent Mugini. "How are you feeling?"

With a groan, the prisoner slowly opened his swollen eyes. When he saw Altan, he hacked and spat out a gob of spit at Altan's feet.

"Wrong answer," said Altan, and dug his nail into the cut.

The prisoner screamed loudly. Altan let go.

"What do you want?" the prisoner demanded. His Mugini was coarse and slurred, a far cry from the polished accent Rin had studied at Sinegard. It took her a moment to decipher his dialect.

"It occurs to me that Khurdalain was never the main target," Altan said casually, resting back on his haunches. "Perhaps you would like to tell us what is."

The prisoner smiled an awful, bloody-faced smile that twisted his burn scars. "*Khurdalain*," he repeated, rolling the Nikara word through his mouth like a wad of phlegm. "Who would want to capture this shit hole?"

"Never mind," said Altan. "Where is the main offensive going?"

The prisoner glowered up at him and snorted.

Altan raised a hand and slapped the prisoner on the blistered side of his face. Rin winced. By targeting the prisoner's sore, open wounds, Altan was making him hurt worse and more acutely than any heavy-handed blows could.

"Where is the other offensive?" Altan repeated.

The prisoner spat blood at Altan's feet.

"*Answer me!*" Altan shouted.

Rin jumped.

The prisoner raised his head. "Nikara swine," he sneered.

Altan grabbed the prisoner by a fistful of hair in the back of his head. He slammed his other fist into the prisoner's already bruised eye. Again. And again. Blood flew across the room, splashed against the dirt floor.

"Stop," Rin squeaked.

Altan turned around.

"Leave the room or shut up," he said.

"At this rate he'll pass out," she responded, her heart hammering. "And we don't have time to revive him."

Altan stared at her for a wild-eyed moment. Then he nodded curtly and turned back to the prisoner.

"Sit up."

The prisoner muttered something none of them could understand.

Altan kicked him in the ribs. "*Sit up!*"

The prisoner spat another gob of blood on Altan's boots. His head lolled to the side. Altan wiped his toe on the ground with deliberate slowness, then knelt down in front of the prisoner. He stuck two fingers under the prisoner's chin and tilted his face up to his own in a gesture that was almost intimate.

"Hey, I'm talking to you," he said. "Hey. Wake up."

He slapped the prisoner's cheeks until the prisoner's eyes fluttered back open.

"I have nothing to say to you," the prisoner sneered.

"You will," Altan said. His voice dropped in pitch, a sharp contrast from his previous shouts. "Do you know what a Speerly is?"

The prisoner's eyes furrowed together in confusion. "What?"

"Surely you know," Altan said softly. His voice became a low, velvety purr. "Surely you've heard tales of us. Surely the island hasn't forgotten. You must have been a child when your people massacred Speer, no? Did you know they did it overnight? Killed every single man, woman, and child."

Sweat beaded at the prisoner's temples, dripping down to mingle with fresh rivulets of blood. Altan snapped his fingers before the prisoner's eyes. "Can you see this? Can you see my fingers? Yes or no."

"Yes," the prisoner said hoarsely.

Altan tilted his head. "They say your people were terrified of the Speerlies. That the generals gave orders that not one single Speerly child should survive, because they were so terrified of what we might become. Do you know why?"

The prisoner stared blankly forward.

Altan snapped again. His thumb and index finger burst into flames.

"This is why," he said.

The prisoner's eyes bulged with terror.

Altan brought his hand close to the prisoner's face, so that the edge of the flame licked threateningly at the gas blisters.

"I will burn you piece by piece," said Altan. His tone was so soft that he could have been speaking to a lover. "I will start with the bottoms of your feet. I will feed you one bit of pain at a time, so you will never lose consciousness. Your wounds will cauterize as soon as they manifest, so you won't die from blood loss. When your feet are charred, coated entirely in black, I'll move on to your fingers. I'll make them drop off one by one. I will line up the charcoal stubs in a string to hang around your neck. When I've finished with your extremities, I'll move on to your testicles. I will singe them so slowly you will go insane from the agony. *Then* you'll sing."

The prisoner's eyes twitched madly, but still he shook his head.

Altan's tone softened even further. "It doesn't have to be like this. Your division let us take you. You don't owe them anything." His voice became soothing and hypnotic, almost gentle. "The others wanted to have you put to death, you know. Publicly executed before the civilians. They would have had you torn apart. An eye for an eye." Altan's voice was so lovely. He could be so beautiful, so charismatic, when he wanted to be. "But I'm not like the others. I'm reasonable. I don't want to hurt you. I just want your cooperation."

The soldier's throat bobbed. His eyes darted across Altan's face; he was hopelessly confused, trying to get a read and concluding nothing. Altan wore two masks at the same time, feigned two contrasting entities, and the prisoner did not know which to expect or pander to.

"Tell me, and I can have you released," Altan said gently. "Tell me, and I'll let you go."

The prisoner maintained his silence.

"No?" Altan searched the prisoner's face. "All right." His flames doubled in intensity, shooting sparks through the air.

The prisoner shrieked. "Golyn Niis!"

Altan kept the flames held perilously close to the prisoner's eyes. "Elaborate."

"We never needed to take Khurdalain," spat the prisoner. "The goal was always Golyn Niis. All your best divisions came flocking to the coast as soon as this war started. Idiots. We never even wanted this beach town."

"But the fleet," said Altan. "Khurdalain has been your point of entry for every offensive. You can't get to Golyn Niis without going through Khurdalain."

"There was another fleet," hissed the prisoner. "There have been many fleets, sailing south of this pathetic city. They found the mountain pass. You poor idiots, did you think you could keep that a secret? They're cutting straight toward Golyn Niis itself. Your war capital will burn, our Armed Forces are cutting directly across your heartland, and you're still holed up here in this pathetic excuse for a city."

Altan drew his hand back.

Rin flinched instinctively, expecting him to lash out again.

But Altan only extinguished his flame and patted the prisoner condescendingly on the head. "Good boy," he said in a low whisper. "Thank you."

He nodded to Rin and Chaghan, indicating they were about to leave.

"Wait," the prisoner said hastily. "You said you'd let me go."

Altan tilted his face up to the ceiling and sighed. A thin trickle of sweat ran from the bone under his ear down his neck.

"Sure," he said. "I'll let you go."

He whipped his hand across the prisoner's neck. A spray of blood flew outward.

The prisoner bore an astonished expression. He made a last startled, choked noise. Then his eyes drooped closed and his head slumped forward. The smell of cooked meat and burned blood filled the air.

Rin tasted bile in the back of her throat. It was a long while before she remembered how to breathe.

Altan rose to his feet. The veins at his neck protruded in the dim light. He took a deep breath and then exhaled slowly, like an opium smoker, like a man who had just filled his lungs with a drug. He turned toward them. His eyes glowed bright red in the darkness. His eyes were nothing human.

"Fine," he said to his lieutenant. "You were right."

Chaghan hadn't moved throughout the entire interrogation.

"I'm rarely wrong," said Chaghan.

PART III

CHAPTER 21

Baji yawned loudly, winced, and pulled his neck far to the side. A series of cracks punctuated the still morning air. There was no room to lie down in the river sampan, so sleep had to be acquired in short, fitful bursts, bent over in cramp-inducing positions. He blinked blearily for a minute, and then reached across the narrow boat with his foot to nudge Rin's leg.

"I can take watch now."

"I'm fine," Rin said. She sat huddled with her hands shoved into her armpits, slumped forward so that her head rested on her knees. She stared blankly out at the running water.

"You really should get some sleep."

"Can't."

"You should try."

"I've tried," Rin said shortly.

Rin could not silence the Talwu's voice in her head. She had heard the Hexagram uttered only once, but she was unlikely to forget a single word. It had been seared into her mind, and no matter how many times she revisited it, she could not interpret it in a way that did not leave her feeling sick with dread.

Abrupt with fire, with death . . . as though burning; as though

*dying . . . the subject is with tears flowing in torrents . . . great joy
in decapitating enemies . . .*

She used to think divination was a pale science, a vague approximation if valuable at all. But the Talwu's words were anything but vague. There was only one possible fate for Golyn Niis.

You have cast the Twenty-Sixth Hexagram. The Net. Chaghan had said the net meant a trap had been laid. But had the trap been laid for Golyn Niis? Had it already been sprung, or were they heading straight toward their deaths?

"You're going to wear yourself out. Fretting won't make these boats run any faster." Baji pulled his head to the side until he heard another satisfying crack. "And it won't make the dead come back to life."

They raced up the Golyn River, making absurd time in a journey that should have taken a month on horseback. Aratsha ferried them along the river at blinding speed. Still, it took them a week to travel the length of the Golyn River to the lush delta where Golyn Niis had been built.

Rin glanced up to look at the boat at the very fore, where Altan sat. He rode beside Chaghan; their heads were tilted together, speaking in low tones as usual. They had been like this since they had left Khurdalain. Chaghan and Qara may have been linked as anchor twins, but it was Altan whom Chaghan seemed bonded to.

"Why isn't Chaghan commander?" she asked.

Baji looked confused. "What do you mean?"

"I don't understand why Chaghan obeys Altan," she said. Against the Woman, he had proclaimed himself the most powerful shaman in existence. She believed it. Chaghan navigated the spirit world like he belonged there, as if he were a god himself. The Cike didn't hesitate to talk back to Altan, but she had never seen any of them dare to so much as contradict Chaghan. Altan commanded their loyalty, but Chaghan enjoyed their fear.

"He was slated to be commander after Tyr," said Baji. "Got shunted to the side after Altan showed up, though."

"And he was fine with that?" Rin couldn't imagine someone like Chaghan relinquishing authority peacefully.

"Of course not. Nearly spit fire when Tyr started favoring the golden boy from Sinegard over him."

"So then why—"

"Why's he happy serving under Altan? He wasn't, at first. He bitched about it for a straight week, until Altan finally got fed up. He asked Tyr for permission for a duel and got it. He took Chaghan out into the valleys for three days."

"What happened?"

Baji snorted. "What happens when anyone fights Trengsin? When Chaghan got back, all that pretty white hair was singed black and he was obeying Altan like a whipped dog. Our friend from the Hinterlands might shatter minds, but he couldn't touch Trengsin. No one can."

Rin dropped her head back onto her knees and closed her eyes against the light from the rising sun. She hadn't slept—hadn't truly rested—since they'd left Khurdalain. But her body couldn't sustain itself any longer. She was so tired . . .

Their boat jolted in the water. Rin snapped up to a sitting position. They had bumped straight into the boat in front of them.

"Something's in the water," Ramsa shouted from the fore.

Rin looked over the side and squinted at the river. The water was the same muddy brown, until she glanced upstream.

At first she thought it was a trick of the light, an illusion of the sun's rays. And then her boat reached an odd patch of colored water, and she draped her fingers over the edge. Then she yanked it back in horror.

They were riding through a river of blood.

Altan and Chaghan both jumped up with startled exclamations. Behind them, Unegen uttered a long, inhuman shriek.

"Oh gods," Baji said, over and over. "Oh gods, oh gods, oh gods."

Then the bodies began to float toward them.

Rin was paralyzed, stricken with an irrational fear that the bodies might be the enemy, that they would rise out of the water and attack them.

Their boat stopped moving completely. They were surrounded by corpses. Soldiers. Civilians. Men. Women. Children. They were uniformly bloated and discolored. Some of their faces were disfigured, slashed apart. Others were simply blank, resigned, bobbing listlessly in the crimson water as if they had never been living, breathing bodies.

Chaghan reached out to examine a young girl's blue lips. His own mouth was pursed dispassionately as if he were tracking a footprint, not touching a rubbery carcass. "These bodies have been in the river for days. Why haven't they drifted out to sea yet?

"It's the Golyn Niis Dam," Unegen suggested. "It's blocking them up."

"But we're still miles out from the city . . ." Rin trailed off.

They fell silent.

Altan stood up at the head of his boat. "Get out. Start running."

The road to Golyn Niis was empty. Qara and Unegen scouted ahead but reported no sign of enemy combatants. Yet evidence of Federation presence was obvious everywhere they looked—trampled grass, abandoned campfires, rectangular patches in the dirt where tents had been erected. Rin felt sure that Federation soldiers were lying in wait for them, setting an ambush, but as they drew closer to the city, she realized that made no sense; the Federation wouldn't have known they were coming, and they wouldn't have set such an elaborate trap for such a small squadron.

She would have preferred an ambush. The silence was worse.

If Golyn Niis were still under siege, the Federation would be on guard. They would be prepared for skirmishes. They would have posted guards to make sure no reinforcements could reach the resistance inside.

There would *be* a resistance.

But the Federation seemed to have simply packed up and walked away. They hadn't even bothered to leave behind a skeleton patrol. Which meant that the Federation didn't care who came into Golyn Niis.

Which meant that whatever lay behind those city walls, it wasn't worth guarding.

When the Cike finally succeeded in dragging open the heavy gates, an appalling stink assaulted them like a slap to the face. Rin knew the smell. She had experienced it at Sinegard and Khurdalain. She knew what to expect now. It had been a fool's hope to expect anything different, but still she could not fully register the sight that awaited them when they passed through the barrier.

All of them stood still at the gates, unwilling to take one step farther inside.

For a long time none of them could speak.

Then Ramsa fell to his knees and began to cackle with laughter.

"Khurdalain," he gasped. "We were all so obsessed with holding *Khurdalain*."

He doubled over, sides shaking with mirth, and beat his fists against the dirt.

Rin envied him.

Golyn Niis was a city of corpses.

The bodies had been arranged deliberately, as if the Federation had wanted to leave a greeting message for the next people to walk into the city. The destruction possessed a strange artfulness, a sadistic symmetry. Corpses were piled in neat, even rows, forming pyramids of ten, then nine, then eight. Corpses were stacked against the wall. Corpses were placed across the street in tidy lines. Corpses were arranged as far as the eye could see.

Nothing human moved. The only sounds in the city were wind rustling through debris, the buzzing of flies, and the squawking of carrion birds.

Rin's eyes watered. The stench was overwhelming. She looked to Altan, but his face was a mask. He marched them stoically down the main street into the city center, as if he was determined to witness the full extent of the destruction.

They marched in silence.

The Federation handiwork became more elaborate the deeper they traveled into the city. Close to the city square, the Federation had arrayed the corpses in states of incredible desecration, grotesque positions that defied human imagination. Corpses nailed to boards. Corpses hung by their tongues from hooks. Corpses dismembered in every possible way; headless, limbless, displaying mutilations that must have been performed while the victim was still alive. Fingers removed, then stacked in a small pile beside stubby hands. An entire line of castrated men, severed penises placed delicately on their slack-jawed mouths.

One sees great joy in decapitating enemies.

There were so many beheadings. Heads stacked up in neat little piles, not yet so rotted that they had become skulls, but no longer resembling human faces. Whatever heads retained enough flesh to form expressions wore identical looks of terrible dullness, as if they had never been alive.

As though burning; as though dying.

Perhaps due to some initial desire for sanitation, or mere curiosity, the Federation had tried to ignite several corpse pyramids. But they had given up before the job was finished. Perhaps they did not want to waste the oil. Perhaps the stink became unbearable. The bodies were grotesque, half-charred spectacles; hair had turned to ash, and the top layers of skin had turned a crinkling black, but the worst part was that there was something beneath the ashes that looked identifiably human.

The subject is with tears flowing in torrents, groaning in sorrow.

In the square they found bizarrely short skeletons—not corpses, but skeletons gleaming pristine white. They looked at first like children's bones, but upon closer examination, Enki identified them as adult torsos. He bent down and touched the dirt where one skeleton was fixed to the ground. The top half of the body had been stripped clean so the bones glistened in the sunlight, while the lower half remained intact in the dirt.

"They were buried," he said, disgusted. "They were buried up to the waist and set upon by dogs."

Rin could not understand how the Federation had found so many different ways to inflict suffering. But each corner they turned revealed another instance in the string of horrors, barbarian savagery matched only by inventiveness. A family, arms still around each other, impaled upon the same spear. Babies lying at the bottoms of vats, their skin a horrible shade of crimson, floating in the water in which they'd boiled to death.

In the hours that had passed, the only living creatures they encountered were dogs unnaturally fattened by feeding on corpses. Dogs, and vultures.

"Orders?" Unegen finally asked Altan.

They looked to their commander.

Altan hadn't spoken since they had walked through the city gates. His skin had turned a ghostly shade of gray. He might have been ill. He was sweating profusely, his left arm trembling. When they reached another pile of charred corpses, he convulsed, sank to his knees, and could not keep walking.

This was not Altan's first genocide.

This is Speer again, Rin thought. Altan must have been imagining the massacre of Speer in his mind, imagining the way his people were slaughtered overnight like cattle.

After a long time Chaghan extended his hand to Altan.

Altan grasped it and rose to his feet. He swallowed, closed his eyes. A mask of detachment spread across his expression once more with a curious ripple, like a facade of indifference had formed a seal over the surface of his face, locking any vulnerabilities within.

"Spread out," Altan ordered. His voice was impossibly level. "Find any survivors."

Surrounded by death, spreading out was the last thing any of them wanted to do.

Suni opened his mouth to protest. "But the Federation—"

"The Federation isn't here. They've been marching inland for a steady week. Our people are dead. Find me survivors."

They found evidence of a last desperate battle near the southern gate. The victors were clear. The Militia corpses had been given the same deliberate treatment as the carcasses of the civilians. Corpses had been stacked in the middle of the square, neat little piles with bodies arranged carefully on top of one another.

Rin saw the broken flag of the Militia lying on the ground, burned and smeared with blood. The flag bearer's hand was detached at the wrist; the rest of his body lay several feet away, eyes blank and unseeing.

The flag bore the dragon crest of the Red Emperor, the symbol of the Nikara Empire. In the lower left corner was stitched the number two in Old Nikara calligraphy. It was the insignia of the Second Division.

Rin's heart skipped a beat.

Kitay's division.

Rin dropped to her knees and touched the flag. A barking noise sounded from behind a pile of corpses. She looked up just as a dark, flea-matted mongrel came running at her. It was the size of a small wolf. Its gut was grotesquely round, like it had been gorging for days.

It dashed past Rin toward the flag bearer's corpse, sniffing hopefully.

Rin watched it rooting around, salivating eagerly, and something inside her snapped.

"*Get away!*" she shrieked, kicking out at the dog.

Any Sinegardian animal would have slunk away in fear. But this dog had lost all fear of human beings. This dog had lived amid a juicy feast of carnage for too long. Perhaps it assumed that she, too, was close to death. Perhaps it thought fresh meat would taste better than rotting flesh.

It snarled and lunged at her.

Rin was caught off guard by the dog's tremendous weight; it knocked her to the ground. It slobbered from open jaws as it lunged for her artery, but she raised her arms in defense and it sank its teeth into her left forearm instead. She screamed out loud, but the dog did not let go; with her right arm she reached for her sword, unsheathed it, and shoved it upward.

Her sword found its way through the dog's ribs. The dog's jaws went slack.

She stabbed again. The dog fell off her.

She jumped to her feet and jammed her sword down, piercing the dog's side. It was in its death throes now. She stabbed it again, this time in the neck. A spray of blood exploded outward, coating her face with its warm wetness. She was using her sword like a dagger now, bringing her arm down again and again just to feel bones and muscle give way to metal, just to hurt and *break* something . . .

"Rin!"

Someone grabbed her sword arm. She whirled on him, but Suni pulled her arms behind her back and held her tightly, so that she could not move until her sobbing had subsided.

"You're lucky it didn't get your sword arm," said Enki. "Keep this on for a week. See me if it starts to smell."

Rin flexed her arm. Enki had bound the dog bite tightly with a poultice that stung like she had stuck her arm in a hornet's nest.

"It's good for you," he said when she grimaced. "It'll prevent infection. We don't need you to go frothing mad."

"I think I'd like to go frothing mad," said Rin. "I'd like to lose my head. I think I'd be happier."

"Don't talk like that," Enki said sternly. "You have work to do."

But was it really work, what they were doing? Or were they deluding themselves that by finding the survivors, they could atone for the simple truth that they were too late?

She continued her miserable work of combing through the empty streets, upending debris, searching homes whose doors had been smashed in. After hours of looking she stopped hoping to find Kitay alive, and started to hope she wouldn't find his corpse during her patrols, because the sight of him flayed, dismembered, jammed into a wheelbarrow with a pile of other corpses, half-burned, would be worse than never finding him at all.

She walked Golyn Niis alone in a daze, trying to both see and not see. In time she found herself inured to the smell, and eventually the sight of bodies was not a shock, just another array of faces to be scanned for someone she knew.

All the while she called Kitay's name. She screamed it every time she saw a hint of motion, anything that could be alive: a cat disappearing into an alley, a pack of crows taking off suddenly, startled by the return of humans who weren't dead or dying. She screamed it for days.

And then from the ruins, so faintly she thought it was an echo, she heard her name in response.

"Remember that time I said the Trials were as bad as Speer?" Kitay asked. "I was wrong. This is as bad as Speer. This is worse than Speer."

It wasn't remotely funny, and neither of them laughed.

Rin's eyes and throat were sore from weeping. She had been clutching Kitay's hand for hours, fingers wound tightly around his, and she never wanted to let go. They sat side by side in a hastily constructed shelter half a mile outside the city, the only place they could escape the stench of death that permeated Golyn Niis. Kitay's survival was nothing short of a miracle. He and a small band of soldiers from the Second Division had hidden for days under the bodies of their slain comrades, too afraid to venture out in case the Federation patrols should return.

When it looked like they could sneak away from the killing fields, they hid in the demolished slums of the eastern side of the city. They had pulled a cellar door away and filled the open space with bricks, so from the outside it just looked like a wall. That was why the Cike hadn't seen them on their first pass through the city.

Only a handful of Kitay's squadron was still alive. He didn't know if the city contained any more survivors.

"Have you seen Nezha?" Kitay finally asked. "I heard he was being shipped to Khurdalain."

Rin opened her mouth to respond, but a horrible prickling feeling spread from the bridge of her nose to under her eyes, and then she was choking under wild, heaving sobs, and she couldn't form any words at all.

Kitay said nothing, just held his arms out in wordless sympathy. She collapsed into them. It was absurd that he should be comforting her, that she should be the one crying, after all that Kitay had survived. But Kitay was numb; for Kitay the suffering had been normalized, and he couldn't grieve any more than he already had. He was still holding her when Qara ducked into the tent.

"You're Chen Kitay?" She wasn't really asking, she just needed to say something to break the silence.

"Yes."

"You were with the Second Division when . . . ?" Qara trailed off. Kitay nodded.

"We need you to brief us. Can you walk?"

Under the open sky, in front of a silent audience of Altan and the twins, Kitay recounted in a halting voice the massacre at Golyn Niis.

"The city's defense was doomed from the start," Kitay said. "We thought we still had weeks. But you could have given us months, and the same thing would have happened."

Golyn Niis had been defended by an amalgamation of the Second, Ninth, and Eleventh Divisions. In this case, greater numbers did not mean greater strength. Perhaps even worse than in Khurdalain, the soldiers of the different provinces felt little sense of cohesion or purpose. The commanding officers were rivals, paranoid with distrust, unwilling to share intelligence.

"Irjah begged the Warlords over and over again to put aside their differences. He couldn't make them see reason." Kitay swallowed. "The first two skirmishes went badly. They took us by surprise. They surrounded the city from the southeast. We hadn't been expecting them so early. We didn't think they had found the mountain pass. But they came at night, and they . . . they captured Irjah. They flayed him alive over the city wall so that everyone could see. That broke our resistance. Most of the soldiers wanted to flee after that.

"After Irjah was dead, the Ninth and Eleventh surrendered en masse. I don't blame them. They were outnumbered, and they thought they'd get off easier if they didn't resist. Thought maybe it'd be better to become prisoners than to die." Kitay shuddered violently. "They were so wrong. The Federation general took their surrender with all the usual etiquette. Confiscated their arms, corralled the soldiers into prison camps. The next morning they were marched up the mountain and beheaded. There were a lot of deserters from the Second after that. A couple of us stayed to fight. It was pointless, but . . . it was better than surrendering. We couldn't dishonor Irjah. Not like that."

"Wait," Chaghan interrupted. "Did they take the Empress?"

"The Empress fled," Kitay said. "She took twenty of her guards and stole out of the city the night after Irjah died."

Qara and Chaghan made synchronous noises of disbelief, but Kitay shook his head warily. "Who can blame her? It was that or let those monsters get their hands on her, and who knows what they would have done to her . . ."

Chaghan did not look convinced.

"Pathetic," he spat, and Rin agreed with him. The idea that the Empress had fled from a city while her people were burned, killed, murdered, raped went against everything Rin had been taught about warfare. A general did not abandon his soldiers. An Empress did not abandon her people.

Again, the Talwu's words rang true.

A leader abandons their people. A ruler begins a campaign. . . . Joy in decapitating enemies. This signifies evil.

Was there any other way to interpret the Hexagram, in the face of the evidence of destruction before them? Rin had been torturing herself with the Talwu's words, trying to construe them in any way that didn't point to the massacre at Golyn Niis, but she had been deluding herself. The Talwu had told them exactly what to expect.

She should have known that when the Empress had abandoned the Nikara, then all truly was lost.

But the Empress was not the only one who had abandoned Golyn Niis. The entire army had surrendered the city. Within a week Golyn Niis had more or less been delivered to the Federation on the platter, and the entirety of its half million people subjected to the whims of the invading forces.

Those whims turned out to have little to do with the city itself. Instead, the Federation simply wanted to squeeze Golyn Niis for whatever resources they could find in preparation for a deeper march inland. They sacked the marketplace, rounded up the livestock, and demanded that families bring out their stores of rice and grain. Whatever couldn't be loaded up on their supply wagons, they burned or left out to spoil.

Then they disposed of the people.

"They decided that beheadings took too long, so they started doing things more efficiently," said Kitay. "They started with gas. You should probably know this, actually; they've got this thing, this weapon that emits yellow-green fog—"

"I know," Altan said. "We saw the same thing in Khurdalain."

"They took out practically the entire Second Division in one night," said Kitay. "Some of us put up a last stand near the south gate. When the gas cleared, nothing was alive. I went there afterward to find survivors. At first I didn't know what I was looking at. All over the ground, you could see animals. Mice, rats, rodents of every kind. So many of them. They'd crawled out of their holes to die. When the Militia was gone, nothing stood between the soldiers and our people. The Federation had fun. They made it a sport. They threw babies in the air to see if they could cleave them in half before they hit the ground. They had contests to see how many civilians they could round up and decapitate in an hour. They raced to see who could stack bodies the fastest." Kitay's voice cracked. "Could I have some water?"

Qara wordlessly handed him her canteen.

"How did Mugen become like this?" Chaghan asked wonderingly. "What did you ever do to make them hate you so much?"

"It's not anything we did," said Altan. His left hand, Rin noticed, was shaking again. "It's how the Federation soldiers were trained. When you believe your life means nothing except for your usefulness to your Emperor, the lives of your enemies mean even less."

"The Federation soldiers don't feel anything." Kitay nodded in agreement. "They don't think of themselves as people. They are parts of a machine. They do as they are commanded, and the only time they feel joy is when reveling in another person's suffering. There is no reasoning with them. There is no attempting to understand them. They are accustomed to propagating such grotesque evil that they cannot properly be called human." Kitay's voice trembled.

"When they were cutting my squadron down, I looked into the eyes of one of them. I thought I could make him recognize me as a fellow man. As a person, not just an opponent. And he stared back at me, and I realized I couldn't connect with him at all. There was nothing human in those eyes."

Once the survivors began to realize that the Militia had arrived, they emerged from their hiding holes in miserable, straggling groups.

The few survivors of Golyn Niis had been driven deep into the city, hiding in disguised shelters like Kitay or locked up in makeshift prisons and then forgotten when the Federation soldiers decided to continue their march inland. After discovering two or three such holding rooms, Altan ordered them—Cike and civilians alike—to carefully search the city.

No one disagreed with the order. They all knew, Rin suspected, that it would be horrible to die alone, chained to walls when their captors had long since departed.

"I guess we're saving people for once," Baji said. "Feels nice."

Altan himself led a squad to take on the nearly impossible task of clearing away the bodies. He claimed it was to ward against rot and disease, but Rin suspected it was because he wanted to give them a proper funeral—and because there was so little else that he could do for the city.

They had no time to dig mass graves on the scale necessary before the stench of rotting bodies became unbearable. So they stacked the corpses into large pyres, great bonfires of bodies that burned constantly. Golyn Niis turned from a city of corpses to a city of ash.

But the sheer number of the dead was staggering. The corpses Altan burned barely made a dent in the piles of rotting bodies inside the city walls. Rin didn't think it was possible to truly cleanse Golyn Niis unless they burned the entire city to the ground.

Eventually they might have to. But not while there could still be survivors.

Rin was outside the city walls trying to find a fresh source of water that wasn't spoiled with blood when Kitay pulled her aside and reported that they had found Venka. She had been kept in a "relaxation house," which was likely the only reason why the Federation had let a division soldier live. Kitay did not elaborate on what a "relaxation house" was, but he didn't need to.

Rin could hardly recognize Venka when she went to see her that night. Her lovely hair was shorn short, as if someone had hacked at it with a knife. Her lively eyes were now dull and glassy. Both her arms had been broken at the wrist. She wore them in slings. Rin saw the angle at which Venka's arms had been twisted, and knew there was only one way they could have gotten like that.

Venka hardly stirred when Rin entered her room. Only when Rin closed the door did she flinch.

"Hi," Rin said in a small voice.

Venka looked up dully and said nothing.

"I thought you'd want someone to talk to," said Rin, though the words sounded hollow and insufficient even as they left her mouth.

Venka glared at her.

Rin struggled for words. She could think of no questions that were not inane. *Are you all right?* Of course Venka was not all right. *How did you survive?* By having the body of a woman. *What happened to you?* But she already knew.

"Did you know they called us public toilets?" Venka asked suddenly.

Rin stopped two paces from the door. Comprehension dawned on her, and her blood turned to ice. "*What?*"

"They thought I couldn't understand Mugini," Venka said with a horrifying attempt at a chuckle. "That's what they called me, when they were in me."

"Venka . . ."

"Do you know how badly it hurt? They were in me, they were in me for hours and they wouldn't stop. I blacked out over and over but every time I awoke they were still going, a different man would be on top of me, or maybe the same man . . . they were all the same after a while. It was a nightmare, and I couldn't wake up."

Rin's mouth filled with the taste of bile. "I'm so sorry—" she tried, but Venka didn't seem to hear her.

"I'm not the worst," Venka said. "I fought back. I was trouble. So they saved me for last. They wanted to break me first. They made me watch. I saw women disemboweled. I saw the soldiers slice off their breasts. I saw them nail women alive to walls. I saw them mutilate young girls, when they had tired of their mothers. If their vaginas were too small, they cut them open to make it easier to rape them." Venka's voice rose in pitch. "There was a pregnant woman in the house with us. She was seven months to term. Eight. At first the soldiers let her live so she'd take care of us. Wash us. Feed us. She was the only kind face in that house. They didn't touch her because she was pregnant, not at first. Then one day the general decided he'd had enough of the other girls. He came for her. You'd think she'd have learned by then, after watching what the soldiers did to us. You'd think she would know there wasn't any point in resisting."

Rin didn't want to hear any more. She wanted to bury her head under her arms and block everything out. But Venka continued, as if now that she had started her testimony she couldn't stop. "She kicked and dragged. And then she slapped him. The general howled and grabbed at her stomach. Not with his knife. With his fingers. His nails. He knocked her down and he tore and tore." Venka turned her head away. "And he pulled out her stomach, and her intestines, and then finally the baby . . . and the baby was still moving. We saw everything from the hallway."

Rin stopped breathing.

"I was glad," Venka said. "Glad that she was dead, before the general ripped her baby in half the way you'd split an orange." Underneath her slings, Venka's fingers clenched and spasmed. "He made me mop it up."

"Gods. Venka." Rin couldn't look her in the eye. "I'm so sorry."

"*Don't pity me!*" Venka shrieked suddenly. She made a movement as if trying to reach for Rin's arm, as if she had forgotten that her arms were broken. She stood up and walked toward Rin so that they were face-to-face, nose to nose.

Her expression was as unhinged as it had been that day when they fought in the ring.

"I don't need your pity. I need you to kill them for me. You *have* to kill them for me," Venka hissed. "Swear it. Swear on your blood that you will *burn them*."

"Venka, I can't . . ."

"I know you can." Venka's voice climbed in pitch. "I heard what they said about you. You have to burn them. Whatever it takes. Swear it on your life. Swear it. Swear it for me."

Her eyes were like shattered glass.

It took all of Rin's courage to meet her gaze.

"I swear."

* * *

Rin left Venka's room and set off at a run.

She couldn't breathe. She couldn't speak.

She needed Altan.

She didn't know why she thought that he would offer the relief she was looking for, but among them only Altan had gone through this once before. Altan had been on Speer when it burned, Altan had seen his people killed . . . Altan, surely, could tell her that the Earth might keep on turning, that the sun would continue to rise and set, that the existence of such abominable evil, such disregard for human life did not mean the entire world was shrouded in darkness. Altan, surely, could tell her they still had something worth fighting for.

"In the library," Suni told her, pointing to an ancient-looking tower two blocks past the city gates.

The door to the library was closed, and nobody responded when she knocked.

Rin turned the handle slowly and peered within.

The great inner chamber was filled with lamps, yet none were lit. The only light came from the moonbeams shining in through tall glass windows. The room was filled with a sickly sweet smoke that tugged at her memory, so thick and cloying that Rin nearly choked.

In a corner among stacks of books, Altan was sprawled, legs out and head tilted listlessly. His shirt was off.

Her breath hitched in her throat.

His chest was a crisscross of scars. Many were jagged battle wounds. Others were startlingly neat, symmetrical and clean as if carved deliberately into his skin.

A pipe lay in his hand. As she watched, he brought it to his lips and inhaled deeply, crimson eyes rolling upward as he did so. He let the smoke fill his lungs and then exhaled slowly with a low, satisfied sigh.

"Altan?" she said quietly.

He didn't seem to hear her at first. Rin crossed the room and slowly knelt down next to him. The smell was nauseatingly familiar:

opium nuggets, sweet like rotted fruit. It gave her memories of Tikany, of living corpses wasting away in drug dens.

Finally, Altan looked in her direction. His face twisted into a droll, uninterested smile, and even in the ruins of Golyn Niis, even in this city of corpses, Rin thought that the sight of Altan then was the most terrible thing she'd ever seen.

CHAPTER 22

"You knew?" Rin asked.

"We all did," Ramsa murmured. He touched her shoulder tentatively, attempting a comforting gesture, but it didn't help. "He tries to hide it. Doesn't do a very good job."

Rin moaned and pressed her forehead into her knees. She could hardly see through her tears. It hurt to inhale now; it felt like her rib cage was being crushed, like the despair was pressing against her chest, weighing her down so that she could barely breathe.

This had to be the end. Their wartime capital had fallen, her friends were dead or broken, and Altan . . .

"*Why?*" she wailed. "Doesn't he know what it *does* to you?"

"He knows." Ramsa let his hand drop. He twisted his fingers in his lap. "I don't think he can help it."

Rin knew that was true, but she couldn't accept it.

She knew the horrors of opium addiction. She'd seen the Fangs' clientele—promising young scholars, well-to-do merchants, talented men—whose lives had been ruined by opium nuggets. She'd seen proud government officials reduced in the span of months to shriveled, penniless men begging in the streets to fund their next fix.

But she couldn't reconcile those images with her commander.

Altan was invincible. Altan was the best martial artist in the country. Altan wasn't—Altan *couldn't be*—

"He's supposed to be our commander," she said hoarsely. "How can he fight when he—when he's like *that*?"

"We cover for him," Ramsa said quietly. "He never used to do it more than once a month."

All those times he'd smelled like smoke. All those times he'd been missing when she tried to find him.

He'd just been sprawled in his office, sucking in and out, glassy and empty and *gone*.

"It's disgusting," she said. "It's—it's *pathetic*."

"Don't say that," Ramsa said sharply. He curled his fingers into a fist. "Take that back."

"He's our commander! He has a duty to us! How could he—"

But Ramsa cut her off. "I don't know how Altan survived that island. But I do know whatever happened to him is unimaginable. You didn't know you were a Speerly until months ago. But Altan lost everyone in his life overnight. You don't get over that kind of pain. So it's what he needs. So it's a vulnerability. I won't judge him. I don't dare, because I don't have the right. And neither do you."

After two weeks of sifting through rubble, breaking into locked basements, and relocating corpses, the Cike found fewer than a thousand survivors in the city that had once been home to half a million. Too many days had passed. They gave up hope of finding any more.

For the first time since the start of the war, the Cike had no operations planned.

"What are we waiting around for?" Baji asked several times a day.

"Orders," Qara always answered.

But no commands were forthcoming. Altan was usually absent, sometimes disappearing for entire days. When he was present, he was in no state to give orders. Chaghan took over smoothly, assigned the Cike routine duties in the interim. Most of them were told to keep watch. They all knew that the enemy was already moving inland to finish what they had started, and that there was nothing in Golyn Niis to guard but ruins, but still they obeyed.

Rin sat over the gate, clutching a spear to keep herself upright as she watched the path leading to the city. She had the twilight watch, which was just as well, because she could not sleep if she tried. Each time she closed her eyes she saw blood. Dried blood in the streets. Blood in the Golyn River. Corpses on hooks. Infants in barrels.

She couldn't eat, either. The blandest foods still tasted like carcasses. Only once did they have meat; Baji caught two rabbits in the woods, flayed them, and staked them on a narrow piece of wood to roast. When Rin smelled them, she dry-heaved for several long minutes. She could not dissociate the rabbits' flesh from the charred flesh of bodies in the square. She could not walk Golyn Niis without imagining the deaths in the moment of the execution. She could not see the hundreds of decapitated heads on poles without seeing the soldier who had walked down the row of kneeling prisoners, methodically bringing his sword down again and again as if reaping corn. She could not pass the babies in their barrel graves without hearing their uncomprehending screams.

The entire time, her own mind screamed the unanswerable question: *Why?*

The cruelty could not register for her. Bloodlust, she understood. Bloodlust, she was guilty of. She had lost herself in battle, too; she had gone further than she should have, she had hurt others when she should have stopped.

But this—viciousness on this scale, wanton slaughter of this magnitude, against innocents who hadn't even lifted a finger in self-defense, *this* she could not imagine doing.

They surrendered, she wanted to scream at her disappeared enemy. *They dropped their weapons. They posed no threat to you. Why did you have to do this?*

A rational explanation eluded her.

Because the answer could not be rational. It was not founded in military strategy. It was not because of a shortage of food rations, or because of the risk of insurgency or backlash. It was, simply, what happened when one race decided that the other was insignificant.

The Federation had massacred Golyn Niis for the simple reason that they did not think of the Nikara as *human*. And if your opponent was not human, if your opponent was a cockroach, what did it matter how many of them you killed? What was the difference between crushing an ant and setting an anthill on fire? Why shouldn't you pull wings off insects for your own enjoyment? The bug might feel pain, but what did that matter to you?

If you were the victim, what could you say to make your tormentor recognize you as human? How did you get your enemy to recognize you at all?

And why should an oppressor care?

Warfare was about absolutes. Us or them. Victory or defeat. There was no middle way. There was no mercy. No surrender.

This was the same logic, Rin realized, that had justified the destruction of Speer. To the Federation, to wipe out an entire race overnight was not an atrocity at all. Only a necessity.

"You're insane."

Rin's head jerked up. She had sunk into another exhausted daze. She blinked twice and squinted out into the darkness until the source of the voice shifted from amorphous shadows to two recognizable forms.

Altan and Chaghan stood underneath the gate, Chaghan with his arms tightly crossed, Altan slouched against the wall. Heart hammering, Rin ducked under the low wall so they wouldn't see her if they looked up.

"What if it wasn't just us?" Altan asked in a low, eager voice. Rin was stunned; Altan sounded alert, alive, like he hadn't been in days. "What if there were more of us?"

"Not this again," said Chaghan.

"What if there were *thousands* of the Cike, soldiers as powerful as you and me, soldiers who could call the gods?"

"Altan . . ."

"What if I could raise an entire army of shamans?"

Rin's eyes widened. An *army*?

Chaghan made a choking noise that might have been a laugh. "How do you propose to do that?"

"You know precisely how," said Altan. "You know why I sent you to the mountain."

"You said you only wanted the Gatekeeper." Chaghan's voice grew agitated. "You didn't say you wanted to release every madman in there."

"They're not madmen—"

"They are not men at all! By now they are demigods! They are like bolts of lightning, like hurricanes of spiritual power. If I'd known what you were planning, I wouldn't have—"

"Bullshit, Chaghan. You knew *exactly* what I was planning."

"We were supposed to release the Gatekeeper *together*." Chaghan sounded wounded.

"And we will. Just as we'll release everyone else. Feylen. Huleinin. All of them."

"*Feylen?* After what he tried to do? You don't know what you're saying. You are speaking of atrocities."

"Atrocities?" Altan asked coolly. "You've seen the bodies here, and you accuse *me* of atrocities?"

Chaghan's voice rose steadily in pitch. "What Mugen has done is *human* cruelty. But humans alone are only capable of so much destruction. The beings locked inside the Chuluu Korikh are capable of ruin on a different scale altogether."

Altan barked out a laugh. "Do you have *eyes*? Do you see what they've done to Golyn Niis? A ruler should do anything necessary to protect their people. I will not be Tearza, Chaghan. *I will not let them kill us off like dogs.*"

Rin heard a scuffling noise. Feet shuffling against dry leaves.

Limbs brushing against limbs. Were they *fighting*? Hardly daring to breathe, Rin peeked out from over the wall.

Chaghan grasped Altan by the collar with both hands, pulling him down so that they were face-to-face. Altan was half a foot taller than Chaghan, could have snapped him in half with ease, and yet he did not lift a hand in defense.

Rin stared at them in disbelief. Nobody touched Altan like that.

"This isn't *Speer* again," Chaghan hissed. His face was so close to Altan's that their noses almost touched. "Even Tearza wouldn't unleash her god to save one island. But you are sentencing thousands of people to death."

"I'm trying to *win* this war—"

"What for? Look around, Trengsin! No one is going to pat you on the back and tell you good job. There's no one *left*. This country is going to shit, and no one cares—"

"The Empress cares," said Altan. "I sent a falcon, she approved my plan—"

"Who cares what your Empress says?" Chaghan screamed. His hands shook wildly. "*Fuck* your Empress! Your Empress fled!"

"She's one of us," Altan said. "You know she is. If we have her, and we have the Gatekeeper, then we can lead this army—"

"No one can lead that army." Chaghan let go of Altan's collar. "Those people in the mountain are not like you. They're not like Suni. You can't control them, and you're not going to try. I won't let you."

Chaghan raised his hands to push Altan again, but Altan grabbed them this time, seized his wrists and lowered them easily. He did not let them go. "Do you really think you can stop me?"

"This isn't you," Chaghan said. "This is about Speer. This is about your revenge. That's all you Speerlies do, you hate and burn and destroy without consequence. Tearza was the only one of you with any foresight. Maybe the Federation was right about you, maybe it was best they burned down your island—"

"How dare you," Altan said, his voice so quiet Rin pressed herself against the wall as if she could somehow get closer and make sure she was hearing right. Altan's fingers tightened around Chaghan's wrists. "You've crossed the line."

"I'm your Seer," Chaghan said. "I give you counsel, whether you want to hear it or not."

"The Seer does not command," Altan said. "The Seer does not *disobey*. I have no place for a disloyal lieutenant. If you won't help me, then I'll send you away. Go north. Go to the dam. Take your sister and do as we planned."

"Altan, listen to reason," Chaghan pleaded. "You don't have to do this."

"Do as I command," Altan said curtly. "Go, or leave the Cike."

Rin sank back behind the wall, heart hammering.

She abandoned her post as soon as she heard Altan's footsteps fading into the distance. Once she could no longer see his form from the gate, she darted down the steps and raced out onto the open road. She caught Chaghan and Qara as they were saddling a recovered gelding.

"Let's go," Chaghan told his sister when he saw Rin approaching, but Rin grabbed the reins before Qara could prod the horse forward.

"Where are you going?" she demanded.

"Away," Chaghan said tersely. "Please let go."

"I need to talk to you."

"We have orders to leave."

"I overheard you with Altan."

Qara muttered something in her own language.

Chaghan scowled. "Have you ever been able to mind your own business?"

Rin tightened her grip on the reins. "What army is he talking about? Why won't you help him?"

Chaghan's eyes narrowed. "You have no idea what you're getting into."

"So tell me. Who is Feylen?" Rin continued loudly. "Who is Huleinin? What did he mean, he'll release the Gatekeeper?"

"Altan is going to burn down Nikan. I will not be responsible."

"*Burn down Nikan?*" Rin repeated. "How—"

"Your commander has gone mad," Chaghan said bluntly. "That is as much as you need to know. And you know the worst part? I think he's meant to do this all along. I've been blind. This is what he's wanted since the Federation marched on Sinegard."

"And you're just going to let him?"

Chaghan recoiled violently, as if he'd been slapped. Rin had a fear that he might yank on the reins and ride away, but Chaghan merely sat there, mouth slightly open.

She had never seen Chaghan speechless before. It scared her.

She wouldn't have expected Chaghan to shrink from cruelty. Chaghan, alone among the Cike, had never displayed an ounce of fear about his power, about losing control. Chaghan reveled in his abilities. He relished them.

What could be so unthinkable that it horrified even Chaghan?

Without taking his eyes off Rin, Chaghan reached down, grasped the reins, and swung himself off the horse. She took two steps backward as he walked toward her. He stopped much closer to her than she would have liked. He studied her in silence for a long moment.

"Do you understand the source of Altan's power?" he asked finally.

Rin frowned. "He's a Speerly. It's obvious."

"Even the average Speerly was not half as powerful as Altan is," said Chaghan. "Have you ever asked yourself why Altan alone among Speerlies survived? Why he was allowed to live when the rest of his kin were burned and dismembered?"

Rin shook her head.

"After the First Poppy War, the Federation became obsessed with your people," said Chaghan. "They couldn't believe their Armed Forces had been bested by this tiny island nation. That's what spurred their interest in shamanism. There has never been a Federation shaman. The Federation needed to know how the Speerlies got their powers. When they occupied the Snake Province, they built a research base opposite the island and spent the decades in between the Poppy Wars kidnapping Speerlies, experimenting on them, trying to figure out what made them special. Altan was one of those experiments."

Rin's chest felt very tight. She dreaded what might come next, but Chaghan continued, his voice as flat and emotionless as if he were reciting history lessons. "By the time the Hesperians liberated the facilities, Altan had spent half his life in a lab. The Federation scientists drugged him daily to keep him sedated. They starved him. They tortured him to make him comply. He wasn't the only Speerly they took, but he was the only one who survived. Do you know how?"

Rin shook her head. "I . . ."

Chaghan continued, ruthless. "Did you know they strapped him down and made him watch as they took the others apart to find out what made them tick? What are Speerlies made of? The Federation was determined to find out. Did you know they kept them alive as long as they could, even when they had peeled their flesh away from their rib cages, so they could see how their muscles moved while they were splayed out like rabbits?"

"He never told me," Rin whispered.

"And he never would have." Chaghan said. "Altan likes to suffer in silence. Altan likes to let his hatred fester, likes to incubate it as long as he can. Now do you understand the source of his power? It is not because he is a Speerly. It is nothing genetic. Altan is so powerful because he hates so deeply and so thoroughly that it constitutes every part of his being. Your Phoenix is the god of fire, but it is also the god of rage. Of vengeance. Altan doesn't need opium to call the Phoenix because the Phoenix is always alive inside him. You asked me why I wouldn't stop him. Now you understand. You can't stop an avenger. You can't reason with a madman. You think I am running, and I admit to you that I am afraid. I am afraid of what he might do in his quest for vengeance. And I am afraid that he is right."

*   *   *

When she found Altan, lying in that same corner of the ancient library he had been last time, she said nothing. She crossed the moonlit room and took the pipe from his languid fingers. She sat down cross-legged, leaning against the shelves of ancient scrolls. Then she took a long draught herself. The effect took a long while to set in, but when it did, she wondered why she had ever meditated at all.

She understood, now, why Altan needed opium.

Small wonder he was addicted. Smoking the pipe had to be the only time that he was not consumed with his misery, with scars that would never heal. The haze induced by the smoke was the only time that he could feel nothing, the only time that he could forget.

"How are you doing?" Altan mumbled.

"I hate them," she said. "I hate them so much. I hate them so much it hurts. I hate them with every drop of my blood. I hate them with every bone in my body."

Altan blew out a long stream of smoke. He didn't look like a human so much as he did a simple vessel for the fumes, an inanimate extension of the pipe.

"It doesn't stop hurting," he said.

She sucked in another deep breath of the wonderful sweetness.

"I understand now," she said.

"Do you?"

"I'm sorry about before."

Her words were vague, but Altan seemed to know what she meant. He took the pipe back from her and inhaled again, and that was acknowledgment enough.

It was a long while before he spoke again.

"I am about to do something terrible," he said. "And you will have a choice. You can choose to come with me to the prison under the stone. I believe you know what I intend to do there."

"Yes." She knew, without asking, what was imprisoned in the Chuluu Korikh.

Unnatural criminals, who have committed unnatural crimes.

If she went with him, she would help him to unleash monsters. Monsters worse than the chimei. Monsters worse than anything in the Emperor's Menagerie—because these monsters were not beasts, mindless things that could be leashed and controlled, but warriors. Shamans. The gods walking in humans, with no regard for the mortal world.

"Or you can stay in Golyn Niis. You can fight with the remnants of the Nikara army and you can try to win this war without the help of the gods. You can remain Jiang's good girl, you can heed his warnings, and you can shy away from the power that you know you have." He extended his hand to her. "But I need your help. I need another Speerly."

She glanced down at his slender brown fingers.

If she helped him free this army, would that make her a monster? Would they be guilty of everything Chaghan had accused them of?

Perhaps. But what else did they have to lose? The invaders who had already pumped her country full of opium and left it to rot had returned to finish the job.

She reached for his hand, curled her fingers around his. The sensation of his skin under hers was a feeling unlike anything she had dared to imagine. Alone in the library, with only the ancient scrolls of Old Nikan to bear witness, she pledged her allegiance.

"I'm with you," she said.

CHAPTER 23

THE CHULUU KORIKH

From *The Seejin Classification of Deities*, compiled in the Annals of the Red Emperor, recorded by Vachir Mogoi, High Historian of Sinegard

Long before the days of the Red Emperor, this country was not yet a great empire, but a sparse land populated by a small scattering of tribes. These tribesmen were horse-riding nomads from the north, who had been cast out of the Hinterlands by the hordes of the great khan. Now they struggled to survive in this strange, warm land.

They were ignorant of many things: the cycles of the rain, the tides of the Murui River, the variations of soil. They knew not how to plow the land or to sow seeds so they could grow food instead of hunt for it. They needed guidance. They needed the gods.

But the deities of the Pantheon were yet reluctant to grant their aid to mankind.

"Men are selfish and petty," argued Erlang Shen, Grand Marshal of the Heavenly Forces. "Their life spans are so short that they give no thought to the future of the land. If we lend them aid, they will drain this earth and squabble among themselves. There will be no peace."

"But they are suffering now." Erlang Shen's twin sister, the beautiful Sanshengmu, led the opposing faction. "We have the power to help them. Why do we withhold it?"

"You are blind, sister," said Erlang Shen. "You think too highly of mortals. They give nothing to the universe, and the universe owes them nothing in return. If they cannot survive, then let them die."

He issued a heavenly order forbidding any entity in the Pantheon from interfering with mortal matters. But Sanshengmu, always the gentler of the two, was convinced that her brother was too quick to judge mankind. She hatched a plan to descend to Earth in secret, in hopes of proving to the Pantheon that men were worthy of help from the gods. However, Erlang Shen was alerted to Sanshengmu's plot at the last moment, and he gave chase. In her haste to escape from her brother, Sanshengmu landed badly on Earth.

She lay on the road for three days. Her mortal guise was of a woman of uncommon beauty. In those times, that was a dangerous thing to be.

The first man who found her, a soldier, raped her and left her for dead.

The second man, a merchant, took her clothes but left her behind, as she would have been too heavy for his wagon.

The third man was a hunter. When he saw Sanshengmu he took off his cloak and wrapped her in it. Then he carried her back to his tent.

"Why are you helping me?" Sanshengmu asked. "You are a human. You live only to prey upon each other. You have no compassion. All you do is satisfy your own greed."

"Not all humans," said the hunter. "Not me."

By the time they reached his tent, Sanshengmu had fallen in love.

She married the hunter. She taught the men of the hunter's

tribe many things: how to chant at the sky for rain, how to read the patterns of the weather in the cracked shell of a tortoise, how to burn incense to appease the deities of agriculture in return for a bountiful harvest.

The hunter's tribe flourished and spread across the fertile land of Nikan. Word spread of the living goddess who had come to Earth. Sanshengmu's worshippers increased in number across the country. The men of Nikan lit incense and built statues in her honor, the first divine entity they had ever known of.

And in time, she bore the hunter a child.

From his throne in the heavens, Erlang Shen watched, and grew enraged.

When Sanshengmu's son reached his first birthday, Erlang Shen journeyed down to the world of man. He set fire to the banquet tent, driving out the guests in a panicked terror. He impaled the hunter with his great three-pronged spear and killed him. He took Sanshengmu's son and hurled him off the side of a mountain. Then he grasped his horrified sister by the neck and lifted her in the air.

"You cannot kill me," choked Sanshengmu. "You are bound to me. We are two halves of one whole. You cannot survive my death."

"No," acknowledged Erlang Shen. "But I can imprison you. Since you love the world of men so much, I will build for you an earthly prison, where you will pass an eternity. This will be your punishment for daring to love a mortal."

As he spoke, a great mountain formed in the air. He flung his twin sister away from him, and the mountain sank on top of her, an unbreakable prison of stone. Sanshengmu tried and tried to escape, but inside her prison, she could not access her magic.

She languished in that stone prison for years. And every moment was torture to the goddess, who had once flown free through the heavens.

There are many stories about Sanshengmu. There are stories of her son, the Lotus Warrior, and how he was the first shaman to walk Nikan, a liaison between gods and men. There are stories of his war against his uncle, Erlang Shen, in order to free his mother.

There are stories, too, about the Chuluu Korikh. There are stories of the monkey king, the arrogant shaman who was locked for five thousand years within by the Jade Emperor as punishment for his impudence. One could say that this was the beginning of the age of stories, because that was the beginning of the age of shamans.

Much is true. Much more is not.

But one thing can be said to be fact. To this day, of all the places on this Earth, only the Chuluu Korikh may contain a god.

"Are you finally going to tell me where you're headed?" Kitay asked. "Or did you call me here just to say goodbye?"

Rin was packing her equipment into traveling bags, deliberately avoiding eye contact with Kitay. She had avoided him the past week while she and Altan planned their journey.

Altan had forbidden her to speak of it to anyone outside the Cike. He and Rin would travel to the Chuluu Korikh alone. But if they succeeded, Rin wanted Kitay to know what was coming. She wanted him to know when to flee.

"We're leaving as soon as the gelding is ready," she said. Chaghan and Qara had departed Golyn Niis on the only halfway decent horse that the Federation hadn't taken with them. It had taken days to find another gelding that wasn't diseased or dying, and days more to nurture it back to a state fit for travel.

"Can I ask where to?" Kitay asked. He tried not to display his annoyance, but she knew him too well to overlook it; irritation was written across his face. Kitay was not used to missing information; she knew he resented her for it.

She hesitated, and then said, "The Kukhonin range."

"*Kukhonin?*" Kitay repeated.

"Two days' ride south from here." She rummaged around in her bag to avoid looking at him. She had packed an enormous amount of poppy seed, everything from Enki's stores that she could hold. Of course, none of it would be useful inside the Chuluu Korikh itself, but once they left the mountain, once they had freed every shaman inside . . .

"I know where the Kukhonin range is," Kitay said impatiently. "I want to know why you're riding in the opposite direction from Mugen's main column."

You have to tell him. Rin could not see a way of warning Kitay without divulging part of Altan's plan. Otherwise he would insist on finding out for himself, and his curiosity would spell the death of him. She set the bag down, straightened up, and met Kitay's eyes.

"Altan wants to raise an army."

Kitay made a noise of disbelief. "Come again?"

"It's . . . they're . . . You wouldn't understand if I told you." How was she to explain this to him? Kitay had never studied Lore. Kitay had never truly believed in the gods, not even after the battle at Sinegard. Kitay thought that shamanism was a metaphor for arcane martial arts, that Rin and Altan's abilities were sleights of hand and parlor tricks. Kitay did not know what lay in the Pantheon. Kitay did not understand the danger they were about to unleash.

"Just—look, I'm trying to warn you—"

"No, you're trying to deceive me. You don't get to deceive me," Kitay said very loudly. "I have seen cities burning. I have seen you do what mortals should not be able to do. I have seen you raise fire. I think I have the right to know. Try me."

"Fine."

She told him.

Amazingly, he believed her.

"This sounds like a plan where many things could go wrong," said Kitay when she finished. "How does Altan even know this army will fight for him?"

"They're Nikara," said Rin. "They have to. They've fought for the Empire before."

"The same Empire that had them buried alive in the first place?"

"Not buried alive," she said. "Immured."

"Oh, sorry," Kitay amended, "*immured*. Enclosed in stone in some magic mountain, because they became so powerful that a fucking *mountain* was the only thing that could stop them tearing apart entire villages. *This* is the army you're just going to set loose on the country. *This* is what you think is going to save Nikan. Who came up with this, you or your opium-addled commander? Because this sure as hell isn't the kind of plan you come up with sober, I can tell you that."

Rin crossed her arms tightly against her chest. Kitay wasn't saying anything she hadn't already considered. What could anyone predict about maddened souls who had been entombed for years? The shamans of the Chuluu Korikh might do nothing. They might destroy half the country out of spite.

But Altan was certain they would fight for him.

They have no right to begrudge the Empress, Altan had said. *All shamans know the risks when they journey to the gods. Everyone in the Cike knows that at the end of the line, they are destined for the Stone Mountain.*

And the alternative was the extermination of every Nikara alive. The massacre of Golyn Niis made it obvious that the Federation did not want to take any prisoners. They wanted the massive piece of land that was the Nikara Empire. They were not interested in cohabitation with its former occupants. She knew the risks, and she had weighed them and concluded that she didn't care. She had thrown her lot in with Altan, for better or worse.

"You can't change my mind," she said. "I'm telling you this as a favor. When we come out of that mountain, I don't know how much control we'll have, only that we'll be powerful. Do not try to stop us. Do not try to join us. When we come, you should flee."

* * *

"The rendezvous point will be at the base of the Kukhonin Mountains," Altan told the assembled Cike. "If we don't meet you there in seven days' time, assume we were killed. Do not go inside the mountain yourselves. Wait for a bird from Qara and do as the message commands. Chaghan is commander in my stead."

"Where *is* Chaghan?" Unegen ventured to ask.

"With Qara." Altan's face betrayed nothing. "They've gone north on my orders. You'll know when they're back."

"When will that be?"

"When they've done their job."

Rin waited by their horse, watched Altan speaking with a self-assured aura that she had not seen since Sinegard. Altan, as he presented himself now, was not that broken boy with the opium pipe. He was not the despairing Speerly reliving the genocide of his people. He was not a victim. Altan was different now than he had been even in Khurdalain. He was no longer frustrated, pacing around his office like a cornered animal, no longer constrained under Jun's thumb. Altan had orders now, a mission, a singular purpose. He didn't have to hold back anymore. He had been let off his leash. Altan was going to take his anger to a final, terrible conclusion.

She had no doubts they would succeed. She just didn't know if the country would survive his plan.

"Good luck," said Enki. "Say hi to Feylen for us."

"Great guy," Unegen said wistfully. "Until, you know, he tried to flatten everything in a twenty-mile radius."

"Don't exaggerate," said Ramsa. "It was only ten."

They rode as fast as the old gelding would allow. At midday they passed a boulder with two lines etched into its side. She would have missed it if Altan had not pointed it out.

"Chaghan's work," said Altan. "Proof that the way is safe."

"You sent Chaghan here?"

"Yes. Before we left the Night Castle for Khurdalain."

"Why?"

"Chaghan and I . . . Chaghan had a theory," said Altan. "About the Trifecta. Before Sinegard, when he realized Tyr had died, he'd seen something on the spirit horizon. He thought he'd seen the Gatekeeper. He saw the same disturbance a week later, and then it disappeared. He thought the Gatekeeper must have intentionally closed himself in the Chuluu Korikh. We thought we might extract him, find out the truth—maybe discover the truth behind the Trifecta, see what's happened to the Gatekeeper and the Emperor, find out what the Empress did to them. Chaghan didn't know I wanted to free anyone else."

"You lied to him."

Altan shrugged. "Chaghan believes what he wants to believe."

"Chaghan also . . . He said . . ." She trailed off, unsure of how to phrase her question.

"What?" Altan demanded.

"He said they trained you like a dog. At Sinegard."

Altan laughed drily. "He phrased it like that, did he?"

"He said they fed you opium."

Altan stiffened.

"They trained soldiers at Sinegard," he said. "With me, they did their job."

They might have done their job too well, Rin thought. Like the Cike, the masters at Sinegard had conjured a more frightening power than they were equipped to handle. They'd done more than train a Speerly. They'd created an avenger.

Altan was a commander who would burn down the world to destroy his enemy.

This should have bothered her. Three years ago, if she had known what she knew about Altan now, she would have run in the opposite direction.

But now, she had seen and suffered too much. The Empire didn't need someone reasonable. It needed someone mad enough to try to save it.

They stopped riding when it became too dark to see the path in front of them. They had ventured onto a trail so lightly trodden it could hardly be called a road, and their horse could have easily cut its hooves on a jagged rock or sent them tumbling into a ravine. Their gelding staggered when they dismounted. Altan poured out a pan of water for it, but only after Rin's prodding did it begin to halfheartedly drink.

"He'll die if we ride him any harder," Rin said. She knew very little about horses, but she could tell when an animal was on the verge of collapse. One of the military steeds at Khurdalain, perhaps, could have easily made the trip, but this horse was a miserable pack animal—an old beast so thin its ribs showed through its matted coat.

"We just need him for one more day," said Altan. "He can die after."

Rin fed the gelding a handful of oats from their pack. Meanwhile Altan built their camp with austere, methodical efficiency. He collected fallen pine needles and dry leaves to insulate against the cold. He formed a frame out of broken tree limbs and draped a spare cloak over it to shield against overnight snowfall. He pulled from his pack dry kindling and oil, quickly dug a pit, and arranged the flammables inside. He extended his hand. A flare caught immediately. Casually, as if he were doing nothing harder than waving a fan, Altan increased the volume of the flame until they were sitting before a roaring bonfire.

Rin held her hands out, let the heat seep through into her bones. She hadn't noticed how cold she'd become over the day; she realized she hadn't been able to feel her toes until now.

"Are you warm?" Altan asked.

She nodded quickly. "Thanks."

He watched her in silence for a moment. She felt the heat of his gaze on her, and tried not to flush. She was not used to receiving Altan's full attention; he had been distracted with Chaghan ever since Khurdalain, ever since their falling-out. But things were reversed now. Chaghan had abandoned Altan, and Rin stood by his side. She felt a thrill of vindictive joy when she considered this. Suddenly guilty, she tried to quash it down.

"You've been to the mountain before?"

"Only once," Altan said. "A year ago. I helped Tyr bring Feylen in."

"Feylen's the one who went crazy?"

"They all go crazy, in the end," he said. "The Cike die in battle, or they get immured. Most commanders assume their title when they've disposed of their old master. If Tyr hadn't died, I probably would have locked him in myself. It's always a pain when it happens."

"Why aren't they just killed?" she asked.

"You can't kill a shaman who's been fully possessed," said Altan. "When that happens, the shaman isn't human anymore. They're not mortal. They're vessels of the divine. You can behead them, stab them, hang them, but the body will keep moving. You dismember the body, and still the pieces will skitter to rejoin the others. The best you can do is bind them, incapacitate them, and overpower them until you get them into the mountain."

Rin imagined herself bound and blindfolded, dragged involuntarily along this same mountain path into an eternal stone prison. She shuddered. She could understand this sort of cruelty from the Federation, but from her own commander?

"And you're all right with that?"

"Of course I'm not all right with that," he snapped. "But it's the job. It's *my* job. I'm supposed to bring the Cike to the mountain when they've become unfit to serve. The Cike controls itself. The Cike is the Empire's way of eliminating the threat of rogue shamans."

Altan twisted his fingers together. "Every Cike commander is charged with two things: to obey the will of the Empress, and to cull the force when it's time. Jun was right. There's no place for the Cike in modern warfare. We're too small. We can't achieve anything a well-trained Militia force couldn't. Fire powder, cannons, and steel—these things win wars, not a handful of shamans. The only unique role of the Cike is to do what no other military force can do. We can subdue ourselves, which is the only reason why we're allowed to exist."

Rin thought of Suni—poor, gentle, and horrifically strong Suni, who was so clearly unstable. How long before he would meet the same fate that had befallen Feylen? When would Suni's madness outweigh his usefulness to the Empire?

"But I won't be like the commanders of before," Altan said. His fingers clenched to form fists. "I won't turn from my people because they've drawn more power than they should have. How is that fair? Suni and Baji were sent to the Baghra desert because Jiang got scared of them. That's what he does—erases his mistakes, runs from them. But Tyr trained them instead, gave them back a shred of rationality. So there must be a way of taming the gods. The Feylen that I knew would not kill his own people. There must be a way to bring him back from madness. There *has* to be."

He spoke with such conviction. He looked so sure, so absolutely sure that he could control this sleeping army the same way he had calmed Suni in that mess hall, had brought him back to the world of mortals with nothing more than whispers and words.

She forced herself to believe him, because the alternative was too terrible to comprehend.

They reached the Chuluu Korikh on the afternoon of the second day, hours earlier than they had planned. Altan was pleased at this; he was pleased at everything today, forging ahead with an ecstatic, giddy energy. He acted as if he had waited years for this day. For all Rin knew, he had.

When the terrain became too treacherous to keep riding, they dismounted and let the animal go. The gelding strode away with a grievous air to find somewhere to die.

They hiked for the better part of the afternoon. The ice and snow thickened the higher up they climbed. Rin was reminded of the treacherously icy stairs at Sinegard, how one misstep could mean a shattered spine. But here, no first-years had scattered salt across the ice to make the ground safe. If they slipped now, they were guaranteed a quick, icy death.

Altan used his trident as a staff, stabbing at the ground in front of him before he stepped forward. Rin followed gingerly in the path he had marked as safe. She suggested that they simply melt the ice with Speerly fire. Altan tried it. It took too long.

The sky had just begun to darken when Altan paused before a stretch of wall.

"Wait. This is it."

Rin froze in her steps, teeth chattering madly. She glanced around. She could see no marker, no indication that this was the special entrance. But Altan sounded certain.

He backtracked several steps and then began scrubbing at the mountainside, wiping off snow to get at the smooth stone face underneath. He grumbled with exasperation and pressed a flaming hand against the rock. The fire gradually melted a clean circle in the ice with Altan's hand at its center.

Rin could now see a crevice carved into the rock. It had been barely visible under a thick coat of snow and ice. A traveler could have walked past it twenty times and never seen it.

"Tyr said to stop when we reached the crag that looked like an eagle's beak," Altan said. He gestured toward the precipice they stood upon. It did, in fact, look like the profile of one of Qara's birds. "I almost forgot."

Rin dug two strips of dry cloth out of her travel sack, dribbled a vial of oil over them, and busied herself with wrapping the heads of a couple of wooden sticks. "You've never been inside?"

"Tyr had me wait outside," said Altan. He stood back from the entrance. He had cleanly melted the ice away from the stone face, revealing a circular door embedded in the side of the mountain. "The only person alive who's ever been inside is Chaghan. I've no idea how he got this door open. You ready?"

Rin yanked the last cloth knot tight with her teeth and nodded.

Altan turned around, braced his back against the stone door, bent his legs, and pushed. His face strained with the effort.

For a second nothing happened. Then, with a ponderous screech, the rock slid at an angle into its stone bed.

When the rock ground to a halt, Rin and Altan stood before the great maw of darkness. The tunnel was so black inside it seemed to swallow the sunlight whole. Glancing into the dark interior, Rin felt a sense of dread that had nothing to do with the darkness. Inside this mountain, there was no calling the Phoenix. They would have no access to the Pantheon. No way to call the power.

"Last chance to turn back," said Altan.

She scoffed, handed him a torch, and strode forward.

Rin had barely made it ten feet in when she took one step too wide. The dark passageway turned out to be perilously narrow. She felt something crumble under her foot, and scrambled back against the wall. She held her torch out over the precipice and was immediately overcome with a horrible sense of vertigo. There was no visible bottom to the abyss; it dropped away into nothing.

"It's hollow all the way down," said Altan, standing close behind her. He put a hand on her shoulder. "Stick to me. Watch your feet. Chaghan said we'd reach a wider platform in about twenty paces."

She pressed herself against the cliff wall and let Altan squeeze past her, following him gingerly down the steps.

"What else did Chaghan say?"

"That we would find this." Altan held out his torch.

A lone pulley lift hung in the middle of the mountain. Rin held her torch out as far as it would go, and the light illuminated something black and shiny on the platform surface.

"That's oil. This is a lamp," Rin realized. She drew her arm back.

"Careful," Altan hissed just as Rin flung her torch out onto the lift.

The ancient oil blazed immediately to life. Fire snaked through the darkness across predetermined oil patterns in a hypnotizing sequence, revealing several similar pulley lamps hanging at various heights. Only after several long minutes was the entire mountain illuminated, revealing an intricate architecture to the stone prison. Below the passageway where they stood, Rin could see circles upon circles of plinths, extending down as far as the light reached. Around and around the inside of the mountain went a spiraling pathway that led to countless stone tombs.

The pattern was oddly familiar. Rin had seen this before.

It was a stone version of the Pantheon in miniature, multiplied in a spiraling helix. It was a perverse Pantheon, for the gods were not alive here but arrested in suspended animation.

Rin felt a sudden burst of panic. She took a deep breath, trying to dispel the feeling, but the overwhelming sense of suffocation only grew.

"I feel it, too," Altan said quietly. "It's the mountain. We've been sealed off."

Back in Tikany, Rin had once fallen out of a tree and hit her head so hard against the ground that she lost her hearing temporarily. She'd seen Kesegi shouting at her, gesturing at his throat, but nothing had come through. It was the same here. Something was missing. She had been denied access to something.

She could not imagine what it was like to be trapped here for years, decades upon decades, unable to die but unable to leave the material world. This was a place that did not allow dreaming. This was a place of never-ending nightmares.

What a horrible fate to be entombed here.

Rin's fingers brushed against something round. Under the pressure of her touch, it shifted and began to turn. She shone her torch on it and signaled for Altan's attention.

"Look."

It was a stone cylinder. Rin was reminded of the prayer wheels in front of the pagoda at the Academy. But this cylinder was much larger, rising up to her shoulder. Rin held the torch up to the stone and examined it closely. Deep grooves had been cut into its sides. She placed a hand on one side and dug her heels into the dirt, pushed hard.

With a screech that sounded like a scream, the wheel began to turn.

The grooves were words. No—names. Names upon names, each one followed by a string of numbers. It was a record. A registry of every soul that had been sealed inside the Chuluu Korikh.

There must have been a hundred names carved into that wheel.

Altan held the torch up to her right. "It's not the only one."

She looked up and saw that the fire illuminated another record wheel.

Then another. Then another.

They stretched through the entire first tier of the Stone Mountain.

Thousands and thousands of names. Names dating past the reign of the Dragon Emperor. Names dating past the Red Emperor himself.

Rin almost staggered at the significance.

There were people here who had not been conscious since the birth of the Nikara Empire.

"The investiture of the gods," said Altan. He was trembling. "The sheer power in this mountain . . . no one could stop them, not even the Federation . . ."

And not even us, Rin thought.

If they woke the Chuluu Korikh, they would have an army of madmen, of primordial spigots of psychic energy. This was an army they would not be able to control. This was an army that could raze the world.

Rin traced her fingers against the first record wheel, the one closest to the entrance.

At the top, in very careful, deliberate writing, was the most recent entry.

She recognized that handwriting.

"I found him," she said.

"Who, the Gatekeeper?" Altan looked confused.

"It's him," she said. "*Of course* it's him."

She ran her fingers over the engraved stone, and a deep flood of relief shot through her.

Jiang Ziya.

She had found him, finally found him. Her master was sealed inside one of these plinths. She grabbed the torch back from Altan and started at a run down the steps. Whispers echoed past her as she ran. She thought she could sense things coming through from the other side, the things that had been whispering through the void Jiang summoned at Sinegard.

She felt in the air an overwhelming *want*.

They must have immured the shamans starting at the bottom of the prison. Jiang could not be far from where they stood. Rin ran faster, felt the stone scrape under her feet. Up before her, her torch illuminated a plinth carved in the image of a stooped gatekeeper. She came to a sudden halt.

This had to be Jiang.

Altan caught up to her. "Don't just take off like that."

"He's here," she said, shining her torch up at the plinth. "He's in there."

"Move," said Altan.

She had barely stepped out of the way when Altan slammed the end of his trident into the plinth.

When the rubble cleared, Jiang's serene form was revealed under a layer of crumbling dust. He lay perfectly still against the rock, the sides of his mouth curved faintly upward as if he found something deeply amusing. He might have been sleeping.

He opened his eyes, looked them up and down, and blinked. "You might have knocked first."

Rin stepped toward him. "Master?"

Jiang tilted his head sideways. "Have you gotten taller?"

"We're here to rescue you," said Rin, although the words

sounded stupid as soon as she uttered them. No one could have forced Jiang into the mountain. He must have wanted to be there.

But she didn't care why he had come here; she had found him, she had released him, she had his attention now. "We need your help. *Please.*"

Jiang stepped forward out of the stone and shook his limbs as if working out the kinks. He brushed the dust meticulously off his robes. Then he uttered mildly, "You should not be here. It's not your time."

"You don't understand—"

"And you do not listen." He was not smiling anymore. "The Seal is breaking. I can feel it—it's almost gone. If I leave this mountain, all sorts of terrible things will come into your world."

"So it's true," Altan said. "You're the Gatekeeper."

Jiang looked irritated. "What did I just say about not listening?"

But Altan was flushed with excitement. "You are the most powerful shaman in Nikara history! You can unlock this entire mountain! You could command this army!"

"*That's* your plan?" Jiang gaped at him as if in disbelief that anyone could be this stupid. "Are you mad?"

"We . . ." Altan faltered, then regained his composure. "I'm not—"

Jiang buried his face in his palm, like an exasperated schoolteacher. "The boy wants to set everyone in this mountain free. The boy wants to unleash the contents of the Chuluu Korikh on the world."

"It's that, or let Nikan fall," Altan snapped.

"Then let it."

"*What?*"

"You don't know what the Federation is capable of," Rin said. "You didn't see what they did to Golyn Niis."

"I saw more than you think," said Jiang. "But this is not the way. This path leads only to darkness."

"How can there be more darkness?" she screamed in frustration. Her voice echoed off the cavernous walls. "How can things possibly get worse than this? Even you took the risks, you opened the void . . ."

"That was my mistake," Jiang said regretfully, like a child who had been chastened. "I never should have done that. I should have let them take Sinegard."

"Don't you dare," Rin hissed. "You opened the void, you let the beasts through, and you ran and hid here to let us deal with the consequences. When are you going to stop hiding? When are you going to stop being such a damn *coward*? What are you running from?"

Jiang looked pained. "It's easy to be brave. Harder to know when not to fight. I've learned that lesson."

"Master, *please* . . ."

"If you unleash this on Mugen, you will ensure that this war will continue for generations," said Jiang. "You will do more than burn entire provinces to the ground. You will rip apart the very fabric of the universe. These are not men entombed in this mountain; these are gods. They will treat the material world as a plaything. They will shape nature according to their will. They will level mountains and redraw rivers. They will turn the mortal world into the same chaotic flow of primal forces that constitutes the Pantheon. But in the Pantheon, the gods are balanced. Life and death, light and dark—each of the sixty-four entities has its opposite. Bring the gods into your world, and that balance will shatter. You will turn your world to ash, and only demons will live in the rubble."

When Jiang finished speaking, the silence rang heavily in the darkness.

"I can control them," said Altan, though even to Rin he sounded hesitant, like a boy insisting to himself that he could fly. "There are men in those bodies. The gods can't run free. I've done it with my people. Suni should have been locked up here years ago, but I've tamed him, I can talk them back from the madness—"

"You *are* mad." Jiang's voice was almost a whisper, containing as much awe as disbelief. "You're blinded by your own desire for vengeance. Why are you doing this?" He reached out and grasped Altan's shoulder. "For the Empire? For love of the country? Which is it, Trengsin? What story have you told yourself?"

"I want to save Nikan," Altan insisted. He repeated in a strained voice, as if trying to convince himself, "I want to save Nikan."

"No, you don't," said Jiang. "You want to raze Mugen."

"They're the same thing!"

"There is a world of difference between them, and the fact that you don't see that is why you can't do this. Your patriotism is a farce. You dress up your crusade with moral arguments, when in truth you would let millions die if it means you get your so-called justice. That's what will happen if you open the Chuluu Korikh, you know," said Jiang. "It won't be just Mugen that pays to sate your need for retribution, but anyone unlucky enough to be caught in this storm of insanity. Chaos does not discriminate, Trengsin, and that's why this prison was designed to never be unlocked." He sighed. "But of course, you don't care."

Altan could not have looked more shocked if Jiang had struck him across the face.

"You have not cared about anything for a very long time," Jiang continued. He regarded Altan with pity. "You are broken. You're hardly yourself anymore."

"I'm trying to save my country," Altan reiterated hollowly. "And you're a coward."

"I am terrified," Jiang acknowledged. "But only because I'm starting to remember who I once was. Don't go down that path. Your country is ash. You can't bring it back with blood."

Altan gaped at him, unable to respond.

Jiang tilted his head to the side. "Irjah knew, didn't he?"

Altan blinked rapidly. He looked terrified. "What? Irjah didn't—Irjah never—"

"Oh, he knew." Jiang sighed. "He must have known. Daji would have told him—Daji saw what I didn't, Daji would have made sure Irjah knew how to keep you tame."

Rin looked between them, confused. The blood had drained

from Altan's face; his features twisted with rage. "How dare you—you dare allege—"

"It's my fault," Jiang said. "I should have tried harder to help you."

Altan's voice cracked. "I didn't need to be *helped.*"

"You needed it more than anything," Jiang said sadly. "I'm so sorry. I should have fought to save you. You were a scared little boy, and they turned you into a weapon. And now . . . now you're lost. But not *her.* She can still be saved. Don't burn her with yourself."

They both looked to her then.

Rin glanced between them. So this was her choice. The paths before her were clear. Altan or Jiang. Commander or master. Victory and revenge, or . . . or whatever Jiang had promised her.

But what had he ever promised her? Only wisdom. Only understanding. Enlightenment. But those meant only further warnings, petty excuses to hold her back from exercising a power that she knew she could access . . .

"I taught you better than this." Jiang put a hand on her shoulder. He sounded as if he were pleading. "Didn't I? Rin?"

He could have helped them. He could have stopped the massacre at Golyn Niis. He could have saved Nezha.

But Jiang had hidden. His country had needed him, and he had fled to ensconce himself here, without any regard for those he left behind.

He had abandoned her.

He hadn't even said goodbye.

But Altan . . . Altan had not given up on her.

Altan had verbally abused her and hit her, but he had faith in her power. Altan had only ever wanted to make her stronger.

"I'm sorry, sir," she said. "But I have my orders."

Jiang exhaled, and his hand fell away from her shoulder. As always under his gaze, she felt as if she were suffocating, as if he could see through to every part of her. He weighed her with those pale eyes then, and she failed him.

And even though she had made her choice, she couldn't bear his disappointment. She looked away.

"No, I am sorry," Jiang said. "I'm so sorry. I tried to warn you."

He stepped backward over the ruins of his plinth. He closed his eyes.

"Master, please—"

He began to chant. At his feet the broken stone began to move as if liquid, assuming again the form of a smooth, unbroken plinth that built slowly from the ground up.

Rin ran forward. "*Master!*"

But Jiang was still, silent. Then the stone covered his face completely.

"He's wrong."

Altan's voice trembled, whether from fear or naked rage, she didn't know. "That isn't why—I'm not . . . We don't need him. We'll wake the others. They'll fight for me. And you—you'll fight for me, won't you? Rin?"

"Of course I will," she whispered, but Altan was already bashing at the next plinth with his trident, slamming the metal down over and over with naked desperation.

"Wake up," he shouted, voice cracking. "Wake up, come on . . ."

The shaman in the plinth had to be Feylen, the mad and murderous one. That should have posed a deterrent, but Altan certainly didn't seem to care as he slammed his trident down again into the thin stone veneer that lay over Feylen's face.

The rocks came crumbling down, and the second shaman woke.

Rin held her torch out hesitantly. When she saw the figure inside she cringed in revulsion.

Feylen was barely recognizable as human. Jiang had only just immured himself; his body was still passably that of a man, displaying no signs of decay. But Feylen . . . Feylen's body was a dead one, grayed and hardened after months of entombment without nourishment or oxygen. He had not decayed, but he had petrified.

Blue veins protruded against ash-gray skin. Rin doubted any blood still flowed through those veins.

Feylen's build was slender, thin and stooped, and his face looked like it might have been pleasant once. But now his skin was pulled taut over his cheekbones, eyes sunken in deep craters in his skull.

And then he opened his eyes, and Rin's breath hitched in her throat.

Feylen's eyes glowed brilliantly in the darkness, an unnerving blue like two fragments of the sky.

"It's me," Altan said. "Trengsin." She could hear the way he fought to keep his voice level. "Do you remember me?"

"We remember voices," Feylen said slowly. His voice was scratchy from months without use; it sounded like a steel blade dragged against the ancient stone of the mountain. He cocked his head at an unnatural angle, as if trying to tip maggots out of his ear. "We remember fire. And we remember you, Trengsin. We remember your hand across our mouth and your other hand at our throat."

The way Feylen spoke made Rin clench the hilt of her sword with fear. He didn't speak like a man who had fought by Altan's side.

He referred to himself as *we*.

Altan seemed to have realized this, too. "Do you remember who you are?"

Feylen frowned at this as if he had forgotten. He pondered a long time before he rasped out, "We are a spirit of the wind. We may take the body of a dragon or the body of a man. We rule the skies of this world. We carry the four winds in a bag and we fly as our whims take us."

"You're Feylen of the Cike. You serve the Empress, and you served under Tyr's command. I need your help," Altan said. "I need you to fight for me again."

"To . . . fight?"

"There's a war," Altan said, "and we need the power of the gods."

"The power of the gods," Feylen drawled slowly. Then he laughed.

It wasn't a human laugh. It was a high-pitched echo that sounded off the mountain walls like the shrieking of bats.

"We fought for you the first time," he said. "We fought for the Empire. For your thrice-damned Empress. What did that get us? A slap on the back, and a trip to this mountain."

"You did try to send the Night Castle tumbling down a cliff," Altan pointed out.

"We were confused. We didn't know where we were." Feylen sounded rueful. "But no one helped us . . . no one calmed us. No, instead you helped put us in here. When Tyr subdued us, you held the rope. You dragged us here like cattle. And he stood there and watched the stone close across our face."

"That wasn't my decision," Altan said. "Tyr thought—"

"Tyr got *scared*. The man asked for our power, and backed off when it became too much."

Altan swallowed. "I didn't want this for you."

"You promised us you wouldn't hurt us. I thought you cared about us. We were scared. We were vulnerable. And you bound us in the night, you subdued us with your flames . . . can you imagine the pain? The terror? All we ever did was fight for you, and you repaid us with eternal torture."

"We put you to sleep," Altan said. "We gave you rest."

"Rest? Do you think this is rest?" Feylen hissed. "Do you have any idea what this mountain is like? Try stepping into that stone, see if you can last even an hour. Gods were not meant to be contained, least of all us. We are the *wind*. We blow in each and every direction. We obey no master. Do you know what torment this is? Do you know what the *boredom* is like?"

He stepped forward and opened his hands out toward Altan.

Rin tensed, but nothing happened.

Perhaps the god Feylen had summoned was capable of immense power. Perhaps he could have leveled villages, might have ripped Altan apart under normal circumstances. But they were inside the mountain. Whatever Feylen was capable of, whatever he would have done, the gods had no power here.

"I know how terrible it must be to be cut off from the Pantheon," said Altan. "But if you fight for me, if you promise to contain yourself, then you never have to suffer that again."

"We have become divine," said Feylen. "Do you think we care what happens to mortals?"

"I don't need you to care about mortals," said Altan. "I need you to remember *me*. I need the power of your god, but I need more the man inside. I need the person in control. I know you're in there, Feylen."

"In control? You speak to us of *control*?" Feylen gnashed his teeth when he spoke, like every word was a curse. "We cannot be controlled like pack animals for your use. You're in over your head, little Speerly. You've brought down forces you don't understand into your pathetic little material world, and your world would be infinitely more interesting if someone *smashed it up for a bit.*"

The color drained from Altan's face.

"Rin, get back," he said quietly.

Jiang was right. Chaghan had been right. An entire army of these creatures would have spelled the end of the world.

She had never felt so *wrong*.

We can't let this thing leave the mountain.

The same thought seemed to strike Feylen at precisely that moment. He looked between them and the stream of light two tiers up, through which they could just hear the wind howling outside, and he smiled crookedly.

"Ah," he said. "Left it wide open, haven't you?"

His luminous eyes came alive with malicious glee, and he regarded the exit with the yearning of a drowning man desperate to come up for air.

"Feylen, please." Altan stretched out a hand, and his voice was quiet when he spoke to Feylen, as if he thought he could calm him the way he had calmed Suni.

"You cannot threaten us. We can rip you apart," sneered Feylen.

"I know you can," said Altan. "But I trust that you won't. I'm trusting the person inside."

"You are a fool to think me human."

"Me," said Altan. "You said *me*."

Feylen's face spasmed. The blue light dimmed from his eyes. His features morphed just so slightly; the sneer disappeared, and his mouth worked as if trying to decide what commands to obey.

Altan lifted his trident out to the side, far away from Feylen. Then, with a slow deliberateness, he flung the weapon away from him. It clattered against the wall, echoed in the silence of the mountain.

Feylen stared at the weapon in wide-eyed disbelief.

"I'm trusting you with my life," said Altan. "I know you're in there, Feylen."

Slowly, he stretched his hand out again.

And Feylen grasped it.

The contact sent tremors through Feylen's body. When he looked up, he had that same terrified expression she'd seen in Suni. His eyes were wide, dark and imploring, like a child seeking a protector; a lost soul desperately seeking an anchor back to the mortal world.

"Altan?" he whispered.

"I'm here." Altan walked forward. As before, he approached the god without fear, despite full knowledge of what it could do to him.

"I can't die," Feylen whispered. His voice contained none of that grating quality now; it was tremulous, so vulnerable there was no doubt that this Feylen was human. "It's awful, Trengsin. Why can't I die? I should never have summoned that god . . . Our minds are meant to be our own, not shared with these *things* . . . I do not live here in this mountain . . . but *I can't die*."

Rin felt sick.

Jiang was right. The gods had no place in their world. No wonder the Speerlies had driven themselves mad. No wonder Jiang was so terrified of pulling the gods down into the mortal realm.

The Pantheon was where they belonged; the Pantheon was where they should stay. This was a power mankind never should have meddled with.

What were they thinking? They should leave, now, while Feylen was still under control; they should pull the stone door closed so that he could never escape.

But Altan showed none of her fear. Altan had his soldier back.

"I can't let you die yet," Altan said. "I need you to fight for me. Can you do that?"

Feylen had not let go of Altan's arm; he drew him closer, as if into an embrace. He leaned in and brushed his lips against Altan's ear, and whispered so that Rin could barely hear what he said: "Kill yourself, Trengsin. Die while you still can."

His eyes met Rin's over Altan's shoulder. They glinted a bright blue.

"*Altan!*" Rin screamed.

And Feylen wrenched his commander across the plinth and flung him toward the abyss.

It was not a strong throw. Feylen's muscles were atrophied from months of disuse; he moved clumsily, like newborn fawn, a god tottering about in a mortal body.

But Altan careened wildly over the side, flailing in the air for balance, and Feylen pushed past him and scrambled up the stone steps toward the exit. His face was wild with a gleeful malice, ecstatic.

Rin threw herself across the stone; she landed stomach-first on floor, arms extended, and the next thing she felt was terrible pain as Altan's fingers closed around her wrist just before he plunged into the darkness.

His weight wrenched her arm down. She cried out in agony as her elbow slammed against stone.

But then Altan's other arm shot up from the darkness. She strained down. Their fingers clasped together.

Rocks clattered off the edge of the precipice, falling away into the abyss, but Altan hung steady by both of her arms. They slid forward and for one sick moment she feared his weight might pull the both of them over the edge, but then her foot caught in a groove and they came to a stop.

"I've got you," she panted.

"Let go," Altan said.

"What?"

"I'm going to swing myself up," he said. "Let my left arm go." She obeyed.

Altan kicked himself to the side to generate momentum and then threw his other hand up to grasp the edge. She lay straining against the floor, legs digging into the stone to keep herself from sliding forward while he pulled himself over the edge of the precipice. He slammed one arm over the top and dug his elbow into the floor. Grunting, he hauled his legs over the edge in a single fluid movement.

Sobbing with relief, Rin helped him to his feet, but he brushed her off.

"Feylen," he hissed, and set out at an uneven sprint up the stone pathway.

Rin followed him, but it was pointless. When they ran, the only footsteps they could hear were their own, because Feylen had long disappeared out the mouth of the Chuluu Korikh.

They'd given him free rein in the world.

But Altan had overpowered him once. Surely they could do so again. They *had* to.

They stumbled out the stone door and skidded to a halt before a wall of steel.

Federation soldiers thronged the mountainside.

Their general barked a command and the soldiers pressed forward with their shields linked to create a barrier, backing Rin and Altan inside the stone mountain.

She caught Altan's stricken expression for a brief moment before he was buried beneath a crowd of armor and swords.

She had no time to wonder why the Federation soldiers were

there or how they had known to arrive; all questions disappeared from her mind with the immediacy of combat. The fighting instinct took over—the world became a matter of blades and parries, just another melee—

Yet even as she drew her sword she knew it was hopeless.

The Federation had chosen precisely the right place to kill a Speerly.

Altan and Rin had no advantage in here. The Phoenix could not reach them through the thick walls of stone. Swallowing the poppy would be useless. They might pray to their god, but no one would answer.

A pair of gauntleted arms reached around Rin from behind, pinning her arms to her sides. From the corner of her eye she saw Altan backed against the wall, no fewer than five blades at his neck.

He might have been the best martial artist in Nikan. But without his fire, without his trident, he was still only one man.

Rin jammed her elbow into her captor's stomach, wriggled free, and whipped her sword outward at the nearest soldier. Their blades clashed; she landed a lucky, wild swing. He tumbled, yelling, into the abyss with her sword embedded in his knee. Rin made a grab for her weapon, but it was too late.

The next soldier swung wide overhead. She ducked into close quarters, reaching for the knife in her belt.

The soldier cracked the hilt of his blade down on her shoulder and sent her sprawling across the floor. She fumbled blindly against the rock.

Then someone slammed a shield against the back of her head.

CHAPTER 24

She woke in darkness. She was lying on a flat, swaying surface—a wagon? A ship? Though she was certain her eyes were open, she could see nothing. Had she been sealed inside something, or was it simply nighttime? She had no idea how much time had passed. She tried to move and discovered that she was bound: hands tied tightly behind her back, legs strapped together. She tried to sit up, and the muscles around her left shoulder screamed in pain. She choked back a whimper and lay down until the throbbing subsided.

Then she tried moving horizontally instead. Her legs were stiff; the one she lay on was numb from lack of blood flow, and when she shifted so that it would regain feeling, it hurt like a thousand needles were being slowly inserted into her foot. She could not move her legs separately so she writhed back and forth like a worm, inching about until her feet kicked against the sides of something. She pushed against it and writhed the other way.

She was sure now that she was in a wagon.

With great effort she pulled herself to a sitting position. The top of her head bumped against something scratchy. A canvas sheet. Or a tarp? Now that her eyes had adjusted, she could see that it was not dark outside after all; the wagon cover simply blocked out the sunlight.

She strained against the tarp until a crack of light flooded in through the side. Trembling with effort, she pressed her eye to the slit.

It took her a while to comprehend what she saw.

The road looked like something out of a dream. It was as if a great gust of wind had blown through a small city, turning households inside out, distributing the contents at random on the grass by the trail. A pair of ornate wooden chairs lay tipped over next to a set of woolen stockings. A dining table sat beside a carved chess set, jade pieces scattered across the dirt. Paintings. Toys. Entire trunks of clothing lay open by the roadside. She saw a wedding dress. A matching set of silken sleepwear.

It was a trail of fleeing villagers. Whatever Nikara had lived in this area, they had long gone, and they had flung things by the roadside as they became too heavy to carry. As desperation for survival outweighed their attachment to their possessions, the Nikara had dropped off their belongings one by one.

Was this Feylen's doing, or the Federation's? Rin's stomach curdled at the idea that she might be responsible for this. But if the Wind God had indeed caused this destruction, then he had long moved on. The air was calm when they rode, and no freak winds or tornadoes materialized to rip them to pieces.

Perhaps he was wreaking havoc on the world elsewhere. Perhaps he had fled north to bide his time, to heal and adjust to his long-awaited freedom. Who could predict the will of a god?

Had the Federation razed Tikany to the ground yet? Had the Fangs heard rumors of the advancing army early enough to run before the Federation tore their village apart? What about Kesegi?

She thought the Federation soldiers might loot the debris. But they were moving so fast that the officers yelled at their troops when they stopped to pick things up. Wherever they were going, they wanted to get there soon.

Among the abandoned chests and furniture, Rin saw a man sitting by the road. He slouched beside a bamboo carrying pole, the kind farmers used to balance buckets of water for irrigation. He had fashioned a large sign out of the back of a painting, on which he'd scrawled in messy calligraphy FIVE INGOTS.

"Two girls," he said in a slow chant. "Two girls, healthy girls, for sale."

Two toddlers peered out over the tops of the wooden buckets. They stared wonderingly at the passing soldiers. One noticed Rin peeking out from under the tarp, and she blinked her luminous eyes in uncomprehending curiosity. She lifted her tiny fingers and waved at them, just as a soldier shouted out in excitement.

Rin shrank back into the wagon. Tears leaked out the sides of her eyes. She couldn't breathe. She squeezed her eyes shut. She did not want to see what became of those girls.

"Rin?"

For the first time she noticed that Altan was curled up in the other corner of the wagon. She could barely see him under the darkness of the tarp. She inched clumsily toward him like a caterpillar.

"Where are we?" he asked.

"I can't tell," she said. "But we're nowhere near the Kukhonin range. We're traveling over flat roads."

"We're in a wagon?"

"I think so. I don't know how many of them there are."

"It doesn't matter. I'll get us out. I'm going to burn through these ropes," he announced. "Get back."

She wriggled to the other side of the wagon just as Altan ignited a small flame from his arms. His bonds caught fire at the edges, began slowly to blacken.

Smoke filled the wagon. Rin's eyes teared up; she could not stop herself from coughing. Minutes passed.

"Just a bit longer," Altan said.

The smoke curled off the rope in thick tendrils. Rin glanced about the tarp, panicked. If the smoke didn't escape out the sides, they might suffocate before Altan broke through his bonds. But if it did . . .

She heard shouting above her. The language was Mugini but the commands were too terse and abrupt for her to translate.

Someone yanked the tarp off.

Altan's flames exploded into full force, just as a soldier drenched him with an entire bucket full of water. A great sizzling noise filled the air.

Altan screamed.

Someone clamped a damp cloth over Rin's mouth. She kicked and struggled, holding her breath, but they jabbed something sharp into her bruised shoulder and she could not help inhaling sharply in pain. Then her nostrils filled with the sweet smell of gas.

Lights. Lights so bright they hurt like knives jabbing into her eyes. Rin tried to squirm away from the source, but nothing happened. For a moment she thrashed in vain, terrified that she'd been paralyzed, until she realized she was tied down with restraints. Strapped to some flat bed. Rin's peripheral vision was limited to the top half of the room. If she strained, she could just see Altan's head adjacent to hers.

Rin's eyes darted around in terror. Shelves filled the sides of the room. They brimmed with jars that contained feet, heads, organs, and fingers, all meticulously labeled. A massive glass chamber stood in the corner. Inside was the body of an adult man. Rin stared at him for a minute before she realized the man was long dead; it was only a corpse that was being preserved in chemicals, like pickled vegetables. His eyes were still frozen in an expression of horror; mouth wide in an underwater scream. The label at the top of the jar read in fine, neat handwriting: *Nikara Man, 32*.

The jars on the shelves were labeled similarly. *Liver, Nikara Child, 12. Lungs, Nikara Woman, 51.* She wondered dully if that was how she would end up, neatly parceled in this operating room. *Nikara Woman, 19.*

"I'm back." Altan had awoken beside her. His voice was a dry whisper. "I never thought I'd be back."

Rin's insides twisted with dread. "Where are we?"

"Please," Altan said. "Don't make me explain this to you."

She knew, then, exactly where they were.

Chaghan's words echoed in her mind.

After the First Poppy War, the Federation became obsessed with your people . . . They spent the decades in between the Poppy Wars kidnapping Speerlies, experimenting on them, trying to figure out what made them special.

The Federation soldiers had brought them to that same research facility that Altan had been abducted to as a child. The place that had left him with a crippling addiction to opium. The place that had been liberated by the Hesperians. The place that *should* have been destroyed after the Second Poppy War.

Snake Province must have fallen, she realized with a sinking feeling. The Federation had occupied more ground than she'd feared.

The Hesperians were long gone. The Federation was back. The monsters had returned to their lair.

"You know the worst part?" Altan said. "We're so close to home. To Speer. We're on the coastline. We're right by the sea. When they first brought us here, there weren't so many cells . . . they put us in a room with a window facing the water. I could see the constellations. Every night. I saw the star of the Phoenix and thought that if I could just slip away, I could swim and keep swimming and find my way back home."

Rin thought of a four-year-old Altan, locked in this place, staring out at the night sky while around him his friends were strapped down and dissected. She wanted to reach out and touch him, but no matter how hard she strained against those straps, she couldn't move. "Altan . . ."

"I thought someone would come and get us," he continued, and Rin didn't think he was talking to her anymore. He spoke like he was recounting a nightmare to the empty air. "Even when they killed the others, I thought that maybe . . . maybe my parents would still come for me. But when the Hesperian troops liberated me, they told me I could never go back. They told me there was nothing on the island but bones and ash."

He fell quiet.

Rin was at a loss for words. She felt like she needed to say something, something to rouse him, turn his attention to seeking a way out of this place, but anything that came to mind was laughably inadequate. What kind of consolation could she possibly give?

"Good! You're awake."

A high, tremulous voice interrupted her thoughts. Whoever it was spoke from directly behind her, out of her line of sight. Rin's eyes bulged and she strained against the straps.

"Oh, I'm sorry—but of course you cannot see me."

The owner of the voice moved to stand directly above her. He was a very thin white-haired man in a doctor's uniform. His beard was trimmed meticulously to a sharp point ending two inches below his chin. His dark eyes glittered with a bright intelligence.

"Is this better?" He smiled benignly, as if greeting an old friend. "I am Eyimchi Shiro, chief medical officer of this camp. You may call me Dr. Shiro."

He spoke Nikara, not Mugini. He had a very prim Sinegardian accent, as if he'd learned the language fifty years ago. His tone was stilted, artificially cheerful.

When Rin did not respond, the doctor shrugged and turned to the other table.

"Oh, Altan," he said. "I had no idea you'd be coming back. This is a wonderful surprise! I couldn't believe it when they told me. They said, 'Dr. Shiro, we've found a Speerly!' And I said, 'You've got to be joking! There are no more Speerlies!'" Shiro chuckled mildly.

Rin strained to see Altan's face. He was awake; his eyes were open, but he glared at the ceiling without looking at Shiro.

"They have been so scared of you, you know," Shiro continued cheerfully. "What do they call you? The monster of Nikan? The Phoenix incarnate? My countrymen love exaggerations, and they love you Nikara shamans even more. You are a myth, a legend! You are so special! Why do you act so sullen?"

Altan said nothing.

Shiro seemed to deflate slightly, but then he grinned and patted Altan on the cheek. "Of course. You must be tired. Do not worry. We will fix you up in just a moment. I have *just the thing . . .*"

He hummed happily as he bustled over to the corner of the operating room. He perused his shelves, plucking out various vials and instruments. Rin heard a popping noise, and then the sound of a candle being lit. She could not see what Shiro was doing with his hands until he returned to stand above Altan.

"Did you miss me?" he inquired.

Altan said nothing.

"Hm." Shiro lifted a syringe over Altan's face, tapping the glass so that both of them could see the liquid inside. "Did you miss this?"

Altan's eyes bulged.

Shiro held Altan's wrist down with a gentle touch, almost as a mother would caress her child. His skilled fingers prodded for a vein. With his other hand he brought the needle to Altan's arm and pushed.

Only then did Altan scream.

"Stop!" Rin shrieked. Spittle flew out the sides of her mouth. "*Stop it!*"

"My dear!" Shiro set the empty syringe down and rushed to her side. "Calm! Calm down! He will be fine."

"*You're killing him!*" She thrashed wildly against her bonds, but they held firm.

Tears leaked from her eyes. Shiro wiped them meticulously away, keeping his fingers out of reach of her gnashing teeth.

"Killing? Don't be dramatic. I just gave him some of his favorite medicine." Shiro tapped his temple and winked at her. "You know he enjoys it. You traveled with him, didn't you? This drug is not anything new to him. He will be fine in a few minutes."

They both looked to Altan. Altan's breathing had stabilized, but he certainly did not look fine.

"Why are you doing this?" Rin choked. She'd thought she

understood Federation cruelty by now. She had seen Golyn Niis. She'd seen the evidence of Mugenese scientists' handiwork. But to look this evil in the eye, to watch Shiro inflict such pain on Altan and *smile* about it . . . Rin could not comprehend it. "What do you *want* from us?"

Shiro sighed. "Is it not obvious?" He patted her cheek. "I want knowledge. Our work here will advance medical technology by decades. When else do you get such a good chance to do research? An endless supply of cadavers! Boundless opportunities for experimentation! I can answer every question I've ever had about the human body! I can devise ways to prevent death!"

Rin gaped at him in disbelief. "*You are cutting my people open.*"

"*Your* people?" Shiro snorted. "Don't degrade yourself. You're nothing like those pathetic Nikara. You Speerlies are so fascinating. Composed of such lovely material." Shiro fondly brushed the hair from Altan's sweaty forehead. "Such beautiful skin. Such fascinating eyes. The Empress doesn't know what she has."

He pressed two fingers against Rin's neck to take her pulse. She swallowed down the bile that rose up at his touch.

"I wonder if you might oblige me," he said gently. "Show me the fire. I know you can."

"*What?*"

"You Speerlies are so special," Shiro confided. His voice had taken on a low, husky tone. He spoke as if to an infant, or a lover. "So strong. So unique. They say you are a god's chosen people. What makes you this way?"

Hatred, Rin thought. *Hatred, and a history of suffering inflicted by people like you.*

"You know my country has never achieved feats of shamanism," Shiro said. "Do you have any idea why?"

"Because the gods wouldn't bother with scum like you," Rin spat.

Shiro brushed at the air, as if swatting the insult away. He must have heard so many Nikara curses by now that they meant nothing to him.

"We will do it like this," he said. "I will request you to show me the way to the gods. Each time you refuse, I will give him another injection of the drug. You know how he will feel it."

Altan made a low, guttural noise from his bed. His entire body tensed and spasmed.

Shiro murmured something into his ear and stroked Altan's forehead, as tenderly as a mother might comfort an ailing child.

Hours passed. Shiro posed his questions about shamanism to Rin again and again, but she maintained a stony front. She would not reveal the secrets behind the Pantheon. She would not place yet another weapon in Mugen's hands.

Instead she cursed and spat, called him a monster, called him every vile thing she could think of. Jima hadn't taught them to curse in Mugini, but Shiro caught the gist.

"Come now," Shiro said dismissively. "It's not like you've never seen this before."

She paused, spittle dripping from her mouth. "I don't know what you mean."

Shiro touched his fingers to Altan's neck to feel his pulse, pulled his eyelids back and pursed his lips as if confirming something. "His tolerance is astounding. Inhuman. He's been smoking opium for years."

"Because of what *you* did to him," she screeched.

"And afterward? After he was liberated?" Shiro sounded like a disappointed teacher. "They had the last Speerly in their hands, and they never tried to wean him off the drug? It's obvious—someone's been feeding it to him for years. Clever of them. Oh, don't look at me like that. The Federation weren't the first to use opium to control a population. The Nikara originated this technique."

"What are you *talking* about?"

"They didn't teach you?" Shiro looked amused. "But of course. Of course they wouldn't. Nikan likes to scrub out all that is embarrassing about its past."

He crossed the room to stand over her, brushing his fingers along the shelves as he walked. "How do you think the Red Emperor kept the Speerlies on their leash? Use your head, my dear. When Speer lost its independence, the Red Emperor sent crates of opium over to the Speerlies as an offering. A gift, from the colonizing state to the tributary. This was deliberate. Previously the Speerlies had only ever ingested their local bark in their ceremonies. They were used to such mild hallucinogens that to them, smoking opium was like drinking wood alcohol. When they tried it, they immediately became addicted. They did anything they could to get more of it. They were slaves to the opium just as much as they were slaves to the Emperor."

Rin's mind reeled. She could not think of any response.

She wanted to call Shiro a liar. She wanted to scream at him to stop. But it made sense.

It made so much sense.

"So you see, our countries are not so different after all," Shiro said smugly. "The only difference is that we revere shamans, we desire to learn from them, while your Empire is terrified and paranoid about the power it possesses. Your Empire has culled you and exploited you and made you eliminate each other. I will unleash you. I will grant you freedom to call the god as you have never been allowed to before."

"If you give me freedom," she snarled, "the first thing I will do is burn you alive."

Her connection to the Phoenix was the last advantage she had. The Federation had raped and burned her country. The Federation had destroyed her school and killed her friends. By now they had mostly likely razed her hometown to the ground. Only the Pantheon remained sacred, the one thing in the universe that Mugen still had no access to.

Rin had been tortured, bound, beaten, and starved, but her

mind was her own. Her god was her own. She would die before she betrayed it.

Eventually, Shiro grew bored of her. He summoned the guards to drag the prisoners into a cell. "I will see you both tomorrow," he said cheerfully. "And we will try this again."

Rin spat on his coat as the guards marched her out. Another guard followed with Altan's inert form thrown over his shoulder like an animal carcass.

One guard chained Rin's leg to the wall and slammed the cell door shut on them. Beside her Altan jerked and moaned, muttering incoherently under his breath. Rin cradled his head in her lap and kept a miserable vigil over her fallen commander.

Altan did not come to his senses for hours. Many times he cried out, spoke words in the Speerly language that she didn't understand.

Then he moaned her name. "*Rin*."

"I'm here," she said, stroking his forehead.

"Did he hurt you?" he demanded.

She choked back a sob. "No. No—he wanted me to talk, teach him about the Pantheon. I didn't, but he said he'd just keep hurting you . . ."

"It's not the drug that hurts," he said. "It's when it wears off."

Then, with a sickening pang in her stomach, she understood.

Altan was not lapsing when he smoked opium. No—smoking opium was the only time when he was not in pain. He had lived his entire life in perpetual pain, always longing to have another dose.

She had never understood how horrendously difficult it was to be Altan Trengsin, to live under the strain of a furious god constantly screaming for destruction in the back of his mind, while an indifferent narcotic deity whispered promises in his blood.

That's why the Speerlies became addicted to opium so easily, she realized. Not because they needed it for their fire. Because for some of them, it was the only time they could get away from their horrible god.

Deep down, she had known this, had suspected this ever since she'd learned that Altan didn't need drugs like the rest of the Cike did, that Altan's eyes were perpetually bright like poppy flowers.

Altan should have been locked into the Chuluu Korikh himself a long time ago.

But she hadn't wanted to believe, because she needed to trust that her commander was sane.

Because without Altan, what was she?

In the hours that followed, when the drug seeped out of his bloodstream, Altan suffered. He sweated. He writhed. He seized so violently that Rin had to restrain him to keep him from hurting himself. He screamed. He begged for Shiro to come back. He begged for Rin to help him die.

"You can't," she said, panicking. "We have to escape here. We have to get out."

His eyes were blank, defeated. "Resistance here means suffering, Rin. There is no escape. There is no future. The best you can hope for is that Shiro gets bored and grants you a painless death."

She almost did it then.

She wanted to end his misery. She couldn't see him tortured like this anymore, couldn't watch the man she had admired since she set eyes on him reduced to *this*.

She found herself kneeling over his inert torso, hands around his neck. All she had to do was put pressure into her arms. Force the air out of his throat. Choke the life out of him.

He would hardly feel it. He could hardly feel anything anymore.

Even as her fingers grasped his skin, he did not resist. He wanted it to end.

She had done this once before. She had killed the likeness of him in the guise of the chimei.

But Altan had been fighting then. Then, Altan had been a threat. He was not a threat now, only the tragic, glaring proof that her heroes inevitably let her down.

Altan Trengsin was not invincible after all.

He had been so good at following orders. They told him to jump and he flew. They told him to fight and he *destroyed*.

But here at the end, without a purpose and without a ruler, Altan Trengsin was broken.

Rin's fingers tensed, but then she trembled and pushed his limp form violently away from her.

"How are my darling Speerlies doing? Ready for another round?"

Shiro approached their cell, beaming. He was coming from the lab at the opposite end of the hallway. He held several round metallic containers in his arms.

They didn't respond.

"Would you like to know what those canisters are for?" Shiro asked. His voice remained artificially bright. "Any guesses? Here's a hint. It's a weapon."

Rin glowered at the doctor. Altan stared at the floor.

Shiro continued, unfazed. "It's the plague, children. Surely you know what the plague does? First your nose begins to run, and then great welts start growing on your arms, your legs, between your legs . . . you die from shock when the wounds rupture, or from your own poisoned blood. It takes quite a long time to die down, once it's caught on. But perhaps that was before your time. Nikan has been plague free for a while now, hasn't it?"

Shiro tapped the metal bars. "It took us a devilishly long time to figure out how it spread. Fleas, can you believe that? Fleas, that latch onto rats, and then spread their little plague particles over everything they touch. Of course, now that we know how it spreads, it's only a hop step to turning it into a weapon. Obviously it will not do to have the weapon run around without control—we *do* plan to inhabit your country one day—but when released in some densely populated areas, with the right critical mass . . . well, this war will be over much sooner than we anticipated, won't it?"

Shiro leaned forward, head resting against the bars. "You have nothing to fight for anymore," he said quietly. "Your country is lost. Why do you hold your silence? You have an easy way out of this place. Just cooperate with me. Tell me how you summon the fire."

"I'll die first," Rin spat.

"What are you defending?" Shiro asked. "You owe Nikan nothing. What were you to them? What were the Speerlies to them, ever? Freaks! Outcasts!"

Rin stood up. "We fight for the Empress," she said. "I'm a Militia soldier until the day I die."

"The Empress?" Shiro looked faintly puzzled. "Have you really not figured it out?"

"Figured *what* out?" Rin snapped, even as Altan silently mouthed *no*.

But she had taken the bait, she had risen to the doctor's provocation, and she could tell from the way Shiro's eyes gleamed that he had been waiting for this moment.

"Have you even asked how we knew you were at the Chuluu Korikh?" Shiro asked. "Who must have given us that information? Who was the *only other person* who knew of that wonderful mountain?"

Rin gaped at him, openmouthed, while the truth pieced itself together in her mind. She could see Altan puzzling it out, too. His eyes widened as he came to the same realization that she did.

"No," said Altan. "You're lying."

"Your precious Empress betrayed you," Shiro said with relish. "You were a trade."

"That's impossible," said Altan. "We served her. We *killed* for her."

"Your Empress gave you up, you and your precious band of shamans. You were *sold*, my dear Speerlies, just like Speer was sold. Just like your Empire was sold."

"*You're lying!*"

Altan flung himself at the bars. Fire ignited across his body, flared out in tentacles that almost reached the guards. Altan continued to scream, and the fire licked wider and wider, and although the metal did not melt, Rin thought she saw the bars begin to bend.

Shiro shouted a command in Mugini.

Three guards rushed to the cell. As one worked to unlock the gate, another sloshed a bucket of water over Altan. Once he was doused, the third rushed in to pull Altan's arms back behind his head while the first jammed a needle into his neck. Altan jerked and dropped to the floor.

The guards turned to Rin.

Rin thought she saw Shiro's mouth moving, yelling, "No, not her," before she, too, felt the needle sink into her neck.

The rush she felt was nothing like poppy seeds.

With poppy seeds, she still had to concentrate on clearing her mind. With poppy seeds it took conscious effort to ascend to the Pantheon.

Heroin was nowhere near as subtle. Heroin evicted her from her own body so that she had no choice but to seek refuge in the realm of spirit.

And she realized, with a fierce joy, that in attempting to sedate her, Shiro's guards had set her *free*.

She found Altan in the other realm. She *felt* him. She knew the pattern of him as well as she knew her own.

She had not always known the shape of him. She had loved the version of him she'd constructed for herself. She had admired him. She had idolized him. She had adored an idea of him, an archetype, a version of him that was invulnerable.

But now she knew the truth, she knew the realness of Altan and his vulnerabilities and most of all his *pain* . . . and still she loved him.

She had mirrored herself against him, molded herself after him; one Speerly after another. She had emulated his cruelty, his hatred, and his vulnerability. She knew him, finally knew all of him, and that was how she found him.

Altan?

Rin.

She could feel him all around her; a hard edge, a deeply wounded aura, and yet a comforting presence.

Altan's form appeared before her as if he stood across a very large field. He walked, or floated, toward her. Space and distance did not exist in this realm, not really, but her mind had to interpret it as such for her to orient herself.

She did not have to read the anguish in his eyes. She felt it. Altan did not keep his spirit closed off, the way Chaghan did; he was an open book, available for her to peruse, as if he were offering himself up for her to try to understand.

She understood. She understood his pain and his misery, and she understood why all he wanted to do now was die.

But she had no patience for it.

Rin had given up the luxury of fear a long, long time ago. She had wanted to give up so many times. It would have been easier. It would have been painless.

But throughout everything, the one thing she had held on to was her anger, and she knew one truth: She would not die like this. She would not die without vengeance.

"They killed our people," she said. "They sold us. Since Tearza, Speer has been a pawn in the Empire's geopolitical chess game. We were disposable. We were tools. Tell me that doesn't make you furious."

He looked exhausted. "I am sick with fury," he said. "And I am sick knowing that there is nothing I can do."

"You've blinded yourself. You're a *Speerly.* You have power," she said. "You have the anger of all of Speer. Show me how to use it. *Give it to me.*"

"You'll die."

"Then I will die on my feet," she said. "I will die with flames in my hand and fury in my heart. I will die fighting for the legacy of my people, rather than on Shiro's operating table, drugged and wasted. I will not die a coward. And neither will you. Altan, look at me. We are not like Jiang. We are not like *Tearza.*"

Altan lifted his head then.

"Mai'rinnen Tearza," he whispered. "The queen who abandoned her people."

"Would you abandon them?" she pressed. "You heard what Shiro said. The Empress didn't just sell us out. She sold the entire Cike. Shiro won't stop until he has every Nikara shaman locked up in this hellhole. When you are gone, who will protect them? Who will protect Ramsa? Suni? *Chaghan?*"

She felt it from him then—a stab of defiance. A flicker of resolve.

That was all she needed.

"The Phoenix isn't only the god of fire," he said. "It is the god of revenge. And there is a power, born of centuries of festering hatred, that only a Speerly can access. I have tapped into it many times, but never in full. It would consume you. It would burn at you until there was nothing left."

"Give it to me," she said immediately, hungrily.

"I can't," he said. "It's not mine to give. That power belongs to the Speerlies."

"Then take me to them," Rin demanded.

And so he took her back.

In the realm of dreams, time ceased to hold meaning. Altan took her back centuries. He took her back into the only spaces where their ancestors still existed, in ancient memory.

Being led by Altan was not the same as being led by Chaghan. Chaghan was a sure guide, more native to the spirit world than the world of the living. With Chaghan, she had felt as if she were being dragged along, and that if she didn't obey, Chaghan would have shattered her mind. But with Altan . . . Altan did not feel even like a separate presence. Rather, he and she made two parts of a much greater whole. They were two small instances of the grand, ancient entity of all that was Speer, hurtling through the world of spirit to rejoin their kind.

When space and time again became tangible concepts to her,

Rin perceived that they were at a campfire. She saw drums, she heard people chanting and singing, and she knew that song, she had been taught that song when she was a little girl, she could not believe she had ever forgotten that song . . . all Speerlies could sing that song before their fifth birthday.

No—not her. Rin had never learned that song. This was not her recollection; she was living inside the remembrance of a Speerly who had lived many, many years ago. This was a shared memory. This was an illusion.

So was this dance. And so, too, was the man who held her by the fire. He danced with her, spinning her about in great arcs, then pulling her back against his warm chest. He could not be Altan, and yet he had Altan's face, and she was certain that she had always known him.

She had never been taught to dance, but somehow she knew the steps.

The night sky was lit up with stars like little torches. A million tiny campfires scattered across the darkness. A thousand Isles of Speer, a thousand fireside dances.

Years ago Jiang had told her that the spirits of the dead dissolved back into the void. But not the spirits of Speer. The Speerlies refused to let go of their illusions, refused to forget about the material world, because Speer's shamans couldn't be at peace until they got their vengeance.

She saw faces in the shadow. She saw a sad-looking woman who looked like her, sitting beside an old man wearing a crescent pendant around his neck. Rin tried to look closer but their faces were blurred, those of people she only half remembered.

"Is this what it was like?" she asked out loud.

The voices of the ghosts answered as one. *This was the golden age of Speer. This was Speer before Tearza. Before the massacre.*

She could have wept at the beauty of it.

There was no madness here. Only fires and dances.

"We could stay here," Altan said. "We could stay here forever. We wouldn't have to go back."

In that moment it was all she wanted.

Their bodies would waste away and become nothing. Shiro would deposit their corpses into a waste chamber and incinerate them. Then, when the last part of them had been given to the Phoenix, once their ashes were scattered in the winds, they would be free.

"We could," she agreed. "We could be lost to history. But you'd never do that, would you?"

"They wouldn't take us now," he said. "Do you feel them? Can you feel their anger?"

She could. The ghosts of Speer were so sad, but they were also furious.

"This is why we are strong. We draw our strength from centuries and centuries of unforgotten injustices. Our task—our very reason for being—is to make those deaths mean something. After us, there will be no Speer. Only a memory."

She had thought she understood Altan's power, but only now did she realize the *depth* of it. The weight of it. He was burdened with the legacy of a million souls forgotten by history, vengeful souls screaming for justice.

The ghosts of Speer were chanting now, a deep and sorrowful song in the language she was born too late to understand, but connected to her very bones. The ghosts spoke to them for an eternity. Years passed. No time passed at all. Their ancestors imparted all that they knew of Speer, all that had ever been remembered of their people. They instilled in her centuries of history and culture and religion.

They told her what she had to do.

"Our god is an angry god," said the woman who looked like Rin. "It will not let this injustice rest. It demands vengeance."

"You must go to the isle," said the old man with the crescent pendant. "You must go to the temple. Find the Pantheon. Call the Phoenix, and wake the ancient fault lines on which Speer lies. The Phoenix will only answer to you. It has to."

The man and woman faded back into the blur of brown faces.

The ghosts of Speer began to sing as one, mouths moving in unison.

Rin could not determine the meaning of the song from the words, but she felt it. It was a song of vengeance. It was a horrible song. It was a wonderful song.

The ghosts gave Rin their blessing, and it made the rush from the heroin feel like a feathery touch in comparison.

She had been granted a power beyond imagination.

She had the strength of their ancestors. She held within her every Speerly who had died on that terrible day, and every Speerly who had ever lived on the Dead Island.

They were the Phoenix's chosen people. The Phoenix thrived on anger, and Rin possessed that in abundance.

She reached for Altan. They were of one mind and one purpose.

They forced their way back into the world of the living.

Their eyes flared open at the same time.

One of Shiro's assistants had been bending over them, back on the table in Shiro's laboratory. The flames roiling from their bodies immolated him immediately, catching his hair and clothes so that when he reeled away from them, screaming, every bit of him was on fire.

Flames licked out in every direction. They caught the chemicals in the laboratory and combusted, shattering glass. They caught the alcohol used to sterilize wounds and spread rapidly on the fumes. The jar in the corner bearing the pickled man trembled from the heat and exploded, spilling its vile contents out onto the floor. The fumes of the embalming fluid caught fire, too, lighting up the room in an earnest blaze.

The lab assistant ran into the hallway, screaming for Shiro to save him.

Rin writhed and twisted where she lay. The straps keeping her down could not bear the heat of the flame at such a close angle. They snapped and she fell off the table, picked herself up, and turned just as Shiro rushed into the room clutching a reloading crossbow.

He shifted his aim from Altan to Rin and back again.

Rin tensed, but Shiro did not pull the trigger—whether out of inexperience or reluctance, Rin did not know.

"Beautiful," he marveled in a low voice. The fire reflected in his hungry eyes, and for a moment made him seem as if he, too, possessed the scarlet eyes of the Speerlies.

"*Shiro!*" Altan roared.

The doctor did not move as Altan advanced. Rather he lowered his crossbow, held his arms out to Altan as if welcoming a son into his embrace.

Altan grabbed his tormentor by the face. And squeezed. Flames poured from his hands, white-hot flames, surrounding the doctor's head like a crown. First Altan's hands left fingerprints of black against around Shiro's temples, and then the heat burned through bone and Altan's fingers bored holes through Shiro's skull. Shiro's eyes bulged. His arms twitched madly. He dropped the crossbow.

Altan pressed Shiro's skull between his hands. Shiro's head split open with a wet crack.

The twitching stopped.

Altan dropped the body and stepped away from it. He turned to Rin. His eyes burned a brighter red than they ever had before.

"Okay," he said. "Now we run."

Rin scooped the crossbow off the ground and followed Altan out of the operating room.

"Where's the exit?"

"No clue," Altan said. "Look for light."

They ran for their lives, turning corners at random. The research facility was a massive complex, far larger than Rin had imagined. As they ran, Rin saw that the hallway containing their cells was only one corridor in the mazelike interior; they passed empty barracks, many operating tables, and storage rooms stacked with canisters of gas.

Alarm bells sounded across the entire complex, alerting the soldiers to the breach.

Finally they found an exit: a side door in an empty corridor. It was boarded shut, but Altan pushed Rin aside and then kicked it down. She jumped out and helped him climb through.

"Over there!"

A Federation patrol group caught sight of them and raced in their direction.

Altan grabbed the crossbow from Rin and aimed it at the patrol group. Three soldiers dropped to the ground, but the others advanced over their comrades' dead bodies.

The crossbow made a hollow clicking noise.

"Shit," Altan said.

The patrol group drew closer.

Rin and Altan were starved, weakened, still half-drugged. And yet they fought, back to back. They moved as perfect complements to each other. They achieved a better synchronization than Rin had even with Nezha, for Nezha knew how she moved only by observing her. Altan didn't have to—Altan knew by *instinct* who she was, how she would fight, because they were the same. They were two parts of a whole. They were Speerlies.

They dispatched the patrol of five, only to see another squadron of twenty approach them from the side of the building.

"Well, we can't kill all of them," said Altan.

Rin wasn't sure about that. They kept running anyway.

Her feet were scraped raw from the cobbled floor. Altan gripped her arm as they ran, dragging her forward.

The cobblestones became sand, then wooden planks. They were at a port. They were by the sea.

They needed to get to the water, to the sea. Needed to swim across the narrow strait. Speer was so close . . .

You must go to the isle. You must go to the temple.

They reached the end of the pier. And stopped.

The night was lit up with torches.

* * *

It seemed as if the entire Federation army had assembled by the docks—Mugenese soldiers behind the pier, Mugenese ships in the water. There were hundreds of them. They were hundreds against two. The odds were not simply bad, they were insurmountable.

Rin felt a sensation of crushing despair. She couldn't breathe under the weight of it. This was where it ended. This was Speer's last stand.

Altan hadn't let go of her arm. Blood dripped from his eyes, blood dropped from his mouth.

"Look." He pointed. "Do you see that star? That's the constellation of the Phoenix."

She raised her head.

"Take it as your guide," he said. "Speer is southeast of here. It'll be a long swim."

"What are you talking about?" she demanded. "We'll swim together. You'll guide me."

His hand closed around her fingers. He held them tight for a moment and then let go.

"No," he said. "I'll finish my duty."

Panic twisted her insides.

"Altan, no."

She couldn't stop the onslaught of hot tears, but Altan wasn't looking at her. He was gazing out at the assembled army.

"Tearza didn't save our people," he said. "I couldn't save our people. But this comes close."

"Altan, please . . ."

"It will be harder for you," Altan said. "You'll have to live with the consequences. But you're brave . . . you're the bravest person I've ever met."

"Don't leave me," she begged.

He leaned forward and grasped her face in both hands.

She thought for a bizarre moment that he was going to kiss her.

He didn't. He pressed his forehead against hers for a long time.

She closed her eyes. She drank in the sensation of her skin against his. She seared it into her memory.

"You're so much stronger than I am," said Altan. Then he let her go.

She shook her head frantically. "No, I'm not, it's *you*, I need *you*—"

"Someone's got to destroy that research facility, Rin."

He stepped away from her. Arms stretched forward, he walked toward the fleet.

"No," Rin begged. "*No!*"

Altan took off at a run.

A hail of arrows erupted from the Federation force.

At the same moment Altan lit up like a torch.

He called the Phoenix and the Phoenix came; enveloping him, embracing him, loving him, bringing him back into the fold.

Altan was a silhouette in the light, a shadow of a man. She thought she saw him look back toward her. She thought she saw him smile.

She thought she heard a bird's cackle.

Rin saw in the flames the image of Mai'rinnen Tearza. She was weeping.

The fire doesn't give, the fire takes, and takes, and takes.

Rin screamed a wordless scream. Her voice was lost in the fire.

A great column of flame erupted from the site of Altan's immolation.

A wave of heat rolled out in every direction, bowling over the Federation soldiers like they were straw. It hit Rin like a punch to the gut, and she pitched backward into the inky black water.

CHAPTER 25

She swam for hours. Days. An eternity. She remembered only the beginning, the initial shock as her body slammed into the water, how she thought she had died because she could not make her body obey, and because her skin prickled where it hit the water as if she had been flayed alive. If she craned her head she could see the research base burning. It was a beautiful burn, crimson and gold licking up in tendrils to the softly dark sky.

At first Rin swam the way she had been trained to at the Academy—a stroke with a minimized profile so her arms would not exit the water. The Federation archers would shoot her dead in the water if they saw her, if there were any left alive . . . Then the fatigue set in, and she simply moved her limbs to keep afloat, to keep drifting, without any consideration for technique. Her strokes became mechanical, automated, and formless.

Even the water had warmed from the heat of Altan's conflagration. It felt like a bath, like a soft bed. She drifted, and thought it might be nice to drown. The ocean floor would be quiet. Nothing would hurt. There would be no Phoenix, no war, nothing at all, only silence . . . In those warm, dark depths she would feel no loss at all . . .

But the sight of Altan walking to his death was seared into

her memory; it burned at the forefront of her thoughts, more raw and painful than the salt water seeping into her open wounds. He commanded her from the grave, whispering orders even now . . . She did not know if she merely hallucinated his voice, or if he was truly with her, guiding her.

Keep swimming, follow the wings, don't stop, don't give up, keep moving . . .

She trained her eyes on the constellation of the Phoenix. *Southeast. You must swim to the southeast.*

The stars became torches, and the torches became fire, and she thought she saw her god. "I feel you," said the Phoenix, undulating before her. "I sense your sacrifice, your pain, and I want it, bring it to me . . . you are close, so close."

Rin reached a shaking hand toward the god, but then something jolted in her mind, something primal and terrified.

Stay away, screamed the Woman. *Stay far away from here.*

No, Rin thought. *You can't keep me away. I'm coming.*

She floated senselessly in the black water; arms and legs spread-eagled to remain afloat. She wavered in and out of reality. Her spirit went flying. She lost all sense of direction; she had no destination. She went wherever she was pulled, as if by a magnetic power, as if by an entity beyond her control.

She saw visions.

She saw a storm cloud that looked like a man gathering over the mountains, with four cyclones branching off like limbs, and when she stared at the source, two intelligent spots of cerulean peered back at her—too bright to be natural, too malicious to be anything but a god.

She saw a great dam with four gorges, the largest structure she had ever seen. She saw water gushing in every direction, flooding the plains. She saw Chaghan and Qara standing somewhere high, watching the fragments of the broken dam stream into the shifting river mouth.

She brushed against them, wondering, and Chaghan jerked his head up.

"Altan?" Chaghan asked hopefully.

Qara looked to her brother. "What is it?"

Chaghan ignored his sister, gazing around as if he could see Rin. But his pale eyes went straight through her. He was looking for something that no longer existed.

"Altan, are you there?"

She tried to say something, but no sound came out. She didn't have a mouth. She didn't have a body. Scared, she flitted away, and then the void was pulling her through again so that she couldn't have gone back if she'd tried.

She flew through the present to the past.

She saw a great temple, a temple built of stone and blood.

She saw a familiar woman, tall and magnificent, brown-skinned and long-limbed. She wore a crown of scarlet feathers and ash-colored beads. She was weeping.

"I won't," said the woman. "I will not sacrifice the world for the sake of this island."

The Phoenix shrieked with a fury so great that Rin trembled under its naked rage.

"I will not be defied. I will smite those who have broken their promises. And *you* . . . you have broken the greatest vow of all," hissed the god. "I condemn you. You will never know peace."

The woman screamed, collapsed to her knees, and clutched at something within her, as if trying to claw her very heart out. She glowed from inside like a burning coal; light poured through her eyes, her mouth, until cracks appeared in her skin and she shattered like rock.

Rin would have screamed, too, if she had a mouth.

The Phoenix turned its attention to her, just as the void dragged her away again.

She hurtled through time and space.

She saw a shock of white hair, and then everything stood still.

The Gatekeeper hung in a vacuum, frozen in a state of suspended animation, a place next to nowhere and on the way to everywhere.

"Why did you abandon us?" she cried. "You could have helped us. You could have saved us."

His eyes shot open and found her.

She did not know how long he stared at her. His eyes bored into the back of her soul, searched through all of her. And she stared back. She stared back, and what was she saw nearly broke her.

Jiang was no mortal. He was something old, something ancient, something very, very powerful. And yet at the same time he was her teacher, he was that frail and ageless man whom she knew as human.

He reached out for her and she almost touched him, but her fingers glided through his and touched nothing, and she thought with a sickening fright that she was drifting away again. But he uttered a word, and she hung still.

Then their fingers met, and she had a body again, and she could feel, feel his hands cup her cheeks and his forehead press against hers. She felt it acutely when he grasped her shoulders and shook her, hard.

"Wake up," he said. "You're going to drown."

She hauled herself out of the water onto hot sand.

She took a breath, and her throat burned as if she had drunk a gallon of peppercorn sauce. She whimpered and swallowed, and it felt like a fistful of rocks was trying to scrape its way down her esophagus. She curled into herself, rolled over, hauled herself to her feet, and attempted a step forward.

Something crunched under her foot. She lurched forward and tripped onto the ground. Dazed, she glanced around. Her ankle had wedged inside something. She wiggled her foot and lifted it up.

She dragged a skull out of the sand.

She had stepped inside a dead man's jaw.

She shrieked and fell backward. Her vision pulsed black. Her eyes were open but they had shut down, refusing all sensory input. Bright flashes of light swam before her eyes. Her fingers scrabbled through the sand. It was full of hard little objects. She lifted them out and brought them to her eyes, squinting until her vision returned.

They weren't pebbles.

Little bits of white stuck up in the sand everywhere she looked. Bones. Bones, everywhere.

She was kneeling in a massive graveyard.

She trembled so hard the sand beneath her vibrated. She doubled over onto her knees and gagged. Her stomach was so shrunken that with every dry heave, she felt as if she had been stabbed with a knife.

Get out of the target line. Was that Altan's voice echoing in her head, or her own thoughts? The voice was harsh, commanding. She obeyed. *You are visible against white sand. Take cover in the trees.*

She dragged herself across the sand, heaving every time her fingers rolled over a skull. She shook with tearless sobs, too dehydrated to cry.

Go to the temple. You'll find the way. All paths lead to the temple.

Paths? What paths? Whatever walkways had once existed had long ago been reclaimed by the island. She knelt there, staring stupidly at the foliage.

You're not looking hard enough.

She crawled up and down the tree line on her hands and knees, trying to find any indication of something that might have been a trail. Her fingers found a flat rock, the size of her head, just visible under a veneer of grass. Then another. And another.

She hauled herself to her feet and stumbled along the path, holding the surrounding trees for support. The rocks were hard and jagged, and they cut her feet so that she left bloody footprints as she walked.

Her head swam; she had been so long without food or drink that she hardly remembered she had a body anymore. She saw, or imagined, grotesque animals, animals that should not exist. Birds with two heads. Rodents with many tails. Spiders with a thousand eyes.

She continued following the path until she felt as if she'd walked the length of the entire island. *All paths lead to the temple*, the ancestors had told her. But when she came to the clearing at the center, she found only ruins among the sand. She saw shattered rocks engraved in a calligraphy she could not read, a stone entrance that led nowhere.

The Federation must have torn down the temple twenty years ago. It must have been the first thing they did, after they had butchered the Speerlies. The Federation had to destroy the Speerlies' place of worship. They had to remove their source of power, to ruin and smash it so completely so that no one on Speer could seek the Phoenix for help.

Rin ran through the ruins, searching for a door, some remnant of the holy area, but she found nothing. Nothing was there.

She sank to the ground, too numb to move. No. Not like this. Not after all she had been through. She had almost begun to cry when she felt the sand giving way under her hands. It was sliding. Falling somewhere.

She laughed suddenly. She laughed so hard that she gasped in pain. She fell over on her side and clutched her stomach, shrieking with relief.

The temple was underground.

She fashioned herself a torch from a stick of dry wood and held it before her as she descended the stairs of the temple. She climbed down for a long time. The air became cool and dry. She rounded a corner and could no longer see sunlight. She found it difficult to breathe.

She thought of the Chuluu Korikh, and her head reeled. She had to lean against the stone and took several heaving breaths before her panic subsided. This was not the prison under the stone. She was not walking away from her god. No—she was getting closer.

The inner chamber was entirely devoid of sound. She could hear none of the ocean, not the rustling of wind or sounds of wildlife above. But silent though it was, the temple was the opposite of the Chuluu Korikh. The silence in the temple was lucid, enhancing. It helped her focus. She could almost see her way upward, as if the path to the gods were as mundane as the dirt on which she trod.

The wall formed a circle, just like the Pantheon, but she saw only one plinth.

The Speerlies needed only one.

The entire room was a shrine to the Phoenix. Its likeness had been carved in stone in the far wall, a bas-relief thrice her size. The bird's head was turned sideways, its profile etched into the chamber. Its eye was huge, wild, and mad. Fear struck her as she looked into that eye. It seemed furious. It seemed alive.

Rin's hands moved instinctively to her belt, but she didn't have poppy with her. She realized she didn't need it, the same way that Altan had never needed it. Her very presence inside the temple placed her halfway to the gods already. She entered the trance simply by gazing into the furious eyes of the Phoenix.

Her spirit flew up until it was stopped.

When she saw the Woman, this time she spoke first.

"Not this again," Rin said. "You can't stop me. You know where I stand."

"I warn you one more time," said the ghost of Mai'rinnen Tearza. "Do not give yourself to the Phoenix."

"Shut up and let me through," Rin said. Starved and dehydrated, she had no patience for warnings.

Tearza touched her cheek. Her expression was desperate. "To give your soul to the Phoenix is to enter hell. It consumes you. You will burn eternally."

"I'm already in hell," Rin said hoarsely. "And I don't care."

Tearza's face twisted in grief. "Blood of my blood. Daughter of mine. Do not go down this path."

"I'm *not going* down your path. You did nothing," said Rin. "You were too scared to do what you needed to do. You sold our people. You acted from cowardice."

"Not cowardice," Tearza said. "I acted from a higher principle."

"You acted from selfishness!" Rin screamed. "If you hadn't given up Speer, our people might still be alive right now!"

"If I hadn't given up Speer, the world would be burning down," said Tearza. "When I was young, I thought that I would have done it. I sat where you sit now. I came to this temple and prayed to our god. And the Phoenix came to me, too, for I was his chosen ruler. But I realized what I was about to do, and I turned the fire on myself. I burned away my body, my power, and Speer's hope for freedom. I gave my country to the Red Emperor. And I maintained peace."

"How is death and slavery *peace*?" Rin spat. "I have lost my friends and my country. I have lost everything I care about. I don't want peace, I want revenge."

"Revenge will only bring you pain."

"What do you know?" Rin sneered. "Do you think you brought peace? You left your people to become slaves. You let the Red Emperor exploit and abuse and mistreat them for a millennium. You set Speer on a path that made centuries of suffering inevitable. If you hadn't been such a fucking coward, I wouldn't have to do this. And Altan would still be alive."

Mai'rinnen Tearza's eyes blazed red, but Rin moved first. A wall of flame erupted between them. Tearza's spirit dissolved in the fire.

And then she was before her god.

The Phoenix was so much more beautiful up close, and so much more terrible. As she watched, it unfurled its great wings behind her back and spread them. They stretched to the ends of the room. The Phoenix tilted its head to the side and fixed her with its ember eyes. Rin saw entire civilizations rise and fall in those eyes. She saw cities built from the ground up, then burning, then crumbling into ash.

"I've been waiting for you for a long time," said her god.

"I would have come sooner," said Rin. "But I was warned against you. My master . . ."

"Your master was a coward. But not your commander."

"You know what Altan did," Rin said in a low whisper. "You have him forever now."

"The boy could never have done what you are able to do," said the Phoenix. "The boy was broken in body and spirit. The boy was a coward."

"But he called you—"

"And I answered. I gave him what he wanted."

Altan had won. Altan had achieved in death what he couldn't do in life because Altan, Rin suspected, had been tired of living. He couldn't wage the protracted war of vengeance that the Phoenix demanded, so he'd sought a martyr's death and gotten it.

It's harder to keep living.

"And what do *you* want from me?" the Phoenix inquired.

"I want an end to the Federation."

"How do you intend to achieve that?"

She glowered at the god. The Phoenix was playing with her, forcing her to spell out her demand. Forcing her to specify exactly what abomination she wanted to commit.

Rin forced the last parts of what was human out of her soul and gave way to her hatred. Hating was so easy. It filled a hole inside her. It let her feel something again. It felt so good.

"Total victory," she said. "It's what you want, isn't it?"

"What I want?" The Phoenix sounded amused. "The gods do not *want* anything. The gods merely exist. We cannot help what we are; we are pure essence, pure element. You humans inflict everything on yourselves, and then blame us afterward. Every calamity has been man-made. We do not force you to do anything. We have only ever helped."

"This is my destiny," Rin said with conviction. "I'm the last Speerly. I have to do this. It is written."

"Nothing is written," said the Phoenix. "You humans always think you're destined for things, for tragedy or for greatness.

Destiny is a myth. Destiny is the *only* myth. The gods choose nothing. You *chose*. You chose to take the exam. You chose to come to Sinegard. You chose to pledge Lore, you chose to study the paths of the gods, and you chose to follow your commander's demands over your master's warnings. At every critical juncture you were given an option; you were given a way out. Yet you picked precisely the roads that led you here. You are at this temple, kneeling before me, only because you wanted to be. And you know that should you give the command, I will call something terrible. I will wreak a disaster to destroy the island of Mugen completely, as thoroughly as Speer was destroyed. By your choice, many will die."

"Many more will live," Rin said, and she was nearly certain that it was true. And even if it wasn't, she was willing to take that gamble. She knew she would bear full responsibility for the murders she was about to commit, bear the weight of them for as long as she lived.

But it was worth it.

For the sake of her vengeance, it was worth it. This was divine retribution for what the Federation had wreaked on her people. This was her justice.

"They aren't people," she whispered. "They're animals. I want you to make them burn. Every last one."

"And what will you give me in return?" inquired the Phoenix. "The price to alter the fabric of the world is steep."

What did a god, especially the Phoenix, want? What did any god ever want?

"I can give you worship," she promised. "I can give you an unending flow of blood."

The Phoenix inclined its head. Its want was tangible, as great as her hatred. The Phoenix could not help what it craved; it was an agent of destruction, and it needed an avatar. Rin could give it one.

Don't, cried the ghost of Mai'rinnen Tearza.

"Do it," Rin whispered.

"Your will is mine," said the Phoenix.

For one moment, glorious air rushed into the chamber, sweet air, filling her lungs.

Then she burned. The pain was immediate and intense. There was no time for her to even gasp. It was as if a roaring wall of flame had attacked every part of her at once, forcing her onto her knees and then onto the floor when her knees buckled.

She writhed and contorted at the base of the carving, clawing at the floor, trying to find some grounding against the pain. It was relentless, however, consuming her in waves of greater and greater intensity. She would have screamed, but she couldn't force air into her seizing throat.

It seemed to last for an eternity. Rin cried and whimpered, silently begging the impassive figure looming over her . . . anything, death even, would be better than this; she just wanted it to stop.

But death wasn't coming; she wasn't dying, she wasn't hurt, even; she could see no change in her body even though it felt as if she were being consumed by fire . . . no, she was whole, but something was burning inside. Something was disappearing.

Then Rin felt herself jerked back by a force infinitely greater than she was; her head flung back, arms stretched out to the sides. She had become a conduit. An open door without a gatekeeper. The power came not from her but from the terrible source on the other side; she was merely the portal that let it into this world. She erupted in a column of flame. The fire filled the temple, gushed out the doors and into the night where many miles away Federation children lay sleeping in their beds.

The whole world was on fire.

She had not just altered the fabric of the universe, had not simply rewritten the script. She had *torn* it, ripped a great gaping hole in the cloth of reality, and set fire to it with the ravenous rage of an uncontrollable god.

Once, the fabric had contained the stories of millions of lives— the lives of every man, woman, and child on the longbow island—

civilians who had gone to bed easy, knowing that what their soldiers did across the narrow sea was a far-off dream, fulfilling the promise of their Emperor of some great destiny that they had been conditioned to believe in since birth.

In an instant, the script had written their stories to the end.

At one point in time those people existed.

And then they didn't.

Because nothing was written. The Phoenix had told Rin that, and the Phoenix had *shown* Rin that.

And now the unrealized futures of millions were scorched out of existence, like a sky full of stars suddenly darkened.

She could not abide the terrible guilt of it, so she closed her mind off to the reality. She burned away the part of her that would have felt remorse for those deaths, because if she felt them, if she felt each and every single one of them, it would have torn her apart. The lives were so many that she ceased to acknowledge them for what they were.

Those weren't lives.

She thought of the pathetic little noise a candle wick made when she licked her fingers and pinched it. She thought of incense sticks fizzling out when they had burned to the end. She thought of the flies that she had crushed under her finger.

Those weren't lives.

The death of one soldier was a tragedy, because she could imagine the pain he felt at the very end: the hopes he had, the finest details like the way he put on his uniform, whether he had a family, whether he had kids whom he told he would see right after he came back from the war. His life was an entire world constructed around him, and the passing of that was a tragedy.

But she could not possibly multiply that by thousands. That kind of thinking did not compute. The scale was unimaginable. So she didn't bother to try.

The part of her that was capable of considering that no longer worked.

Those weren't lives.

They were numbers.

They were a necessary subtraction.

Hours later, it seemed, the pain slowly subsided. Rin drew breath in great, hoarse gasps. Air had never tasted so sweet. She uncurled herself from the fetal position she'd withdrawn into and slowly pulled herself up, clutching at the carving for support.

She tried to stand. Her legs trembled. Flames erupted wherever her hands touched stone. She lit sparks every time she moved. Whatever gift the Phoenix had given her, she couldn't control it, couldn't contain it or use it in discrete bits. It was a flood of divine fire pouring straight from the heavens, and she barely functioned as the channel. She could hardly keep from dissolving into the flames herself.

The fire was everywhere: in her eyes, streaming from her nostrils and mouth. A burning sensation consumed her throat and she opened her mouth to scream. The fire burst out of her mouth, on and on, a blazing ball in the air before her.

Somehow she dragged herself out of the temple. Then she collapsed into the sand.

CHAPTER 26

When Rin woke inside yet another unfamiliar room, she was seized with a panic so great that she could not breathe. Not this again. No. She had been caught again, she was back in Mugen's clutches, and they were going to cut her to pieces and splay her out like a rabbit . . .

But when she flung her arms outward, no restraints kept them down. And when she tried to sit up, nothing stopped her. She was bound by no chains. The weight she felt on her chest was a thin blanket, not a strap.

She was lying on a bed. Not tied down to an operating table. Not shackled to a floor.

It was only a bed.

She curled in on herself, clutched her knees to her chest, and rocked back and forth until her breathing slowed and she had calmed enough to take stock of her surroundings.

The room was small, dark, and windowless. Wooden floors. Wooden ceiling, wooden walls. The floor moved beneath her, tilting back and forth gently, the way a mother rocked an infant. She thought at first that she had been drugged again, for what else could explain the way the room shifted rhythmically even when she lay still?

It took her a while to realize that she might be out at sea.

She flexed her limbs gingerly, and a fresh wave of pain rolled over her. She tried it again, and it hurt less this time. Amazingly, none of her limbs were broken. She was all of herself. She was whole, intact.

She rolled to her side and gingerly placed her bare feet on the cool floor. She took a deep breath and tried to stand, but her legs gave out under her and she immediately collapsed against the small bed. She had never been out on open sea before. She was suddenly nauseated, and although her stomach was empty, she dry-heaved over the side of the bed for several minutes before she finally got a grip on herself.

Her stained, tattered shift was gone. Someone had dressed her in a clean set of black robes. She thought the cloth felt oddly familiar, until she examined the fabric and realized she had worn robes like this before. They were Cike robes.

For the first time, the possibility struck her that she was not on enemy ground.

Hoping against hope, not daring to wish, Rin slid off the bed and found the strength to stand. She approached the door. Her arm trembled as she tried the handle.

It swung free.

She walked up the first staircase she saw and climbed onto a wooden deck, and when she saw the open sky above her, purple in the evening light, she could have cried.

"She awakens!"

She turned her head, dazed. She knew that voice.

Ramsa waved to her from the other end of the deck. He held a mop in one hand, a bucket in the other. He smiled widely at her, dropped the mop, and started at a run toward her.

The sight of him was so unexpected that for a long moment Rin stood still, staring at him in confusion. Then she walked tentatively toward him, hand outstretched. It had been so long since she had seen any of the Cike that she was half-convinced that

Ramsa was an illusion, some terrible trick conjured by Shiro to torture her.

She would have welcomed the mirage anyway, if she could at least hold on to *something*.

But he was real—no sooner had he reached her than Ramsa knocked her hand aside and wrapped his skinny arms around her in a tight embrace. And as she pressed her face into his thin shoulder, every part of him felt and looked so real: his bony frame, the warmth of his skin, the scarring around his eyepatch. He was solid. He was *there*.

She was not dreaming.

Ramsa broke away and stared at her eyes, frowning. "Shit," he said. "*Shit*."

"What?"

"Your eyes," he said.

"What about them?"

"They look like Altan's."

At the sound of that name she began to cry in earnest.

"Hey. Hey, now," Ramsa said, patting her awkwardly on the head. "It's all right. You're safe."

"How did you . . . *where*?" She choked out incoherent questions in between her sobs.

"Well, we're several miles out from the southern coast," said Ramsa. "Aratsha has been navigating for us. We think it's best if we stay off the shore for a while. Things are getting messy on the mainland."

"'We' . . . ?" Rin repeated with bated breath. *Could it be?*

Ramsa nodded, grinning broadly. "We're all here. Everyone else is belowdecks. Well—except the twins, but they'll join us in a few days."

"How?" Rin demanded. The Cike hadn't known what happened at the Chuluu Korikh. They couldn't have known what happened in the research facility. How could they have known to come to Speer?

"We waited at the rendezvous point like Altan commanded," Ramsa explained. "When you didn't show, we knew something had happened. Unegen tracked the Federation soldiers all the way to that . . . that place. We staked the whole thing out, sent Unegen in to try to figure out a way to grab you, but then . . ." Ramsa trailed off. "Well. You know."

"That was Altan," Rin said. She felt a fresh pang of grief the moment she said it, and her face crumpled.

"We saw," Ramsa said softly. "We figured that was him."

"He saved me."

"Yeah."

Ramsa hesitated. "So he's definitely . . ."

She began to sob.

"Fuck," Ramsa said quietly. "Chaghan's . . . someone's going to have to tell Chaghan."

"Where is he?"

"Close. Qara sent us a message with a raven but it didn't say much, except that they're coming. We'll rendezvous with them soon. She'll know how to find us."

She looked up at him. "How did you find *me*?"

"After a lot of corpse digging." Ramsa shot her a thin smile. "We searched the rubble for survivors for two days. Nothing. Then your friend had the idea to sail to the island, and that's where we stumbled upon you. You were lying on a sheet of glass, Rin. Sand all around you, and you were on a sheet of clear crystal. It was something like a story. A fairy tale."

Not a fairy tale, she thought. She had burned so hot that she had melted down the sand around her. That was no story. It was a nightmare.

"How long have I been out?"

"About three days. We put you up in the captain's cabin."

Three days? How long had she been without food? Her legs nearly gave way under her then, and she hastily shifted to lean against the rail. Her head felt very, very light. She turned to face the sea. The spray of ocean mist felt wonderful against her face. She lost herself for a minute, basked in lingering rays of the sun, until she remembered herself.

In a small voice she asked, "What did I do?"

Ramsa's smile slid off his face.

He looked uneasy, trying to decide upon words, but then another familiar voice spoke from behind her.

"We were rather hoping you'd tell us."

And then there was Kitay.

Lovely, wonderful Kitay. Amazingly unharmed Kitay.

There was a hard glint to his eyes that she had never seen in him before. He looked as if he had aged five years. He looked like his father. He was like a sword that had been sharpened, metal that had been tempered.

"You're okay," she whispered.

"I made them take me along after you left with Altan," Kitay said with a wry smile. "They took some convincing."

"Good thing he did, too," said Ramsa. "It was his idea to search the island."

"And I was right," said Kitay. "I've never been so glad to be right." He rushed forward and hugged Rin tightly. "You didn't give up on me at Golyn Niis. I couldn't give up on you."

All Rin wanted to do was stand forever in that embrace. She wanted to forget everything, to forget the war, to forget her gods. It was enough to simply *be*, to know that her friends were alive and that the entire world was not so dark after all.

But she could not remain inside this happy delusion.

More powerful than her desire to forget was her desire to know. What had the Phoenix done? What, precisely, had she accomplished in the temple?

"I need to know what I did," she said. "Right now."

Ramsa looked uncomfortable. There was something he wasn't telling her. "Why don't you come back belowdecks?" he suggested, shooting Kitay a glance. "Everyone else is in the mess. It's probably best if we talk about this together."

Rin began to follow him, but Kitay reached for her wrist. He leveled a grim look at Ramsa.

"Actually," said Kitay, "I'd rather talk to her alone."

Ramsa shot Rin a confused glance, but she hesitantly nodded her assent.

"Sure." Ramsa backed away. "We'll be belowdecks when you're ready."

Kitay remained silent until Ramsa had walked out of earshot. Rin watched his expression but couldn't tell what he was thinking. What was wrong with him? Why didn't he look happier to see her? She thought she might go mad from anxiety if he didn't say something.

"So it's true," he said finally. "You can really call gods."

His eyes hadn't left her face. She wished she had a mirror, so that she could see her own crimson eyes.

"What is it? What are you not telling me?"

"Do you really have no idea?" Kitay whispered.

She shrank from him, suddenly fearful. She had some idea. She had more than an idea. But she needed confirmation.

"I don't know what you're talking about," she said.

"Come with me," Kitay said. She followed him the length of the deck until they stood on the other side of the ship.

Then he pointed out to the horizon.

"There."

Far out over the water sprouted the most unnatural-looking cloud Rin had ever seen. It was a massive, dense plume of ash, spreading over the earth like a flood. It looked like a thundercloud, but it was erupting upward from a dark landmass, not concentrated in the sky. Great rolls of gray and black smoke billowed out, like a slow-growing mushroom. Illuminated from behind by red rays of the setting sun, it looked like it was bleeding bright rivulets of blood into the ocean.

It looked like something alive, like a vengeful smoke giant arisen from the depths of the ocean. It was somehow beautiful, the way that the Empress was beautiful: lovely and terrible all at once. Rin could not tear her eyes away.

"What is that? What happened?"

"I didn't see it happen," said Kitay. "I only felt it. Even miles away from the shore, I felt it. A great trembling under my feet. A sudden jolt, and then everything was still. When we went outside, the sky was pitch-black. The ash blotted out the sun for days. This is the first sunset I've seen since we found you."

Rin's insides curdled. That small, dark landmass, there in the distance . . . that was Mugen?

"What is it?" she asked in a small voice. "The cloud?"

"Pyroclastic flows. Ash clouds. Do you remember the old fire mountain eruptions we studied in Yim's class?" Kitay asked.

She nodded.

"That's what happened. The landmass under the island was stable for millennia, and then it erupted without warning. I've spent days trying to puzzle out how it happened, Rin. Trying to imagine how it must have felt for the people on the island. I'll bet most of the population was incinerated in their homes. The survivors wouldn't have lasted much longer. The whole island is trapped in a firestorm of poisonous vapors and molten debris," said Kitay. His voice was oddly flat. "We couldn't get nearer if we tried. We would choke. The ship would burn from the heat a mile off."

"So Mugen is gone?" Rin breathed. "They're all dead?"

"If they aren't, they will be soon," said Kitay. "I've imagined it so many times. I've pieced things together from what we studied. The fire mountain would have emitted an avalanche of hot ash and volcanic gas. It would have swallowed their country whole. If they didn't burn to death, they choked. If they didn't choke to death, they were buried under rubble. And if all of that didn't kill them, then they'll starve to death, because sure as hell nothing is going to grow on that island now, because the ash would have decimated the island agriculture. When the lava dries, the island will be a solid tomb."

Rin stared out at the plume of ash, watched the smoke yet unfurling, bit by bit, like an eternally burning furnace.

The Federation of Mugen had become, in some perverse way, like the Chuluu Korikh. The island across the narrow strait had turned into a stone mountain of its own. The citizens of the Federation were prisoners arrested in suspended animation, never to reawaken.

Had she really destroyed that island? She felt a swell of panicked confusion. Impossible. It couldn't be. That kind of natural disaster could not have been her doing. This was a freak coincidence. An accident.

Had she truly done this?

But she had *felt* it, precisely at the moment of eruption. She had triggered it. She had willed it into being. She had felt each one of those lives wink out of existence. She had felt the Phoenix's exhilaration, experienced vicariously its frenzied bloodlust.

She had destroyed an entire country with the power of her anger. She had done to Mugen what the Federation did to Speer.

"The Dead Island was dangerously close to that ash cloud," Kitay said finally. "It's a miracle you're alive."

"No, it's not," she said. "It's the will of the gods."

Kitay looked as if he was struggling with his words. Rin watched him, confused. Why wasn't Kitay relieved to see her? Why did he look as if something terrible had happened? She had survived! She was okay! She had made it out of the temple!

"I need to know what you did," he said finally. "Did you will that?"

She trembled without knowing why, and then nodded. What was the point in lying to Kitay now? What was the point in lying to anyone? They all knew what she was capable of. And, she realized, she *wanted* them to know.

"Was that your will?" Kitay demanded.

"I told you," she whispered. "I went to my god. I told it what I wanted."

He looked aghast.

"You're saying—so your god, it—it made you do this?"

"My god didn't *make* me do anything," she said. "The gods can't make our choices for us. They can only offer their power, and we can wield it. And I did, and this is what I chose." She swallowed. "I don't regret it."

But Kitay's face had drained of color. "You just killed thousands of innocent people."

"They *tortured* me! They killed Altan!"

"You did to Mugen the same thing that they did to Speer."

"They deserved it!"

"How could anyone deserve that?" Kitay yelled. "*How*, Rin?"

She was amazed. How could he be angry with her now? Did he have *any idea* what she had been through?

"You don't know what they did," she said in a low whisper. "What they were planning. They were going to kill us all. They don't care about human lives. They—"

"They're monsters! I know! I was at Golyn Niis! I lay amid the corpses for days! But *you*—" Kitay swallowed, choking on his words. "You turned around and did the exact same thing. Civilians. Innocents. Children, Rin. You just buried an *entire country* and you don't feel a *thing*."

"*They were monsters!*" Rin shrieked. "*They were not human!*"

Kitay opened his mouth. No sound came out. He closed it. When he finally spoke again, it sounded as if he was close to tears.

"Have you ever considered," he said slowly, "that that was exactly what they thought of us?"

They glared at each other, breathing heavily. Blood thundered in Rin's ears.

How dare he? How *dare* he stand there like this and accuse her of atrocities? He had not seen the inside of that laboratory, he had not known how Shiro had planned to wipe out every Nikara alive . . . he had not seen Altan walk off that dock and light up like a human torch.

She had achieved revenge for her people. She had *saved* the Empire. Kitay would not judge her for it. She wouldn't let him.

516 R. F. KUANG

"Get out of my way," she snapped. "I need to go find my people."

Kitay looked exhausted. "What for, Rin?"

"We have work to do," she said tightly. "This isn't over."

"Are you serious? Have you listened to anything I've said? Mugen's *finished*!" Kitay shouted.

"Not Mugen," she said. "Mugen is not the final enemy."

"What are you talking about?"

"I want a war against the Empress."

"The *Empress*?" Kitay looked dumbfounded.

"Su Daji betrayed our location to the Federation," she said. "That's why they found us, they knew we'd be at the Chuluu Korikh—"

"That's insane," said Kitay.

"But they said it! The Mugenese, they said—"

Kitay stared at her. "And it never occurred to you that they had good incentive to lie?"

"Not about that. They knew who we were. Where we'd be. Only she knew that." Her breathing quickened. The anger had returned. "I need to know why she did it. And then I need to punish her for it. I need to make her *suffer*."

"Are you listening to yourself? Does it matter who sold who?" Kitay grasped her by her shoulders and shook her hard. "Look around you. Look at what's happened to this world. All of our friends are *dead*. Nezha. Raban. Irjah. Altan." Rin flinched at each name, but Kitay continued, relentless. "Our entire *world* has been torn apart, and you still want to go to war?"

"War's already here. A traitor sits on the throne of the Empire," she said stubbornly. "I will see her burn."

Kitay let go of her arm, and the expression on his face stunned her.

He looked at her as if looking at a stranger. He looked scared of her.

"I don't know what happened to you in that temple," he said. "But you are not Fang Runin."

* * *

Kitay left her on the deck. He did not seek her out again.

Rin saw the Cike in the galley belowdecks, but she did not join them. She was too drained, exhausted. She went back to her cabin and locked herself inside.

She thought—hoped, really—that Kitay would seek her out, but he didn't. When she cried, there was no one to comfort her. She choked on her tears and buried her face in the mattress. She stifled her screams in the hard straw padding, then decided she didn't care who heard her, and screamed out loud into the dark.

Baji came to the door, bearing a tray of food. She refused it.

An hour later Enki forced his way into her quarters. He enjoined her to eat. Again she refused. He argued she wouldn't do any of them any favors by starving to death.

She agreed to eat if he would give her opium.

"I don't think that's such a good idea," Enki said, looking over Rin's gaunt face, her tangled, matted hair.

"It's not that," she said. "I don't need seeds. I need the smoke."

"I can make you a sleeping draught."

"I don't need to sleep," she insisted. "I need to *feel nothing.*"

Because the Phoenix had not left her when she crawled out of that temple. The Phoenix spoke to her even now, a constant presence in her mind, hungry and frenzied. It had been ecstatic, out there on the deck. It had seen the cloud of ash and read it as worship.

Rin could not separate her thoughts from the Phoenix's desire. She could resist it, in which case she thought she'd go mad. Or she could embrace it and love it.

If Jiang could see me now, she realized, *he would have me locked in the Chuluu Korikh.*

That was, after all, where she belonged.

Jiang would say that self-immurement was the noble thing to do.

No fucking way, she thought.

She would never step voluntarily into the Chuluu Korikh, not while the Empress Su Daji walked this earth. Not while Feylen ran free.

She was the only one powerful enough to stop them, because she had now attained a power that Altan had only ever dreamed of.

She saw now that the Phoenix was right: Altan *had* been weak. Altan, despite how hard he tried, could only ever have been weak. He was crippled by those years spent in captivity. He did not choose his anger freely; it was inflicted on him, blow after blow, torture after torture, until he reacted precisely the way an injured wolf might, rising up to bite the hand that hit him.

Altan's anger was wild and undirected; he was a walking vessel for the Phoenix. He never had any choice in his quest for vengeance. Altan could not negotiate with the god like she did.

She was sane, she was convinced of it. She was whole. She had lost much, yes, but she still had her own mind. She made her decisions. She *chose* to accept the Phoenix. She chose to let it invade her mind.

But if she wanted her thoughts to herself, then she had to think nothing at all. If she wanted a reprieve from the Phoenix's bloodlust, she needed the pipe.

She mused out loud to the darkness as she sucked in that sickly sweet drug.

In, out. In, out.

I have become something wonderful, she thought. *I have become something terrible.*

Was she now a goddess or a monster?

Perhaps neither. Perhaps both.

Rin was curled up on her bed when the twins finally boarded the ship. She did not know they had even arrived until they appeared at her cabin door unannounced.

"So you made it," Chaghan said.

She sat up. They had caught her in a rare state, a sober state. She had not touched the pipe for hours, but only because she had been asleep.

Qara dashed inside and embraced her.

Rin accepted the embrace, eyes wide in shock. Qara had always been so reticent. So distant. She lifted her arm awkwardly, trying to decide if she should pat Qara on the shoulder.

But Qara drew back just as abruptly.

"You're burning," she said.

"I can't turn it off," Rin said. "It's with me. It's always with me."

Qara touched Rin's shoulders softly. She gave her a knowing look, a pitying look. "You went to the temple."

"I did it," Rin said. "That cloud of ash. That was me."

"I know," Qara said. "We felt it."

"Feylen," she said abruptly. "Feylen's out, Feylen escaped, we tried to stop him but—"

"We know," said Chaghan. "We felt that, too."

He stood stiffly at the doorway. He looked as if he were choking on something.

"Where's Altan?" he finally asked.

She said nothing. She just sat there, matching his gaze.

Chaghan blinked and made a noise like an animal that had been kicked.

"That's not possible," he said very quietly.

"He's dead, Chaghan," Rin said. She felt very tired. "Give it up. He's gone."

"But I would have felt it. I would have *felt* him go," he insisted.

"That's what we all think," she said flatly.

"You're lying."

"Why would I? I was there. I saw it happen."

Chaghan abruptly stalked out of the room and slammed the door behind him.

Qara glanced down at Rin. She didn't wear her normal irate expression then. She just looked sad.

"You understand," she said.

Rin more than understood.

"What did you do? What happened?" she asked Qara finally.

"We won the war in the north," said Qara, twisting her hands in her lap. "We followed orders."

Altan's last, desperate operation had involved not one but two prongs. To the south, he had taken Rin to open the Chuluu Korikh. And to the north, he sent the twins.

They had flooded the Murui River. That river delta Rin had seen from the spirit realm was the Four Gorges Dam, the largest set of levees that held the Murui back from inundating all four surrounding provinces with river water. Altan had ordered the breaking of the levees to divert the river south into an older channel, cutting off the Federation supply route to the south.

It was almost exactly like a battle plan Rin had suggested in Strategy class in her first year. She remembered Venka's objections. *You can't just break a dam like that. Dams take years to rebuild. The entire river delta will flood, not just that valley. You're talking about famine. Dysentery.*

Rin drew her knees to her chest. "I suppose there's no point asking if you evacuated the countryside first."

Qara laughed without smiling. "Did *you*?"

Qara's words hit her like a blow. There was no reasoning through what she had done. It had happened. It was a decision that had been ripped out of her. And she had . . . and she had . . .

She began to quiver. "What have I done, Qara?"

Until now the sheer scale of the atrocity had not computed for her, not really. The number of lives lost, the enormity of what she had invoked—it was an abstract concept, an unreal impossibility.

Was it *worth* it? Was it enough to atone for Golyn Niis? For Speer?

How could she compare the lives lost? One genocide against another—how did they balance on the scale of justice? And who was she, to imagine that she could make that comparison?

She seized Qara's wrist. "What have I *done*?"

"The same thing that we did," said Qara. "We won a war."

"No, I *killed* . . ." Rin choked. She couldn't finish saying it.

But Qara suddenly looked angry. "What do you want from me? Do you want forgiveness? I can't give you that."

"I just . . ."

"Would you like to compare death tolls?" she asked sharply. "Would you like to argue about whose guilt is greater? You created an eruption, and we caused a flood. Entire villages, drowned in an instant. Flattened. You destroyed the enemy. *We killed the Nikara*."

Rin could only stare at her.

Qara wrenched her arm out of Rin's grip. "Get that look off your face. We made our decisions, and we survived with our country intact. Worth it is worth it."

"But we *murdered*—"

"*We won a war!*" Qara shouted. "We avenged him, Rin. He's gone, but avenged."

When Rin didn't respond, Qara seized her by both shoulders. Her fingers dug painfully into her flesh.

"This is what you have to tell yourself," Qara said fiercely. "You have to believe that it was necessary. That it stopped something worse. And even if it wasn't, it's the lie we'll tell ourselves, starting today and every day afterward. You made your choice. There's nothing you can do about it now. It's over."

That was what Rin had told herself on the island. It was what she had told herself when talking to Kitay.

And later, in the dead of night, when she couldn't sleep for the nightmares and had to reach for her pipe, she would do as Qara said and keep telling herself what was done was done. But Qara was wrong about one thing:

It was not over. It couldn't be over—because Federation troops were still on the mainland, scattered throughout the south; because even Chaghan and Qara hadn't managed to drown them all. And now they had no leader to obey and no home to return to, which made them desperate, unpredictable . . . and dangerous.

And somewhere on the mainland sat an Empress on a makeshift throne, taking refuge in a new wartime capital because Sinegard had been destroyed by a conflict she'd invented. Perhaps by now she had heard the longbow island was gone. Was she distressed to lose an ally? Relieved to be freed from an enemy? Perhaps she had already taken credit for a victory she hadn't planned; perhaps she was using it to cement her hold on power.

Mugen was gone, but the Cike's enemies had multiplied. And they were rogue agents now, no longer loyal to the crown that had sold them.

Nothing was over.

The Cike had never before acknowledged the passing of their commander. By nature of their occupation, a change in leadership was an unavoidably messy affair. Past Cike commanders had either gone frothing mad and had to be dragged into the Chuluu Korikh against their will, or been killed on assignment and never come back.

Few had died with such grace as Altan Trengsin.

They said their goodbyes at sunrise. The entire contingent gathered on the front deck, solemn in their black robes. The ritual was no Nikara ceremony. It was a Speerly ceremony.

Qara spoke for all of them. She conducted the ceremony, because Chaghan, the Seer, refused to. Because Chaghan could not.

"The Speerlies used to burn the dead," she said. "They believed that their bodies were only temporary. *From ash we come, and to ash we return.* To the Speerlies, death was not an end but only a great reunion. Altan has left us to go home. Altan has returned to Speer."

Qara cast her arms over the waters. She began to chant, not in the language of the Speerlies but in the rhythmic language of the Hinterlands. Her birds circled overhead in silent tribute. And the wind itself seemed to cease, the rocking of the waves halted, as if the very universe stood still for the loss of Altan.

The Cike stood in a line, all in their identical black uniforms, watching Qara wordlessly. Ramsa's arms were folded tightly over his narrow chest, shoulders hunched as if he could withdraw into himself. Baji silently put a hand on his shoulder.

Rin and Chaghan stood at the back of the deck, removed from the rest of their division.

Kitay was nowhere to be seen.

"We should have his ashes," Chaghan said bitterly.

"His ashes are already in the sea," Rin said.

Chaghan glared at her. His eyes were red with grief, bloodshot. His pale skin was pulled over his high cheekbones so tightly that he looked even more skeletal than he usually did. He appeared as if he had not eaten in days. He appeared as if he might blow away with the wind.

Rin wondered how long it would take for him to stop blaming her in his mind for Altan's death.

"I guess he gave as good as he got," Chaghan said, nodding toward the ashen mess that was the Federation of Mugen. "Trengsin got his revenge in the end."

"No, he didn't."

Chaghan stiffened. "Explain."

"Mugen didn't betray him," she said. "Mugen didn't draw him to that mountain. Mugen didn't sell Speer. The Empress did."

"Su Daji?" Chaghan said incredulously. "Why? What would she have to gain?"

"I don't know. I intend to find out."

"*Tenega*," Chaghan swore. He looked as if he had just realized something. He crossed his thin arms against his chest, muttering in his own language. "But of course."

"What?"

"You drew the Hexagram of the Net," he said. "The Net signifies traps, betrayals. The wires of your capture were laid out ahead of you. She must have sent a missive to the Federation the minute Altan got it in his head to go to that damned mountain. *One is ready to move, but his footprints run crisscross.* You two were pawns in someone else's game this entire time."

"We were not *pawns*," Rin snapped. "And don't act like you saw this coming." She felt a sudden flash of anger then—at Chaghan's lecturing tone, his retrospective musing, as if he'd seen it all, like he'd expected this to happen, like he'd known better than Altan all along. "Your Hexagrams only make sense in hindsight and give no guidance when they're cast. Your Hexagrams are fucking useless."

Chaghan stiffened. "My Hexagrams are not useless. I see the shape of the world. I understand the changing nature of reality. I have read countless Hexagrams for the Cike's commanders—"

She snorted. "And in all the Hexagrams you read for Altan, you never foresaw that he might die?"

To her surprise, Chaghan flinched.

She knew it wasn't fair, to hurl accusations when Altan's death was hardly Chaghan's fault, but she needed to lash out, needed to blame it on someone other than herself.

She couldn't stand Chaghan with his attitude that he knew better, that he'd foreseen this tragedy, because he *hadn't*. She and Altan had gone to the mountain blind, and he had let them.

"I told you," Chaghan said. "The Hexagrams can't foresee the future. They're portraits of the world as it is, descriptions of the forces at hand. The gods of the Pantheon represent sixty-four fundamental forces, and the Hexagrams reflect their undulations.

"And none of those undulations screamed, *Don't go to this mountain, you'll be killed*?"

"I *did* warn him," Chaghan said quietly.

"You could have tried harder," Rin said bitterly, even though she knew that, too, was an unfair accusation, and that she was saying it only to hurt Chaghan. "You could have told him he was about to die."

"All of Altan's Hexagrams spoke of death," said Chaghan. "I didn't expect that this time it would mark his own."

She laughed out loud. "Aren't you supposed to be a Seer? Do you ever see *anything* useful?"

"I saw Golyn Niis, didn't I?" Chaghan snapped.

But the moment those words left his mouth he made a choking noise, and his features twisted with grief.

Rin didn't say what they were both thinking—that maybe if they hadn't gone to Golyn Niis, Altan wouldn't have died.

She wished they had just fought the war out at Khurdalain. She wished they had abandoned the Empire completely and escaped back to the Night Castle, let the Federation ravage the countryside while they waited out the turmoil in the mountains, safe and insulated and *alive*.

Chaghan looked so miserable that Rin's anger dissipated. Chaghan had, after all, tried to stop Altan. He'd failed. Neither of them could have talked Altan out of his frenzied death drive.

There was no way Chaghan could have predicted Altan's future because the future was not written. Altan made his choices; at Khurdalain, at Golyn Niis, and finally on that pier, and neither of them could have stopped him.

"I should have known," Chaghan said finally. "*We have an enemy whom we love.*"

"What?"

"I read it in Altan's Hexagram. Months ago."

"It meant the Empress," she said.

"Perhaps," he said, and turned his gaze out to the sea.

They watched Qara's falcons in silence. The birds flew in great circles overhead, as if they were guides, as if they could lead a spirit toward the heavens.

Rin thought of the parade from so long ago, of the puppets of the animals of the Emperor's Menagerie. Of the majestic kirin, that noble lion-headed beast, which appeared in the skies upon the death of a great leader.

Would a kirin appear for Altan?

Did he deserve one?

She found that she could not answer.

"The Empress should be the least of your concerns," said Chaghan after a while. "Feylen's getting stronger. And he always was powerful. Almost more so than Altan."

Rin thought of that storm cloud she'd seen over the mountains. Those malicious blue eyes. "What does he want?"

"Who knows? The God of the Four Winds is one of the most mercurial entities of the Pantheon. His moods are entirely unpredictable. He will become a gentle breeze one day, and rip apart entire villages the next. He will sink ships and topple cities. He might be the end of this country."

Chaghan spoke lightly, casually, as if he couldn't care less if Nikan was destroyed the very next day. Rin had expected blame and accusation, but she heard none; only detachment, as if the Hinterlander held no stake in Nikan's affairs now that Altan was gone. Maybe he didn't.

"We'll stop him," Rin said.

Chaghan gave an indifferent shrug. "Good luck. It'll take all of you."

"Then will you command us?"

Chaghan shook his head "It couldn't be me. Even back when I was Tyr's lieutenant, I knew it could never be me. I was Altan's Seer, but I was never slated to be a commander."

"Why not?"

"A foreigner in charge of the Empire's most lethal division? Not likely." Chaghan folded his arms across his chest. "No, Altan named his successor before we left for Golyn Niis."

Rin jerked her head up. That was news. "Who?"

Chaghan looked like he couldn't believe she had asked.

"It's you," he said, as if it were obvious.

Rin felt like he had punched her in the solar plexus.

Altan had named her as his successor. Entrusted his legacy to her. He had written and signed the order in blood before they had even left Khurdalain.

"I am the commander of the Cike," she said, and then had to repeat the words to herself before their meaning sank in. She held a status equivalent to the generals of the Warlords. She had the power to order the Cike to do as she wished. "*I command the Cike.*"

Chaghan looked sideways at her. His expression was grim. "You are going to paint the world in Altan's blood, aren't you?"

"I'm going to find and kill everyone responsible," said Rin. "You cannot stop me."

Chaghan laughed a dry, cutting laugh. "Oh, I'm not going to stop you."

He held out his hand.

She grasped it, and the drowned land and the ash-choked sky bore witness to the pact between Seer and Speerly.

They had come to an understanding, she and Chaghan. They were no longer opposed, vying for Altan's favor. They were allies, now, bound by the mutual atrocities they had committed.

They had a god to kill. A world to reshape. An Empress to overthrow.

They were bound by the blood they had spilled. They were bound by their suffering. They were bound by what had happened to them.

No.

This had not *happened* to her.

We do not force you to do anything, the Phoenix had whispered, and it had spoken the truth. The Phoenix, for all its power, could not compel Tearza to obey it. And it could not have compelled Rin, because she had agreed wholeheartedly to the bargain.

Jiang was wrong. She was not dabbling in forces she could not control, for the gods were not dangerous. The gods had no power at all, except what she gave them. The gods could affect the universe only through humans like her. Her destiny had not been written in the stars, or in the registers of the Pantheon. She had made her choices fully and autonomously. And though she called upon the gods to aid her in battle, they were her tools from beginning to end.

She was no victim of destiny. She was the last Speerly, commander of the Cike, and a shaman who called the gods to do her bidding.

And she would call the gods to do such terrible things.

ACKNOWLEDGMENTS

Hannah Bowman is an incredible agent, editor, and advocate. Without her, more characters would have lived. The team at Liza Dawson Associates has been wonderful to me. David Pomerico and Natasha Bardon are sharp, insightful editors who made this manuscript infinitely better. Laura Cherkas is an eagle-eyed copyeditor, who caught far too many continuity errors. Thank you all for giving me a chance.

Jeanne Cavelos, my personal Gandalf, transformed me from a person who liked to write into a person who is a writer. I hope Elijahcorn is treating you well. Kij Johnson is a genius, and I want to be just like her when I grow up. Barbara Webb is ridiculously cool. (I hope Ethan and Nick find happiness.) My office-hour chats with Dr. John Glavin always inspired and motivated me. Thank you all for encouraging me to try harder and write better.

My Odyssey 2016 class put me in actual, physical pain. I miss you all! It's been very hard to talk to you ever since you gained omnipotence, Bob. To the Binobos—Huw, Jae, Jake, Marlee, Greg, Becca, Caitlin—thanks for the laughs, the happy-hour margaritas, and multiple *Pacific Rim* viewings. Bennett: Look! The word *Scargon* finally made it into a book. One day his story will be told. PS: I love you. The Tomatoes—Farah Naz, Linden,

Pablo, Richard, Jeremy, Josh—are my shining stars, my lifelines, and my best friends. Thank you all for being there for me.

Finally, to Mom and Dad: I love you very much. I can never repay you for the sacrifices you've made to give me the life that I have, but I can try to make you proud. Immigrants, we get the job done.

About the author

Read on

About the book

Insights,
Interviews
& More...

Meet R. F. Kuang

Seattle Sophia theme photography Studio

R. F. KUANG studies modern
Chinese history. She has a BA
from Georgetown University and
is currently a graduate student in
the United Kingdom on a Marshall
Scholarship. *The Poppy War* is her
debut novel. ✑

A Note from the Author

Since *The Poppy War* came out, many readers have emailed me asking for nonfiction resources on the Rape of Nanjing, Sino-Japanese relations, and the history of World War II in China. As a graduate student of this very subject, I'm delighted that *The Poppy War* has stoked such an interest in China's wartime history. I also happen to have many, many nonfiction recommendations (largely because I've been forced to read them for class!), some of which I'll list here as an accompanying reading guide. I've tried to choose books that would be most engaging and accessible to lay readers approaching this history for the first time.

Iris Chang's gorgeously written and bestselling *The Rape of Nanking: The Forgotten Holocaust of World War II* was one of the first books that brought the (then rather neglected) history of the Nanjing Massacre to the attention of Western readers. Almost every scene from the chapters of Golyn Niis came from Chang's account of the Nanjing Massacre. Very little was made up—most of what you see truly happened.

Descriptions of the battle at Khurdalain, particularly the bombing scene and the challenges of urban warfare, were based largely on accounts from the Battle of Shanghai in 1937. Peter Harmsen's *Shanghai 1937: Stalingrad on the Yangtze* is a riveting account of those first few weeks of the war. On the topic of sexual assault, abuse, and slavery by the Japanese military, look into Yoshimi Yoshiaki's *Comfort Women: Sexual Slavery in the Japanese Military During World War II* and ▶

A Note from the Author
(continued)

George Hicks's *The Comfort Women: Japan's Brutal Regime of Enforced Prostitution in the Second World War.*

For broader, comprehensive histories of China's War of Resistance against Japan, I highly recommend Rana Mitter's *Forgotten Ally: China's World War II, 1937–1945* and Hans van de Ven's *China at War: Triumph and Tragedy in the Emergence of the New China.* Readers who are fascinated by military particularities and don't mind a bit more of a challenge will enjoy *The Battle for China: Essays on the Military History of the Sino-Japanese War of 1937–1945,* edited by Mark Peattie, Edward Drea, and Hans van de Ven. I particularly enjoyed the essay on Japanese air tactics and was disappointed I didn't get to discuss them in *The Poppy War.*

I wrote *The Poppy War* after several long discussions with my Chinese grandparents about their experiences during World War II. The last few years—from publishing *The Poppy War* to finishing my master's thesis on the complicated remembrance to the Rape of Nanjing to starting my MPhil in Chinese studies at Cambridge—have been a long, often painful process of excavating both familial and national history to understand where I—we—come from. It's a history that isn't often taught in American classrooms, and which often isn't known even to members of the Chinese diaspora. I hope my work does a little bit to change that. Thank you for reading.

Reading Group Discussion Questions

1. R. F. Kuang's academic background is evident throughout the novel. Do you see any connection between modern Chinese history and the world and system that Kuang creates?

2. *The Art of War* by Sun Tzu appears often (in a slightly different form) in *The Poppy War*—how does this text interact with the book? How does *The Art of War* influence the society's political climate as one of its core principles? What is the significance of the Nikara military's inability to follow through on those principles?

3. What track would you pledge as a student of Sinegard?

4. There are several great relationships at play in this book: Rin and Jiang, Rin and Kitay, Rin and Nezha, and Rin and Altan. How do these relationships affect Rin? How do the relationships change and grow? Is one person in the relationship more powerful than the other?

5. Human connection is a huge theme in this novel. After graduating Sinegard, Rin—being an outsider in many ways—finally finds a place where she belongs. How does ▶

her previous experience of exclusion affect the relationship with her found family? What does Rin gain by being part of this group? Or would it be safe to say she is *never* part of a group?

6. Who would you say has the most control in the book? How do control and power play together in this novel?

7. There are many underlying sociopolitical themes at play in *The Poppy War*, including race and colorism. What challenges does Rin experience being darker skinned than most of the children in her society? How does it affect her experiences? How does it affect your reading of the book?

8. Do you agree with Tearza's decision? Or do you agree with Rin's decision to obtain power from the Phoenix, even though it comes at a terrible cost? What would you have done in this situation?

9. Where do you hope the story goes in book two, *The Dragon Republic?*

Discover great authors, exclusive offers, and more at hc.com.